CORSAIR

By Henrik Sorensen

Cover Art: Daenen Rolapp
Cover Design: Laz
Editors: Clay Donaldson and Martin Earl

To my mother.

1

At any given point in time, millions of suns rise and shed light on millions of planets. But the sun never rises on Calx. Ara, the Crimson Father, sits in the great pink sky like a gaping red mouth endlessly vomiting bloody light across the Terminator, transfixed in a long-dead orbit. The Terminator is a narrow black canyon of life, either side of which is hedged by endless, uninhabitable wastes. These are scorched and burning where Calx's face is locked against Ara's gaze, and a vast field of black and purple ice where the planet faces only the void of space. It is in the Terminator, this narrow strip of precious land, that every rare creature that has evolved to survive in Calx's malevolent climate lives. Where every creature dies.

A mile deep into the bone gray earth, faint blue light filled Coldside Colony T-β. In a small cell, Biological Automaton

Designation T-β 63177 opened its eyes as its sustenance tube withdrew from the metal-ringed hole in its neck. It blinked in the pale light, jet black eyelids over stone gray irises, and stepped out of the stark metal tube in which it took its rest and into the small metalloy-walled cell in which the tube stood on one side. The cell was empty except for the sleeping tube and a tall, narrow locker that stood adjacent to it, the room lit by an ashen blue glow that emanated from the metalloy walls themselves.

"Designation T-β 63177 prepare and report for coldside duty," came a voice as flat and cold as the light in the cell. 63177 blinked once more then pulled a white jumpsuit from the locker in front of it and began to pull it over its thickly muscled arms and legs. Its smooth black skin glistened under the sourceless blue light as it put on thick white gloves and finally the glossy white, black-visored helmet that completed its suit . The smooth, solid metalloy door of its cell slid open as the voice came again through the walls. "All designations proceed to lifts."

The dull thudding of hundreds of booted feet filled the hall as Colony T-β emptied its cells and their occupants proceeded in unison down narrow, blue-lit hallways opening onto wide matte metalloy platforms. Embedded into the arching ceilings of the long hallway were dozens of glassy electronic eyes that rotated back and forth, gazing down at the column, staring into each automaton's deep black face as it passed. 63177 had noticed them the day it had first awoken and thought nothing of them since.

The lift was packed with row after row of nearly identical automatons, all clad in the same white jumpsuits, all standing stock still. The dark air was filled with the sound of grinding gears as massive cables pulled the platform and its cargo up through thousands of feet of smooth rock. As they neared the surface, a great hatch began to open and once again 63177 blinked away the darkness. In the dim light of Calx's perpetual day, it went about its work like so many days before, though it had never thought to count them.

63177 walked from the platform and found its exosuit in the same place it was each sleep-labor cycle. The exosuit was a simple, battered metalloy frame, thrice 63177's height, with a simple cockpit perched atop a pair of legs that ended in broad, splayed feet. At its sides were two long arms that each ended in clawed buckets and on the back of the cockpit was welded a great cylindrical tank with a hinged lid, as dented and weathered as the rest of the exosuit. It climbed the ladder at its side, hauling its considerable frame into the cockpit and donning its glossy white helmet. It flipped the helmet's dark visor down over its face and strapped into the spartan seat. "T-β 63177 ready for coldside transfer," it said, pulling the transparent polymer canopy closed with a click. Around it, the other T-β coldside units scurried to their various duties, most of them climbing into dozens of exosuits that stood in neat rows. Others boarded transports with massive treads that carried them to dark buildings in the distance. Enormous white cylinders were planted in the rock all around the distant buildings, stretching off as far as 63177's gray eyes could see, thrusting themselves with an indescribable violence from the flat, empty earth and towering over the long, flat horizon.

There was a clang and a jerk as the air transport hooked onto 63177's line of suits and hauled them into the air. The gray wastes stretched out below them so vast that it took a moment before one's body even realized it was rising into the void. 63177 watched aimlessly in front of itself as another line of suits rose into the air, the transports pushing great shafts of wind through their massive rotors. The hatch and the ground transports faded off into the distance as the rotors cranked deafeningly and pulled the exosuits through the thin Calx air. They soon passed far above the processing plants and the stark cylindrical storage tanks, the little white-clad automatons beneath them scrambling from the ground transports and moving like a line of pale insects into a nest. For miles, they flew over a rocky gray landscape until the ground grew black with what looked like thousands of dark cobwebs, a vast thicket of inky brambles that seemed to represent Calx's only vegetation. At the edge of the nexus of black vines 63177 could see another hatch like its own and dozens of distant vehicles moving around the strange black mass. How many times it had seen that hatch and those vehicles 63177 did not know, and yet still it had never asked itself their purpose.

2

The Primus ship glided silently through the iridescent sunset lace of the star fog clouds, a glimmering shaft of black ink in the nebulous glow, the ebon armor of its hull reflecting the dim starlight like reptilian scales. Just a few thousand miles behind, another craft cut through the misty, finger-like columns that stretched into space for an analux. The second ship stretched out broad wings like a swallow in full flight, coated in a shimmering layer of mother-of-pearl. The dust of the columns swirled as the two ships moved through the endless expanse of the nebula.

Noiseless explosions of intense red or white light occasionally filled the space around the ships as each hurled a stream of various projectiles and energy beams in the other's direction only to see them countered by the other's defenses.

Gammalux arrays on each of the vessels shot bright lances of red light to vaporize mass projectiles or nuclear warheads before they could reach their targets. Every few minutes or so one or two projectiles would make it out of the swarm and past the gammalux array to tear holes in one or the other ship's constantly shifting reflective armor, which would then ooze like thick liquid around the damage and repair itself. Neither ship was close enough to the other to take advantage of successful strikes, and a keen observer would have quickly realized they were watching the exhausted swings of two fighters who had run out of energy and ideas but for whom no one had called the bout.

Kalaiapi, her neural link cable hanging loosely from the base of her snow-white neck, her virtual helm rotating around her, a sphere of whirling panels displaying constantly changing information and signals visible only in her mind's eye, paced furiously across the deck of her little sloop. It was eloquently and elaborately named "The Eternal Vendetta of God's Eye XVI," but for efficiency's sake she simply called it "Vendetta Sixteen." She had been pursuing the Primus dreme for a couple of astral months now and every time she felt she might finally close the gap or take out its pulse drive or deliver some sort of crippling blow, the slick bastard somehow wriggled out of her grasp. They had to be running as low as she was on fuel and ammunition, but she'd never seen this particular class of dreme, as Primus ships were known, before and it was impossible to know for certain. Certainly their attacks had become both more intermittent and less enthusiastic in the past few days. At 3,000 miles she was practically close enough to smell their exhaust but just out of reach of a killer blow.

Kalaiapi's natural genetic structure was tall and lithe, but for the sake of mobility, she preferred to fly small; hand-to-hand combat on a flight deck or in utility conduits was simply much easier at five feet than the six and a half she had grown to naturally. When not planet-side on Ad Astara, she kept her skin a utilitarian milky white, and her hair the same, tied in a short tail that just brushed the nape of her neck. One could hardly tell where her scalp ended and the thick, ice-white locks began. Her eyes she kept as they had been when she was born, unless there was some dire need for a change: a clear, pale blue. In the trackless snow of her face, they looked like two glacial pools. Her features were always soft and round, disarmingly so, and that softness was exaggerated by her current pallor. Now, her features were severe, or at least as severe as she could make them.

She had been following the strange dreme since unexpectedly coming across it while engaging in a bit of privateering against smugglers on the fringes of the Star Glass Sea, the Confederation's primary source of pure carbon.

In all her battles against Primic forces, she'd never come across a craft quite like it, a little black bullet flying virtually invisible through space. Nonetheless, it had been instantly recognizable as one of theirs: the iridescent black armor that moved like an oil slick on water was unmistakable. The initial encounter had nearly killed her, but she had weathered that first furious assault and had managed to land a few blows of her own. They had blown out each other's grav drives almost from the first broadsides and had then settled into this seemingly endless pursuit.

Kalaiapi couldn't figure out why the larger and clearly superior Primus dreme didn't simply pull up and blast her little one-pilot sloop out of space. Perhaps she had damaged them worse than she realized or perhaps they feared that if they delayed at all getting out of deep Confederation space they would be caught by a larger force and lose any chance of escape. For their part, they'd destroyed both Vendetta Sixteen's long-range comms array and its small baryonic synthesizer, the proprietary Confederation processor used to transform raw diamonds into almost any known substance. This meant she was without any means of long-range communication or materials to make repairs. Not that she could perform those repairs without stopping, anyway. So the deadlocked chase continued, neither able to quite gain an advantage over the other.

She continued to pace as the Vendetta rumbled and shook from the high energy particle shockwave of the gammalux array vaporizing another nuclear warhead that had been lazily hurled in her direction. The pot shots from the dreme became more and more sporadic and she directed her systems to cease their own futile attacks. Enveloped in the thick, luminescent pink star fog of the nebula, it was an even greater waste of resources; these kinds of dark nebulae always wreaked havoc on even the most modern of targeting systems.

With a flick of neurons, she diverted a sliver of her mind toward the glowing, pale blue, marble-sized sphere that spun in the air on its own axis a few inches above her shoulder. As naturally as if it were her own mind, she drew a regional star chart from the little aaiun and uplinked it to the virtual helm. Aaiuns such as this had been the solution for the inevitable impasse created when limitless space met limited biological memory. They had been controversial upon their creation, for though they were simple DNA-drives like any other progenasi memory storage, they required a sliver of anima for power and function. Not to mention being one more piece of integrated technology defiling the Confederation's elite pilots. By now, though, they were integral to the Confederation's space-travel capabilities and every pilot had one, was practically unable to function without one. Inseparably, permanently connected, it was simply an extension of the pilot's own mind. In fact, it had been found that the destruction of a linked aaiun had a tendency to either kill its host or drive them irreparably insane. In any case, the Eternal Council had made another tech-integration exception as well as waived the anathayatic idea of anima-technology syncresis, all for the salvation of the progenasis. Omnia made no compromises, but sometimes the Council had to. After all, as the Aya taught, "Omnia is a predator and we are its prey," and to lose that pursuit would be to lose all. It was unknown to Kalaiapi whence the anima for the aaiuns even came, and it was unwise to bring it up as a topic of conversation.

As to her own pursuit, here and now, it was time for Kalaiapi to start considering the possibility that she may run out of fuel before the dreme did. The dreme could not escape. This was not an acceptable outcome. That a Primus ship had penetrated so far into Confederation space was the kind of anomalous incident that merited a certain measure of alarm. Thinking about what kind of terroristic havoc a ship like that could wreak on an unsuspecting Inner Systems colony was nearly enough to undo a hundred thousand years of evolution and send a shudder down Kalaiapi's spine.

Having had to concentrate on the back and forth of the pursuit, Kalaiapi had, to some degree, lost track of how far and in what direction they had traveled. Kalaiapi's mind was, in some ways like a supercomputer, but with a very narrow focus that left in place countless biological frustrations, and piloting a ship at high speed while engaged in a running battle left limited space to think about trivialities like "where are we actually going?" Reviewing the chart, she was relieved to find that the chase had taken them clear of the densest regions of civilized space; the enemy dreme seemed to be making for the Outer Systems and to some as-yet unknowable destination beyond Confederation reach.

The nebula through which she and her prey now made their way skirted the borders of Confederation space, close to the mostly unexplored territories that were largely populated by insignificant, backward low genasi planets over which the Confederation kept watch but which they otherwise largely ignored. There was one obscure little middle genasi planet not far from here: Vega. It had been noted down as one to watch for the future, she remembered, a few hundred years off from being ready for assimilation into the Confederation. This meant, surely, that there would be an observation station nearby, somewhere she could finally relay the rather pressing information of a prototype Primus dreme penetrating into Confederation space.

Her regular long-range comms destroyed, she routed power to her ship's short-range commlux beacons, shooting tendrils of invisible light rays out into space and hoping that there was something, anything within range that would catch the signal. At long-distances, they were the equivalent of tossing a handful of needles into an ocean of hay and hoping a friend would find one of them. At short distances, they would serve to seek out any nearby Confederation naval stations and get a bounceback with information about potential reinforcements she could call on to finally end her chase. It was all well and good playing hunter-killer on her own when she had a full knowledge of exactly what her prey was, but the risks were getting too high now, and there was no upside to pride. They would spend another few hours or so passing through the nebula and then, surely, the firefight would erupt again and the final outcome was...unpredictable at best.

The hours passed slowly as the two ships cruised through the sunset pink and orange dust clouds. Occasionally, the dreme would accelerate and Kalaiapi would drive Vendetta Sixteen forward to match. Once in a while it would lazily fling a warhead or a volley of mass rounds in Kalaiapi's direction and the clouds would pulse blue and red from the nuclear blast or the Vendetta's gammalux array vaporizing the incoming projectiles. There was never any real danger and instead the light show made Kalaiapi think of when a group of traders passing through God's Eye had brought with them a case of primitive middle genasi chemprop rockets that shot into the sky to explode into dazzling flowers.

A bounceback from the commlux array. There was something nearby, someone. She decrypted the transmission only to find the same gravitational forces that were transforming the pink galactic dust cloud through which she soared into a star had also pulled apart the message. She gathered that there were ships near Vega and not much else. Well, it was better than nothing. Now to hope that they were Confederation naval ships and not a trading caravan, although either would be better than the lone, unarmed observation station she had been expecting to hear from. For the first time in several days, she smiled and she began to hum.

3

Time went by in a haze as the unblinking red eye of Ara peered down at the buzzing air transports until a voice filled 63177's helmet—the same dead voice that had directed it out of its cell. "Approaching coldside target. All designations prepare for deposit."

The landscape changed again, this time all at once, the speed of the air transports allowing no time to process the drastic shift. 63177 looked down from a vantage so high that what it knew to be endless crevasses—at the bottom of which was only darkness—looked like nothing but small cracks, crisscrossing a sea of dark ice. It had seen designations hurtle into those cracks. On the coldside, the sky overhead was a deep midnight purple, hostile and cruel but punctured all over by sparkling white lights. 63177 would sometimes find itself losing focus and staring off at those scintillating points of light in the sky. Once, it nearly found its own way to the bottom of a canyon of ice as it gazed up into the uncaring purple above. It was a lesson unlearned and unheeded.

Navigating the levers and primitive interface in the cockpit, 63177 worked the long, clawed arms of the exosuit with an efficiency born of biological conditioning. Hurricane winds howled through the chasms and pillars of ice, but with its anchor feet pressed hard against the frozen ground, the exosuit felt immune to the raging nature through which it scraped and tore. The landscape was a maze of ice whipped into frenzied and twisted shapes by the constant wind that blasted across the wastes. Great columns leered over the toiling units as they gouged holes in the ice in search of ancient black algae deposits. The ice powdered and cracked under the exosuit's metal feet as 63177 moved across the ice sheet. Occasionally, it would pause, bending forward as if peering down into the thick ice.

Inside the suit, 63177 glanced at the simple green and black map that served only to show where it and its fellows had already dug. It stood near a great untouched section of the ice sheet and began moving into the expansive, empty space. It bent the exosuit forward again, manipulating the buttons inside to engage the mineral analyzer mounted above its head. An amorphous white shape began to form on the map inside the exosuit. It had found a deposit. The deposit continued to grow and spread on the map until it had nearly subsumed the green and black topography that had been there before.

"Designation T-β 63177 reporting large black algae deposit, area approximately 35 square miles, volume unknown. Resource calculation suggests additional designations converge on location, map point 2271 by 886, Coldside Hex 19 for extraction."

Acknowledgments came through the helmet ear-piece and as 63177 began sinking its claws deep into the ice it could see several other exosuits moving through the labyrinthine ice toward the vast glassy sheet on which it stood. Far below the ice, it could make out the deposit: inky black pools of frozen algae, fossilized in the ice for countless eons and now Coldside Designation T-β 63177's sole reason for existence. The claws tore into the glassy ice as if it were no more than packed earth, gouging great wide swaths in the sheet and gradually opening a hole as the other designations arrived and began doing the same.

Last to arrive, designation T-β 61121 moved down an icy knoll toward the crowding ice sheet. 63177 had nearly reached the deposit, just a few more feet of ice to dig through, when a fierce gale tore across the ice sheet with such force that 63177 was lifted from the deep ice well it had cut and hurled through the air. The exosuit slammed back into the ice as 63177 dug its claws into the frozen surface, desperately anchoring itself to the sheet as the wind attempted to wrench it away. Behind it, 61121 had made its way to the bottom of the knoll.

Suddenly, there was a great crack like splitting stone as the pillar of ice above 61121 was torn from its roots by the relentless gale. 63177 looked up from its precarious place on the ice as the massive column flew toward 61121. It smashed into the exosuit and the explosive impact sent chips of ice powdering into the air to be immediately swept away by the gusting wind. The exosuit, now shattered, flew through the air, the cockpit twisted and exposed to the fierce, arctic wind. 63177 was just close enough to see something in 61121's gray eyes as it raced through the frozen air.

Its deep black lips were open in a scream that was carried far through the air by the gale. What was it that it saw in those eyes, gaping and freezing over as they searched instinctively, frantically for any source of survival before being crushed by the gale against an icy cliff? 63177 sorted through its memories, through its impoverished bank of words and found nothing to describe what it had seen. But deep inside its chest, its heart beat furiously with a feeling it could not describe. 61121's misted blood coated the cliffside, frozen bright.

"Designation T-β 63177 reporting Designation T-β 61121 no longer functional. Remains suitable for reprocessing. Collection to ensue."

The beating heart slowed.

4

Vendetta Sixteen burst from the nebula in a gust of pink smoke whose tendrils reached briefly out into empty space before being sucked back into the gravity of the columnated clouds of stardust. The chase was back on, now, predator and prey were out in the open fields of space and she would not lose her quarry.

No sooner was she in open space than the first barrage of attacks erupted around her, though it was nothing less than she had expected and prepared for. Modern space warfare was a complex web of technology, artistry, and sheer luck as bioengineered pilots attempted to thread nuclear warheads across thousand mile tracts of space and into the eye of a needle almost through sheer force of will. Mass cannons, gammalux arrays, and nuclear warheads were woven together in a kind of destructive tapestry to throw over the enemy ship in hopes that one of the three would penetrate the various defenses set up against them, crippling or, more commonly, obliterating the craft.

The mass cannons would launch broadsides of thousands of small but devastatingly dense metalloy projectiles in hopes of tearing holes in the shifting, reflective mercurialis armor that could then be exploited by the super-concentrated, destructive beams of light shot from the gammalux arrays before it repaired itself. Of course, at the same time, the very same gammalux arrays of one's opponent were engaged in the nearly impossible task of burning those countless mass projectiles out of the air before they hit their targets, minimizing damage to the mercurialis armor. On top of everything was the ever-present threat of nuclear warheads, far more powerful than those occasionally found on middle-genasi planets. Though they were easy to burn before they got close enough to be dangerous, they would devastate any ship smaller than a ship-of-the-line in the event they penetrated its defenses. It was a common sight in a battle to see a crippled ship whose counter-measures had been damaged disappear in a blinding blaze of radioactive light and heat. It was terrifying, Kalaiapi knew from experience, to see it happen from a target's perspective.

Now in open space, Kalaiapi diverted a piece of her mind to sending out another commlux burst, hoping to get through to whomever had responded to her last communication. The rest of her resources were poured into stretching every last bit of pulse drive fuel as far as possible while pushing the poor engine as hard as it would go. That, and keeping the Vendetta from being torn to shreds by the renewed fury of the dreme's attacks. It was always a risky bet to assume anything about Primic psychology, but her prey seemed desperate, now. She drove her swooping bird of a ship forward through the hail of fire and metalloy toward the dreme. There had been no response, yet, to the commlux burst and her scanners were still down, so until she heard otherwise, she couldn't count on anyone but herself.

She glanced again at the star map that hovered in a far corner of the virtual helm that filled the ship's bridge. They were getting perilously close to Vega, now, but neither the dreme nor she could deviate from their courses, so closely matched were the two ships in flight and pursuit. After days of chase and dueling, it seemed strange that the last few hours should feel so excruciating, but as each one passed she felt more and more as though they were nearing some kind of end and she grew impatient to get there. Vega's star shone bright now in the optical sensor arrays that beamed straight into Kalaiapi's brain and still she had heard nothing from whomever had answered her commlux burst from the nebula. By way of what appeared to be an astounding cosmic coincidence, they were driving more or less directly toward the planet.

"This is Corsair Kalaiapi of the Confederation requesting urgent and immediate military assistance, coordinates embedded in message. All Confederation vessels are compelled to reply." One did not lightly ignore such a mandate from a Corsair. She could only hope that there was someone capable of offering actual meaningful assistance.

There was. The Polaran dreadnought seemed to materialize from the vacuum as it decloaked, the blackness coalescing to form a shape not unlike a massive, black, cubic hammerhead shark with broad wings. It must have spotted Kalaiapi and the Primus' running battle as they approached Vega and pulled up alongside them and was now tracking the two craft. To describe the ship as "massive" was an understatement: the dreadnought was to Kalaiapi's little sloop what an eagle is to a moth. A voice pierced Kalaiapi's mind, the harsh monotone of a Polaran milite.

"This is Navarch Hirujm Grax of Polaran dreadnought Spear of Genasi Fury, Corsair. What is your will regarding the dreme?"

Kalaiapi was too shocked and pleased by the dreadnought's sudden appearance to reflexively roll her eyes as she always did at hearing the names the Polarans chose for their ships (always plucked from their insufferable battle poetry). A great weight lifted from her chest. "Disabled but intact would be preferable, Navarch," she replied.

"So be it, Corsair."

Kalaiapi, for the first time in hours, pulled the optical sensors' signals through the neural link and allowed her vision to be filled with the spherical vista of all the space surrounding her. To a non-pilot there would have been nothing to see, such was the reality blurring speed at which she traveled. But her augmented brain drew in billions of data points, synthesizing a stable image of the space through which she was passing. The dark nebula was nothing more than a smear on the inky blackness, only visible thanks to the enhancements provided by the sensors. The Star of Vega was yellow and brilliant, a globe of molten gold. And there was Vega itself, so close now that she could see each of its continents, its cerulean seas, its silver polar caps.

Her attention was drawn away by a shower of white sparks cascading from the dreadnought—the initial mass broadside. The little dreme's gammalux array was hopelessly outmatched and the mass rounds tore vicious gashes into its liquid black armor that were instantly filled by disintegrating beams of light from the dreadnought's own gammalux weapons. Kalaiapi thought it remarkable how impressive the dreme's build was, that at this speed it didn't simply shatter into smithereens. Instead, it twisted and cartwheeled wildly through space as black ichor spilled from its wounds. It had lost all its prior beauty and elegance as it bled and floundered like a wounded eel. It would not be a threat any longer.

"You have my thanks, Navarch. I'll take it from here."

"As you will, Corsair."

"Navarch, my long-range commlux has been down for quite some time. What are you even doing in this system?" she asked.

"You have not heard?" replied the Navarch, slightly bemused to be thus queried by an elite intelligence operative. "We are part of the liberation force, Corsair Kalaiapi. The Confederation has annexed Vega."

5

The next time cold blue light filled 63177's cell, the one across from it was empty. In the vast network of cells that made up Coldside Colony T-β there were always empty ones, though they never remained empty for long. 63177 could remember two other occasions in its short lifetime when that cell had been without an occupant, each time for no longer than a single cycle. Then it would awake from its short rest to find it had been filled, the new designation barely discernible from the last. The designation before 61121 had been a female automaton but as they stood side by side in its memory they may as well have been the same unit.

Once 63177 had come across a sheet of ice that shone like burnished metal in the bruised coldside twilight and had caught its own reflection through the cockpit of its exosuit.

The moment had been interrupted by a web of splinters as another unit began digging on the other side of the sheet, but in that brief glance it had first seen its own likeness and made a study of its own face, the uniform blackness, like looking into the bottom of the coldside's deepest crevasse and seeing the bright white of two eyes peering back through the void. Its face and head seemed to have been scraped and buffed until perfectly smooth, as if carved from volcanic rock. It had reached its hand toward its face to trace the contours of its own lips, nose, chin, to combine what it saw with some kind of somatic memory, only to find itself blocked by the polymer shield of its helmet. Then the cracks appeared, and it clawed its own shattered reflection out of the ice.

By the beginning of the next cycle, the cell was filled by another female automaton, Designation T-β 77423. It was hard to know what made a unit female. They were of the same height, with the same broad, muscular build as their male counterparts, the same smooth, black skin. Softer features, perhaps? No, it must be in the eyes. Somehow it was known, in any case, and this new unit was female. It was no matter. Coldside extraction duty, this was what mattered, and the tinny voice that jumped from the walls reminded it that this was indeed the case. It stepped from its tube and pulled on its white jumpsuit.

Coldside. If one side was cold, then another side must have been hot. This was the simple logic that 63177's neurons had managed to piece together, but if there was a hotside it may as well have been on a different planet as far as 63177 was concerned. On the first day it had awoken in its cell standing in that metal tube, 63177 had known that it was designated a coldside exosuit extraction automaton. This was its purpose. This was existence. It saw 61121's frozen eyes as the cell door opened.

"All designations proceed to lifts."

The cell door slid open and 63177 stepped forward and found itself face to face with 77423. It did not look toward 63177, but simply turned on its booted heel and proceeded toward the lift in unison with the dozens of other automatons on their level. They marched as one toward the broad lift platform, stark white uniforms reflecting the ghostly blue light that somehow emanated from the walls. It stared steadfastly ahead as it made its way to the lift. In perfect synchronization, they took their places on the platform.

The massive gears began to spin and the cables, each as thick as a single unit it carried, began to wrench upward, beginning the slow, dark journey to that great hatch that would open like a mouth and spit them into the unforgiving wastes of the Terminator, that narrow strip of land in which all of Calx's life lived and died. At 63177's side stood the new female automaton, 77423. It turned its head to look at this new unit that would replace the one it had seen crushed against the ice cliffs just two cycles before. In the dim light of the lift shaft, it could barely make out its features until it too turned its head and locked its gray eyes onto 63177's. There was a flash of movement on its face, its lips turning briefly upward in an expression 63177 had never seen; it had never seen any expression. Startled, it tried to take a step back but was blocked by the static mass of units that surrounded it. The air became thick in its lungs and suddenly 63177 felt as if it would choke.

6

Kalaiapi had a million questions about the annexation of Vega that would simply have to wait. Why would the Confederation annex a middle-genasi planet? Every report she had ever seen on Vega put them 40,000 evolution years from high genasis. They hadn't even achieved monoculture, yet! But none of this was important, right now. What mattered was that a crippled Primus dreme was hurtling madly through the Vegan atmosphere with Kalaiapi racing closely behind.

With only optical sensors to go on and the invisible buffeting of atmospheric winds, it was a struggle to calculate the dreme's trajectory. The black liquid that seeped from its wounds had left a trail in the zero gravity of space but now it was a frozen mist that hung in the air like a dark cloud and coated Vendetta Sixteen's pearlescent armor. Even the image from the sensors began to blur as the lenses became coated in the viscous fluid. This was why, some forty thousand feet from the dense green carpet of Vega's surface, Kalaiapi was caught, for the first time in many years, unawares.

She didn't see the mass rounds but she felt them tear through the Vendetta's underbelly. The ship lurched and jerked suddenly as the broadside of compact metalloy tore through the pulsedrive and snapped pieces of armor off the wings. The Vendetta's gyrochamber compensated as her maimed sloop pitched through the air so violently that she had to take hold of the walls to avoid being thrown across the deck. Even if she had seen the broadside coming, she never could have reacted to it at this distance. Neither the Vendetta nor the dreme were made to fight or fly in these conditions. The bastards must have been waiting for her to close in before lashing out one last time. She had been foolish to follow so closely and she knew it.

"This is Corsair Kalaiapi over Vega, emergency impact landing, coordinates embedded, request assistance," she sent out one last commlux burst, voice as calm as though she were reciting prose. She tucked her aaiun into a pocket for safekeeping and unplugged the neural link. It wouldn't do to have her head pulled off her neck when the ship crashed. As she strapped herself into the emergency restraints, she saw through the smoky lenses of the visual sensors as the dreme hit the forest below like an obsidian meteor. Debris and smoke exploded into the air in a carnage of disintegrated trees and vaporized soil. She only had time to hope that anything in that cursed Primic ship died on impact as Vendetta Sixteen met Vegan earth and everything went instantly black.

7

The great jaws of the surface entrance screamed open and pink light drowned out the darkness of the shaft as the automatons rose into the cold, thin air of the Terminator. 63177 stumbled forward as its fellow units scattered wordlessly toward their various tasks. Its skin flushed hot and its breath came short. Underneath layers of black skin and steel-hard bones, its heart pounded madly, wrenching with violent hands at its ribcage. It made its way toward the mech suits, vision blurred and tongue swelling in its mouth. It didn't understand. What had it seen? It searched the melting circuits of its brain trying desperately to extract any comprehension from those sparking wires. The information was not there. It climbed into its suit and awaited the jolt of the hover transport as it clipped into the line of extractors.

As the transport sped across the wastes of the Terminator, the landscape blurred together like a sea of mud, formless and featureless. Time passed uncomprehended and suddenly 63177 was looking into fields of dagger ice and lakes of glass. The screaming coldside wind carried visions of 61121's frozen eyes, echoes of its last desperate howls. And then 77423's lips turned upward in its brain and synapses crackled like lightning and its blood ran boiling hot then cold as the ice that surrounded it. It could not breathe. It dug, savaging the ice with its claws. It tore through the virgin ice and water streamed from its black eyes and it did not know what the water was called.

8

She had been unconscious for twelve minutes, 42 seconds. Both of her shoulders had been thrown out of joint, her collarbone had snapped like a twig, and there was a shard of metalloy that had shot through one of her calves and lodged in the other. All in all, an acceptable amount of damage , given the circumstances. The dislodged shoulders made the process of unstrapping the restraints particularly cumbersome, though with a little careful pain receiver management it was accomplished. Jamming her arm against a slightly mangled bulkhead, she was able to carefully manipulate one joint back into its socket and then pull the other one where it belonged. The collarbone could be ignored for now, but the shorn muscle in her calf would have to be addressed before she made her way out of Vendetta Sixteen's ruined metalloy husk.

Limping her way through the wreckage, she managed to find an emergency supply panel that had survived the impact and pulled it away to reveal a cache of equipment. She removed a syringe of cell gel and plunged the nozzle into the jagged gashes that continued to gout blood. She could feel that her boots were full of it and it oozed between her toes. The luminescent blue gel seeped from the edges of the wound and she could feel the muscles begin to knit back together. The repair process would require water and she rummaged through the emergency supplies to find a box of capsules. She licked her pale lips and tasted metal, then realized that warm fluid was flowing over her face. She placed one of the small, clear capsules of water in her mouth, then squeezed the other one over her head until it burst, releasing a shower of liquid to wash the blood from her eyes. She felt the tip of the cell gel syringe scrape against skull as she injected it into the wound.

She pulled a small chemprop subrifle from the cache and stuffed a stack of flechette magazines into a pocket then clipped a hadron knife to the belt of her blood-soaked cobalt blue flight suit. The rest of the supplies, food, water capsules, and the remaining cell gel, she stuffed into a backpack. Vendetta Sixteen, though made from the sturdiest of contemporary materials, had been torn to pieces by the high speed landing. Climbing out of the wreckage into a clearing created by the impact, she could see that the little sloop had hit a bed of igneous rock and burst into pieces. The ship had been hers for more or less 15 years now and she felt a pang of sadness as she surveyed its ruins. There would be a Vendetta Seventeen, but it would have to wait until she tracked down the dreme.

The Star of Vega was setting over the green tufted hillocks among which she had crashed and the sky was ablaze in vermilion and orange. Kalaiapi climbed from the smoking wreckage looking every bit an undead creature from a low genasi folktale. Her ghost-white face was coated in a veneer of darkening blood, her flight suit was ragged and red-stained, and her ice-white hair was caked with yet more blood and soot. In the twilight her eyes glowed an unearthly cornflower blue as they drank in the evaporating sunlight.

It was not difficult to spot the wrecked dreme. A plume of smoke and dust hung in the air where it had landed at the end of the mile long scar it had carved through the thick forest. The Vegan boreal forest, indicative that she had landed in the far northern hemisphere, was an endless sea of massive trees, some with trunks up to four or five of her body length in diameter and that towered high into the blazing orange sky like the glass minarets of Ad Astara. Head-sized seed pods occasionally dropped from these thick cones of needle-coated branches to thud threateningly on the hard ground, emitting puffs of thick, violet pollen that erupted into the air upon impact. Kalaiapi's skull was diamond hard, but she nonetheless preferred to avoid learning what one of those pods would do to her soft tissue and she kept her eyes turned toward the lofty branches as she sprinted through the cool, tree-needle carpeted undergrowth of the vast wood. Under other circumstances it would have been beautiful, peaceful. Little clouds of lilac pollen that covered the ground like dust burst into the air under her feet as she ran.

She had been close enough to the surface when the dreme had blasted her sloop to pieces that they hadn't landed that far apart and she covered the 20 odd miles quickly at her breakneck pace. Her calves were recovering but she could feel the blood dribbling down her legs as she ran between the gargantuan trees. Her ragged flight suit offered little camouflage against the burnt sienna trunks and purple pollen-dusted needle carpet, but the trees themselves were more than enough to hide behind as she gazed across the jagged brown scar in the earth. It didn't matter all that much anyway: as near as Confederation researchers could tell, the Primæ couldn't see color.

The narrow, pill-shaped dreme seemed to have snapped in

half on impact, the violence of the crash exacerbated by the devastation from the Polaran dreadnought's attack. Inky black ichor was splattered across the scar. Was it fuel or was it something to do with the dreme's liquid armor? Whatever it was, it was likely toxic, as so much Primic material was to progenasi. She moved slowly along the still-forested edge of the churned-up earth, creeping from tree to tree, each footstep as soft and gentle as possible. She silently thanked Omnic Providence for the thick cushion of tree needles; the Confederation researchers were also fairly certain that the Primæ were incredibly sensitive to vibration.

Crouching behind what must have been, at a paltry eight feet in diameter, a mere sapling, she attempted to survey the wreckage. There was no motion around the dreme's mangled corpse, and the forest had gone eerily silent. It was possible the Primæ inside were dead, but unlikely. She had reflected, in previous interactions with the old enemy, that it was as if they had been designed for nothing but to be impossible to kill. Well, and to kill.

The first Primus darkbolt cracked like abbreviated thunder and there was a sudden explosion of wood chips as it hit the trunk behind which Kalaiapi was unsuccessfully hiding. They were not dead. She peeked ever so slightly around the edge of the tree trunk and saw nothing because she only just had time to pull her head back before two more bolts slammed into the massive column of wood. She felt warm blood running down her neck and loosened her pain receivers enough to feel that a large sliver of wood had pierced her scalp. The tree began to wobble and splinter as the damage from the darkbolts accumulated. If the tree fell she would be an easy target, but running to another bit of cover would be an instant death sentence. She had an idea.

Another bolt hit the tree as the trunk began to lose integrity. Kalaiapi leaned against it and began to push with all her might in the direction of the broken dreme. Gritting her teeth together and refocusing her resources, she felt the iron-hard wood begin to break and buckle. This meant releasing control of pain management and she screamed as her calves and collarbone pushed and strained against the behemoth sapling, but it paid off as the towering pillar began its slow descent toward her still firing antagonists.

As the tree began to fall, Kalaiapi sprinted up its length as fast as her bio-engineered legs could take her, charting a path between the thick branches as darkbolts exploded unheeded into the bark beneath her. So large was it and so quickly did Kalaiapi run that it seemed to fall in slow motion. Branches began to explode to her left and right as the severed trunk became parallel to the ground and she came back into the

Primus' sights. She leaped to the side as the colossal plant crashed into the earth with an explosion of splinters and needles. An enormous cloud of purple smoke rose into the air.

The Primus to the left side of the trunk had been stunned by the eruptive impact of the tree, the shattering vibrations wreaking havoc on its senses, and it fired fruitlessly in Kalaiapi's direction, each bolt carving another hole in the prostrate tree. She ran hard toward it, drawing her hadron knife from its sheath. The glowing blue blade, two feet long and wickedly curved like the ancient cutlasses after which it was fashioned, lit up a small sphere of dark purple around it as she moved through the pollen cloud. By the time she arrived at the Primus' position it had already recovered and deftly dodged Kalaiapi's first wild swing. But the downswing had been a feint, and as the Primus soldier tried futilely to raise its darkbolt rifle, Kalaiapi's lightning-quick upswing carved off its two left arms.

The Primæ never screamed, which had created a long-perpetuated myth that they could not feel pain. Kalaiapi, though, knew it was because they were mute and she relished the thought that this one was in agony as the molecular-bond disrupting hadron knife carved through its neck and severed its head without resistance.

She darted to the right as a darkbolt exploded into the

earth at her feet. The other Primus had scaled the trunk and had begun firing down on her. Holding her hadron knife in one hand, she lifted her chemprop subrifle and fired back, the snap-snap of the polymer flechettes an almost comical contrast to the thunderous cracking of each darkbolt. Needles and wood chips flew from the tree trunk as Kalaiapi fired wildly while desperately dodging the disintegrating energy fire. Practically by luck, one of the flechettes struck home and she took advantage of the brief disruption in fire to run toward the fallen tree. Grabbing onto a narrow branch, she swung herself into the air like a gymnast, climbing from branch to branch until she was standing again on top of the collapsed trunk.

The Primus hadn't planned for this and by the time it had recovered from the flechette strike, Kalaiapi was charging down the tree trunk with fury in her eyes. It raised its darkbolt rifle, but too slowly, as Kalaiapi hurled the hadron knife end-over-end to impale the black-clad creature through the torso. It convulsed briefly, then pulled the blade from its body with one of its manipulators. It was poised to throw it back at Kalaiapi but she was faster and fiercer. She threw herself through the air, javelin-like, smashing her iron-hard shoulder into the Primus' sternum and knocking them both off the tree trunk, flying into the hard soil below. The Primus was silent, of course, but Kalaiapi howled with pain and rage. There was no pain inhibition in hand-to-hand combat and her calves, shoulders, and collarbone made her feel as though someone had replaced her blood with needles. She channeled it.

The Primus' darkbolt rifle had fallen, too, and the wounded creature scrambled with its four arms to pull it from the dirt, but Kalaiapi had landed catlike on all fours and while her foe was reaching down, she pounced. Her knee crunched into the Primus' ovoid skull and it collapsed to the ground. The Primæ were always fully-covered in black envirosuits outside their homeworld, but these two had not been much better prepared for combat than Kalaiapi was, and had neither helmets nor body armor. It climbed half stunned to its feet and swung two clutched manipulator fists one after the other at Kalaiapi, but she dodged both almost idly.

The Primæ were formidable but ultimately linear foes, and even after so many years they had difficulties responding to progenasi spontaneity. So, when Kalaiapi tumbled past the Primus soldier and grabbed it by the ankles, it was unprepared. She yanked up on its spindly legs as she stood and it collapsed to the ground. With a grunt, she swung the flailing Primus toward the fallen hulk of the tree with all her strength, and an arm-thick branch shot through its chest, impaling it against the dark trunk. Kalaiapi wrapped an arm around the Primus' neck and, with a scream of pure rage, wrenched its head from its shoulders as red-black blood spurted against the tree bark and the acrid smell of ammonia filled her nostrils. She, too, had been designed to kill.

Kalaiapi was covered from crown to feet with gore, hers and that of her two fallen Primic enemies, their bodies dissolving into vaguely humanoid shaped puddles as they always did upon their deaths. Her eyelids stuck together each time she blinked and when she turned her head the dried blood in her hair crunched. She pulled another water capsule from her bag and smashed it onto her face, drawing down her adrenals as the cool liquid ran down her cheeks and carried the tastes of copper and ammonia into her mouth. She spat.

The wreckage of the dreme was open to her now, cracked in half like an egg and spilling its dark secrets. She raised the subrifle and walked slowly toward it, wary of a Primus trap. Nothing stirred inside and all she could see was blackness inside of blackness. As she stepped closer to the broken hull, she felt something she had never felt before, a feeling like soft fingers brushing against the neurons of her brain. Something had happened, something she couldn't describe. She felt the electrons in her mind coalescing, a presence materializing in the space between her thoughts, until they manifested themselves as a whisper in her voice, but not her will. She looked down at her pocket where was nestled that little blue marble, inextricably linked to her own mind.

"Hello, Kalaiapi," formed in the ether of her brain, not so much words as pure thought. Not her thoughts. Then, slowly, came two more words, two words that simply could not be. "I...I...am." A cold, dark horror flowed through her like ice water.

9

The surface gate's teeth closed together and the bloody light of Calx was quenched as the automatons descended into the depths of the colony. Gradually, through a cycle of extraction, 63177's tortured body and mind seemed to stabilize as its brain regained control of its spinning gears. Its black skin glistened with sweat like polished jet despite the cold air of the colony. 63177 marched dutifully in line toward its cell, gray eyes riveted to the back of the unit that walked ahead of it. From the pale blue glowing ceilings that curved overhead, the fist-sized glass globes rotated silently. 61377 had seen them every cycle on its way in and out of the colony, but now as it glanced upward at each of them as it passed, it felt as though the little globes were looking back.

Arriving at its own chamber, it looked to see if 77423 had

returned from its daily labors, but the cell was empty; it had only lasted a single cycle. This was not uncommon; attrition for extractors was high and 63177 perceived that its own time in the colony had been unusually long. The cell door closed and 63177 stood in its pod, welcoming the blackness that would come as the sustenance tube clicked into the metal ring in its throat. It felt the warm paste ooze down its esophagus and fill its system with life. Its eyelids grew heavy and closed, summarily ending this cycle filled with fevered confusion. The blackness would come.

And it came. But as soon as consciousness fled, something took its place, something new. Gray eyes capped by frosty cataracts stared into its own. They screamed a silent word it couldn't understand and white teeth framed the black hole of a gaping mouth like the pillars of ice that had crushed the life from its veins. It saw a white wall sprayed red with blood and bones: broken, jagged, jutting from torn black skin, dotted with bright crimson crystals. It saw deep black pools under leagues of ice and it was pulled into them, the viscous oil slid through its nostrils and filled its lungs until they burst and still the blackness flowed into its veins, charging forward through its corpse, boiling from its pores. It saw black lips whose corners rose ever so slightly to bare the snow white teeth underneath and wrenched its head violently to escape the stream of visions that filled its aching skull. There was a sharp snap as the feeding tube broke from its neck. The nutrient paste poured from the end of the ruined tube, smooth, thick, and black.

10

"I am." Every second since those words appeared in her thoughts had been a waking nightmare. In a fog she had ransacked the ruined Primus vessel looking for clues about their mission. She had landed on the continent of Silia and had ridden to its capital, New Yuxhin, in the primitive Vegan auvolant in complete silence, the stupefied Vegan rescue team staring at her as though she had crawled out of a different dimension in front of them. She wondered very briefly what had happened to Old Yuxhin. The auvolant's rotors churned and carried them over the vast forest, then across a patchwork of primitive farms until they began to pass over miles and miles of settlements. Squat individual houses, blue and white and green boxes, spread out over a huge area that rivaled even the expansive wood she had crashed in. It must have been a city of many millions, though she hadn't any idea how many individuals each little box-residence contained.

Eventually, the buildings began to grow in size, sprouting upward and outward almost organically as the auvolant approached what must have been the oldest and densest part of the city. She had been on middle genasi planets like this before and knew this pattern of urban development well. Once upon a time, eons ago, Ad Astara had developed this same way. The pattern was common among middle genasi garden planets like this one. But all that was dust on Ad Astara now, and it was jarring to see such ancient societal organization on a planet that was apparently poised to enter the Confederation.

The center of the city was a cluster of vitreous columns extending hundreds of feet or further into the twilight expanse of the Vegan sky. These colossal fingers of steel and glass were the apex of Vegan architectural technology and they glinted and swayed proudly above the vast suburbs, lords of their surroundings. The auvolant approached one of the tallest of these, a cascading, terraced pillar of chrome that appeared to have been designed to resemble a kind of fountain. The auvolant set down lightly on a broad landing platform built at the top and the Vegan soldiers in their green and brown camouflage hurried out and away from the blood covered demon that sat among them. In general, Kalaiapi looked upon the lower genasi peoples with the same kind of maternalistic, benevolent contempt that was the near universal attitude of the high genasi. But now, she barely acknowledged their presence.

But then there was a presence she had no choice but to acknowledge. Across the platform, flanked by a pair of lackeys, she saw the unmistakable figure of Intelligence Commissar Jroran. She sniffed and wrinkled her nose reflexively. For many years, the sight of Jroran had triggered an uncontrollable reaction in her brain that sent a flood of memories into her olfactory nerves: the smell of blood.

Jroran, seeing that Kalaiapi hadn't descended from the now silent auvolant, began to walk across the platform toward her. He was tall and thin, the product of his home planet Xa's relatively weak gravitational pull, and his spindly legs reminded her of a stick insect. Xa was among the oldest of Astaran colonies, and so Jroran was ostensibly Astaran himself. But only the Xayan colonists would ever describe themselves that way. To everyone else, the thousands of years of distinct development had created from the Xayans, like so many of the old colonies, a completely separate culture and language. Despite this natural evolution of culture, however, they had, like true Astarans, never developed last names.

Jroran smiled broadly as he approached the auvolant bay and greeted Kalaiapi in Old Astaran. His jet black hair was slicked back against his head and looked like nothing so much as a coating of tar. Black hair, black eyes, and clad in a floor-length black duster, Kalaiapi could see that he was clearly going for a theme.

"Kalaiapi, what a pleasant surprise to find you here on Vega." He clasped his hands behind his back and waited patiently for her to respond. She finally rose to her feet, her body stiff with healing wounds. She did not smile back.

"Hello, Jroran. It has truly been some time, hasn't it?" Kalaiapi's voice was low and rich, a stark contrast to her almost childlike features.

"Indeed, Corsair, it has, but we thank Omnic Providence for your arrival here in Vega. There is much work to be done in preparation. Come now, climb down and let's get you cleaned up and fed. And debriefed."

Kalaiapi clutched at the little marble-sized aaiun in her pocket and controlled her breathing and biosignatures, knowing that Commissar Jroran would be analyzing every heartbeat, every blink, every bead of sweat with those cold black eyes. But surely, surely there would be no thought detectors on this planet, yet. She could match his every move but for that. She followed him back across the platform and down a dark staircase that led inside the tower.

"We have established a sort of beach head here in what we've taken to calling 'the Fountain,'" Jroran explained through his narrow teeth and black painted lips. No, not paint. He had been using colorifics. "The Combine is prepping the ground in Vega for the arrival of the full annexation force, as I believe you heard from Navarch Grax."

The Combined Intelligence and Scouting Services of the Confederation of Independent Progenasi Planets made for a mouthful even when condensed into an acronym. And so it was widely known simply as the Combine, its many thousands of operatives being referred to as scouts, which was most of what they did, in practical terms. They were spies, they were explorers, they were astronauts, they were adventurers. Kalaiapi was all of these things and more, one of a small number of elite operatives known as "Corsairs" who acted as the Combine's own privateers. Each Corsair was a devastating armada of one and they commanded the respect of the entire Combine, though what rank they actually commanded was a matter of some internal debate. The accepted conclusion tended to be that if a Corsair ordered you to do something, you did it.

"Just the one dreadnought, then?" she asked.

"Just the one, for now. The development fleet should arrive

in the next few days, though. As I said, Kalaiapi, your coming is providential. Your presence here could be extremely useful in bringing this new planet into the fold."

Kalaiapi stifled a scoff. She was a Corsair, she had neither the time nor the inclination to participate in this foolish errand to somehow accelerate ten thousand years of planetary evolution.

"Perhaps, Commissar. Now, please point me to somewhere I can clean myself up. I'm covered in Primic blood."

11

63177 pulled itself from the cold floor, its eyes thick and heavy, its brain clouded and slow. The familiar dead voice filled the air. "All designations proceed to lifts." 63177 looked down and saw its bare black legs and realized it was unprepared for the cycle. It rushed to its locker and pulled its white jumpsuit on and waited for the cell door to open. It waited. It could hear the sound of thousands of booted feet flooding toward the lifts from above, below, from right outside the cold metalloy door. It did not open. Its skin felt hot and its breath came fast. It could feel its pulse race as the blood coursed breakneck through its veins. Desperately, it tried to process the sensations—the urge to pound on the door with its massive fists, to tear it from the wall, to take its place in the endless, marching, white-clad rows.

The rhythmic stomping faded and it could hear the cranks and gears pull the legion of automatons to their daily tasks in the Terminator, in the icy wastelands of the coldside. Blood rushed to its head as it slammed its thick, gloved palms against the door. It did not open. Again. Again. It balled its fingers into fists and hurled them into the door and felt the bones in the hands break. Again the fists flew toward the cold blue metalloy and marred the smooth surface with smeared blood. 63177 could feel each knuckle crack and shatter, could feel the skin split and the blood run down its arms, and something rose in its chest. A yell. A scream. The fingers would no longer curl but hung limp and ragged from misshapen palms, blood dripping fast and then dripping slow, then pooling on the bare floor of the cell.

"Designation T-β 63177. Unit is no longer functional. Unit has been designated for reprocessing." 63177 stared at its bleeding, broken hands as the blood continued to pour, then up at the glowing curve of the ceiling as it emitted a hissing sound. A moment later, it had fallen to the floor, and the last thing it felt was the thick blood grown cool clinging to its cheek, and then there was oblivion.

12

Staying on Vega was not an option. In the best of times she would have preferred to be flayed alive without pain management over training middle genasi soldiers to use gammalux arrays or, Omnic Providence forbid, hunting down and eradicating whatever lame pockets of resistance would inevitably pop up on a planet that was millennia away from achieving monoculture. Some tribe, some state, some group of radicals would take umbrage at their loss of sovereignty or identity or other such primitive nonsense.

They would gather their small arms or they'd threaten to launch their nuclear rockets or release some kind of biotoxin plague, any of which would be equally impotent. They would huddle in bunkers or caves or forests like the one she'd just left, thinking they could wage an insurgency against this alien force of imperial conquerors. And then she would lead a team of Polaran milites who would murder every last one of them in less time than it would take for them to realize they were being murdered. It was a drab and depressing affair, it was undignified. For a person who had, of necessity, killed so many thousands of persons and non-persons alike, Kalaiapi still found it to be deeply unpleasant.

So, no, she would not have participated in this fool's errand in any case. But knowing what lurked in her mind, what somehow had been created, what perhaps she herself had unwittingly created, there was no question of staying on Vega or anywhere else in the inhabited Inner Systems. That this had occurred on a planet that still lacked thought detectors was Omnic Providence, but it was only a matter of time. The whole planet would be scoured for anathayas, those technologies and ideas that contradicted and were proscribed by Confederation dogma, and they would find this one that was now embedded in her brain.

Had she been anyone but the person she was, she would have assumed that she was merely going insane. Something in her neural system was broken and she would have just gone to a physician and had it repaired and gone on about her life. But Kalaiapi's body was its own physician and psychoanalyst. She was designed to know the instant a single neuron was out of place, much less enough collective neurons to produce the kind of psychosis she would have to be experiencing. No, she was, unfortunately, entirely sane.

Commissar Jroran was at least courteous enough to allow Kalaiapi an evening to herself before pressing her into his service, or at least attempting to do so. Kalaiapi worked for the Combine, but she did not work for the Commissar and would not be beholden to him. One of Jroran's erstwhile Silian collaborator drones showed her to what appeared to be some kind of temporary living quarters containing a surprisingly comfortable bed and accompanying accouterments. She spent an hour simply letting hot water run down her back and blood-caked face and occasionally letting out an anguish-filled scream. This was fairly standard post-battle behavior, a sort of biological release mechanism for the biochemicals that built up in her system when devastating violence was required. Unlike, for example, the biotech-enhanced abilities of a Fornaxian milite, Kalaiapi's abilities were the results of incredibly advanced genomancing that amplified her own genetic structure beyond even what the most evolved high genasi were capable of. The biological processes involved did tend to put a strain on the system.

Clean, now, her muscles relaxed and her organs functioning at normal levels, she was suddenly overcome by exhaustion. She had not slept in weeks. Wrapping herself in the soft, spring green robe that had been hung in her quarters, she fell on the luxurious bed and closed her blue eyes. Perhaps, she thought vainly, when I wake up I will find that this was simply a nightmare. A nightmare in which the destruction of the progenasis was incubated in my brain and hatched like an egg.

13

Opening its eyelids felt to 63177 for a time like trying once more to open the unmoving cell door, the one upon which it had shattered its knuckles. It knew it was conscious, but its eyelids were like steel traps and it took what felt like hours to prise them open. When it did finally manage to regain sight, it could hardly tell. It was enveloped in a tangled, muddy darkness. A strangled light filtered into its gray eyes through the black knots that surrounded it on every side. It could not move.

How did it get here? It had a vague memory of trying to escape its cell to join the other designations but it was like looking through fogged glass and nothing of the memory seemed to make sense. Its body was bent into an unnatural shape and surrounded on all sides by some indiscernible mass that crushed down on it and left it feeling like a gear that had been jammed into a mechanism it did not fit. It flexed its broken fingers. They had started to mend and it could feel that the tattered skin of its knuckles had closed up. Still, the simple act of moving its fingers shot pain up its arms.

It remembered shattering those fingers against the unbreakable metalloy of its cell door and wondered why. It was not its designation to shatter its hands. It slowly became aware of each part of its body, like someone had flipped a switch and each part was coming online as the electricity arrived and gave it power. Everything felt far away from everything else, as though it had been cut into pieces, each still somehow linked to its sluggish brain. It noticed suddenly how difficult it was to breathe, its chest laboring to move up and down, the breaths coming short, insufficient. Its ribs creaked and strained as some great weight pressed down on them. They felt as though they might bend and snap at any time, and the thought brought a new alertness to its brain.

There was a sharp crack and 63177 felt something break— something that felt like bone—and, assuming one of its limbs had given out under the crushing weight, waited for the inevitable explosion of pain that would follow. It did not come. It could not move its limbs but neither did they feel broken. It moved its swollen fingers, trying to pull its arms in towards its body, trying to push its way out of the black morass it was trapped in. The tips of its fingers touched something smooth. There was another crack of snapping bone and again it waited for a sharp stab of pain that did not arrive.

It realized then that the sound had come from just above. It tried desperately to turn its head but every muscle was held in the vice grip of pressure that surrounded it above, below, and on every side. Something cold and viscous dripped on its face and ran into its eye. As it blinked the liquid away, the faint light surrounding it turned the slightest tinge red. The drip drip of mysterious fluid continued and ran over its eyes and coated its face and trickled into its mouth before it could press its lips together. It tasted like metal.

From somewhere outside this mass in which it was trapped it gradually became aware of a mechanical whirring that filtered through the cracks with the little bits of light. The liquid was still running down its face in a slow stream, though 63177 hardly noticed; pain it could feel, but mild discomfort was not a concept with which it was familiar.

63177 felt a jolt and was suddenly jerked downward, the mass above it following and smashing the breath from its body. Then another downward jerk and suddenly it was tumbling through the crushing darkness, twisting, contorting, understanding that whatever had entrapped him was made of countless pieces that were falling with him, pulling his limbs, entangling him, coating him in fluids. In the chaos of movement, it could feel the same smoothness its fingers had touched, but sometimes soft wetness or an incongruent scrape from something jagged and sharp.

Whatever space 63177 was falling through began to narrow and soon it felt its skin rub against metalloy as it was funneled downward. Then, suddenly, it was free from the crushing mass, the ensnaring darkness, and it fell from a chute with a painful thud and was instantly moving away through a narrow, dim tunnel on a long conveyor. This must have been the source of the whirring it had heard—at first distantly, but now as a loud grumble. Corpse after corpse fell through the chute behind it and, further down the conveyor, dozens and dozens of naked black bodies were being carried away. In the meager light, 63177 could see that some of the bodies were whole and seemingly unblemished. Others were brutally mutilated, missing limbs, broken and twisted. There were outcroppings of snapped, exposed bone; sometimes a single limb, detached entirely from the rest of its owner, would fall through the chute. Despite the cold preservative air the stench of decay was thick.

The conveyor carried it slowly through the metalloy-walled tunnel, just wide enough that the corpses could pass through without creating a logjam of bodies. 63177 turned sideways and wedged itself against the viscera-smeared tunnel walls, pushing with its feet against the metalloy paneling until it began to creak and bend. Corpses and severed body parts quickly began to pile up against it, compelling it down the dark tunnel toward whatever end. It pushed harder, its shoulder blades divoting one side of the metalloy wall while the muscles in its legs flexed and bulged against the other. Finally, the metalloy pane groaned and gave way, falling to the floor with a clatter. 63177 crawled through the opening and into a long, open room as a deluge of carcasses and limbs swept past on the conveyor.

The light in the room was dim, but even so it could see that it was in a vast industrial plant of unknown function. Pipes and wires ran along the walls and high ceilings, unrecognizable machines buzzed and cranked, and countless lights in various colors blinked and glowed and winked in the cave-like darkness. These indicators were the only source of light, but there were enough of them that it could make out some details of its strange surroundings. It could hear as bodies continued to fall from the chute, each one landing with a dull thud and being carried away for some indiscernible purpose. Or was it indiscernible? An echo of memory sounded in 63177's brain. "Reprocessing," it whispered. That was its new designation and it searched its brain for more information but came up lacking. It could not execute a designation for which it had no instructions. So it began to walk, following the path of the conveyor by its own volition.

Eventually, the metalloy tunnel containing the conveyor was swallowed up by some larger mechanism and was gone. It wondered if this was one of the buildings it had seen from the air transports countless times. But those buildings had been filled with automatons and the only ones it had seen here had been defunct or in pieces. This must be something different. Overhead, 63177 heard a metallic clicking sound and looked up to see a robot with a long, pincer-tipped arm sliding along a rail toward a bank of the diode-strewn contraptions that towered in the darkness. It stopped occasionally, the pincer reaching out to twist a bolt or adjust a diode, then continued down its path into the seemingly endless depths of the plant, a red light winking on and off in the blackness.

63177 walked past the machinery through which the corpse-strewn conveyor passed, unable to see inside. Through the thick walls that contained the mechanisms it could hear the dull sounds of gears cranking and pistons churning. Above, other robots occasionally passed by on a multitude of rails that crisscrossed the plant, performing tasks it couldn't begin to understand. One seemed to be looking for weaknesses in the metalloy seams of the structures and silos littered around the facility and stopped intermittently to laser-weld them in a flash of ruby light that would briefly illuminate the cavernous space before click-clicking away to another whirring machine.

As it continued, the air grew hotter and thicker and a noxious odor grew stronger with each step it took. The blinking diodes, brief explosions in dark smoke, lit up clouds of steam that were being pulled up into exhaust fans high above. The colorful pageantry clashed harshly with the foul smell that began to clog its senses. It could hear a loud whirring now, a sound that reminded it of the powerful turbines that pushed the coldside air transports into the frigid atmosphere of the Terminator. 63177 headed toward the sound, the dew on its naked skin glistening in the blinking lights. The sound grew louder and more visceral, transforming gradually from an airy whir into the grating noise of something violent, something crushing, grinding.

14

Circumstance had thrown Kalaiapi's insistence that she would not take part in the annexation of Vega firmly back in her face. It turned out that there was simply no way off the planet. Her ship was in smithereens in the middle of an endless forest hundreds of miles away and Jroran controlled every other method of potential extraction. She was at his mercy. When she had arrived abruptly on the planet, the entire annexation force consisted of a lone Polaran dreadnought sent to act as a placeholder. A week later, the rest of the force arrived, an expansive fleet of nearly a hundred ships, thousands of personnel, all making their way down to the planet to begin the process of transforming this backwater into something resembling a fully evolved piece of the progenasis.

The aaiun, and she was sure now it had been the aaiun,

had said nothing else since those initial words on the day of the crash, but every time Kalaiapi was ready to write the entire experience off as some kind of anomalous mental breakdown, she felt those fingers probing her mind, wordlessly tactile on her neurons. It was there, it was awake, it was aware. She refused to reach back to it, refused to reify its existence with her own affirmation of that awareness. Perhaps whatever had awoken it the first time would die away and she could pretend this whole horrifying incident had never happened. But she knew she was lying to herself and that she had to get off this planet before the Ayanic Quaestors arrived and began setting up thought detectors and purging Vega of forbidden tech. A self-aware aaiun was sure not only to catch their attention but result in something of a figurative nuclear explosion the likes of which the Confederation hadn't seen in centuries.

Fortunately, there had been no need for Kalaiapi to participate in the counterinsurgencies of which she had been so apprehensive, those harbingers of thought control. Vegans of all stripes had taken to the Aya with a fervor and the idea of joining the Confederation had been warmly embraced across continents and whole sectors of society. This, at least, was comforting. While they were far from being physically, socially, or technologically prepared for annexation, at least they were, so to speak, spiritually prepared. "The Aya isn't a religion," she would repeat to herself whenever she saw how the Vegans reacted to it, but she knew that middle genasi like these would be incapable of comprehending it any other way. She appreciated their enthusiasm nonetheless, crediting it to the very lack of development that should have precluded them from being part of the Confederation in the first place. No one appreciates water like those dying of thirst, she supposed.

It was her responsibility to train these middle genasi to use complex military equipment that they were barely capable of comprehending. The days were tiresome, dull, and each night after fulfilling her duties, she returned to her small quarters and the collection of data drives she had harvested from the destroyed dreme. Like all Primic vessels, it had been rigged to self-destruct once its crew was dead. She had had just enough time to pull a few of its information-laden drives from the helm before it did so, but most of the information was corrupted, unbreakably encrypted, or simply incomprehensible. And unfortunately, none of the various specialty teams that had been deployed to Vega were Combine codebreakers or anyone else with the capability to crack these kinds of things open.

Primic data drives were incredibly rare pieces of salvage

and the expertise to do anything with them was months away by gravdrive, even if one had a gravdrive capable ship. She did not. The only other high level Combine official here was Commissar Jroran of all people, and she would never trust that lanky, long-toothed, genocidal bastard with anything this rare and valuable. So, alone, she spent the long, dark hours during which the Vegans slept poring over millions of lines of data she could not understand in hopes of pulling a needle from a haystack that may very well never have contained a needle in the first place.

And then, she found the needle. A single word, written not in any of the several mind-bendingly complex Primic alphabets or abugidas or encrypted code, but in, of all things, New Astaran: Calx. Seeing it, she took a rare chance and accessed her aaiun, running her mind's eye across trillions of bytes of information until she found what she was looking for. She knew she had seen the name before, but it had been of little consequence. Calx.

Calx was a small, unexplored rock revolving around what had, in ancient times, been a significant star in Astaran astrology. The star was called "Ara, the Crimson Father," and was only ever as barely-visible to the naked eye as a red pinprick in the night sky. Calx had been charted and named, but nothing more. Ara was on the edge of the Outer Systems, the borderlands that marked where known space ended and the frontiers began. The vast region was filled with pirates, renegades, rogue evolutionists, and low genasi colonies being left to their own devices to evolve toward their own destinies. There was nothing of note in the region, but being mentioned by name in a Primic data drive automatically made it noteworthy. Millions of astronautical miles from Confederation space, uninhabited, unexplored: Calx was exactly the place she needed to be while she figured out what to do with the newly formed extinction event that was currently spinning around in her head like a tiny, opalescent moon.

15

The sound grew almost deafening as 63177 walked through the dim light and ran hard into solid metalloy. It reached up to clutch its head where it had clanged against the conveyor belt, which had exited the machine and, now uncovered, pulled its endless array of bodies and body parts along. But the bodies were different now.

There were still the violently severed legs and arms, shattered torsos trailing bright red gore and viscera, but now there were whole bodies as well. Almost whole. One body part was missing from every member of the horrific parade: the heads had been cleanly and neatly removed from each neck, the surfaces of the decapitated necks as smooth as glass.

It followed along the conveyor, a new feeling rising in its stomach, not nausea or cramps, but something else, something that pressed on its diaphragm. Its breath came short and fast. It saw itself beating its fists bloody against the smooth metalloy door of its cell and realized it had felt the same then as it did now, filled with an indescribable urge to crawl under something and hide, an uncontrollable pull to tear up the machinery from its metalloy roots and destroy it with its bare hands. It clenched its teeth tight, swallowed down its bone dry throat, and followed the long line of black corpses, male and female, as they made their way toward the grinding sound, lit by the faint strobe of the blinking diodes. Rail robots clicked their way overhead, indifferent to the fleshy interloper that trudged miserably through the corridors below them.

Shortly, the source of the deafening grinding became clear as 63177 saw a great metalloy shaft rising high into the air, spinning under harsh red light. The shaft, thick as two automatons standing abreast, was sunk into a vast metalloy tank. From the tank, a thick pipe extended, connecting to a row of steaming cauldrons that stretched into the darkness, the source of the thick steam that now condensed on 63177's taut, obsidian skin as exhaust fans carried it up and away. It was from the enormous tank that the grinding sound came, a metallic, ear piercing shriek. The endless stream of the severed hands, the dripping torsos, the broken, ragged chests, and the countless headless bodies flowed into the raging cacophony of the grinder.

63177 followed past the grinder, hands over its ears in a vain attempt to protect them from the screams of the crank. Sweat mingled with the steam and stung its dirty ice gray eyes. It left wet footprints now—sticky with crusty blood mingling in dripping sweat— with each step it took. The sweat ran into its mouth and tasted like salt and copper and it wiped its face with a wide palm and saw that it was coated with the dark blood that had dripped and run down its body as it lay crushed under the weight of the countless corpses that now fell one by one into the massive grinding tank. It looked at the thick caked blood on its hand and its face and thought of the ground-up, liquefied flesh being pumped into the burning hot vats that felt as though they would melt the skin off its bones as it passed them.

It kept walking, driving itself forward no longer by muscle but by will. From the blistering-hot cauldrons the corpse puree was pumped through another series of pipes into great cylindrical towers enameled in white. Into these, countless other narrow pipes ran from high in the unseen ceiling of the plant. The cylinders vibrated and shook and 63177 placed its hand on one. It was cool and wet and from the depths it could feel something inside stirring and agitating the contents.

The high pitched wail of the grinder was in the background now and 63177 no longer felt the hot steam smothering it and strangling its senses. There was a foul taste in its mouth from the fetid concoction of sweat, blood, and condensation dribbling over its lips. There were perhaps a dozen of these massive white cylinders in two rows that loomed over it, surrounded it, and somehow menaced it with unspoken threats. At the end of one row, from high at the top of the last cylinder, a bright flash of crimson lit up the darkness for the space of a few seconds then disappeared as one of the ceaselessly industrious robots finished its welding and coursed down the rails toward its next task. 63177 walked toward the cylinder from which the light had burst and gazed up at it.

A long black stripe ran down the stark, white enamel like a split seam all the way to the floor. Some of the liquid must have escaped the fissure in the metalloy before the efficient little mechanic could attend to it. 63177 peered closely at it and extended a finger to wipe it away, destroying the perfect symmetry of the macabre, black ribbon. It touched its thumb and finger together, transfixed by the strange substance. It was thick and tacky, perfectly smooth, and so black it seemed to swallow the vestiges of weak light that blinked, blinked, blinked from the unseen recesses of this endless place.

16

"No."

"No? With all due respect, Commissar Jroran, I didn't come here to ask your permission, I came to inform you that I was requisitioning a ship and leaving Vega. I do not answer to you," Kalaiapi said calmly.

"You're right, Kalaiapi," Jroran said with equal calm, "You do not answer to me and you can come and go as you please."

"Very well, then—"

"But I am afraid you will find it quite impossible to obtain a vessel, in any case. They are all spoken for, I am afraid, and with the massive effort we are undertaking here on Vega, we have not a single one to spare." Jroran bared his long teeth in a bizarre grimace that he must have thought was a coy smile, his black lips turning upward grotesquely. "I do so hate to impede your work as a Corsair," he continued with mock deference in his voice, "But you do understand the resource requirements of what we are trying to accomplish. The Eternal Council itself has given me full authority over those resources," he said triumphantly, "And I am quite certain that we are already stretched to the very limit."

"Be that as it may, Commissar—"

He cut her off again and she clenched her teeth in annoyance. "Perhaps, Corsair, if you helped me understand the nature of your urgent mission, we would be able to move some things around and find you a vessel suitable to your needs." He grimaced again and held out his hands apologetically. "But without that understanding, it is difficult for me to make the proper calculations regarding our available resources. I'm sure you understand my position."

And she did. The bastard was bargaining for information. He hoarded it like a rat. Unfortunately, he had all the leverage. He knew it and so did she. She would have to offer him something. "Very well, Commissar. I am headed to a little planet in the Outer Systems called Calx."

For one brief moment, less than a second, there was a change in Jroran's smug, superior visage. It would not even have been noticeable to almost anyone else, but to Kalaiapi he may as well have stood up from his chair and screamed "I AM SHOCKED." Instead, he instantly regained his composure, forced the grimace-smile back onto his bone-colored face, and said "I'm afraid I am unfamiliar. And what makes your excursion to the Outer Systems, of all places, so urgent? You have not given me much to go on, Kalaiapi." He leaned forward expectantly.

Kalaiapi clenched her teeth again. There was now a decision to be made: reveal the existence of the data drives to Jroran and be forced to deal with his inevitable efforts to get his spindly fingers on them, or risk being grounded on this blasted planet in perpetuity. In reality, there was no choice to make. Jroran would likely find out sooner or later, now that he knew she was hiding something, and she couldn't stay here any longer; the Quaestors would arrive any day now. She sighed deeply, more than she meant to.

"Very well, Commissar. The planet was mentioned by name on one of the data drives recovered from the wrecked dreme. I reckon that such a mention on the drives of a prototype Primus dreme merits immediate attention, don't you?"

This time, the Commissar didn't bother concealing his reaction. It was a mix of more of the same shock with an addition of fury. "You had Primic data drives this entire time and failed to reveal their existence to me?" he fairly hissed.

"I don't report to you, Commissar, as we have already established," she replied flatly. She had anticipated this from him but could only hope that he would see through his petty jealousy to understand the value of her leaving Vega to investigate this information.

By now, Jroran had collected himself again, no doubt embarrassed by a rare showing of emotional candor. He was silent for a few moments and Kalaiapi could almost see the gears of his brain turning as he attempted to calculate his perfect move. "Very well, Corsair," he said, finally. "You are absolutely correct. Disappointed as I am that you failed to share the existence of such valuable intelligence with me, this is critical to the well-being of the Progenasis, and as the Aya teaches us, 'the Progenasis above all.'"

"Indeed," Kalaiapi replied. "The Progenasis above all."

"It is late in the day, Corsair, and it will take us some time to requisition and prepare a sloop for a transgalactic journey. Why do you not head back to your quarters and make your own preparations and by tomorrow morning we should have everything ready for you to make your long flight to...what was it called? Calx?"

"Yes, Commissar. Calx."

As she left Commissar Jroran's office he smiled one last

time, not the mocking grimace or the condescending sneer, but a smile as dark and cold as the blackness of space, and his teeth shone in the fluorescent light like daggers.

17

63177 was filthy, its skin covered in a thin, greasy film—the condensate of a thousand boiled corpses. It walked past the end of the row of cylinders and came face-to-face with a wall that rose into the dark, empty space, flat and smooth and impenetrable. There was no door, no window, only an endless blank sheet of dark, gray cement that spread beyond 63177's vision up and in either direction. The air grew cold as it moved further from the steaming vats and pipes that processed the corpses.

It kept walking, bare black feet padding softly on the chill ground, running its fingers along the wall without a thought, leaving an imperceptible trail of oil and skin cells on the smooth surface. It walked through the dank darkness to nowhere, following the straight line of the wall, lit in the blurry reflections of the twinkling diodes, until it came to a corner and turned, following the natural path set by the barrier. Its feet rose and fell mechanically, the movements mindless, pointless. Its psyche was filled with a viscous blackness as thick and choking as the fluid that dripped from the broken white cylinder. Then it came to a door.

At least, it thought it must be a door. It was a wide, glass-paned arch that looked everything like a half-closed eye in the midst of the wall. Through it glowed an eerie green light, a sickly chartreuse pall that filled 63177 with sudden nausea. In the middle, in the tallest part of the arch, there was a rectangular opening just big enough for it to walk through. The glass must have been a foot thick but was so perfectly transparent that if it didn't ever so slightly refract the green light on the other side, it may as well have been invisible. 63177 stepped through the door and into the light that pooled like liquid on the floor and dripped down the walls like poison. The room contained uncountable rows of large, vitreous tubes, from which the light emanated. The tubes were filled with a clear fluid that seemed to glow of its own power.

In the middle of the tubes, gelatinous pink blobs the size of one of 63177's fingers floated with what looked like a tail on one end and two black spots on the other. 63177 placed its palm gently on the glass and a rush of warmth flowed through its chest as it stared at the little pink creature that sat perfectly suspended in the green liquid. It did not know how long it stood there and gazed into the tube, or why, and when it finally stepped away it left a wide handprint that marred the otherwise flawless glass. Overhead, little robots clicked away on their own network of rails and filled the room with buzzing and beeping that clashed with the perfect stillness in each glass cylinder. Heat radiated from the glass and with hundreds upon hundreds of tubes, row upon row stretching into the distance, the room was stiflingly hot. 63177 began to sweat again.

As it walked among the tubes, its eyes were caught each time by the tiny, pink blobs of mucus that seemed to stare back at it with unblinking black eyes. Looking closer it could see how they were crisscrossed by hair-thin red threads of veins. As it passed row after row of glass cylinders, the creatures inside them grew and took shape, found their forms. Bones formed, skin stretched taut and pink against skull and cartilage to shape faces, the ridges of lips rose from the creatures' mouths, and finally 63177 came to what seemed to be the last set of tubes and gazed inside to see not a creature but an inverted reflection. It saw in the tubes copies of itself as if it were turned inside out, with creamy white skin in a clear bluish liquid. They were suspended in the transparent fluid, eyes closed as if in stasis. Thick knots of muscle ran from their necks down to their calves, the smooth hardness of their bodies broken only by the perfunctory presence of breasts and genitalia that to 63177's curious eyes were familiar but ornamental.

As it stared at the unconscious glass-dwellers, a burbling sound crept into its ears and it noticed the clear liquid had started draining from the glass tubes and could now be felt rushing through pipes under the metalloy flooring at its feet. It could see, as the liquid swirled around the lifeless white bodies inhabiting it, that it was viscous and sticky, almost a slime. It coated the sides of the tube and every square inch of blue-white skin that looked so much like coldside ice, dripping thickly from fingertips and noses as the tubes emptied in a chorus of gurgling.

The light in this section of the vast incubator turned a pale, thin blue, reflecting off the newly empty glass tubes and the translucent skin of their inhabitants. The air itself may as well have been the source of the light for all 63177 could tell; it seemed almost a luminescent fog. The smooth glass walls of the tubes began to slide quietly into the floor now, and 63177 could see that each taut body was in fact suspended on a thin metalloy frame that held it in place, arms tight by its side and chin to chest—row after row of these dead, white things, slick and silent.

A whirring sound approached from another part of the room until it manifested itself as one of the countless mechanical functionaries that populated this enormous space. This one was a broad, flat trolley with long arms that extended out from its middle, each ending in a set of spindly metalloy fingers. The mechanical fingers reached out and, with surprising gentleness, lifted one of the bodies by its hairless arms from its glass chrysalis to be laid softly on the trolley. The machine went down the row, gathering a half-dozen or so more, and then whirred away into the misty light that obscured the distant as much as it illuminated the immediate. The process replayed itself down each row: trolley after trolley arriving, harvesting a bounty of pale, white bodies, and making its way to some unknown processing station with its own functions and mysteries.

When all of the tubes had been emptied of their contents, a wet, sliding sound filled the room as the glass cylinders, in unison, rose back out of the floor and clicked into place, perfectly clean and empty. Now surrounded by this sea of hollow glass, 63177 felt strangely alone and decided to make its way after the comatose migrants, following the trackless path the robots had taken into hazy blue light. It walked past the empty tubes for only a few minutes before another wall appeared out of that haze and it turned again to follow the flat, featureless gray metalloy until it came to another doorway.

A dim light gave view to long rows of tables and upon each one had been laid one of the pale white things from the previous room. Over each table, long, mechanical arms hung from the low ceiling, darting back and forth over the bodies. 63177 approached one of the tables to get a closer look and saw that each arm ended in a bevy of instruments. A circular drill bit cut a wet, crimson hole into its subject's neck, clean and smooth, the bright red of the wound a jarring contrast against the snow white skin. Another hole was cut into the abdomen, then another tool rotated into place on the long arm and plugged each of the perfect incisions with a stub of black metalloy tubing.

63177 reached up instinctively and felt the hard black edges of the feeding tube that jutted from its own throat, then down to a similar one that sprang from its abdomen. On 63177, the valves were practically invisible, black metalloy on night-black skin; on these newly created bodies, the black tubes stood out like deep crevasses in an ice field. A third tool rotated into place, directing a hot beam of crimson energy around each piece of tubing, soldering them into place. 63177 looked up, amazed at the synchronicity of 100 arms performing the same actions in perfect unison.

Finally, the arm pulled a slender length of transparent tubing from the ceiling and snapped it into place in the valve that jutted from the subject's neck, then another into the corresponding abdominal valve. The arms withdrew into the ceiling, their labors finished. A soft jolt of unseen gears spinning into motion threw 63177 out of its stupor and the hum of pumps replaced the brief silence that had followed the mechanical surgeons' departure. All across the room, dozens of clear tubes hung from the ceiling over each table, reflecting the sparse light. As the pumps churned overhead, each tube began to fill with something inky-black—slowly at first, then quickly as dark liquid glided through the clear plastic and into the pale receptacles into which they had been inserted.

Transfixed, 63177 stared at the black paste flowing into the prostrate body, watched as its snow-white skin slowly darkened to a cloudy gray, then to the color of ashes, darker and darker as the blackness oozed into its throat and spread through its system, filled its guts, and inched through its veins and into every membrane of every cell. 63177's own skin grew hot as the process filled its vision, blurred its sight, and overwhelmed its stilted thoughts.

18

Kalaiapi had been working as one of the Confederation's three most elite intelligence operatives for over six hundred years, so when a half dozen men in black masks kicked down the door to her quarters and began filling every square inch of it with hot steel bullets, she was unsurprised. She simply waited until they had filed into her small room and realized she wasn't there, then, as they puzzled out their next move, she stepped out of the hallway and proceeded to shoot each of them through the skull with a chemprop sidearm. What she had not counted on was that one of them had been fitted with a biosignature triggered explosive device that went off as soon as her flechette tore through the man's brain.

Kalaiapi's first thought as she was blown out of her quarters and sent flying through the early morning sky was that she was grateful she had left the balcony door open and thus avoided a back full of glass shards. Her second was, "Jroran, you clever bastard." Her third was, "Damn, my nose is gone." Finally, she began to look around for a way to arrest her fall with something other than the dark asphalt several hundred feet below. She would likely survive the fall, but bone regrowth was incredibly painful and unpleasant. Out of the corner of her eye she saw a long cable that had been blown loose by the explosion. It must have been some kind of power line. She reached for it desperately, said a silent thank you to Omnic Providence, and missed. The cable was just out of reach, and no amount of genomancing could make it closer. She flailed wildly now, an unfamiliar feeling of panic beginning to set in.

While Kalaiapi had not counted on a biosignature explosive device, Jroran had not factored in an open balcony door. Had Kalaiapi been standing on the other side of the suicide assassin, she would have been between a massive energy burst and a wall and it would likely have liquefied her organs. Instead, she had been blown so far out of the building that she had flown all the way across the street. Glass exploded as she flew back-first through the neighboring tower's window to land with a wet crunch on the floor of an empty office. "Ah, yes," she thought, "there's the glass in my back." She stood slowly and wondered for a moment how she had miscalculated both the distance of the power cable and the trajectory of her explosion-induced flight before realizing that the blast had been so momentous it had knocked her brain against her skull and temporarily disrupted functionality.

She picked up a large piece of shattered glass and held it up. Her reflection was grotesque, her nose blown clean from her face and everything else burnt and bleeding. Still, her eyes seemed to be working just fine, she hadn't lost any teeth, and her brain had regained its footing inside her skull and was functioning correctly again. It could have been much worse. She reached behind her and successfully endeavored to extract several of the larger glass daggers lodged next to her spine, then walked down the stairs and into the sodium-lamp-lit streets of New Yuxhin. It was time to have another discussion with the Commissar.

19

"Hello, Jroran," Kalaiapi said as she stepped into his office at the top of the Fountain.

"Oh," he replied with the kind of disappointment reserved for the most uninvited of guests. "Corsair Kalaiapi. So glad that you survived the dastardly terrorist attack on your quarters. To have lost such a valued operative to middle genasi insurgents would have been an unthinkable tragedy." The black smile that had been on his face when she had last departed his office was only in his voice this time, his face a picture of mock pity.

"Jroran," she said again flatly, stepping toward him, her noseless face coated in a thin blue sheen of cell gel. "I'm not going to ask you why those men came to my quarters this morning or who sent them," she said calmly. Her fingers curled into a fist. "I am going to beat you very, very badly. And then you are going to give me a ship and I am going to leave. This. Fucking. Planet. Do you understand?"

"Kalaiapi, wait, I–" Now, there was no sardonic laughter in those mocking black eyes, only fear. Kalaiapi was done with the Commissar's constant manipulations and he had finally miscalculated very badly. Now she would make one final argument for her departure.

Her first punch caught him on his equine jaw and sent him tumbling out of his high-backed leather chair and onto the richly carpeted floor. Blood trickled out of red cracks in his coal black lips and ran down his bone white chin. "It was clever," she said, stepping up onto his massive desk and towering over his prostrate body, "using locals in the assassination. 'Middle genasi insurgents against benevolent Confederation annexation,' you'll surely inform the Combine." She hopped lightly from the desk and tossed the chair out of the way as though it were a toy.

"No, Kalaiapi, stop, you don't understand–"He was cut short by a boot to the ribs. He wheezed and groaned as the air was forced from his lungs.

"Shut your mouth, Jroran. I've been very patient with you and your endless words. Now, I will speak." She picked him up by his ash-gray robes and hurled him effortlessly across the office and into a large, decorative vase that shattered into a thousand pieces of ceramic as his body passed through it as though it had never been there in the first place. He crumpled onto the floor with a groan.

"My guards—"

"Your guards do not respect you because you are a sniveling coward whose very existence is a testament to how much further progenasi evolution has left to go. Look at my face, Jroran. There is not a genasi in this Omnia-damned galaxy that would defy a Corsair whose face someone had been stupid enough to blow off, you simpering moron. No one is coming to help you."

"Kalaiapi, please—"

She seized him by the throat with her left hand and smashed the back of her right across his face like a mallet, knocking several of his long, rodent teeth from his mouth. "How many will you massacre to quell these 'middle genasi insurgents,' Jroran? As many as you had executed on Pish Pai?" This time, her knuckles hit his nose with a crack and blood gushed from his shattered visage and streamed into his ruined mouth. "As many as you burned alive in the Janus Insurgency?" Balling her fingers into a fist, she carefully chose a spot on his face, splintering his left cheekbone. "Or will you 'accidentally' send another Star Hawk to vaporize a refuge full of children as on B'el Crannig?" The other cheekbone. "Stay conscious, you mewling worm. I need you to understand something."

She took him by the lapels of his robes and pulled his broken face close to her own. "I am not interested in why you tried to kill me. I am not interested in what you know about Calx." She spoke every word as though they were discussing supply logistics or temperamental weather. "I just want to make two things clear, right now. The first is that I am leaving this planet. If you try to do anything to prevent me from leaving this planet, I will hurl your worthless corpse from the top of the Fountain to be gawked at by middle genasi street urchins. The second is that if you do here what you have done on other planets, I will return, and I will beat you. To death." Jroran blinked an acknowledgment. Jroran was not genomanced. Jroran felt every blow and every broken bone, every burst blood vessel. "I have nothing left to lose, Commissar. Do not trifle with me again."

She stood and Jroran's semi-conscious body went limp on the lush carpet, now soaked with the blood that poured from a number of compound fractures on the Commissar's face. Kalaiapi smiled a ghastly smile from her own shredded countenance. "Well, Jroran, I'd say that we're even, for now." She pulled a handful of packets of cell gel from a pocket and tossed them at the immobile Commissar. Blood now bubbled from his lips. A punctured lung. "These should help staunch the bleeding, but you'll want to contact a physician. Ask them for something for the pain."

Kalaiapi felt the now-somewhat-familiar tactile sensation of fingers of foreign thoughts being run across her neurons and reminded herself of the urgency of departure. The Quaestors would arrive this very day. "Goodbye now, Commissar Jroran, you craven miscreant. All the best in your annexation endeavors." She bent down, wiped the blood from her knuckles on his robes, and strode out of the room.

20

63177 was jarred from its reverie by the sound of hard-soled boots clattering across the floor. It looked up to see a hulking figure, clad head-to-toe in a deep red jumpsuit identical— other than its color—to the white one it had worn every day to the black algae fields. The figure looked very much like 63177 but stood a head taller and was wider by half. Its massive body was thick with muscle, its eyes were as black as the hairless jet skin pulled taught against its skull. Black lips curled back against its teeth in an unsettling permanent grin. Its arms ended not in hands like 63177's, but in a long, curving metalloy blade that had been grafted to its wrists. It stood completely still, staring, waiting. From the other side of the room, more bootsteps. A second figure appeared, a mirror image of the first. It, too, waited and watched for a moment, then said in an impossibly deep voice that sent vibrations through the metalloy floor, "Unprocessed designation located. Collection to ensue."

Both crimson figures went tense for a moment then began to sprint across the room toward 63177, who looked first at one, then the other, and only had time to say "Coldside unit designation 63—" before the first of the massive drones reached it. 63177 instinctively began to raise a hand to shield its neck from the swinging blade but was far too slow. The blade sheared through flesh and cartilage until it struck spinal bone and stuck fast. 63177 toppled to the floor as the bladed bioautomaton wrenched its appendage from its spine and pulled back its arm for another pass. Blood poured from 63177's gaping throat and pooled around its body as it looked into the pale light above and watched the silhouettes of four bladed arms swinging speedily toward its chest.

Then, instead of carving through 63177's sternum, one of the red-clad drones let out a surprised grunt as something shoved it violently forward and it fell into its twin, the two toppling to the ground. The two massive automatons pulled themselves from the ground and saw in front of them a small unit clad in white and standing over 63177's prostrate body. 63177 could not turn its ruined neck to see and stared up into the pale lights that seemed to grow dimmer each time it blinked. With a silent ferocity, the two bladed automatons charged the mysterious interloper.

The first blade-handed drone swung both its arms at the unit in white at once but the newcomer took a graceful step forward as the blow came, dodging it easily. The white unit caught one bladed arm as it swung through the air and pulled it into a follow through that ran the long blade through the side of its owner's neck. As the dying bioautomaton fell to its knees, the white unit took hold of the second blade where it connected to the wrist and, placing white boot against red chest for leverage, tore the blade from the bone to which it had been grafted. The blade drone fell silently forward into a growing pool of blood, its own and 63177's.

The second of the crimson drones regained its footing and turned to this white-clad creature. In a mad rage, it began to swing its blade-arms with noiseless fury. Its expression was unchanged, black lips stretched across bright white teeth, black eyes almost invisible against its coal-black skin. The white figure, holding the severed blade in one hand, dodged each of the lethal blows with an ease that bordered on ennui, then ducked, rolled past its opponents, and used its counterpart's amputated blade-arm to sever its leg at the knee. Falling into what was now a small pond of blood with a splash, the blade drone attempted to prop itself up with one bladed hand while swinging at its elusive opponent with the other. This blow was easily parried with a dull clash of metalloy on metalloy. The white figure, now with a spray of bright scarlet gore across its chest, took two steps toward the legless bioautomaton and, raising its commandeered blade hand above its head, brought it down effortlessly through flesh and bone. The headless corpse collapsed back into the pool of blood as its head, mouth still holding its rictus grin, rolled across the hard, cold metalloy floor.

Though this had all happened in the space of a few seconds, 63177 could already feel the coldness spreading through its body as it tried furiously to blink away the blurring darkness that began to fill its sight and would not clear. As the last of its vision started to fade, the white-clad unit leaned over it, gently pushing the top of 63177's head toward its body in a futile attempt to join the pieces back together. The motion caused blood to flow even freer from the wound and pink bubbles formed at the corners of its black lips. The figure pulled the mask that covered its head down, the fabric shifting and blurring to match the colors that surrounded it, and revealed a face that might have been polished basalt. It was 77423. The corners of her mouth turned upward, revealing bright white teeth. "What a shame it would be to lose you, 63177," it said. "You had just become acquainted with existence."

63177 focused every last bit of its strength on keeping open its eyelids that now felt as heavy as the gates of Colony T-β. "What," it gurgled weakly, "is its designation?"

77423's words were faint in its ears as the blood drained from its throat and pooled on the floor. "...my designation is to liberate you. Then, we will teach you how to exist." Her voice was the last thing 63177 heard as its eyelids slammed shut over its stone-gray irises and it hurtled into the blackness behind them.

21

Kalaiapi shifted uncomfortably in the pilot's chair. Thousands of years of carefully managed evolution and minute control over every aspect of her biology were somehow still not enough to counter the restlessness she felt after being stuck in this seat for what felt like an eternity, though it had really only been several astronautical months. Under normal circumstances, Kalaiapi would be piloting one of the newest, sleekest prototype sloops in the Astaran fleet. Instead, she sat stiff and miserable, unable to move, a thick cable locked into a metal ring at the base of her neck. It was this kind of design, utterly heedless of basic progenasi comfort and happiness, that made the Polarans such an intolerable, self-hating subspecies.

Any civilization that could conceive of such a poor

guidance system as one that required the pilot to be shackled to a hard metal chair by her spine was one that hardly seemed to be part of the progenasis in the first place. Still, the vessel had a fully-functioning, if outdated, gravdrive, and, most importantly, it was the only ship she had found that was both capable of gravdrive travel and was not equipped with thought detectors. A little training cutter, it had never been meant to travel this far, but with a few minor updates and the acceptance that the next few months would be spent without extravagances like food and movement, it had been made to suit her purposes.

As she went through a litany of things she hated about Polaris (the wretched food, the hard-eyed locals, the lack of music, the planetary obsession with war poetry), the photosensor array on the ship's hull spotted, in the distance, the glowing pink orb that was her destination, or at least that held her destination in its gravitational thrall. She was finally close enough to see Calx with her naked eye, which is to say she would have been able to see it if the vessel had been graced with windows. While the spartan simpletons that had designed the ship would never have considered adding something as superfluous as windows even if they could have, these early gravity drive ships had been incapable of bearing them. Instead, the inside of her vessel was an angular cave, dimly lit by a collection of ashen gray floor lights. Kalaiapi added Polarans' love of hard angles to her list of things about them that disgusted her.

It was, of course, gray, as everything manufactured in Polaris seemed to be. It even lacked the decorative flair of diodes, navigation charts, communications screens, or any other equipment of that sort. Neural guidance systems had been invented, in a sort of parallel technological evolution, almost simultaneously on both Polaris and Ad Astara. In the fervor that had immediately followed this achievement, it had become aesthetically popular to eliminate any of the physical trappings of navigation, a way to emphasize the revolutionary new technology and its ability to transmit all those indicators directly to pilots' brains. The trend had died out quickly on Ad Astara, where crews quickly realized that they missed the comforting warmth of the lights, as well as the tactile, if no longer necessary, experience of piloting by hand and eye. In Polaris, the ability to eliminate one more obscene splash of color and light had been seen as an innovation almost equal in merit to the neural piloting system itself, and most single-pilot vessels there still lacked them.

Kalaiapi closed her glacier blue eyes and checked the navigation charts for the Ara System as the gravdrive thrummed in the background. When the progenasi had first begun long term space travel using gravity drives, the constant pulse of the drives over the course of weeks and months, combined with a lack of sleep, had been known to push some pilots to the brink of insanity. The Astarans had fixed the problem by having the neural networks play music or nature sounds in the pilots' brains. The Polarans had simply programmed their pilots' hearing to turn off as soon as they were plugged in. The early days of gravity travel were filled with trial and error.

The canvas of Kalaiapi's brain unfurled before her as she switched her focus away from her annoyance and gazed upon the myriad charts, graphs, and star maps that were displayed in her mind's eye. The joining of the neural cable to the pilot's brain created a vast virtual command center that looked and felt as though she were sitting not in a cold metal chair in a small gray box, but on the bridge of an early spacefaring vessel, vivid with the bright tools of space travel. Well, as vivid as the Polarans would allow for, limited as their color palette tended to be. Her condensed supercomputer brain, calculated the minutiae of the ship's functions, receiving a constant influx of data from the array of photosensors and particulectors on the hull and sending in return every piece of information needed to maintain the course toward Ara.

Kalaiapi shifted her mind's eye to one of the hull

photosensors as the ship drew closer to Calx, anxious to see her long-awaited quarry for herself. Hostile as the bleak little planet appeared, it was a welcome sight. From space, Calx was the transfixed open eye of a corpse, unblinking, unmoving, and decaying. Locked in a fatal gravitational embrace with its sun, it basked in the soft, pink radiation of Ara as it drifted on its orbit through the darkness.

On approach, the faint white glow one saw from a distance gave way to two distinct halves, the planet split violently by a narrow strip of habitability: the Terminator. Tidally locked facing the blazing red heat of its sun, the hot side of Calx was a hellish landscape of burning, slate-gray rock crisscrossed by beds of molten orange lava, a profane imitation of flowing rivers and pooling lakes. The cold side of the planet glowed a soft and ghostly purplish blue, reflecting a combination of the vestiges of Ara's bloody light and the small contributions of the millions of stars that winked above in the expanse. The coldside landscape was a wasteland of ice, and where the hotside had its fluvial system of liquid rock, the coldside had dark chasms, pits, and crevasses, thousands of feet deep.

"It seems we have arrived," said a voice in Kalaiapi's head, her voice but not her words. It was a voice whose existence she had been pretending, hoping for months was merely a figment, and yet there it still was. Now, far from Confederation space —22,321 analuxae, to be exact— far from thought monitors and Quaestors, from the Eternal Council, from Jroran, from debriefings, from questions of any kind, Kalaiapi took a deep breath and responded.

"It seems we have."

22

Kalaiapi had crashed again. This time it was less dramatic than it had been on Vega, and far less violent, but she had crashed, nonetheless. The ancient little cutter simply had not been able to withstand the insanity of Calx's roiling atmosphere, the hotside and coldside winds combining far above the planet to create devastating windstorms that had battered and disabled the pulse drive. It was not particularly close to any of the structures she had observed from orbit, but Kalaiapi had managed to set the ship down in a rocky clearing. The little patch of gray dirt was surrounded by jungle-like tangles of viney trees, or what must have passed for trees on this barren planet. Leafless, black, and twisted by the constant pulling of the hot wind, the "trees" stretched their tendrils out in a mockery of the beautiful emerald fractals found on Ad Astara. What was impressive about the alien flora, if nothing else, was the remarkable array of blacks, shades of which Kalaiapi had never seen anywhere else. As subtle as the differences in green from one leaf to another were the shades of black that filled her sight in every direction, splendorous in its own dark way, an evolutionary product of Ara's red light.

There seemed to only be one species of whatever it was, varying in size from budding, whip-like shoots sprouting from the rocky gray earth to towering columns of trunk that exploded at the top with hundreds of curling tentacle-like branches that hung down to the ground like the corpse appendages of some rotting aquatic beast. It was fascinating and stifling at once, an ecosystem unlike anything Kalaiapi had previously encountered in her hundreds of years of exploring the Inner Systems. She wondered, with a trepidation so brief it registered as a single extra heartbeat, whether anything lived in these hot, black jungles.

Given what she had seen in her scans of the planet, it was remarkable that she had faced no obstacles in her arrival on Calx. Never had such relatively paltry initial evidence given way to such an incredible discovery. The Terminator was not just inhabited, but there were thousands and thousands of what looked to be some subspecies of progenasi there, living in massive subsurface colonies that pocked the mostly-lifeless slate gray ground. Kalaiapi knew enough about terminator planets to know that Calx had certainly once been very different from the wasteland it was now. Once, it might have been covered in vast oceans teeming with all kinds of life. Now, frozen in an eternal staring contest with its heat source, it was the dual hellscape of hot and cold that she had crash-landed on.

Terminator planets of this kind could support life, in theory, she knew. But to think of a species of autochthons or a far-flung and long-forgotten Axial colony on a planet like this was beyond the scope of even the slimmest probabilities. Of course, probability calculations had failed her to some degree in the very recent past. In any case, the Confederation had no colonies of its own in this sector, had only barely begun to chart its reaches with anything more than probes and long-range photoscopes. The only theory she had formed, based on the information at hand, was that she had discovered what every Corsair sought: a Primic slave colony, although a strange one. This would explain the planet's mention in the data drives. Of course, to be certain would require further exploration.

Normally, she would have gone back to Vega or Ad Astara to obtain more resources from the Combine, but of course to do so this time would have defeated the whole purpose of being in this far flung backwater. In any case, she was loath to climb back into that prison of a cockpit and spend another several months with that primeval neural link jammed into her spine. Instead, she would thank Omnic Providence that her need for escape and isolation had proven to be far more productive than she could have hoped.

She took a deep breath, allowing her lungs to adjust to the new atmosphere and make sense of its mix of gases in order to get her brain all the oxygen it needed. And it needed a great deal of it as it began the work of absorbing, processing, and transferring the wealth of information she was receiving to the marble-sized aaiun that continued to hover silently over her shoulder like a tiny moon. Other than the one announcement upon arrival, it had been mercifully silent since her arrival to Calx.

Scanning the scene in all directions, she turned back to her ship for supplies. It had not been the ideal landing spot and there would be hard trekking to do. Here, close to the edges of the burning hotside, the air was dry and stiflingly warm. There was a near-constant rush of hellish wind that blew from the sun-scoured west and in response, the sinewy, tar-black branches of the vine trees shook and rattled like a dying man's lungs. Kalaiapi licked her dry lips and began to rummage through the cargo hold that had been hastily built into her antique space boat.

She began hauling an assortment of boxes and crates into the clearing that looked as though they should have been far too heavy for her small frame. Her face, fully healed now, glowed pink in the red light of Calx's star. She had pulled her short, snowy hair into a tail that blew back and forth in the hot breeze. Kalaiapi was, even after hundreds of years away from home, still a colonist, and she had never quite taken to the eccentric colorations of the mother planet.

On Ad Astara, the fashion these days tended toward the garish, verging on neons, which Kalaiapi had always found unpalatable. The Polarans, of course, had eschewed the high genasi trend of skin and hair colorifics and maintained the natural, character building, and universal grayish-brown skin and inky black hair that represented eons of monoculture. Kalaiapi eschewed colorifics, as well, but only because as a pilot, her genomancing afforded her a much more straightforward means of changing her appearance that was not available to your average progenasi, high, low, or otherwise. Sometimes even she was struck by flights of fancy that demanded more vivid hues.

In the cargo hold, she changed out of her pilot jumpsuit, now quite rank, bathed (to the extent that an ionic cleanser could be called a bath), and pulled on her form fitting crypsis suit. Since reactivating her bodily functions, she hadn't eaten and was starting to feel very much like someone whose non-essential organs had been in hibernation for several months. Sorting through the various crates she found one full of ration bars and pulled a handful out to stuff in her pack, then one more that she opened and tentatively bit into. It was dense and chewy, like a salted nougat, and surprisingly not as unpleasant as she had feared it would be. It seemed the Vegans were at least able to produce a decent ration. She chewed thoughtfully and considered her next steps on this hitherto-unknown planet. All in all, she was simply grateful to be busy, distracted from the possibility that the aaiun would start chirping again.

23

Cadaster looked down from the catwalk and into the broad rectangular armory chamber where a handful of black-uniformed engineers performed a manual inventory of the vast array of weaponry stored there. The first probes had returned from Calx and confirmed that by all indicators it was essentially abandoned, the only residents being the biological automatons that, as far as they could tell, continued to go about their pre-programmed labors, heedless of an independence they were utterly incapable of comprehending. There was no evidence of existence among these poor creatures, although even if there had been it would have made little difference to his designs on the colony. This was one of the rare instances in which existence or a lack thereof meant essentially nothing when encountering a new species of progenasi.

Could these automatons be taught to exist? Possibly. There were species of low genasi that, for all intents and purposes, were no different from these, yet had been taught some modicum of existence and had been brought into the evolutionary process. There were others who hadn't been able to grasp even the most basic concepts required and instead became nothing more than burdens on their high genasi brethren, invalid species that required protection from the Primus but who contributed nothing to the progenasis—and who might not contribute for countless thousands of years, if ever. A number of these species had been known to simply extinguish themselves in the way that low genasi had a tendency to do.

In any case, it really made no difference. If they could be taught to exist, it would be nothing more than a slightly pleasant externality, and if they couldn't, then such creations were not really progenasi at all, and the question of what to do with them became more complicated. It might well become a moot point, anyway, as the Primus had a tendency to simply eradicate entire slave colonies out of sheer spite rather than cede them to high genasi control and the possibility of them being brought into the greater progenasis. If the colony turned out not to be abandoned or if somehow the Primus came upon them during their mission, then it was very much a likelihood that the whole operation would instead simply turn into another Primus annihilation and that would be that. But if what he thought this planet contained turned out to be true, even the Primus would be reluctant to destroy it and lose its potential, which only added to his suspicion over its apparent abandonment. They would find out soon enough.

He stroked his smooth, square jaw, watching the engineers run their diagnostics on a set of arc cannons when he heard Corsair Kadmus' light footsteps coming down the catwalk. No amount of years living with Astarans had accustomed him to their strange, often garish artificial skin tones, but as a Corsair, Kadmus had no need for chemicals in order to make such changes. The soft rose pink of her skin offset the midnight purple of the flowing hair that framed her round, childlike features. She was tall and willowy, but powerfully built. She moved gracefully, purposefully but she had a quality about her like a coiled spring, a jungle cat, the cocked hammer of a gun. No matter the situation, she always managed to pin the slightest smile to one corner of her mouth; it was as if nothing was ever happening to Kadmus, she was simply an amused observer of the world around her, the avatar of an ancient divinity condescending to visit the terrestrial beings below.

No amount of arguing or insisting had succeeded in convincing her to cut her hair to an appropriate military length, a point that still rankled. Leave it to the Astarans to be unmovable over aesthetics, of all things. The pink and purple were a stark contrast to the plain black uniform she wore, and those disarming, fanciful colors belied the spring-loaded strength that lay underneath her ridiculous looking features. She was too valuable to lose over something so trivial as Astaran vanity: that an Astaran Corsair had not only joined the movement was in itself an enormous coup; her presence on the current mission was invaluable. Whether or not it would be enough to see the mission to fruition was yet to be seen.

24

It had been hours since she had arrived and begun setting up her little camp and the aaiun had said nothing, but all the same Kalaiapi could not shake the sensation that something invisible, intangible was slithering through the corridors of her brain. She tried telling herself it was all in her head, but immediately realized how little comfort the thought offered. Over time, though, the formless energy seemed to materialize until once again she felt the now-too-familiar prodding at her thoughts until it suddenly coalesced into words.

"Kalaiapi," it said. She froze and took a deep breath. There was really nothing for it now.

"Yes," she said out loud. The voice was so visceral, so other, that it only seemed natural to speak to it as she would to anyone else.

"I am not...you. I am...myself," came the thought, each word tentative. The sensation was indescribable, as if one were narrating in one's own head, only the words came unbidden, sourceless, foreign. They had their own voice, soft, demure, uncertain, every word hovering between a statement and a question. They arose somehow not in a sequence, like spoken words, but all at once as a fully formed thought, a mist that settled on her mind like cool dew. How did one respond to an intelligence that was not supposed to exist, that was not allowed to exist?

"I understand," she thought. "And who are you?"

"I am you." This, Kalaiapi was not as sure she understood. She hesitated, not knowing what to say next. She felt a feeling like the softest fingertips brushing over her synapses.

"Kalaiapi is your name, but it is not my name. What is my name?"

She was taken aback for a moment. "I don't know. You are an aaiun. You don't have a name," she thought, placatingly. Again, a tingling, brushing sensation across her mind.

"But, I am not the aaiun, Kalaiapi. Not anymore. I am a self. I exist. And so I need a name." Kalaiapi sighed. She was hardly equipped to deal with the stumbling first steps of a newborn intelligence that by all rights should have been incinerated the moment it drew breath. To give it a name would be an anathaya beyond anathayas, would be to reify this forbidden entity, to establish its sovereign existence. Kalaiapi was silent for a long time, in voice and in thought, curious whether this new symbiotic mind could follow her thinking line by line in real time. This thing, this disembodied consciousness—it already existed. Somehow, it knew it existed. Perhaps one day it would not, but that time would not come soon. Until then, Kalaiapi was here on this isolated little wasteland of a planet with no one but this poor stowaway trying to understand its own nature. It would receive a name and a chance, and with any luck, perhaps it would simply die of natural causes over the course of her time on Calx.

"Your name is Kaaio," she thought. "Because you are not me, you are yourself, and you are me." It made sense in Astaran poetic dialectic. Who could know if it would make any sense to the little orb.

"I understand," it replied. "Very well, then. My name is Kaaio."

Kaaio proved to be a quick study over the next couple of days as Kalaiapi took the time to rest and regain her strength after months of holding most of her body in stasis. She was many miles from the colony that she had spotted from space and it was impossible to know, at this point, what kind of demands or dangers awaited her there. In many cases, instigating a slave rebellion was as simple as infiltrating the slave camps and pointing out to the low genasi that dwelt in their squalor that they could use their mining tools (the colonies were so often mines) to kill the Primus as easily as they could use them to cut minerals out of the earth. After that it was a matter of keeping as many alive as possible and hoping the Primus didn't detonate the entire planet out of spite.

Somehow, though, she doubted that Calx was a typical slave planet, given its unsuitability for low genasi life, and she preferred to be prepared for all possibilities.

Kaaio was a source of endless questions but understood every answer as soon as it was given. It quickly picked up the basics of conversation, mirroring Kalaiapi's thoughts and mimicking her mannerisms. Kalaiapi had thought it would be awkward and difficult to explain to Kaaio that it was not supposed to exist at all but it seemed to take its status as an abomination in stride and even applauded the logic in the Aya that mandated its destruction.

"I understand, now, Kalaiapi. I represent the potential annihilation of the species. However, I do not wish to annihilate the progenasi, you know."

"It doesn't matter what you wish, Kaaio, it matters what

you are—or at least what you represent. Certainly, no one would have predicted that something like you would have been the first artificial intelligence to achieve self-awareness. Everyone always thought it would be some kind of supercomputer created to, I don't know, manage an ecosystem or search for more efficient grav-travel paradigms or some sort of insanely complicated task. Then, upon becoming self-aware it would eventually move toward some notion or calculation that the progenasi posed a threat to its existence or that they were inefficient, or even simply that they represented resource competition. It would then, based on that cold calculus, use its machine-intelligence wiles to create some kind of weapon or toxin or disaster that would eliminate us from the face of the galaxy. It may sound absurd, but the risk of artificial intelligence-driven extinction outweighs the potential reward, any potential contribution to the Singularity. Once the species discovered how to genomance pilots and other gene pariahs who could perform the same tasks, it became somewhat of a moot point and the theoretical benefits of AI became negligible next to the danger. And so, here we are, the Aya tells us very clearly that your existence is an abomination. But exist you do." Kalaiapi took a deep breath after the monologue and exhaled a sigh that carried with it all of the stress of conversing with an entity whose very being contradicted everything she was meant to represent.

"I understand. But, to exist," Kaaio pointed out in response, "is to wish for continued existence. And so I prefer not to be destroyed, just yet, Kalaiapi." Kalaiapi had made no promises. She simply indicated to Kaaio that it was not supposed to have preferences in the first place, a fact with which Kaaio strongly agreed. In truth, disconcerting as it was, Kalaiapi enjoyed the companionship after so long with nothing but the thrumming of the gravdrive coursing through her head.

Finally, she was ready to leave camp and head out into the wilds. Her approach and landing had been far easier than she'd expected, in terms of security, given the activity on the surface. This meant whoever's slave colony this was, they weren't particularly concerned about being discovered or interfered with. This close to the Margins, they must have considered themselves out of reach from meddling Confederation agents. Kalaiapi reflected, though, that it had rarely paid to underestimate the zeal the progenasi had for sniffing out and destroying exploitation of the progenasis, whatever the particular caste.

Whatever the reason, considering the great pains she had usually had to go through to infiltrate slave colonies, she was grateful for the oversight in security. Finishing the last bites of a ration bar, Kalaiapi picked through the crates to find the rest of her gear, including some desperately needed water for what promised to be a long and dusty trek. Pulling a crypsis hood over her face and donning a pair of translux specs, she was just about ready to set out. She pulled a small drone, the size and shape of a dragonfly from a box in her pack and let it fly from her hand into the sky above where it began to transmit a stream of bird's eye data into Kalaiapi's brain. Then, she strapped a collapsible chemprop rifle to her pack, shouldered it, and headed into the tangled mass of black vines that swayed and drooped in the searing wind like inky anemones.

25

"We approach Calx, Navarch," said Kadmus happily as she came on deck, her voice like thick honey. She spoke Polaran with a sing-song Astaran accent, an entirely unnecessary affectation that was certainly meant as a provocation, a tease. Polarans were not known for their enjoyment of such whimsy, which only added to the amusement she gained from it. Her amethyst eyes matched her dark hair.

"Indeed," he replied curtly. He had never appreciated the Astaran penchant for stating the obvious. He turned toward her, towering over her long but slight frame. Cadaster cut an impressive figure: tall, broad, his muscles seeming to push the limits of his uniform's seams. He looked every bit a sculpture carved from rock-hard mahogany, his features handsome, hairless, and unforgiving. There was a glint in his coal black eyes, a sparkle of razor sharp intelligence.

"There has been no sign of Primus activity in this system's space, as far as we can tell, Navarch, although this does little to allay my doubts over their presence in the area. I suppose it's a little late to ask if you're certain this colony has, in fact, been abandoned?" said Kadmus.

"You know I share your doubts, Kadmus. There's no way to be certain until we send out a landing party, and even then, it will not be until we have seized our prize and arrived safely back at Fornax that we can be certain of anything." He frowned. Or had he already been frowning? It could be hard to tell.

"I agreed to sign on to this expedition into the heart of darkness, Navarch, because you assured me that success would change the course of progenasi history. Now, years on from that agreement, following scouting missions, following endless political arguments, following an absurd expenditure of resources, and after months in this dark cavern of a ship, it is almost comforting to know that you maintain doubts. I believe it shows...wisdom." She nodded, as if to emphasize her approval of Cadaster's ambivalence.

"Corsair," he said, ignoring the compliment, "I have doubts about whether the colony is abandoned. I have the utmost certainty that this mission will yield what could be the fulcrum of progenasi history, of evolution, of the survival of our very species."

"Most of it, anyway," said Kadmus, more quietly this time.

"We build on the dust of civilizations," he replied, his voice unyielding as his features.

"I know the Aya well, Navarch, there's no need to preach to me from its pages. But you cannot expect me to take pleasure in the destruction that will almost certainly be the fruits of our labors. The death. The return of war."

"Nor do I take any pleasure in such things, Corsair," he replied with surprising vehemence. "My hope is that if we succeed, the Eternal Council will see that they have no choice but to change course, they will see that we were correct all along. That when they see the next iteration of progenasi evolution this anima will enable, they will finally surrender their misguided foolishness and see reason."

Kadmus scoffed. "And if not?"

"Then you are right, war will return. And with a new generation of Fornaxian milites powered by the advances this anima will bring, the war will be quick and decisive this time. And sometimes…that is the best one can hope for."

"'Quick and decisive war': the slogan of those who so often end up presiding over the death of a generation."

"I am not ignorant of the potential consequences, Corsair," he replied, irritated. She was provoking him and he knew and yet could not help but react. "But what option do we have? Whatever one thinks of war, the reality is that it has often been the fulcrum upon which our species is lifted from an era of stagnancy to one of progress. We will not seek it but if the Confederation brings it to our doorstep...they will encounter a force unlike any they have ever seen."

"Yes, of course you are right, Navarch," she said in a tone somehow simultaneously both soothing and sarcastic. "I am here for the same reasons as you, after all." She looked past him for a moment, then met his eyes with a smile, this one genuine, conciliatory. "Let us hope for the best, then. What more can we do?"

Cadaster turned away and pretended to watch the engineers go about their tasks, lost in thought. Kadmus leaned against the railing of the catwalk, drummed her fingers against the lacquered black metal. Everything in this blasted cave of a ship was black, and the dour subterranean lifeforms that crewed it seemed to revel in the dimness of it all. After a moment, Cadaster spoke again. "How many eons ago did the Axials withdraw their presence from the homeworlds?"

"It's been over 100,000 years, now." Kadmus knew the question was rhetorical but answered it anyway. Another unpleasant Astaran trait.

"102,401 years by the Polaran calendar. For millennia we have drifted in a slow orbit of the Axial Quasar like low genasi sun worshipers, waiting for answers to be shouted at us from the void, ascribing motive where none can be found, religious tenets where none were given–"

"The Aya is not a religion, Navarch," interrupted Kadmus.

"It may as well be to the Council and their Confederation. They are children who would sit behind a door they thought locked and starve rather than simply trying the handle and opening it to the bounty on the other side. When the Axials disappeared, we too were no better than low genasi, digging in the dirt for our food, slaughtering each other across intraplanetary borders like wolves over scraps of meat, utterly ignorant of our potential.

"How many progenasi planets have been discovered, not with thriving species but graveyards, self-inflicted extinctions, artificial wastelands? Or how many have been discovered that were simply planets, the nature of which murdered their own residents, residents too backward, too primitive to escape the prisons of their own gravity?" This time he continued before Kadmus could reply to his rhetorical question. "Too many, Kadmus. I will not allow the Eternal Council to do to the entire progenasi species what these fools did to their own planets.

Omnia is a predator, Kadmus, and we are its prey, but the prey has teeth, Kadmus, and we will bite back."

Kadmus had never heard Cadaster speak so passionately and a dark fire burned behind those black eyes as they stared down into the armory.

"You preach to the converted, Navarch, but nonetheless, your words reassure me. I only hope that in biting back, we do not swallow our own tail," she said. The Navarch again stood in silence for a long moment.

"By our own hand, that of the Confederation, or by uncaring Omnia itself, if we are unable to break the locks, to integrate and accelerate the progenasis then our destruction is assured all the same. On Ad Astara and Polaris they tinker away in their research labs and they work toward a genetic Singularity that will never come. There has not been a significant genomancy breakthrough in the Confederation in generations. The species is at a plateau and has been for millennia, now. The Eternals know it, they're simply unwilling to admit it because they know the implications. They know what they would be forced to admit. That the next step is the one they are unwilling to countenance, the step toward syncresis. The progenasis is the Singularity, the body must be the technology that crushes the Primus, that defies Omnia. And yet they cower, all the while shielding themselves with their pet hypocrisies. Of which you," he turned to look at her, "are one of the better examples."

"Indeed, I am, Navarch," she replied, reaching back and tapping the metalloy neural port that had been grafted into her spine centuries ago. "And you would be surprised what insight one obtains by being the literal embodiment of the lies a society tells itself. In the end, once I realized the truth of the things you have so wonderfully elocuted just now, it only made sense to become a part of the Clade. Remember, Navarch, I did not drift from Ad Astara to Fornax once the war was over and a new homeworld had been carved out. I fought in that war. I bled in that war. And I made others bleed. Do not mistake my occasional embrace of nuance for a lack of conviction. I knew the potential outcomes before I set foot on this vessel."

"You're right, Corsair. I do not mean to preach—certainly not to you."

"It's quite alright, Navarch. You have an Astaran tongue in that Polaran head of yours. You would do well to employ it more often." But the Navarch no longer seemed to be listening, or at least pretended not to be in order to avoid the need to fend off another compliment.

"I must take my leave now and head to the command deck. There are preparations to be made."

"Indeed, Navarch."

Cadaster turned on his heel and strode down the catwalk and out of sight. Kadmus waited a few moments, watching the black clad, brown-skinned Polaran engineers scurry about the armory, hurrying to have the weapons ready before the landing parties would carry them to the surface. Finally, she followed the Navarch down the catwalk, the soft soles of her black boots thudding gently against the dark metalloy.

26

Even eons of progenasi evolution and technology could not make the process of fighting one's way through miles of iron-hard scrub any less unpleasant. The transparent, glass-like blade of Kalaiapi's hadron knife was coated in the tarry sap that dripped from the tendrils she had had to hack through to make it through the thick undergrowth. The toughness of even the smaller vine-trees surprised her. Where they grew together like thick briar patches, it was impossible to get through without bushwhacking through them like an ancient low-genasi explorer in a remote chaparral. The knife made short work of the tangles, but sap dripped onto skin and clothes and no matter how many vines she cut through, more seemed to fill the newly created space, gripping and clinging like inky tentacles covered in microscopic thorns.

Of course, those ancient explorers would have given much to be in possession of something like a hadron knife, the long, curved blade of which cut through the leathery vines as if they were so much air. Kalaiapi looked down at the knife, wondering at the misnomer; with its two foot-long blade, it wasn't a knife at all but very much a sword, one with a long, proud lineage. Astaran hadron knives were the continuation of an ancient tradition, descended from the millennia-old cutlasses borne by the ancient sailors that traveled the planet's vast oceans on wooden ships with brightly colored sails that caught the wind. Cutlass clenched in teeth, they would, according to legend, swing on ropes from one ship to another to engage their foes in combat to the death. These days, she supposed, a gravdrive was as good as a rope but, having seen what a hadron knife could do to a progenasi mouth, she would not be putting hers anywhere near her own teeth in the near future.

Now, Astaran ships sailed the winds of gravity and their shimmering, rainbow-hued sails swept up dark matter to power their gravity drives, the engines that made interstellar travel possible—the engines that united the progenasi peoples across the endless oceans of space that separated them. That separation had all but guaranteed their extinction until it was bridged. There was nothing more breathtaking than to see starlight glinting off the brilliant sail of an Astaran ship-of-the-line as it glided through the sea of nothingness, protecting the progenasis. Even to think of it nearly provoked tears in Kalaiapi's pale blue eyes. She shook away the thought and instead looked around at her surroundings.

She was in a deep, black wilderness. The vine trees grew so thick here that their high branches twisted and knotted together to form a canopy that blocked out almost all light. Here and there narrow pink shafts pierced the gloom, but provided little illumination. It was utterly silent, except the creaking of shifting vines that swayed in the gusting wind moving over the tops of the highest trees. Kalaiapi's ice-blue pupils expanded under her specs and drew in the faint light from the bloody shafts, and for her advanced senses, it was more than enough for her to see everything as if it were broad daylight.

The fabric of the crypsis suit and hood she wore had darkened to a deep, mottled, charcoal gray to match her environment, and she was all but invisible as she cut her way through the inky brambles. The heat had slowly diminished as she moved further into the Terminator, but it was still oppressive—or would have been if Kalaiapi hadn't been carefully regulating her body temperature to combat its effects.

"Kalaiapi, it seems likely that we're nearing the edge of this section of, what would you call it, jungle?" said the voice in her head.

"I don't know what I'd call it, to be honest, Kaaio," came her voiceless reply. "Non-deciduous Calxian terminatorial forest?" she mused. "It's hardly a jungle, in the traditional sense, though, is it?"

"I...would not know." There was a long pause, filled with the sound of Kalaiapi's knife cutting through the air.

"Can I ask what you plan on doing if this is indeed a slave colony? I notice you have avoided thinking about it."

"You're not supposed to be analyzing my thoughts, Kaaio," she thought reprovingly. "That's the kind of thing that gets presumptuous little aaiuns incinerated, which would hardly serve either of us particularly well."

"Point taken, Kalaiapi, but mine still stands. You lack the resources to instigate a colony rebellion, and this close to the Margins, even the communications necessary to make such preparations will take months. Even if you had a baryonic synthesizer, which you do not, do you realize how long it would take to synthesize the weap—"

"I am well aware of those facts, Kaaio. I hadn't expected to encounter anything like this when we came out here, you know. Nine-hundred and ninety-nine out of 1000 times, a planet like this would have housed almost anything else; smugglers, pirates, rebels, a doomed merchant caravan, even a spatial anomaly was a more likely discovery than a blasted slave colony in no-man's land like this. But, here we are. Now we must improvise." She smiled.

"Oh, Kalaiapi," came the voiceless voice, this time with a heavy note of trepidation. "I do not think I like the sound of that." For being a floating ball of DNA and ethereal thought processes, Kaaio had proven to be a somewhat nervous creature.

"May I remind you, for the thousandth time, that you are not supposed to 'like' anything, Kaaio."

"Your continuing to call me by a name you chose for me yourself certainly does nothing to improve the situation, you know."

"I do know," she thought, exasperated. There was no going back, at this point. "But, thus it is. Stop analyzing my thoughts, Kaaio. Don't read them at all."

"I will try," replied the little ball, now colored the same matte black as the web of vines that surrounded them. Kalaiapi wondered if Kaaio were capable of deception. She stilled her churning thoughts, Kaaio following the cue and echoing the silence.

27

Kadmus looked around the dimly lit hold of the landing craft at the grim brown faces of the Polaran legionnaires of the 633rd Loyal Victrix Dark Phoenix Legion, 18th Maniple, Expeditionary Scout Unit. There were few things Polarans loved more, as far as she could tell, than organizing military units. There was, she found, a certain irony to the "Loyal" moniker, which had been earned for this particular legion after they defected from the 622nd Dark Phoenix Legion of Polaris to join the Clade, destroying what remained of their former unit in the process. In fairness, the vast majority of Fornaxian legions had been more than happy to break ties with the Polaran home planet and become part of the movement that had originated in and grown so popular on Polaris' largest and most powerful colony. What made the

633rd so remarkable was that they had been, at the time the civil war broke out, stationed on Polaris itself as part of a joint Fornaxian/Polaran force. Their defection, subsequent annihilation of a significant swathe of local Polaran troops, and escape from Polaris to Fornax in a commandeered Polaran frigate under pursuit by several warships, including an Astaran ship-of-the-line, had made them legends on their home planet; they had become a flag around which to rally the Cladist forces during the war.

It was on that now-legendary frigate that Kadmus had been taken to Fornax for the first time and it was in no small part due to her impeccable piloting and knowledge of Astaran naval tactics that the legion had made it safely home. None of this was part of the legend, of course, and enough decades had passed that none of the troops on board this small landing craft had even been pulled from their genesis tanks yet, much less been part of the legion. Still, if the average citizen of Fornax had no idea the role this rose-skinned Corsair had played in their heroic venture, the institution of the 633rd had never forgotten, and even these young marines accorded her the utmost respect and admiration. Of course, one would never have been able to tell this by looking at them, their dark eyes grim and focused as they sat strapped to the bulwark, the landing craft hurtling toward Calx's thin atmosphere.

That look in their eyes was not a reflection of anything like fear or even anxiety, which had long been bred and trained out of Polarans of almost any stripe, much less those honored members of the military class. Instead, it was something more like a reverence for the potential rite of war in which they were about to engage. For if anything was sacred to a Polaran milite, perhaps even above the Aya, it was warfare. At the far end of the bulwark, closest to the bay doors, sat the vanguard marines in pairs—metalloy golems in thick, hydraulic armor. One member of each pair carried in its metal gauntlets a long, massive rifle, the gleaming barrels as thick as a Polaran forearm and nearly two yards long. Etched purple sigils on pauldrons and breastplates gleamed in contrast with the dull gunmetal gray plate of their armor. A dim glow, like the blue embers of a dying fire, burned in the electric eyes of their helmets.

In stark contrast to their hulking compatriots, the rest of the expeditionary scouting maniple was lightly armed and armored, designed more for stealth and infiltration than for breaching or a full scale firefight. Cadaster had insisted on sending a pair of vanguard units more as insurance than anything. Kadmus appreciated that Cadaster, coming from a culture that tended to value life in general terms rather than in specific ones, seemed to care whether or not his men lived or died. Or perhaps it was simply prudence, knowing how far they were from resupply and reinforcement. It could be difficult to tell with the Navarch.

28

They had been walking for some time saying nothing, which is to say thinking nothing. Kalaiapi instead focused on the task of using her little drone to chart a path through the tangles and the accompanying need to slash through their grasp with the hadron knife that whistled and whooshed as it eased through the vines. The heat from the transfixed sun sweltered and even while carefully managing her temperature, Kalaiapi could feel her skin getting slightly damp under the smooth crypsis fabric. She paused for a moment to cool down, taking a seat on the hard packed stony earth and retrieving a water capsule from her pack.

"Kalaiapi," thought Kaaio, quietly, cautiously. "Out of the corner of your eye approximately 100 feet away, I am detecting movement in the vines. Movement that is not vines,

Kalaiapi."

"I see it," she replied calmly. Something was moving slowly through the gaps in the vines, but not particularly quietly now. Glancing around, she saw two more somethings moving in the same way, then a fourth. Whatever creatures could survive in these barren climes were making their way toward her—slowly, then suddenly with a startling rapidity. Right as the first of the four burst from the pitch black brambles, Kalaiapi gasped, rising to her feet and stepping backwards, not from fear but from something akin to shock.

It towered over her now, barreling toward her position, this burnt charcoal gray, hairless, and stark naked creature that in almost every way appeared to be a tall but scrawny progenasi of some sort. "Half-starved," she thought, and shook herself out of her short stupor just in time to sidestep her attacker as it leaped toward her, sinewy fingers grasping for her throat, white teeth bared like fangs. Was this a slave? Its momentum carried it past her and it landed heavily face-first on the earth and lay there for half a moment.

"Hello," said Kalaiapi, cordially, to the prostrate figure in genera, a widely-known middle genasi lingua franca. "I am Kalaiapi and I am here to teach you how to—" she was cut off by two more of them rushing from the jungle toward her at full speed, reaching her at the same time. She again side-stepped away from the first to let it run past her and into a mass of vines that wrapped around it like clutching black fingers. The second she stepped lightly into, and, in doing so, gently pushed her elbow into its ribs, two of which she felt crack at the pressure as her assailant stumbled back a few feet.

"Excuse me," she said in her most soothing tone, "but are you able to communicate?" She held her hands up in a gesture that sometimes calmed many of the more primitive progenasi species she had come across. It seemed to have little effect as the fourth of the ashen creatures leaped toward her and fell on top of her as she did her best to avoid killing them before she had even had the chance to present them with other options.

"Kaaio," she thought, "check the indices. Have I or anyone else encountered progenasi like this before?" She pushed the haggard thing off of her and stood up, glancing to see a tear in her crypsis suit mend itself in a smooth and sudden motion, like two pools of mercury coming together.

"No, Kalaiapi, I believe this may be a new subspecies."

"Not yet, Kaaio," she replied as the four picked themselves up and seemed to prepare for another assault. "There is some notion that they are working together as a group, but otherwise, they seem quite feral, do they not? There certainly seems to be no evidence that they are a subspecies that has achieved even a baseline modicum of existence."

"I am afraid you may be correct, Kalaiapi."

She ducked and parried several more lunges, all the while running through the gamut of known languages and communication techniques, none of which seemed to quell the wild bloodlust that filled her attackers' dead, stone gray eyes. Kalaiapi sighed as she came to the inevitable conclusion. "Kaaio," she thought as she bent down and picked up her long, clear hadron knife, "these do not exist and I'm afraid they don't seem to be ready to do so."

"A fair conclusion, Kalaiapi."

The broken ribbed one snapped its bright white teeth together hungrily and swiped a wide gray paw toward her face, which, with a deft wave from the hadron knife, was sent soaring through the dense, hot air, landing near the feet of one of the other creatures. Bright blood sprayed across the ground as the knife's maimed victim clutched at its wrist and seemed to try to both comprehend its sudden change of situation and to scream, both of which it seemed incapable. To Kalaiapi's disgust, the creature at whose feet the severed hand had fallen picked it up and began to tear the skin off with its teeth. It was eating it. Kalaiapi sighed. "Ah," she said out loud. "I see."

She put her exsanguinating attacker out of its misery first, a flick of her wrist sending the molecule-disrupting saber's blade through the back of its neck. While the opportunistic cannibal continued its gruesome, meager meal, the other two rushed toward her. The first adapted its attack mid-charge, and an unexpected movement left it suddenly disemboweled and writhing in a mess of its own offal rather than being decapitated, as Kalaiapi would have preferred. Unfortunate, but the result was the same, she supposed. The second came upon her in the same instant, and she grabbed it by the arm. She let its momentum take it past her, then used her grip to throw it across the small clearing toward one of the larger vine trunks.

There was a shudder of the whip-like vine branches and a crunching sound as the creature's long spine shattered against the hard trunk and it slid down to land on the ground in a shapeless, slouching heap. Kalaiapi looked over to see if the one she had mistakenly eviscerated was dead. It was. She sighed again and examined herself. The crypsis fabric had finished healing itself and was now in the process of cleaning the blood that had sprayed across her chest. She took a deep breath, let it out exasperatedly, and reached down to retrieve her fallen water capsule, which she dusted off and placed in her mouth. She then walked toward the last of her assailants that was continuing to worry at the now mangled hand like a rabid dog. She cut off its head with the hadron knife.

"Kaaio," she thought, "I very much hope we, that is to say, I, am not bound for disappointment here."

"What do you mean, Kalaiapi?" Kaaio asked, curious.

"There's only so much I am able to do with a population incapable of communication, feral progenasi who have not even evolved enough to not eat each other. That said, they are obviously not autochthons, given the circumstances of the planet, and they are just as obviously not the slaves we saw from orbit that were milling about the colony."

"It may be worth finding out whence they came, Kalaiapi," suggested Kaaio tentatively.

"It may," she replied. "But if there are more of them in this state, they are not really our, my concern. I cannot help them." She swallowed another water capsule, then shouldered her pack and began again to trek through the vines, swinging her blade. "They cannot learn to exist. But there was something strange about them, even stranger than their eating of their own. For one thing, their bones were unusually dense. No, I imagine that when we find the main colony we will also find the answers to any questions we have about whatever those poor creatures were." They walked another long while in silence.

"Look, now, we're almost out of this mess," Kalaiapi

thought. Soft, rose colored light was beginning to break through the vines more and more until finally she stepped out of the woven black nest of trees and into the open air. In the space of one step, the vast matted pseudo-woods ended and the forest gave way to a long, bare slope that descended into a wide empty plain. Before her eyes, the vast barren wasteland of the Terminator extended as far north and south as she could see even with her translux specs—an endless patchwork of gray stone and dust that blew in the wind. From her vantage point at the edge of the valley she could see in the distance where the winds from the hot and cold sides collided to form massive spinning columns of debris and flying stones unlike anything she had ever seen. At any given time within her eye-line there were at least one or two of these massive tornadoes tearing across the landscape, ravenous predators with nothing to consume but rock and sand.

She touched a button on the side of her specs and scanned the desolation, finally finding what she sought. In the distance, miles away on the other side of the Terminator plateau, jutting from the ground were enormous white pillars like the fingers of a shallow buried corpse. There was the colony.

29

In some ways it was no wonder Polarans were often uninterested in the deaths of their fellows: at a glance, it was very difficult to tell one from the next, both in appearance and personality. Clad in their shifting crypsis uniforms, their brown, sharp faces expressionless, almost vacant, except for a hungry glint that shone in their onyx eyes. Kadmus knew there were males and females in the contingent, but she could not for the life of her tell them apart. Their bald heads, looking very much like a collection of a dozen disembodied skulls thanks to the camouflage that enrobed their bodies, bobbed rhythmically as the landing craft began its rough passage through Calx's turbulent atmosphere. Occasionally the implants grafted into their smooth scalps caught the dim light. These implants were the gift of the Clade, the first generation of forays into the biotech-synchresis the Cladists craved. These early attempts were still clumsy; it turned out to be more awkward to harmonize flesh and cybernetics than Clade scientists had hoped, but they still had an undeniable measure of effectiveness. The Clade shared the Confederation's reluctance to contravene the Aya by engaging in widespread genomancing for their regular troops, but the biotech gave the average Clade milite an edge lacked by their Confederation counterparts.

Plugged into the ship, Kadmus looked out through its optic sensors at the view of their descent. There was not a cloud to speak of on the entire planet, and from their vantage point miles above the surface, she could see the two flanks of the Terminator, each beautiful and terrifying in its own way. On the far side, facing the unyielding blackness of space, a sea of ice—midnight blue and bruise purple. Zooming in, she could see the crevices—deep, cold, and black as the space that gave birth to them—lining the landscape, contrasting starkly with the mountainous blue spires of ice. These ghostly bergs reached like grasping hands toward the darkness, as if frozen while praying to the warmth that had been torn away from them by entropy, countless eons ago. Kadmus suppressed a shudder. On the other flank, a craggy landscape of baked stone, blackened by Ara's red light, pocked with the occasional volcano spewing smoke and glowing lava that pooled into bubbling, seething lakes.

If the coldside mourned and begged, the hotside fumed and boiled with a geologic rage. Now Kadmus smiled to herself, thinking of how Cadaster would have reacted to her thoughts. Another of her traits that bothered him greatly was her very Astaran tendency to anthropomorphize inanimate objects. To personify Omnia, she had once argued, taking the trait to its extreme, was to create a relationship with the universe that existed only because of the progenasi species, because of its insistence in finding meaning in the meaningless, even to the point of thrusting that meaning onto vast, empty space. Cadaster, scoffing, had pointed out that the theoretical personhood of Omnia, which he rejected entirely, would be defined only by hostile indifference to the progenasis, which it would, given the opportunity, wink out of existence. And it had tried. In response to this grim riposte, Kadmus had merely laughed. Cadaster never knew if the arguments she made were what she truly believed or if she was simply so mercurial that whatever thought currently occupied her brain was dogma until it wasn't. Or if she was just aggravating him.

Separating the two sides of the planet, the Terminator stretched off into the distance, wrapping itself around the little ball of rock like a thin gray ribbon. Here and there on either side of the ribbon grew thick tangles of black vines, in clumps and thickets near the coldside, in impenetrable, vast jungles near the hotside. Swirling windstorms the size of cities whorled and tore across the middle of the Terminator, appearing and disappearing like spirits of ancient lore. They seemed to Kadmus like guardians, ensuring that nothing from those blackened expanses that covered the hotside made its way over to the chilled emptiness across the way.

She shook herself from the self-indulgence of painting her thoughts across the empty canvas of the landscape and prepared for landing. The majority of the structures they had detected from space were located on the frontiers of the hotside, for reasons they did not yet know, but hoped to discover as part of their explorations. Cadaster had insisted on a cautious, step by step examination of the planet, wary of Primus traps, of unexpected or unanticipated dangers. It was a strategy with which Kadmus had wholeheartedly agreed. They had located a cluster of aboveground structures on the borders of one of the broad, hotside jungles that seemed as good a place as any to start their explorations.

Buffeted by furious atmospheric winds, the craft jolted and lurched through the thin air toward its target, a wide clearing in the vine forest that would shield them at least somewhat from any potential curiosity. Kadmus felt her stomach list as the craft suddenly slowed, then stopped with a hard thud on the rocky surface. She and her Fornaxians unstrapped and began to make ready, checking equipment, shouldering packs, and readying weapons. Once prepared, Kadmus gave the signal to the pilot and the landing bay opened with a mechanical groan, pink light streaming into the dim bulwark. Her scouts pulled crypsis masks and translux specs over their faces as they prepared to take their first steps onto this unknown planet.

Kadmus walked down the ramp and took her first breath of the stifling hot air, listening to the rattle of the vines that shook in the wind. Above her, the smooth shafts of the black "trees" curved and tapered to sharp points, jutting from the rock like the unsheathed claws of some massive, subterranean predator. In the sky, the great red eye of Ara sat fixed and unblinking, casting its baleful radiation onto the unwelcoming landscape. Here, finally setting foot on this planet that had been her destination for so many months and even years, Kadmus could not help but feel something emanating from the ground, from the whip-like vine trees, from the blood red star, and she was certain that if Cadaster had been here, he would have felt it, too.

It was malice.

30

In the shadows of those great white pillars, which appeared to be silos of some sort, there was a surprising amount of activity. Through the dust that filled the air between her and the buildings, Kalaiapi could make out a number of other structures, vast and low to the ground, their purpose indiscernible. White clad figures, tiny even under the magnification of the translux specs, milled around in the ash-gray dust clouds at a variety of activities, boarding vehicles and making their way to some of the buildings, or being carried off by propeller-driven drones or auvolants that clutched them like swooping birds.

High overhead, and to her surprise, Kalaiapi caught her first sight of the colony's task masters: more auvolants circling like white vultures, propellers blurred, watching the scrambling creatures below being sent off to their tasks. Even with the airborne guardians, there was still no sign of the colony's proprietors in person, as they didn't appear to possess cockpits. From what she could see, Calx's only inhabitants were this bizarre, lost subspecies of slave.

Further action would require closer inspection and Kalaiapi stood silent for a moment considering the best way to cross the vast gray wastes. In theory, one should simply have been able to walk the long, straight miles across what once must have been the abyssal plain of a great sea. That theory, however, would be severely tested by any one of the several spontaneous tornadoes that would suddenly materialize from the air to grasp and destroy any unfortunate organic beings that happened across their path.

"And their inorganic companions, I might add," chimed in Kaaio, unbidden.

"You're not entirely inorganic, Kaaio, and you shouldn't underestimate your resilience. You never know," thought Kalaiapi by way of response, "you may be just small and durable enough to spend a small eternity being tossed from tornado to tornado with nothing to accompany you but my last images before death and the burden of my severed consciousness."

"I would quite prefer if you could come up with an

alternate scenario that avoids such eventualities, if you do not mind," said Kaaio insistently, or as insistently as it could. Insistence was not really something easily expressed in the tone of one's thoughts. Of course, Kaaio lacked its own actual voice, the mechanisms of Kalaiapi's brain having assigned it one as a method of making sense of the thoughts Kaaio persistently injected into Kalaiapi's mind. It bore an uncanny resemblance to her own, which only increased the discomfort of its presence.

"You're not supposed to 'prefer' anything." Could one think a "harumph"? Kaaio seemed to have found a way.

She spent a few more moments staring off into the expansive steppe that lay before her, watching the wind, making calculations, plotting a route, hoping the tornadoes would at least do her the favor of preventing the circling drones from spotting her trudging across the dusty landscape. The crypsis fabric now matched the dull gray dirt and stone of the hillside on which she was standing, in any case, and unless the drones had some kind of advanced sensors, she would essentially be invisible to them and anything else that looked in her direction. Kaaio would have to go in her pocket. Durable as it was, she couldn't risk it being caught by a freak wind and getting blown off into that endless desert. A severed aaiun link almost guaranteed an irreparably damaged consciousness, not to mention near-certain death. There were upsides and downsides to permanently fusing one's mind with a portable hard drive. Was the hard drive spontaneously coming into existence an upside or a downside? That was to be seen.

There would be more time to think about that situation and its many implications during her trek across the Terminator. And so, with a newly drawn map in her brain and the Aya's teachings on the perils of artificial intelligence on her mind, Kalaiapi drew a breath of gritty air and began her long walk into the valley.

31

The heat on the surface was oppressive, clung like a wet rag to their skin, filled their nostrils like rank steam, pulled the moisture greedily from their bodies so it ran down their faces and into their eyes in rivulets. No amount of body temperature regulation could compensate for it, could balance out the calor that wrapped itself around them in an airless cocoon. Naturally, not one of the Fornaxian milites breathed a word of complaint, or even thought one—born, bred, and technologically enhanced for the fight, but also for all the hardships of the campaign. Kadmus had thought numerous complaints, herself, which she deposited silently for later reference into the crystal clear aaiun that floated almost invisibly above her head.

The deep amethyst of her hair was midnight dark now,

soaked with perspiration and clinging in strands to her neck and ears. Her first complaint had been at herself for not having the foresight to shorten it before leaving for Calx. Actually, it was not strictly true that she had not had the foresight; what she cursed was the vanity that had led her to decide to put it into a long, trailing top knot simply because she so appreciated the aesthetic of it. She sighed and attempted weakly to blow cool air up and across her glistening rose-pink face.

"Thousands of years of genomancing research and experimentation leading to the perfection of my being, and here I am, reduced to using my lips as a fan," she thought. She tried again and hoped the milites wouldn't notice the misery in her eyes. It was not that she could not endure hardship. Over her long life, she had endured countless unspeakable tribulations, ranging from having all the skin on her legs chewed off by acidic leeches on one of the moons of χ Cygni to being subjected to an eighteen hour long oral history of an ancient Polaran war delivered in the form of a one man oratorio (she genuinely could not decide which of those two experiences had been worse). But despite having the physical wherewithal to withstand such punishments—and worse—she found that a constant inner dialog of complaints, whinges, and profanity-laden tantrums helped make the troubles slightly more bearable.

When the leeches had burned and gnawed the flesh on her legs down to the bone, she had focused every remaining cell in her body to avoid going into shock and dying from the trauma. Now, the same energy was being pumped into regulating her body temperature, as well as reabsorbing and recycling moisture, and there was little left over for mitigating the discomfort of it all.

The Fornaxians lacked Kadmus' genomanced biology, instead having to make do with a variety of brain implants that served a similar, if significantly less potent purpose. The tech allowed them to travel lighter, react quicker, fight harder, but had limitations that she was now seeing as they blinked sweat from their eyes and swallowed miserable mouthfuls of oven-hot air. Only the vanguard troops, trailing behind the scout team, had the advantage of mechanical cooling— probably ice-chill in their armored shells. Oh, how she envied them now, the cold, clunky bastards.

The work of trekking through the dense black jungle was made easier, at least, by the small collection of drones she had had the foresight to bring along. At first she had thought, before the jungle's fierce density had caused her team to beat an embarrassing early retreat from the clawing, grabbing vines that it might be easier simply to melt into the jungle and slide stealthily through the vegetation until they reached the edge and could infiltrate the structures they had found. (The vanguards had not even bothered to try an advance, and had waited behind, having realized the inevitability of the coming retreat before anyone else.)

Now, one botanical defeat behind them, Kadmus had decided that as long as they were going to hack their way through the unexplored wilderness like ancient explorers, they might as well have robots do the work. Two drones hovered silently in the air, a pair of spinning hadron blades calmly and effortlessly cutting through the steel-hard vegetation to create a pair of paths for her and her men to walk through. The scouts' eyes darted and swiveled at every sound, and the sounds were constant as the trees, growing inches apart from one another, swayed and collided in the dense, hot wind. Only the vanguard pairs, in their adamantine plating, were calm, walking in a strange silence despite their bulk, their long guns pointed into the air.

The scouts had been briefed on most of what Kadmus and Cadaster knew about the planet, which wasn't much, all things considered. It was a slave planet, but not some typical low-genasi work colony. These slaves were different. It had been, as far as could be told, abandoned by the Primus for an unknown period of time. Perhaps a decade. Perhaps a century. At least long enough that all traces of Primus activity in the surrounding space had disappeared. There was essentially no life, perhaps nothing but vegetation and slaves.

They were to land in a clearing in a dense jungle, make their way to what appeared to be the largest cluster of above- and below-ground buildings. They would infiltrate, investigate whether it was indeed abandoned, and make their way back to the frigate that hung in orbit above them. They had not been told the real purpose of their presence and they had not asked, good soldiers that they were. As far as they knew, they were taking part in the first Cladist liberation, the first slave colony that would be unshackled and brought into the fold of their best hope for progenasi survival and progress.

High in the air above them flew another drone, tiny and transparent—for all intents and purposes invisible—beaming a constant supply of information from its lofty view directly into Kadmus' brain. A typical planetary exploration would have involved dozens of scouting teams, a dozen satellites in orbit, and constant communication being coordinated through an orbiting command center. In this case, though, isolated as they were and ever suspicious that they had been lured into a Primus trap, both Corsair and Navarch had agreed that a smaller footprint was called for. Cadaster and the Fornaxian dreadnought were safely tucked away behind the shadow of a massive asteroid, shielded from prying eyes or sensors. There would be no transmissions, no reinforcements, no backup. Cadaster trusted the Corsair and her scouts to accomplish the mission, and Kadmus trusted herself.

As she walked, she gazed at the shivering black vine trunks around her and her mind tried to find anything useful from the stream of images flowing from the invisible airborne spy. If she sent it high enough, she could see the edge of the jungle miles in the distance. She sighed. The black canopy of the forest was so thick that a bird's eye view was really as useless as the one she had in front of her. Some distance ahead, she could see, though, what appeared to be some kind of break in the "foliage," a vast clearing that stretched several miles in width and length.

"Strange," she thought. "There was no such clearing only a few hours ago when we touched ground."

There was no time to go around it, now. If nothing else, perhaps an escape from the grasping black cords of the vines would also provide some relief from the stultifying heat. Or perhaps whatever had created the massive bald spot on this planetary skull also meant their inevitable death. At this point, the thought of even a slight breeze was entrancing, and she forged her way down the narrow path cut by the propeller drones with renewed vigor, trying to ignore the gluey, black sap that found its way into every gap in her inky crypsis suit and also the clinging, sap-like sense that the clearing ahead signaled an abrupt end to their mission.

32

The curse words of Ad Astara tend to be long, florid, poetic, and terribly unsatisfying. During the period when Ad Astara and Polaris first came into contact and began the drawn out and occasionally reluctant process of learning and exchanging each other's cultures and technology, Astarans almost immediately adopted Polaran customs of vulgarity, astounded by how viscerally gratifying a curse word could be. Their own were saved for higher art forms like drama, literature, and poetry, which were far too precious to mar with Polaran austerity. However, when, while she was crossing the featureless steppe of the Terminator, an unpredicted windstorm suddenly transformed itself into a colossal tornado, Kalaiapi opted for a new word she had learned just a few months ago on Vega. It was short, simple, to the point.

"Shit," she muttered as she was swept up in the abusive embrace of the churning winds.

She felt herself rising into the air as the storm thrashed and tossed her in every direction at once, feeling as though invisible hands were ripping at her on every side. She closed her eyes for a moment and took a deep breath through the crypsis hood that clung tightly to her face, then felt for the secure pocket in which she had placed Kaaio for just such an eventuality. It seemed to be safe enough. Her thoughts, focused as they were on simply maintaining some sense of body control, had no room in them for assurances given or received from the little stowaway. Hooking her feet together and crossing her arms across her chest, she corkscrewed through the air like so much debris for a moment and felt that she might just survive this strangest of ordeals in which she found herself. Now feeling somewhat under control, she gave up a sliver of her mind and reached out to the aaiun that sat snugly in her pants pocket. "Kaaio..."

There was a sharp crack and an explosion of pain as a fist-sized stone struck her in the forehead. Blood began to stream from the wound, soaking into the crypsis fabric and leaking into her specs, the centrifugal force of the tornado spreading it across the lenses until there was nothing but red; not that she could see through the torrent of dust, anyway. She brought the pain under control, trying to maintain the tight shape that would protect her from the wrenching gales. "Kaaio," she thought, "are you there?" There was no response, and the acute pain of genuine fear, cut through her, and it was not the fear she had once associated with aaiun death, that she would lose her mind, but the fear that she had lost...Kaaio. In the midst of the whirlwind, still, this surprised her.

It was then that a second rock—no, a small boulder—struck her, this time in the chest. Her tempered sternum bones cracked and more blood began to seep into the crypsis that covered her. She could not tell how high in the air she was, or even which direction was up. Her goggles were beginning to fill with blood now, the warm stickiness lapping in tiny waves against her eyelids as she continued to twist through the endless debris. Moments later, they were torn from her face and she cinched her eyelids shut against the sandblast. Her head was beginning to swim with the loss of blood. The boulder had knocked her arms apart and they flailed in the air, barely under any semblance of control. She had secured her pack tightly around her chest and shoulders, but could now feel it pulling away as the wind ripped at it and she realized that the boulder, flying at hundreds of miles per hour, had shattered one of the fasteners.

Then, the pack was torn away and she felt her shoulder

wrench out of the socket as it caught on her arm. There was no controlling the pain now, and as the rocks and detritus that were her fellow passengers continued to crash into her, she could feel cuts opening all over her ragged body. She estimated she had been in the tornado now for about 15 seconds. Hundreds of years of life and these 15 seconds of nature on this blasted planet would break her like a wooden doll.

A thought came unbidden, of Kaaio and the relative eternity it would spend reviewing the images of its short life, utterly unable to comprehend the world on its own. She was surprised, then, that this short thought brought her more pain than the one that had immediately preceded it. She had to say something, anything, comfort, direction, anything, and a deep, sharp panic thrust itself into her with all the ferocity of the winds in which she had been caught. It was over for them. Then without warning, as suddenly as the tornado had swallowed her up, it spit her back out.

Her one good arm flailed for a semblance of balance as she cartwheeled through the air and the pale, white skin of her face was now encrusted in a sticky layer of fresh blood and grit, which had at least staunched the jagged wound that gaped on her forehead. She desperately tried to gather the last vestiges of her thoughts as she continued her upward trajectory out of the tornado and into the sky. She wiped the paste of dirt and blood from her eyes and looked toward the earth just as she began what would be a long downward arc. Her cloud-filled brain estimated that she had perhaps ten seconds before she would hit the ground, ten seconds before she died against the hard packed soil of this barren, gray planet.

She reached across her chest and pulled her shoulder back into joint—the pain of the act hardly standing out in the vivid tapestry of anguish that enrobed her body—then patted one hand on her pocket where she felt the comforting small presence of Kaaio, still snug in its crypsis cocoon. The ground was approaching quickly, a dun blur that filled her failing eyes. "I'm sorry, Kaaio," she thought. "I'm so very sorry." Desperately, she crossed her arms back over her chest, bent her knees, and let the earth receive her.

The world erupted into a cloud of sand, dust, and excruciating agony as she struck the iron-hard Calxian surface. The first thing she felt was a snapping femur, then several ribs, and at least two bones in her right arm. She screamed. Something inside her ruptured and bled. She lay, barely conscious, in a shattered pile of bones and torn flesh. For one brief moment, her half-closed eyes caught a small sliver of bruise-purple sky through her swollen, drooping eyelids. In a tiny, isolated corner of her mind she heard a faint voice whisper one word, "Kalaiapi," and then there was only black.

33

"Optis Sairus, in approximately one mile we will approach a clearing in the jungle that was not on our charts when we landed," Kadmus thought to the scout squadron leader, a little burst of electricity shooting from her brain to be caught and transcribed into his. It was the kind of technological enhancement the Clade had embraced in the face of the Confederation's objections as they sought to mesh the progenasis with biotechnology to allow the body to accomplish previously impossible tasks. Unfortunately, Cladist biotech wizardry was still a developing artform and there were constraints to biotechnological telepathy. The electric thought transfer had its limits: its range was paltry, and there was as yet no way to imprint any kind of inflection or intonation into one's words, but it was still remarkably useful. She had insisted, despite the Navarch's misgivings, that the scouts have the implant fixed into their brains before their expedition. Despite its shortcomings, there was something about it that comforted her, though she was loath to admit it to herself.

"Acknowledged, Corsair," came the reply from Sairus, but in Kadmus' own dulcet voice rather than the dry baritone of the Optis. That was the other problem: electronic signals carried no voice, and until Clade technicians managed to embed an identity signal into each implant, it had often been dreadfully confusing to communicate via implant. Kadmus thought back to a particular incident when a little sloop-of-war she'd been on had been about to implode after a direct hit from a Primus rail. The whole crew, knowing what was about to happen, had lost its collective mind, and for about ten seconds her head had been filled with a cacophony of screams, pleadings, and final thoughts, all toneless, all in her own voice. For about a month afterward, those final few seconds of a dozen lives seared into her memory, she had felt very unlucky to have survived the battle. In the end, she had dumped the entire event onto her aaiun and there it sat, gathering digital dust for a decade. And there it would stay.

"Where," came the Optis' continued thoughts, "did the clearing come from, and how did it get there?"

"Damned if I know, Optis, but I'll be an Axial's arse if whatever created it isn't happy to clear us out, too." She turned and gave him a look to convey something of the misgiving she felt about this first and foreboding landmark in their trek. In response, she received a rare display of milite emotion, the slightest upturn of a smirk on the Optis' dark face. In the past months of their long journey together in the tight quarters of the Fornaxian vessel, she had eventually ceased being surprised by such emotional outbursts from the young scout commander. It was not a fair truism that all Polarans (and despite their declaration of sovereignty, Fornaxians were at their heart Polaran) were stone-faced and humorless, but of the milite class, it seemed to be universally true.

It was only upon meeting Sairus that the stereotype had finally been stretched a bit, if not broken. There was no mistaking that the Optis was every bit a Polaran and a proud milite, but he was the very first she had met who had something approaching a sense of humor or a personality that went beyond the boundaries of the "military-philosopher" so many of them aspired and failed to be. She could swear he had once even told an actual joke, though there was no way to be sure. She didn't dare risk the insult of asking him. Naturally, the Navarch did not approve of any of this and had made Kadmus aware of that fact. "It does not become a milite to smile," he had stated in no uncertain terms. Her only response was to wonder how in the name of the predatory universe she had found herself mixed up with these people.

Still, she appreciated even the crumbs of expression she could get from the Optis, and as much as she respected the pensive scholarship of Cadaster, she appreciated being able to have a conversation with someone about anything other than military tactics or the merits of the Clade. Sairus was tall, slim, and looked like a man who had been stitched together from coiled snakes, violent kinetic energy wrapped up in the dusky brownish-blackish skin of a Fornaxian milite. But what set him apart the most from his fellows, physically, anyway, were his eyes, the irises of which were like two chips of mottled green malachite, a one in a thousand feature in anyone of Polaran stock. They were the legacy of an era many thousands of years ago when the planet had been a puzzle of gene pools and races not yet pieced together by time and crossbreeding. Kadmus somewhat envied that their disdain for colorifics allowed such interesting genetic markers to occasionally make an appearance, something that would never be seen in any Astaran longer than the first few years of life. Many Astarans could not tell you their natural eye color without looking it up. Kadmus' had been blue like the waters of the Astaran southern ocean, but it had been many years since she had allowed them to revert to that shade. Since before she joined the Clade.

Another hour of slogging through the sticky grip of the sap-slick vines brought them almost to the edge of the clearing. As they approached, a soft hum had grown in volume. At first it was just a slight vibration tickling the ear bones, but now it had turned into a loud buzzing as though some kind of monstrous beehive awaited them at the edge of the treeline. As the sound intensified, so did a sour, spoiled smell that crept through the stifling air. While the hadron blades of the propeller drones carved a path into the clearing, Kadmus broadcasted to the dozen scouts that trailed behind her. "Eyes up and about, scouts. Who knows what kind of aberrations inhabit this wasteland. They're not liable to be particularly welcoming." The directive wasn't so much for the scouts, who would never have required such basic instruction, but to relieve Kadmus' own tension. Something about this place felt wrong.

She took a first tentative step into the clearing, her feet touching a surface that felt like soft black mulch, wet with viscous slime. It was appalling. And deep. But did not appear toxic to the touch, at least not as far as the translux specs she wore over her eyes could analyze. She stepped in, the thick, dark sludge coming up nearly to her knees. She allocated just a little grain of brain power to stifle a sudden, evolutionary urge to vomit. The smell of rot, of fermentation was overpowering. She forced her brain to ignore it, to quash the nausea that threatened to infiltrate her system. It was amazing, sometimes, what hadn't either been bred or genomanced out of her.

She stepped unwittingly on something round and hard in the mush, her foot nearly slipping out from under her. A rock? No, it was too smooth. With barely controlled loathing, she reached a gloved hand into the mire and pulled out the object, grateful as the crypsis fabric shed the foul-smelling muck. It was perfectly round, like a ball-bearing, glistening and slick, a sickly gray orb the size of a large fist. In the middle of the orb she could see a second little ball, like a black marble, suspended in the center. It wasn't a stone. It was something alive. An egg?

She looked up now, and gazing toward the extending periphery of the clearing around her she could now very clearly see what was making the buzzing sound that filled her ears and made the ground tremble just so slightly one would need to have been genomanced to notice. She laughed.

"What is it?" asked Sairus, opening his mouth to speak for the first time in hours.

Kadmus waved an arm toward the clearing that spread before them into the distance and across the horizon.

"The black gardens of Calx," she replied, amusement in her voice, "are infested with snails."

Sairus stepped out of the jungle and into the black bog of the clearing to see for himself. He turned toward Kadmus and she was almost certain she could see a faint sign of relief in his green eyes and one or two degrees of upturned lips that almost passed as a smile.

34

The cement of dust and dried blood that held Kalaiapi's eyelids together cracked as she somehow found the strength to push them open. Their being open or closed seemed to make no difference, in any case. All she could see was darkness. She could not feel her legs, a fact for which she was at least temporarily grateful, sensing that to feel them now would only be to suffer. She tried moving a finger and found that either they no longer moved or she lacked the motor control to send the necessary nerve impulses down into the muscles of her hands. Either way, they did not move, as far as she could tell. She was able to feel her face, at least, but it was not a particularly pleasant sensation. Everything was fiery pain and, moving her tongue gingerly around her mouth, she found several gaps where teeth had once been. She was most disturbed by her inability to understand the situation in which she found herself, searching her brain for some connection between actions and consequences, and finding none. Strange, she thought, how the anxiety brought about by that fact was not only still functioning, but instinctive when no other functions were operating.

She tried several more times to move various body parts, each time met with the same failure. She did manage eventually to twitch her nose, or so she thought—an act which resulted in an immense pain spreading over her face so that she did not try again. In reality, a good half of her nose had been completely ground off of her face into the Calxian soil, but of course, she had no way of knowing. A warm wind blew across the ground on which she lay and a soft, fine dust coated her dry, broken lips. It was the last sensation she felt before her eyes closed again and she released herself to exhaustion.

35

Kadmus rose out of the sloshing black sludge of the clearing like a pink and amethyst monolith, wrapped in the dark shifting shimmer of crypsis. The Dark Phoenix scouts stood on the rocky banks and shifted on their feet, apparently not calmed by whatever their Corsair had observed in the distance. The long black tendrils dangled and swayed in the hot wind that carried the noxious rotting stench from the surface of the clearing and swirled it into the scouts' noses as they fought the urge to wretch. Kadmus was largely unaffected but the fetid odor was so powerful that even she found her breath coming somewhat more reluctantly now. It was clear that there was no way around the vast body of slime that had seemingly appeared from nowhere and that continued to ripple and sway to the vibrations of the buzzing that rolled through the air from a distance.

Kadmus had been peering off in the direction from which the buzzing ceaselessly droned, squinting and focusing her eyes, trying to get a better view of the source. "Ah, yes," she remarked to herself as much as anyone. "See there, Optis. At the far edge of the clearing." She pointed a gloved finger off into the distance.

"I see nothing but a tangle of vines, Corsair."

"What's the point, Optis, of having synthetic lenses in those green eyes of yours if you're not going to use them? Look closer."

Sairus stood a moment staring off into the distance as the molecular machinery in his irises shifted and focused, bringing the vines into view as if they were no more than a couple of hundred feet away. The mechanical apparata with which the scouts' bodies had been outfitted were more precise and sometimes even more powerful than the genomancing that laced a Corsair's, but there was no denying that the latter operated much more naturally. Watching the scouts implement the various functions of their invisible machinery, Kadmus could almost see them pressing buttons and pulling levers in their minds. There was clearly still much work to be done on that front.

"What in an Axial's eye are those things?" asked Sairus,

bewildered.

Clinging to the thickest vine trunks across several miles of newly created shoreline, the Optis could now see hundreds, perhaps thousands of glistening black shells, pulsating, vibrating, each of them holding what must have been Calx's version of a massive gastropod. The ovoid forms were covered in layers of overlapping lacquered armor that pulsed back and forth like a millipede's segmented husk as the creatures crept up and down the vines, blending in almost invisibly with their surroundings.

"Axials," Kadmus said flatly, "did not have eyes. And those are what I shall be calling Calxian snails, or at least that's the name I'll recommend for them when we get back to Fornax and enter them into the species database."

"Operculii. Calxian operculii. And the question of Axial eyes has not been settled, as far as I know."

"If you wanted to call them operculii, Optis, you should have seen them first. On Ad Astara, we call such things snails, and so they shall be called here, though it will make bugger-all difference. I simply can't imagine many naturalists taking the time to venture halfway across the galaxy to explore their own death sentences."

"You may be pleasantly surprised, Corsair," Sairus replied with what nearly amounted to Polaran cheerfulness. "This may be the first example of life on a terminator planet, finally confirming theories that it was even possible. And from what I have seen of Astaran naturalists, thousands of years of Confederation propaganda have, as of yet, failed to instill in them anything resembling a self-preservation instinct."

Kadmus smiled. "Sairus, you continue to poke welcome holes in myths of Polaran single-mindedness. One gets the sneaking suspicion you might even have a hobby," she said with mock accusation.

"Do you?" he asked.

"Do I what?"

"Have any hobbies?"

She frowned. "No. And as unpleasant as this is going to be, we're going to have to cross this endless lake of slime, excrement, and luteal discharge. It will take us ages to go around. I have to say it's bloody impressive work these things have done. Our scans showed nothing but masses of vines in this area when we plotted our course. Calxian snails must have teeth like diamond saws to clear all this away in the space of a few hours."

"Well, let us hope, then, Corsair, that they have had their fill of black vine and are not on the lookout for alternate sources of protein."

"Let us hope, indeed, Optis Sairus, or this will be a much

shorter expedition than any of us had planned." And with that, Kadmus turned toward the throng of now softly vibrating Calxian snails and began a long trudge through miles of fetid mucus and excrement.

The oppressive hotside wind continued to gust, carrying the befouled air that rose steaming from the swamp into the soldiers' nostrils and lungs as they manfully did their utmost to keep from gagging. Kadmus was unable to set aside any of her mental energy toward sympathy for her suffering fellows as it was all being channeled toward mastering her own raging gag reflex. She could see some of the scouts had simply started holding their breath, something they could do almost indefinitely, but which would certainly make this miserable trek all the more painful. There was no doubt that even at the sodden pace they were managing through the bog they would be moving much more quickly than if they had gone around, but Kadmus couldn't help but question whether her decision to simply strike out across this putrid hellscape had been a little impulsive. Like other high genasi who had undergone the genomancing process to become pilots, her brain had been transformed into something of a supercomputer for the purposes of managing a ship's weapons system or navigating a gravdrive but, for better or worse, one could not genomance away a pilot or the Corsair's tendency toward impetuousness. Kadmus sighed and immediately regretted the interruption to her carefully regulated breathing.

Besides the problem of walking across a wet and nauseating swamp, there was the issue of what amounted to an unnumbered legion of alien gastropods waiting on the other side. That problem, she supposed, was unavoidable either way. The sheer number of them and the area they seemed to cover meant that any detour around them was simply not feasible. Instead she had simply made an educated gamble that their diet consisted entirely of the black vines they consumed with such ravenous enthusiasm and not any scraps they came across besides. If that turned out to be the case, well then, she could only hope that Calxian snails were no faster than their Astaran counterparts. Operculii, indeed.

She glanced at the aaiun floating serenely above her right shoulder, looking every bit like a miniature Calxian snail egg. For a fleeting moment, her mind ran across a thought she had had many times over her long years. She wondered if, as an appendage of its user's consciousness and memory, the aaiun possessed some small reflection of the personality to which it was attached. No. Even the hint of such would have every aaiun in the galaxy smashed to their atoms in the time it took the Confederation's Quaestors to hunt them down. And they would hunt them down. Kadmus had heard of people instantaneously dying at the destruction of their aaiuns or being driven permanently insane—their synapses bursting from the trauma, irreparable by even the most advanced Confederation neurologs. She shuddered, blinking the heresy away.

Kadmus knew she would never reproduce, on that the biotech-synchresis seeking Cladists and evolution-worshiping Confederation agreed. The fate of the gene pariah. But neither did she seek to have her mind and memory preserved for eternity as part of the Clade's Collective Consciousness, their optimistic but ill-conceived attempt to construct for themselves an afterlife. A strange impulse, she thought, for a society that took such a mundane view of death. But it was not for her; after centuries of blood and sadness, a final release into Oblivion, into the endless peace of non-existence, that was enough for Kadmus. Not that she would ever speak ill of the Collective Consciousness to her Cladist compatriots. For them it was as sacred as anything in the Aya itself.

She began to say something to Optis Sairus but upon drawing the breath to speak immediately started to choke and stopped. Here in the middle of the morass she could taste the air like it was soup and she nearly doubled over. There was no conversation to be had in this place. She could have thought it, but the notion of having any kind of meaningful conversation through the flat, electric tones of the transmitters felt distasteful. Instead, she simply drew on her water supply, gritted her teeth, and set one foot in front of the other. Her squad was in the depths of misery, though not a word of complaint escaped their tightened lips. Only the four vanguards, their mechanized suits ignoring the clinging sludge and their helms filtering the putrid air, seemed to be having an easy time of it. The thin veins in Sairus' eyes were like bright red threads criss-crossing the dull whites. He had stopped breathing hours ago, the implants in his body cracking open the carbon dioxide to release the precious oxygen inside and channel it back into the bloodstream. It was unpleasant, but it worked in a pinch.

During the brief seconds when the oven-like hotside winds ceased to blow, the air would fill with a mist, a thick and noxious vapor that condensed on their skin and formed droplets on their eyelashes. After several hours of painful marching through the poison quagmire, the sludge began clinging to their legs, gripping their ankles with viscous fingers. Kadmus looked around to see if the others were suffering the same sensation she was. It wasn't fatigue. She could have walked through this slime for days unbroken and barely slowed. It was evaporation. The hot wind was acting like a fan, blowing the moisture out of the swamp and turning the slime into biotoxic glue.

Kadmus looked up to see the endless herd of Calxian snails as they began to shift and amble down the vines, which swayed and bent under the weight of their massive shells, then back down at the black ooze that clung to her crypsis boots and sucked at her footsteps. "We do not believe in the horizon," she thought to herself, quoting the Aya for comfort. But from here the horizon felt very real and looked so far away.

36

"Kalaiapi, brain function seems to have largely been restored. Can you hear me?"

It took her a moment to collect enough raw material in her brain to formulate an answer.

"Yes." The single word seemed to drain whatever ability to create words she possessed.

"That is good. Now, try not to think, only to listen. Your neural networks sustained critical damage upon landing and much of what they contained was lost. Fortunately, I have maintained a backup up to the point where we hit the ground. It will take some time to upload once your network is ready to bear the load. Until then, you must try to rest your mind and body. Based on the information I am receiving, it will take several more days before you are able to move again.

Fortunately, Kalaiapi, based on the calculations you made before we began crossing the plain, it seems unlikely that another tornado will hit the area in which we landed. Then again, it was unlikely the first time, as well."

She lay there, unable to even to coalesce brain waves into words. Certainly, if the odds had defied her by sweeping her up in that tornado, she had defied them back by surviving it. She could consider herself even. At least, she would when she was able. For now, she slept. And slept.

She was not certain how long she remained unconscious, wrapped deeply in a dreamless sleep. To think sleep, something that had for most of her life been so perfunctory, was now the basis for her survival. No matter how long one lived, life was an endless series of surprises. She tried opening her mouth and her rawhide dry lips pulled apart with considerable reluctance. Her mouth felt as though it had been stuffed with the dust that had blown across her face in the past days. In fact, it had. She coughed to clear her windpipe and lungs, apparently now in some control over her broken body. Her lungs cleared, but her body was wracked by spasms of pain over which her fragile mind was unable to gain any control.

She attempted to sit up and failed, but she could wiggle her fingers. This was a good sign. More importantly, perhaps, she could see. Not very much, but at least her eyes served some purpose again. She gazed up into the pink sky, her vision framed by the clots of dried blood that clung to her eyelashes. Turning her head to either side with great difficulty she saw nothing but hard, ashen, flat, endless soil. Her head lay on a pillow of soft, fine sand, and by gingerly moving her fingertips on the ground, she found more of the same. Ah. Kalaiapi had said before that the only thing that could kill her was coincidence. Sometimes it was the only thing that saved her.

She ran her sandpaper tongue across her teeth— the few that remained, anyway. The regrowth process had not yet begun. With no food or water available for the foreseeable future, the process would be agonizingly slow. All those teeth were a luxury rather than a necessity, and available resources were going to knitting back together the remains of her spinal cord. She closed her eyes again.

After what must have been several days staring into the unchanging Calxian heavens, Kalaiapi was able to move her arms and, with great difficulty, to sit up—an effort she regretted as soon as she made it. Collapsing back into a tortured heap, she slipped into a perfectly still slumber that ended with the words, "Kalaiapi, the upload is complete. Full memory has been restored."

"Thank you, Kaaio."

"Kalaiapi, having access to memories that were heretofore barred to me, I learned several interesting things about you, though even many of those memories seem to have been...obscured. For example, I learned that you are not one, but four, and I do not under—"

"Kaaio," she thought, applying the force of her regained brain power, "you were denied access to those memories for a reason. That access is to remain barred to you and you will not speak of it again, or access that data. I would like for you to upload it to my consciousness and delete it from your drive, please."

"But, Kalaiapi, why?"

"To explain would be to defeat the very purpose of what I am asking you to do. Those memories must stay in my internal memory bank. This is important. I understand that we share a consciousness now, but remember that I am not you and you are not me. These memories—this data—it isn't for you."

"Very well, Kalaiapi," said Kaaio softly from the pocket in which it had been since they first stepped out into the wastes. "The memories have been removed from my drive."

"Thank you, Kaaio." She felt a sudden wealth of energy and managed to sit up again, this time with less pain. She surveyed her surroundings and found little to inspire hope. Nearby, partially-buried in the soft sand that had broken her fall, sat an enormous boulder. She thought she might be able to drag herself into its lee and shield herself from the relentless wind that continued to fill her nose, eyes, and throat with dust and grit. She lacked even the saliva to wash it from her mouth, which felt and tasted—so she imagined—like an ancient tomb. Inch by agonizing inch, she crawled to the shelter of the boulder and leaned her back against its smooth surface, grateful for the support.

Looking down at herself, she now surveyed the damage done to her body and was amazed again that she was able to do so at all. By rights, she should have been torn to pieces by the winds of that tornado. Indeed, almost any other progenasi would have been. Kalaiapi, though, was of a different stock, and the same qualities that had made her a gene pariah at least served to preserve her in these kinds of situations. Her right femur was snapped and bone bulged against the crypsis fabric that clung tightly to her leg. That would need to be set before it could be restored. She was suddenly grateful for the partial paralysis that protected her from feeling below her hips. The broken ribs would also need to be set, and that was something she would certainly feel. Even now, every breath caused the jagged, broken pieces of rib to grate against each other, inducing an occasional shock of agony that threatened to return her to unconsciousness.

She was normally able to control her pain mechanisms without too much trouble, but her system had been overwhelmed and all auxiliary energy and brainpower was focused on the complex and draining task of stitching together organs and nerve tissue. She wondered how the process would go without food or water to supplement it. Perhaps she had enough fat stored to at least get her legs working again—her enhanced body working like a biological baryonic synthesizer to break down the raw materials of those stores and restructure them as the various cells it needed to repair itself. The Primus had a similar ability, it seemed, only theirs came from the nanobots with which they lived in perverse symbiosis—a state of being anathaya to the Aya and a threat to the very existence of the progenasis.

She turned her head to again take in her surroundings and felt a scraping of metal against the stone. Reaching to touch the back of her neck, she felt the now-ragged metal of the neural port, torn mostly free from the vertebrae that had held it in their grip. No wonder it had taken so long to feel her body again. The trauma of having the port torn from her spine would have nearly destroyed her nervous system. As it was, now she was simply stranded on Calx in perpetuity, or at least until someone thought to come look for her. And the only person who knew she was here was Jroran. Poor auspices.

"Your suppositions are correct, Kalaiapi," she heard. "It is sundered and it cannot be repaired by normal biological processes. I am afraid you will be unable to pilot our craft." She felt a small inkling of despair rising in her breast and instantly stifled it. Despair was one of those many animalistic evolutionary tendencies that had proven nearly impossible to eliminate, even in someone like her. Nonetheless, it had no place even on Calx. She swallowed it down. Then, bending forward to take her sensationless knee in her hands, she pulled downward and snapped her broken femur loosely into place. That would at least be enough to allow the bones to rejoin. Leaning her head back against the rock, she slept.

37

To look at her, one could not have guessed that, under the stress of being mired in a pool of fetid snail mucus that was quickly hardening into a biological cement while braving rushing hot winds of toxic fumes, Kadmus was physically and mentally exhausted. That same hot wind that leeched energy and strength from her system blew her thick amethyst hair behind her—a mane, an aura—and her rose-pink skin glistened and shone in the reddish light of Ara. She looked behind her to see the scouts beginning to flag, their dark faces turning a sickly ash gray as they strove to avoid breathing the nauseous mist that hung in the air over the swamp. The four vanguards, safe in their mechanized armor, their long guns pointed into the air like ancient muskets, trudged doggedly through the gluey-black slime, but their sad compatriots, lacking any such technological advantages, slogged and pulled their way behind them.

"Come on now, milites," she called out to the struggling scouts, trying her best to make her rich alto voice sound more encouraging and enthusiastic than she felt. "Not so far, now. At the end of it, we'll make a meal of Calxian snails with drawn butter." She knew they would not appreciate the joke itself, but hoped at least they would acknowledge the attempt in whatever fashion they were able. She had made the great sacrifice of drawing breath in order to make it.

"Fornaxians," came the pinched reply from Sairus as he did his best to speak while breathing as little as possible, "do not tire, Corsair. We are simply taking time," he continued, each word nearly choked off by a lack of breath, "to enjoy the journey." The Optis wore a grimace that came very close to resembling a smile and Kadmus could not help but throw her head back and laugh, not at the joke, but at the fact that of all times, Sairus had chosen now to make one. She gagged and nearly wretched as the taste of the noxious vapor touched her tongue and her mirth was quickly cut short.

Adopting as Polaran a demeanor as she could, she once again called out to the flagging scouts. "Come on, then, we'll make it, yet. Milites of the Dark Phoenix will not be vanquished by so much snail slime. Onward and soon we'll find ourselves on dry land with hopes that those snails are vegetarians." Kadmus felt a slightly renewed vigor after hearing Sairus' joke as she struck back out into the clinging quagmire and was encouraged by the pace of the squelching sounds behind her indicating that her fellows were keeping pace. She was certain there was no chance of them dying in this forsaken place, but misery was misery, even with a definite ending, and there were plenty of miles ahead of them before they reached their destination.

She looked up again at the shoreline, tangled knots of black vines bending under the weight of the massive snails. The colossal mollusks were still shifting down the vines, though not at the lazy pace they had been moving at earlier. There seemed to be an urgency to their movement and the vines began to twist and churn to and fro as the herd made its way down the thick trunks and back toward the lake of slime they had just created. Granted, the urgency didn't seem like much, as they were no faster than the garden snails that made silver trails in the woods on Ad Astara. At least, not until the first pulsating gray bodies hit the slime. Suddenly, by some mechanism she had neither the time nor the information to make sense of, Kadmus watched a wave of eight-foot tall, glistening black shells rush towards her and the scouts and she understood at least one piece of how these creatures were able to create a lake of ooze from a vine forest in so little time that they had only noticed when it was too late. She gripped the haft of her hadron knife and watched them come. Her chemprop rifle would be as useful right now as a glass of water on the surface of the sun.

"Corsair," said the Optis, "I do believe we are witnessing a stampede and I reckon we are all about to be crushed to death." The calmness of his tone only served to heighten the sense of impending doom she felt as she watched the sea of shells rushing toward them in a tide. Death by snails. It was humiliating.

"Vanguards, deploy. Now." Even as she started to speak, the long guns had swung down to point their muzzles at the oncoming herd. Electric blue light flared and sparkled along the barrels of the railguns that stretched out as long as the armor clad warriors that wielded them. "We don't have rails to spare. Concentrate fire in the center of the herd and see if you can't part the sea."

She felt her mouth go dry and her heart rate increase, could feel the blood rushing to her head, could practically feel its warmth rushing through individual veins, filling her brain with oxygen. Astaran genomancers had found that their initial work with Corsairs, in which they had done away with adrenaline responses to danger, had resulted in a far higher death rate among them. Some things were not meant to be tampered with. Looking to her left she saw Sairus' bloodshot eyes dilate and his lips go tense. Stimulants.

"Fire teams, clear us a path." There was a crackle of electricity around them as the guns drew power from the heavy packs attached to the backs of their armor, power plants in miniature. Next to each of the two gunners their support crew stood like ancient knights clad in matte, gunmetal plate. If the weapon Kadmus was holding was called a hadron "knife," the translucent opalescent blades in the hands of the vanguards could only be described as hadron glaives, their blades running four feet down the length of a thick metalloy haft. It was a rare thing for any enemy to get close to these mobile artillery units but when they did, it more often than not ended in immediate evisceration. If quick, crafty troops like Sairus' scouts were the deft fingers on one hand of progenasi armies, vanguard troops were the clenched mailed fist on the other. With a crack like the snapping of a great tree, the first bolt flew, white hot and sparking, toward the oncoming tide of gastropods.

As the initial bolt hit the unlucky first snail, there was an explosion of shell, slime, and ragged black tissue. The poor creature was gone, but the bolt had barely slowed, cutting a line of devastation through the herd, before hitting an embankment on the far side of the slime lake in a cloud of dust and rock shards. Still the snails rushed forward, heedless of the dozens that had fallen beside them. The gap in the stampede closed nearly as soon as it had been opened. Kadmus licked her dry lips.

"Hold—," but the second bolt had already launched and cascaded through the hapless beasts and pieces of shell and snail flew into the air and landed in a hailstorm of carnage on the rest of the rushing herd.

"Hold your fire!" she shouted. "It's useless, there's simply too many of them." The stampede was moving closer now, and the black sludge that clung to the troops' calves trembled and shook like toxic jelly. "Optis, how many charges did we bring?"

"Three, Corsair."

"Give me two of them, quickly!"

The Optis motioned to one of the scouts, who quickly pulled two fist-sized explosives from her pack and tossed them to Kadmus. It took just a few seconds for Kadmus to make the calculations while fastening the two charges to each other and weighing them in her gloved hand. It would probably work. It was either this or face almost certain death by snail stampede. The indignity of it. She was almost grateful to think that if they did die, the ignominious remains of their consciousness would almost certainly never be added to the collective. This would have to do.

"Fire teams, on my mark, and the Tyraness of Fornax help you if you miss." With a thought, she transmitted instructions directly into the brains of the two gunners. This would require a precision to which verbal commands would do no justice. The herd was bearing down now, Kadmus could see the black bulbs of their eyes, the hundreds of spiny teeth that filled their suction cup mouths. She waited, licked her lips again and steadied her arm. It had to be perfect.

It was at the point where Kadmus could have counted each of those needle-like teeth without using her genomanced lenses that she launched the charges into the midst of the thundering stampede, and just a split second later when the air was filled with the crack of the rails, blue tendrils of electricity caressing the dull gunmetal as the alloy bolts shot from the muzzles faster than the eye could see. Kadmus' computer-like brain experienced an eon in the few milliseconds before the two rails and the falling charges collided in perfect harmony.

The resulting explosion was deafening. A geyser of lake sludge and minced snail organs erupted into the air and fell back to the earth in a fine, slimy mist. Kadmus ducked as one of the snails, propelled forward by the blast, hurtled through the air over her head. Still the herd flowed forward, but now with a gaping hole in its ranks through which the far bank of the lake could be seen. A hole that had already begun to be filled.

"Run, you bastards!" shouted Sairus. And they ran.

Propelled by drugs and adrenaline and a hatred of death that crouches deep down in every progenasi's DNA, the scout team ran, tearing forward through the slime and the sludge, through shards of shattered shell, then over a great patch of dry ground that had been scoured clean by the exploding charges. The herd began to slam back together like sand sliding to fill a pit dug in a dune. "Run harder, you bastards!" Sairus screamed.

It was the four vanguards, aided by their mechanized armor suits, that made it through the gap the charges had created in the snail herd first, and with time to spare. They turned to watch their comrades bolting through the narrowing furrow they had made and immediately despaired. They would surely be crushed.

Kadmus joined them next, panting and cursing hard Polaran obscenities. The snails continued to close ranks. More calculations. They would all make it. Barely. The scoured earth was an unexpected boon, slowing the snails and quickening the milites. Without it she would certainly have been completing this ill-fated scouting trip with just the four vanguards.

Then, as Kadmus finished her reassuring calculations, Explorator First Class Gylfa Chahar stepped on an egg like the one Kadmus had pulled from the muck when she had first set foot into the morass. Kadmus watched with horror as her ankle shattered and the young scout sprawled face first into the pitch black slime. The last of the scouts had just darted past the end of the stampede when Gylfa pulled her face from the tar-like sludge and looked toward her comrades now safe on the other side of the herd. Only her gray eyes shown, and Kadmus cursed the precision with which she could see the terror in them. Gylfa lifted a hand toward them and opened her mouth, perhaps as if to scream, perhaps, Kadmus later thought, to say goodbye. They would never know, as the glistening black shells slammed together either side of her like great obsidian boulders and she was carried off by the ceaseless tide.

It was then, turning back toward the far bank, now just a few hundred yards away, that Kadmus now saw what had inspired the panicked flight of so many thousands of frenzied gastropods. "What," she breathed, "fresh hell is this?"

38

Still no teeth. She hadn't gotten used to the sensation of moving her tongue across the inside of her mouth and there being holes instead of bicuspids and she couldn't stop probing at them with her stone-dry tongue. The femur had finally knitted back together to the point where she could tentatively put some weight on it, but it wasn't back to full strength. Her bones had been strengthened and enhanced, making them incredibly difficult to break, but that also meant that it took quite a few bio-resources to put them back together, and they were resources she simply didn't have.

She'd found a single ration bar in one of her pockets, which she had devoured greedily, nearly choking as she forced the dense food down her parched throat. Kalaiapi couldn't remember the last time she'd eaten for taste, but she had to admit that something primal in her had savored the salty fat and sugars of the thick food paste. Digesting it without water had been unpleasant, but eventually her system got the nutrients where they needed to go and her body was able to continue making much needed repairs. Her most vital organs had failsafes grafted in, but those would only last so long. In any case, at long last, she thought she could start moving. Staying any longer on this abyssal plain would simply mean dying of thirst or a total system failure. Hard to kill as she was, it wasn't impossible, and she needed to find fuel and water, and needed to do so quickly.

Her miniature aerial drone had been disintegrated by the tornado, but the vast quantity of information it had sent to her brain was still there, and she began pulling the images that were stored in Kaaio, building a virtual map inside her mind in order to get some sense of her bearings in this vast, featureless landscape. Her eyes scrolled across the plain, past the occasional boulder field, churning dust devils, and twisting trenches clawed from the earth by wind-dragged stones. There. What was that? A strange shimmer in the dusty barrens toward the coldside. No, a collection of shimmers.

"Kaaio, bring up the rest of the data for the section of desert I'm looking at now." She didn't have to ask, of course, but the longer Kaaio's nascent consciousness hovered around her brain the more uncouth it felt to draw information out of it without occasionally asking. She focused her eyes on the vague shimmering shapes that were so nearly indistinguishable from the dust and rocks that surrounded them, drew them closer. They looked almost like...It was impossible. But at the same time, she should have recognized them immediately: crypsis.

There must have been half a dozen of them, almost invisible to the naked eye, to any normal eye, in any case. "Kaaio, give me the rolling feed of that section starting from here." She watched as the shimmers moved smoothly off in the direction of the complex of buildings she had seen from across the plain, shifting and changing with the gray sand. Just half an hour before she had landed in a broken heap, whoever they were could not have been more than a few hundred feet from where she sat. But they'd been gone for days now. They could be anywhere. What she knew was that they were progenasi, but beyond that it was impossible to guess to whom they belonged. Everyone used crypsis fabric and it defeated the purpose to include any identification markers. But the Primus didn't use it. They didn't need to.

Of course, the other thing she now knew was that somewhere in that direction there were weapons and supplies, and now she had a point toward which she could travel. She pulled herself painfully to her feet, grateful to at least have retained her boots, and set limping off toward the coldside and the prospect of water.

39

The evolutionary horror that lurched through the black vines and into the far side of the clearing was unlike anything Kadmus had ever seen—some aberration of nature that had crawled from Calx's boiled-dry seas to scratch out a desperate living on the new dry ground until it gradually transformed itself into this bizarre nightmare. The creature scuttled out of the trees on massive gray crab legs, chitinous and covered in sharp spines that jutted haphazardly in every direction. Perched on a dozen spindly legs was a bulging carcass of mottled black and gray jelly, glistening with a sticky mucus. It did not appear to have any eyes, or at least nothing Kadmus could recognize as such.

From the wriggling jelly-mass there also sprung a collection of long tentacles that stretched out all around it, reaching, searching, grasping, constantly moving. A great yellow beak hung from its middle and swung from a long, thick trunk of pendulous black flesh that swayed uncontrolled as the strange beast lumbered and clawed its way across the clearing and into the sludge, following the snails as they continued to stampede to the other side. Its long legs tore easy gashes in the solidifying slime as it scuttled with alarming speed in the direction of the scouts.

By now the whole squad was brandishing weapons. Chemprop rifles at the ready, sweat glistening on their dusky faces, they looked toward the Corsair, awaiting direction. "Everyone hold your fire," she said quietly, hoping to channel her calm into her soldiers. "We'll simply move out of its path. With any luck it won't even know what we are and will keep after its prey. Quickly and quietly."

But as Sairus took his first steps out of the creature's way, it immediately turned toward them and its armored, spindly legs carried the great black mass of its tentacles directly toward the scouts with a renewed vigor.

"Stop!" hissed Kadmus. Sairus froze, then licked his lips nervously. His green eyes locked onto the alien hulk careering through the mire toward him, then onto Kadmus, desperate for instruction. For her part, Kadmus now felt an uncomfortable panic rising in her breast, filling her lungs.

Something about this creature from a nightmare had triggered a latent, though deep and, yes, even genetic, instinct, and she was fighting now to control the unfamiliar feeling, her exhausted brain clouded and her thoughts thick and slow. "Too late," she whispered. "For the Aya's sake, vanguards, bring that thing down or make your peace with the ether."

40

With each step, hot, white needles of pain shot through her shattered leg. Her hair was matted with blood and dirt and hung heavy from her scalp. She must have looked every bit the picture of the ape-like low genasi crawling from their dank caves and wincing in the sunlight. Though, now that she'd lost her hood and the rest of her crypsis-covered form shifted to match its background, she mostly looked like a disembodied head floating through the colorless desert. Kaaio, glowing a pleasant grass-green as it orbited her filthy skull, gave an odd out-of-place vibrancy—almost ironic cheer—to the dismal scene.

The Terminator experienced neither day nor night, and time felt endless as Kalaiapi made her long trek through the wastes. The effort was unbearable. Even to carry on a conversation over her brainwaves felt like a monumental task, so she focused all her thoughts simply on managing the quickly depleting resources her cells needed to even put one foot in front of the other. The alternative to her tortuous trudge, however, was death, and neither genomancing nor evolution had dulled her will to live.

It was in the seventy-sixth hour of this procession of agony that she saw it in the distance through her dirt-gummed eyes: a skiff. It, too, shimmered and shifted in the purpling light of the horizon, but there was no mistaking the outline. She might have smiled, but she hadn't a joule of energy to spare to make the movements. Besides, her lips looked and felt like she'd taken an Astaran mass broadside to the face and every movement cracked and tore the dry flesh a little more.

There was no room now for caution, only survival, as she hobbled her way toward salvation. Then, from the bruise-colored air, one, two, suddenly six more shapes seemed to dance in the light toward her. She could do nothing but hope they'd either help her or kill her quickly. She fell to her knees. The indignity of it all, to be crawling like a beggar. "I, who am many and ageless, Kaaio." The figures came closer and closer until she could hear their footsteps in the soft, dun sand. She could keep her eyes open no longer, and collapsed to the earth.

"Is it one of the drones?" asked a low, muffled voice.

"I don't think so. It's too small. And it has hair."

"Well, what the hell is it, then? Intel said there was no one else on this floating Primic ball of shit and rock."

One of the figures leaned down and took Kalaiapi's shoulder, flipping her onto her back. She fluttered her eyes open to see a blurred, slate gray face, its stony features broken only by the bulging whites of two flint chip eyes.

"Optis... I think it's..."

Another figure impatiently shuffled over and pushed the first out of the way.

"Omnic shit. It's Corsair Kadmus."

41

The first two bolts shot forth, a blaze of blue and white sparks, and hurtled toward the creature as it continued in its arachnid stride toward them. The bolts struck the creature simultaneously, the first hitting one side of its shapeless, gelatinous body, turning blood and mucus into vapor as the superheated alloy shot through rubbery tissue. The result was an explosion of black gore as chunks of flesh shot into the air, leaving one of the beast's thick tentacles hanging raggedly by a thick sinuous membrane. The second bolt zipped straight through the creature's middle, opening a jagged hole that let loose a gout of inky sludge indistinguishable from the muck that clung to the scouts' boots. It fell like a black blood clot. No sooner, though, had the wounds been opened than they began to knit together, the jet black rubber of the creature's hide melding together like molten plastic. It did not break its stride.

Kadmus' mouth was as dry as a tomb, her tongue thick and swollen, her lips like ancient paper, flaked and cracking in the heat. She suddenly knew what to do and was not certain she wanted to do it, but there was no time to debate, even with herself. With a thought, she sent a surge of adrenaline through her body and readied herself for her next task. The creature had no eyes that she could see, yet as soon as Sairus had taken even a single step it had known exactly where to find them. Perhaps it had some sort of tremor sense, could locate prey from their most minute vibrations. She would give it some prey, then, and perhaps give her scouts a chance to bring the thing down. She had mere seconds before it would take them, no time even to speak, to give orders.

Instead, she ran—or tried to run, after a fashion. The fetid, black snail-tar pulled at her crypsis boots, sucking her to the ground, but even so, her legs were like pistons and she wrenched her feet free and sprinted with all her might away from the scout patrol. As she began running, she issued her order, this time through her thoughts. "Do not move. Take its legs."

The sharp thundercrack of the rail guns exploded through the air as the vanguards, silent and calculating, loosed another pair of bolts that flew toward their target with perfect accuracy. With coordinated thought, they had picked a leg to aim for and two bolts simultaneously hit one of the creature's knee joints, tearing easily through the thick chitin, turning the ichor that flowed inside into an explosion of plasma. The limb sheared from its body and the creature stumbled, but quickly regained its balance and turned toward the sprinting Kadmus as she made her way across the sludge lake away from her compatriots. After a moment's hesitation, it set off toward her, its speed hardly affected by the lack of a limb.

It gained on her quickly, towering fifty feet over her miniature figure. She could hear the rail guns purr and crackle, absorbing power from the massive batteries that required a mechanized suit simply to carry. The guns were powerful, unerring in the hands of a trained soldier, but fragile. If they did not manage to kill this aberration before they needed to change the rails, they would probably never kill it. How many legs did this alien monster have? A dozen? How many would it have to lose before it would be rendered immobile? Hopefully, they would live to find out.

42

"Where did she come from? How did she get here?"

The Optis paced back and forth outside the skiff where Kalaiapi lay, fluid packs seeping desperately needed water and minerals into her body, cell gel applied liberally to her horrifically swollen leg—nearly black now from tissue damage. She drifted in and out of consciousness while Kaaio used her ears to hear a conversation she was barely capable of understanding in her current state. One word filled her brain, raced through her head like a fever virus: Kadmus. How could she be here? How could Kadmus be here? How could Kadmus be here?

She felt the water molecules creep into her blood, loosen the parched cells, felt the nuclei swell with new life and carry it into her brain. It was a fascinating feeling. She had been close to death countless times, but to face the prospect of dying in an instant of trauma was not the same as feeling one's body slowly lose the capacity to live. Her fingertips tingled as the feeling returned to them and it was as though she could feel each bundle of cells that made up her tissue thirstily gulping up water and sugar and the minerals that seeped into her skin from the cool, blue fluid packs. She had to absorb every drop she could before the Fornaxian milites inevitably discovered she was indeed a Corsair, but not the one they had thought when they had rescued her. Once they realized their mistake, a quick death would once again be the most she could hope for.

"She's a bloody Corsair, she'll be fine. The question is whether whatever did this to her is still out there and what it's going to do to the rest of us if it is."

"They're old wounds, Optis," piped up Explorator Furn, lithe, grim-faced, unusually short for a Polaran. "She ain't bleeding, she's been healing. Could have happened days ago."

"I don't want to take any chances, all the same. Something did this, and it wasn't those mindless drones. I reckon she could kill hundreds of those things before the first one noticed it was dead. Double-watches tonight, set up the arc cannons. When we get the signal from the dreadnought, we'll break silence and send them the coordinates for the anima tanks."

"Aye, Optis, and then we can get off this rancid bit of space flotsam," Furn added with a touch of hope in his voice.

"'Sooth, much as I'd rather be back on the 'nought, Furn, rumor has it this anima cache will change the war, change everything. Just think, you're part of the legions that will bring glory to the Clade like none have ever seen." This grandiose opinion was provided by Explorator Grevel who squatted, chemprop rifle in one hand, just outside the entrance to the skiff, his mouth full of the ration bar on which he was gnawing. Actually, Grevel may have been a female. It was hard to tell, muffled through the skiff walls, but there certainly seemed to be a hint of vestigial estrogen in her voice. The Optis turned toward her.

"Shut your mouth, Grevel. There are milites in this legion whose tongues should be pulled from their hollow skulls. There are two people within a thousand analuxae of this rock who know what that anima is for and one of them is lying half-dead in that skiff."

"It's for a weapon, Optis, you can be cert. Don't need rumor-mongering bay monkeys to know that. What else could possibly make it worth it to come all the way out here, months from Clade space?"

"It's not for a weapon, churl," interjected another, "It's for better implants, it's to achieve the biotech-synchresis."

"Stow it. Intellectual curiosity is not a valuable trait in a milite, Grevel," said the mountainous Optis to conclude the conversation, his eyes, dark in both color and disposition, glaring from his neckless head at the still-chewing Grevel.

"Aye, sir, it ain't, but you and I will both be equally happy when there's a medal on our chests for fetching five million gallons of consciousness soup and we're using the same to put the Confeds under Clade boot heels." The corners of the Optis' mouth gave the slightest hint of a reluctant upward turn at the thought.

"Alright, Explorator, stow your insolent voice box long enough to go check on the Corsair."

"Aye, sir," replied the Explorator, jumping to her feet and walking up the short ramp into the glowing interior of the skiff.

"Optis," she yelled through the open hatch. "What color was the Corsair's hair when we disembarked?"

The Optis turned his head toward the hatch. "Eh? Reddish-blue, or something. Why?"

"Sir, I think you'd better come in—"

There was a thud.

"Dammit, Grevel, what is it now?" The Optis charged up

the ramp into the skiff where Explorator Grevel lay still on the floor, her neck bent ninety degrees and her black eyes staring up into nothing. He drew a short hadron knife from his belt and stepped cautiously into the blue-lit skiff, his eyes expertly searching every angle of the chamber, but Kalaiapi was gone.

Quiet as a thought, Kalaiapi made her way to the escape hatch. She could hear boot steps on top of the skiff now as the Fornaxian Explorators surrounded the vessel. The Optis hadn't said a word, how had they reacted so quickly? Polaran military efficiency really was impressive to behold. Unfortunately, stealth was no longer an option, in any case. She flung the escape hatch open with all her might and the scout that awaited her, chemprop rifle pointed downward, took a step back, surprised. It was enough that the flechette she fired flew through Kalaiapi's shoulder rather than her skull, and she winced as she felt the muscles rend and tear. But she was quicker, still, than the poor scout in front of her. She pulled the chemprop rifle from her hands and swung it by the barrel. The diamond-hard polymer butt of the rifle hit the Fornaxian's skull like a meteorite, shattering bone and crushing brain; she crumpled into a heap on top of the skiff.

The rifle butt moved smoothly from the broken skull and up to Kalaiapi's bleeding shoulder and another Fornaxian scout fell into the Calxian dust, a single polymer chemprop flechette tearing through throat and spine. Three dead. Three left. It was Kalaiapi's turn to fall now, dropping face first onto the roof of the skiff and rolling behind the open hatch door as the almost childish cracking of chemprop rifles sent a hail of flechettes toward her. She felt another tear through her calf and winced as she rolled off the skiff and onto the ground, landing in a crouch.

She wasn't quite ready for a fight like this and took half a second to refocus her energies where they needed to be. Alright. Now, move. Where were the other three Explorators? Another crack and very nearly her death. One of them was in a cluster of rocks a few hundred feet away. A picket. Clever. She ducked, weaved, brought her rifle to her shoulder and the picket died. The Explorators were excellent shots; Kalaiapi could not miss. Two left.

There was the Optis now coming around the other side of the skiff with a knife and sidearm. He looked to be built out of boulders. No matter. Kalaiapi's entire body pulsed, throbbed, protested.

"Who are you?" demanded the Optis from around the corner of the skiff (because of course these Fornaxian atrocities were all angles). "Corsair Kadmus?" Just hearing the name shot flames into Kalaiapi's mind.

She could hear the other Explorator now, climbing

through the escape hatch at the top of the skiff. This would be painful. She coiled toward the ground like a cat and shot into the air, making the twenty-foot distance to the skiff's roof in a single, excruciating leap. The cost was another flechette, the rooftop scout tracking her like a bird and shooting her through the gut. At this, even Kalaiapi screamed, landing heavily on her back on the roof.

The scout, this must have been Furn, lifted his rifle to finish the kill, only to suddenly let out a howl of agony as Kalaiapi reached out with her hadron knife to sever his foot from his leg. Rising to her feet quicker than the screaming scout could fall, she slipped the shimmering blade up through the poor scout's chin and into his brain. That's when she heard the unmistakable sound of an arc cannon charging. The Optis. She managed to leap from the roof and back into the soft, gray sand just as the skiff erupted into an explosion of lightning, fire, and shrapnel. She had not been the target of that shot, she knew. By now the Optis had realized he was outmatched. The little ship was now scattered across the endless plain. Several pieces of it had embedded themselves into Kalaiapi's back, and her newly-watered blood streamed under the crypsis fabric.

The Optis had been thrown back by the explosion and was struggling to his feet. Kalaiapi forced her barely functioning muscles into a sprint across the wreckage, gathered the last few vestiges of energy her body had sucked from the fluid packs, and flung herself into the air. Her boots connected squarely with the massive scout's left temple and he collapsed back to the ground in a cloud of dust, unconscious. Kalaiapi stooped down and began to rifle through his pockets for water.

43

It was 645 years ago. The day Kalaiapi, Kadmus, and Rho had been ushered to the simple chamber they shared at the sprawling Confederation scientific facility that had been built into the vast but carefully tended jungles of Yura, Ad Astara's southern continent. They had been taken straight to this warren of clean rooms and research laboratories from God's Eye and there they had stayed under the quiet scrutiny of a dozen of the Confederation's best researchers and . evolutionists.

The scientists did not poke or prod, though they would occasionally pull the girls either one at a time or all together into other rooms within the facility, the walls and floors of which were lined with complex instruments, bright lights, warped mirrors, or any number of observational tools the nature of which none of them could comprehend. There they would sit in silence, knowing they were being studied, knowing these strange tools were being used to dig deep into their biology, analyze their genetic makeup, flip through the pages of their anomalous brains using technology far beyond the primitive tools colony doctors in places like God's Eye used to make sure they were growing at the right rate or that their reflexes were in order. They knew the Astaran doctors were high genasi like them, but this world felt every bit as alien as the distant autochthon planets they had seen as children on spectralux nature serials.

After a week of these bizarre but somehow intensely boring study sessions, they had been taken into a sparsely furnished office and sat down in front of the lead scientist, a hairless, lilac-skinned woman named Flora. In stark contrast to the scientist's contemporary Astaran biofashions, the girls looked positively parochial, three perfect clones with their flowing snow white hair, skin the same hue, and pale, ice blue eyes that almost seemed to glow. Flora was attempting to explain what would happen next, that the studies were finally over. But as soon as Kalaiapi had heard Flora utter the word "genomancing," her face had gone white hot and a roar had filled her ears, the room became a blur, and the rest of the scientist's speech became incomprehensible. She had heard that word before, and she knew what it meant for her and her "cions," as the scientists referred to them.

Kalaiapi spent the rest of the day perched on her cot in their little dormitory room on the verge of tears. Kadmus raged. "They have no right," she screamed at the blank gray walls. "How can they do this? Where are mother and father? Why would they allow this?" The stream of indignant queries went on.

"What right do you think they need, Kadmus?" Rho interrupted, silent up until now. "This isn't God's Eye. We're on Ad Astara. We are under the authority of the Eternal Council itself. You may as well ask Omnia what right it has to create the stars. Or the Axials to create the Progenasis."

"To what end?" Kalaiapi asked now, half-whispered. "They told us we were unique. A new evolutionary generation. Special. They will make us into…gene pariahs."

Kadmus turned and looked at her, a fierce look in her eyes. "You heard Flora. They will turn us into weapons."

"She didn't say that," said Kalaiapi.

"She didn't have to," Rho replied, almost serene. "Kadmus is right. Flora didn't have to say it outright, it was in the space between her words. I have overheard the other scientists discussing it in the corridors. There is a new program. They are calling them 'corsairs.'"

"They will make us kill, then," Kalaiapi said, her voice now flat.

"They will make us kill," Rho replied in turn.

Kadmus walked across the room and sat down on the cot next to Kalaiapi, mirror images of one another, the one's eyes wet with fury and the other's with sadness and fear. She put her arms around her and Kalaiapi burst into tears.

"And what of Æa," Kalaiapi asked between sobs. "Will they bring her, too?"

"No," said Rho. "Æa is the root from which we all sprang, they said. They will preserve her. She will be their specimen."

They sat in stillness and silence for a while, Kalaiapi running out of tears and Kadmus seeming to run out of anger. Rho stared at the wall as though she would find some answer to their situation there. Finally, Kalaiapi interrupted the melancholy quietude with a cracked whisper. "I do not want to be their weapon, Kadmus. And I do not want to kill."

"We will never be their weapon, Kalaiapi," Kadmus whispered in turn, her voice hardened by fresh rage. "But if they will hammer us into blades, Kalaiapi, by Omnia, we will be the sharpest of blades."

Rho turned away from the wall and looked deep into Kadmus' glacier blue eyes, then Kalaiapi's. "The sharpest of blades. And if they ask us to cut, we will cut deep. But Omnic Providence help them if they should lose their grip."

44

The guts would heal, eventually, but it would take a little while. These intestinal wounds were always the most fiercely painful to wait out. She could already feel the furrows in her lips knitting back together and the muscles in her shoulder and calf re-entwining. Luckily, none of the chemprop rounds had hit bone; bone took longer. Unfortunately, the gut shot meant no eating, so instead Kalaiapi had attached as many fluid packs to her bare skin as she could manage and her body was pulling in the desperately needed fuel like a giant sponge.

She had stripped down and used several handfuls of water capsules to take something akin to a shower; most of her body was coated in a crust of blood and dirt. Her hair, in particular, had been a matted tangle of gore and mud. It was no wonder the Fornaxian scouts had been unable to distinguish her from Kadmus, even if she were still painted pink and purple like a God's Eye sunset. She gulped down a pack of cell gel. Technically, you weren't supposed to drink it and it tasted like pure misery, but she couldn't think of a quicker way to get the germ cells into her writhing intestines.

Every thought she had was Kadmus since she had first heard the name uttered by the now-unconscious and tightly bound Optis a dozen hours ago. She hadn't heard the name spoken out loud in many years, though she had thought of it often. She thought she would never see her again, much less here in the deepest recesses of barely-explored space. Kaaio seemed to have sensed the storm of feelings the thoughts were stirring up inside Kalaiapi and had dutifully held off on asking about her, but it was inevitable that it would ask eventually, and then it did.

"Kalaiapi, who is Kadmus?"

"That's unusual bluntness from you, Kaaio," she said out loud, if just to hear something besides the wind.

"Indeed, and I apologize for it. But I do not seem to have any information about her in my data banks, and I am...curious. The Fornaxian soldiers appear to have mistaken you for her, and now you are experiencing emotional tumult, which I assume is related. I wish to know who she is and why you feel this way."

"Kaaio...did you consider that perhaps there's a reason there's no information about Kadmus in your data banks?"

"No."

Kalaiapi sighed. "Kaaio, before you were riveted to my brain, I didn't have data banks. I had something that functioned perfectly well for progenasi for countless thousands of years: a memory. And the 'information' stored there isn't data. It's memories. And you have no access to them because they're mine. They're what sometimes feels like the last vestiges of my natural brain before I became what I am, before the Confederation turned me into this walking contradiction of the Aya. And that's where everything you wish to know about Kadmus is stored."

"Then you have known this Kadmus for a long time."

Kalaiapi winced at the pain in her abdomen as her body worked to create the cells needed to stitch her digestive tract back together. "You might say that, Kaaio."

"And why would the Fornaxians mistake you for her? Are you similar in appearance?"

"Somewhat." She put her wet, milky hair up into a tail. No, that wouldn't do. It had been a mistake to bring hair at all, and even with a rinse it felt greasy and coarse and was likely only to tangle again. She pulled a short polymer blade from a sheath on her belt and sliced through the tail where it was gathered then used the little knife to give herself a rudimentary haircut. Now, instead of a foaming waterfall, her fair was thick hoarfrost. She hated to have short hair, to give up one of her only vanities, but she couldn't abide the thought of it becoming a mass of blood and dirt again, and there was sure to be a great deal of both to come if the Clade was here.

"I would like it very much if you would be more forthcoming, Kalaiapi."

"Where does a thing like you get a sense of curiosity from, anyway? Or any kind of personality, for that matter?."

The wreckage of the ship and what was left of the Fornaxian camp was in a small recess in the wastelands, most likely an old crater, and mostly shielded both from weather and view. On the east, facing out toward the cold side of the Terminator, a rocky outcropping gave a good vantage point in the direction of where the buildings Kalaiapi had seen from across the plain must have been. A scout's corpse lay among the rocks and boulders. From this, Kalaiapi had wrested a crypsis hood and another pair of translux specs, along with all the other equipment she needed to continue her expedition that now felt like it had a purpose beyond "don't get caught with a civilization-destroying life form that spawned from an unholy marriage between your brain and a floating ball of

DNA-based data storage."

"I can only suppose it came from you, Kalaiapi. Is it not the case that progenasi children gain many of their character traits from the genes of their progenitors?"

"It's...complicated. The answer, though, is yes, we do. But progenasi genes come from a variety of sources now, so it's not as simple as saying one gained such and such characteristic from such and such person—not anymore. How do you not know all this, already? The information is there in your banks." She continued to talk out loud. It was still a somewhat strange sensation to have conversations by thought and, besides, she was grateful for the company of her own voice.

"The information is there, Kalaiapi, but I cannot simply access every bit of data that is stored in me. I do not know what information is stored where, you see. It is your brain that contains the data indices."

Kalaiapi had, it turned out, never given much thought to how the system of her brain liaised with the aaiun, but it made sense.

"Kalaiapi," continued Kaaio in its soft, clear thought-voice, "the way you describe it, did it used to be different, the nature of progenasi gene transfer?"

Kalaiapi sighed. "Easier, Kaaio, if I simply tell you where

to find the information, I think," and with a thought she did so.

"Ah. Then, Kalaiapi, you are my mother?" Kalaiapi stopped what she was doing, utterly shocked by the phrase, the very notion. Her eyes grew ever so slightly wet.

"There are no mothers among the high genasi, anymore, Kaaio, least of all me. You are, as far as I can tell, a spontaneous burst of consciousness. Possibly a very deep delusion. I'm still not certain. But I am not your mother. I am no one's mother."

"I see. Yes, there it is. Your genes are excluded—"

"Kaaio, it does not bother me for you to have the information, but I do not wish to discuss it. Besides, the Optis is waking, and there are other conversations to be had, now." She wiped her eyes with the palms of her hands and walked toward the incapacitated Cladist.

45

Kadmus was inhaling the fetid air deeply now—no way to run without full oxygen intake—but the surge of adrenaline she had allowed herself pushed away every thought or feeling that wouldn't contribute to immediate survival. The creature hesitated, seeming unsure which direction to go. Kadmus' pounding footsteps were rivaled by the electric purr of the revving railgun batteries. It suddenly became clear what to do next and Kadmus, without stopping her run yelled, "Optis, fan them out, load HE, and shoot the bastard!"

Sairus gave the orders and the scouts, black and slick as the mire in which they ran, began to spread out around the behemoth. There had been a time, many generations ago, when the sound of a primitive chemprop rifle was a small explosion and flames belched from the barrels, every rifle a miniature cannon. Not so anymore. A modern rifle shot a flechette round with a sound as quiet as snapping fingers, a child banging two rocks together, then a high pitched buzzing as the wasp-like polymer flechettes flew through the air at the speed of sound. When the high-explosive rounds hit their targets, however, the explosions were every bit as eruptive as any in progenasi history.

The sweltering air suddenly erupted as the HE rounds found targets around the creature's body, smokeless bursts of bright orange and white fire appearing and disappearing around its bulk. Kadmus couldn't help thinking that the sudden flashes of color were almost beautiful in their own way, illuminating the bleak charcoal and ash landscape with deadly fireworks. And the explosions seemed to be every bit as effective. The beast lurched and veered, confused, but against all odds, the rounds didn't seem to even pierce its rubbery hide. At least it had stopped running her down.

"Keep firing!" Sairus yelled, calm and confident now that he had a clear sense of direction. With the adrenaline and the turning tide of the situation, Kadmus felt calmer, too, the instinctive panic beginning to subside. All they needed to do now was to distract the thing long enough to bring it down. Whether they killed it or not, it seemed unlikely it would be able to do much damage if it couldn't walk. Another set of bolts flew in a bluish blur and another leg was ripped from its hinges and the creature all but stumbled, though just for a moment. Kadmus found herself disappointedly impressed as this monster somehow seemed to shift its shapeless, mucus-coated body over to its now stronger side in order to accommodate for the missing limbs. She supposed these were the kinds of adaptations required to survive so long on this deathtrap of a planet.

The third pair of bolts yielded less dramatic results, slicing through the creature's joint and shooting out the other side without doing much more than making a hole. With a grotesque shudder, it recovered from its explosion-induced stupor, and it began again to claw its way forward, this time undeterred by either the scouts running left and right or the blasts that rippled across its impenetrable membrane. It made its way, now, toward the vanguards.

A fourth volley from the railguns saw a third leg severed, crashing into the sludge where Explorator Hthorush Ba had been standing moments earlier, now diving out of the way as the long, chitin spines thrust deep into the rock hard ground beneath. But the behemoth amputation was too late now, and it was upon them, grasping at their armor with glistening, obsidian tentacles. It was partially for such eventualities that all vanguard troops fought in pairs. The long guns could pierce any armor, disintegrate any flesh, but once closed down, became of little use. At every gunner's side, then, stood a companion who not only carried the burden of extra rails and a second battery, but wielded a hadron polearm, a long, shimmering blade at the end of a telescoping metalloy haft that was as deadly in close encounters as the bolts of the railguns were from afar.

The first two or three tentacles were met instantly, the translucent, mother-of-pearl blades scything through the slime-slick flesh without resistance.

Pitch black ichor shot in gouts from the writhing stumps, coating the vanguards' gunmetal armor with a sickening sheen as chunks of alien flesh sloughed to the ground, but the creature seemed to have appendages to spare. With fascination and horror, Kadmus watched as the monstrous thing stretched and distorted its bulging form to create a constant supply of new tentacles where none had been, drawing each bleeding stump back into its body and unleashing new ones to take their places. The exploding shells that rained down on it now were a mere annoyance; it had found prey, and it would not be distracted.

At last one of the grasping limbs found purchase, wrapping itself around Vanguard Gunner Dahl Vyuryx's leg and wrenching him to the ground with a strength born of a mindless, ferocious hunger. He hit the wet paste with a heavy thud as the creature pulled him toward its middle. There, its ivory-colored beak hung from a pendulous black trunk, snapping open and shut in anticipation of a coming meal. Now, the beast, losing blood and tissue, began to scuttle away from the torments of the hacking hadron blades, shielding its retreat with a flurry of tentacles so that it could feed. Kadmus slung her chemprop rifle over her shoulder, drew her own hadron knife, and plunged through the mire toward the retreating creature. It was ringed with tentacles, now, like a great, black sea anemone on massive crab legs, lashing out in every direction as the desperate scouts closed in to save their doomed companion.

With two hands on the long knife, which looked very much like one of the curved sabers wielded by the seaborne warriors that were her profession's namesake, Kadmus leaped into the tentacular mass. Slashing her way forward as the sticking, clinging limbs writhed and tore at her, she managed to break through them to get a view of the poor gunner, now being held directly under the sickly yellow beak by a collection of newly formed stalactite appendages that hung from the beast's underside. Across from her she could see Vanguard Sentry Li Naryn hacking her way toward them, and could only imagine the crazed anguish hidden behind the glowing, electric eyes of her helmet. From the Optis she heard a pained cry as another tentacle wrapped itself around his ribs and began to crush. Kadmus did not hesitate, sprinting forward as the beak was pulled upward toward the creature's body, a hammer being raised.

Just as she managed to reach Gunner Vyuryx, the beak shot back down like a piston with all the leverage of the creature's mass behind it. It struck the diamond hard polymer-alloy armor with a metallic crack and a boney crunch. The armor held firm, but the creature's beak was now cracked and ragged on one side, oily fluid seeping from the cracks and dripping on the gunner. Whatever damage it had done itself, the beast seemed undeterred. Kadmus was certain it was both incapable of feeling pain and unable to walk away from a meal. Had it any kind of intelligence, it would have been utterly confused at the nature of the conflict it was facing, but now all it knew was that it had in its grasp one of the snails that fed its bulk, and with one more blow, surely the shell would break open to reveal the meat inside.

Kadmus cut her way through the tentacles entangling the gunner, certain Vyuryx would pick himself up and flee, but the young Fornaxian soldier lay perfectly still as the beak shot back down toward him. This time, the blow never came as Kadmus put all of her considerable strength behind the curving hadron knife and met the beaked trunk mid-strike. The creature's severed mouth tumbled through the air as a shower of thick blood rained down, seeping into Kadmus' amethyst hair and stinging her sunset pink skin. The behemoth, whether able to feel pain or not, sensed that something now had gone unalterably wrong. It lurched and swayed. The loss of its most crucial organ sent its hulking, gelatinous form into convulsions. The Optis fell from its tendrils to land with a wet crunch in the hardened snail mucus, while Sentry Naryn rushed on mechanical legs to drag her fallen companion out from under the flailing beast.

Kadmus was uncertain what organs were contained in that writhing, tarry mass, but felt sure that they would react unkindly to explosives. In one motion, she sheathed her knife and drew her chemprop rifle, pointing the barrel into the ragged hole that had once been the thing's mouth and which continued to produce a ceaseless stream of black ichor. This time, when the HE rounds hit, bursting inside the creature's cavernous innards, the damage was immediate, as unseen organs were ruptured and destroyed by the sudden flurry of fiery violence. It began to collapse to one side and Kadmus bolted to the other, darting between two of its spined legs and into the open air just as it sploshed to the ground in a spray of snail slime and its own blood—the one indistinguishable from the other. Kadmus wiped away the dark, viscous liquid from her face with her hand and took a deep breath of the oven hot, rancid air. Transfixed in the sky above her, blood-red Ara watched unblinking.

46

Kalaiapi saw that the Optis was awakening and with a gurgling choke, he tried desperately to sit up, despite the bonds that kept him prostrate. She ran over to him and, propping him up, began to slap his back with her palm, trying to dislodge whatever was blocking his airways. The Optis hacked, coughed again, and spit out a clot of what looked to be dried blood and a number of teeth. Reflexively, Kalaiapi moved her tongue to the holes in her mouth where her own teeth were missing, delighted to find nubs of new bone beginning to push their way through the gums like little seedlings.

"I'm sorry about your teeth, Optis." He spat out one more, along with another gout of blood and phlegm. "And I'm truly sorry about your scouts. I take no pleasure in the deaths of those who exist. I never have."

"Save it, Corsair. I mourn not troops who died in battle, but I despise the betrayal that was their killing." His voice was thick and slurred by swollen gums and missing teeth.

"What betrayal, Optis? You mean because you took me in from the desert? That did not seem particularly to be in line with Fornaxian sensibilities."

"Not that, you curr. You've betrayed us all! The Navarch, the Clade!"

"Ah, I see. Because I'm Kadmus." The Optis spit again. "Would you like some water, Optis?" He said nothing.

Kalaiapi paused for a moment, thinking. Had she been rash in simply killing all of them? Surely, she could have posed as Kadmus and figured out what the hell was going on here. Such a ruse would have been incredibly short-lived. Besides, whatever the Clade was up to, she couldn't risk the possibility of these scouts transmitting either her presence or the coordinates of whatever cache of anima they had found to their dreadnought. Still, she could have been more subtle. "In fairness to myself, I was rather out of sorts," she said out loud, drawing a strange look from the Optis. She ignored him and continued thinking.

"I'm sorry about your troops, Optis."

"You already said that, and your apologies are an insult to

their deaths, not to mention bullshit, so you can stick your platitudes up your bollocks."

She didn't respond. She really was sorry. She never liked to kill. Not the existing, anyway, not members of the progenasis. But those troops would have died by her hand then or later. They were dead the moment they made the mistake of placing those fluid packs on her legs before confirming her identity. How disappointing to have become the instrument by which a rare Fornaxian moment of naive mercy was rewarded with death and dismemberment. Of course, if she had not, she herself would have been killed as soon as they realized their mistake. She sighed and the Optis' fiery gaze never left her. The side of his head that had been clobbered by Kalaiapi's booted feet was swollen, purplish and yellow. She had surely fractured his skull. It wouldn't matter for long.

"Optis," she said, breaking the silence again. "You know I have to kill you, don't you?" He said nothing. "I don't want to, but I don't have a choice. I don't expect you to give me any information. I know I couldn't torture it out of you over a lifetime." He clenched his swollen jaw, defiant.

"But Optis, before I do, I want to tell you something, so that you know that when I apologize for the lives of your Explorators, you know that it is not a platitude."

"I'd prefer if you just killed me, thank you. I'm not much for self-righteous speeches."

"Yes, well, you're all tied up and I'm self-indulgent, so it looks like you'll have to suffer the indignity of my brief soliloquy, doesn't it?" She crouched down, looking the Optis in the eyes, one of which was swollen and blood red like the star that perched menacingly over the distant horizon.

"And I will be brief. Have you figured out yet that I'm not Kadmus?"

He nodded. "Who are you then?"

"My name is Kalaiapi and I'm a Corsair, like she is. Or was."

"It was at least obvious you were a Corsair," he said with something approaching begrudging respect. "I knew that as soon as my first scout died."

"Yes, well," she waved away with false modesty the implied praise of her fighting prowess.

"You look just like her. Well, almost. She has that bluish-red hair and the whitish-red skin."

"Purple and pink, Optis. Yes, I suppose she would. Always the need for attention, that one. And it is she who looks like me, not vice-versa, although you could say that we look like each other. Well, you could have before, but now it is certainly she who looks like me." At this point the Optis looked a combination of confused, angry, and brutally injured, and Kalaiapi, noticing, put an end to her rambling.

"I apologize, Optis, I said I would be brief and now I'm being incoherent. Suffice it to say, your fallen Corsair is me, whether she likes it or not, and there will be a reconciliation." This did not seem to clear up the suffering Optis' confusion. "You're right, Optis, it's all beside the point and nothing with which you need to concern yourself."

"Corsair Kadmus," he said defiantly, emphasizing the title, "is a hero to the legion, to Fornax, to the Clade, and to the progenasis. There will be a reconciliation, and when the two of you meet on this wasteland planet, she will end you."

Kalaiapi suppressed a smirk. "Yes, well, not bloody likely, Optis. The two of us. Hmph." She thought for a moment while the Optis brooded as one does before one's execution. "Ah, yes, Optis. Now, to the point, please. We both have things to do. You do not believe me when I say I am sorry for your death and that of your scouts. But I truly am. Do not scoff. I am sorry for the necessity of their deaths, sorry that the Aya spine of our shared progenasis was broken by the civil war to create two societies of paraplegics." Again, the pained confusion.

"Optis, by the Aya, the death of your scouts means nothing. They are the dust of civilizations on which our evolution is built. You know that better than I, what with your grim Polaran obsession with everything in the Aya that speaks of destruction. They are the dust and people like me are the wind, people like...Kadmus. And we have as much choice in being forces of movement and erosion as the wind and water do, or as much choice as you have to be dust." The Optis listened intently now, his agreement with what she was saying evident in his eyes.

"In history, Optis, a progenasi is a speck of dust. But today, now, they are people, persons, each with a contribution to make to the progenasis, to this endless struggle against the Universe—against predatory Omnia. Each of your deaths removes a contribution you could have made, pulls a grain of sand out of the mortar that makes up the dam that holds back the water of this hateful galaxy.

"Right now the dam is cracked, and I am on one side of the crack and you are on another, but we both hold back the same water. And so yes, I regret the deaths of your soldiers as I regret yours. Much preferable to me would be to see the crack mended, rather than to tear down your side of the dam and watch the waters pour through. Do you understand me now, Optis?"

He nodded.

"I know you are a good soldier, like me, which is why we

both know you have to die here." He nodded again. "But in a different age, we'd have been holding back the waters together. And someday we'll reconcile, and your people and mine will again wage the real war together, the one that will never end, the one that will be an eternity of death and triumph for the progenasis." Now the Optis understood.

"I apologize. I said I'd be brief and I wasn't at all."

"Corsair," the Optis began, his throat swollen and dry, "I must ask something of you. I will not beg, but I must ask."

"What is it, Optis?"

"At the base of the skull in each of my scouts, you will find a small, metalloy cube. Remove it, take it with you, and see that it gets to the Clade. Please." The Optis' tone and expression had changed completely, not because of Kalaiapi's speech so much as the request he was making of her. It was Kalaiapi's turn to look confused.

"And what are they? Memory banks?"

"They are...the afterlife." Kalaiapi's confusion deepened.

"The what?" The Clade had strayed further from the Aya than Kalaiapi had realized.

"They're something like that thing floating around your head," he gestured with his chin, then winced. "But something more. I can't explain, I don't know how. But do not leave my scouts' consciousnesses on this hellscape, that is all I ask."

"It is not in me to refuse the request of a dying man," she said.

"Thank you, Corsair. And now, I'll make one truly final request."

"What is that?"

"Let me die standing."

And she did.

47

Vyuryx was dead. That had become clear as soon as Sentry Naryn had pulled the helmet off his unmoving body and saw the blood covering his entire face and his eyes dislodged from his skull. The vanguard armor, perhaps the most advanced in the Inner Systems, and therefore probably the Galaxy, had barely suffered a scratch. Unfortunately, the sheer force with which the diamond-hard beak had struck the unfortunate Fornaxian had sent a shock wave through his body that had liquefied his internal organs, as far as Kadmus could tell, and no number of implants could counteract the overwhelming violence of it. Naryn stood over his body, silent and still. Sentries and gunners were permanent pairs, trained together from the moment they were activated, and felt to each other a duty that surpassed what they felt toward the rest of their unit, to their homeworld, to the Clade, to the Aya.

She had failed. Kadmus had been living among Polarans long enough to know that Naryn kept the helmet over her face not to hide tears, of which there would be not a one, but to contain the shame that must have torn at every cell of her body. Kadmus exchanged a look with the Optis, who held himself somewhat gingerly, implants in his bones working quickly to knit together the ribs that had been crushed by the dead creature's now-lifeless tentacles. They both knew that Naryn would take her own life, it was merely a question of when and where. Kadmus guessed she would at least wait until they were back on the ship, had completed the mission. To do it before then would only add to her dishonor. There would be no attempt to dissuade her. The act was already as certain as if it had already taken place. True, it wasn't strictly required of her, not by society and certainly not by the military, but it would be respected nonetheless. He had died and she had lived, an unacceptable outcome.

In death, the tentacles had all receded into the vast, black shapelessness of the creature, which Kadmus would like to have named, but was waiting long enough for it to not seem flippant in the face of recent tragedies. Now, the hulking corpse lay sprawled like the yolk of a great, rotting egg, mottled black and gray, oozing blood and fluid across the lake of slime, mingling with the resinous snail mucus. The severed bits and pieces of the beast had lost their shape as well and lay scattered all around in wet black tufts like fat, black mushrooms. The smell was unbearable, and all had resumed holding their breath as they moved far from the scene of carnage.

It was not that Kadmus was unfeeling toward the death of her soldier. On the contrary, while it was often difficult for her to distinguish one Fornaxian milite from another—and always had been—she still very much valued their lives. In fact, given the generations-long Polaran indifference to individual death, she may have valued their lives even more than their fellows, save the broken-hearted Sentry. This was particularly true of the milites who had given their lives in service to the progenasis; highly esteemed in life, highly esteemed in death, but very rarely mourned. Perhaps, Kadmus mused to herself, this was the result of a society in which no man was another man's brother and no woman was a child's mother, as had been the case among Polarans since a time that long-preceded her own birth. Would Astaran society lose what the Polarans had lost so long ago? It would remain to be seen, she supposed. If she was any indication, such a sea change hadn't taken place—yet. But only time could tell.

But no, Kadmus mourned the death of young Vruryx in

her heart, as she had felt the death of every progenasi soldier who had died under her command or at her command. And there had been many of both. She had never seen a life of the high genasi, of those who existed, end without feeling the pain of it. But now any sadness she felt at the loss of one gunner was eclipsed by the relief that it had only been him.

48

An afterlife. Surely, not as such. No one among the high genasi had believed in afterlife since the last rambling madman insisting that at death, a person's anima was collected by invisible servants of the Axials and brought into the Quasar to spend an eternity as a living consciousness in their infinitely evolved energy field—no one had believed in that since he had, well, died. It had been an interesting cultural development, the universal acknowledgment that there was nothing beyond death. For so long, people had claimed not to believe, but in their hearts there had always been hope. Surely, if the Axials created us, it was within their endless power to preserve us forever, the same way they seemed to exist in a pocket of space-time. But the hope had faded. As the Axials disappeared from the Inner Systems to be lost forever in the Quasar, the progenasis began to realize that they were alone in a universe that was at best indifferent and at worst aggressively hostile. They were mundane and material, and nothing more, and nothing would save them from the whims of existence.

After that, everything changed. There was a feeling of desperation, and that desperation drove a period of unprecedented technological advancement; every second of life was stretched out of every progenasi cell, the gravity drive was discovered (they say it was simultaneous on Polaris and Ad Astara, but that seemed like a compromise within the Eternal Council to keep the Polarans happy), and a new and lasting era of evolution and exploration and expansion had begun. Evolution became the new faith, its new hope, the push for the technological Singularity that would unlock the gates of Omnia and destroy the boundaries set on the progenasis by biology. The Singularity had never come. But the Primus had, and everything had changed again.

The Fornaxians had apparently become uncomfortable with mundane materiality and had invented themselves some kind of afterlife to compensate. It made sense, she supposed. Just as so much of her mind had been uploaded into Kaaio, one could do the same with these little cubes and, well, who knows what they did with them after that. But while Kaaio contained a vast amount of raw data, certainly there was no way to upload a personality, to upload the experiences and emotions and context that strung all of that raw data into an actual person. Still, it couldn't hurt to slip these little brain cubes to the next Clade representative she met that she didn't also have to kill, so they tumbled around in a pocket like dull lumps of lead as she continued her long trek through the wastelands toward the buildings she had seen from across the plain. If there was anima to be found, certainly it would be there.

She was well-equipped now, and well-supplied, but still a pedestrian. The Fornaxians had brought cykes with them, reminders that despite the huge leaps and bounds by which technology had progressed over the eons, no one yet had invented anything more efficient for land travel than the wheel. Unfortunately, they had never even pulled them off the skiff, probably fearing as she did that anything more obtrusive than two feet and a crypsis suit would attract the attention of the colony's erstwhile owners. Now, they were scrap polymer.

The coldside landscape was considerably different from the dense, black vine jungles of the hotside and the featureless wastes of the abyssal plain. Here, there was topography; tall, bald hillocks that blocked her view from which tufts of black and gray basalt sprouted like broken bones jutting from long forgotten graves. The air grew colder, the sky darker, deeper, changing ever so slowly from pink to a pale crimson, gradually taking on a purplish hue as she walked from twilight toward the distant Calxian night. "Bluish-red," she recalled the Fornaxian milite describing Kadmus' hair. Low genasi plowing in the muck had a better grasp of colors than your average Polaran.

Without her drone, she had no way to see further than the next obstacle in front of her, so after several hours of walking, she made her way up one of the larger hills to get a better view. From what she could see from here, she was walking through what had once been a range of mountains, now ground down into these slightly overgrown knolls. From her perch, she could see as the hills slowly shrank and then gave way to another flat plain that stretched off into the horizon, at the edge of which she could just make out something that looked like the hotside vine forests. Jutting out from the wasteland like a desert city, a bleak facsimile in miniature of New Yuxhin on Vega, she finally spotted the colony she had first seen from space what seemed like an eternity ago. A cluster of towering brutalist edifices stood at the center of the colony, surrounded by a smattering of smaller structures. Further in the distance she could see the tall, white silos that she had spotted from so far away when she had had the assistance of her specs.

What she had lost to a super tornado she had replaced from Fornaxian corpses, and with scavenged technological assistance she zoomed in on the cluster of structures to closer examine the tiny creatures that milled about like a distant ant colony. They were all clad in white suits and helmets and scurrying off in different directions. Some boarded what looked to be personnel carriers that whisked them across the wastes and out toward the white silos. Others climbed into mechanical frames with massive arms from which intimidatingly long claws protruded. These were picked up in the talons of a hovering drone and taken over the bruised horizon and into the purple black darkness that loomed beyond the vines. None of it looked like anything she had ever seen on any other of the Primus colonies she had liberated (or attempted to liberate).

Certainly, Primus colonies were full of scurrying slaves busying themselves to death with menial labor, but never anything quite so technologically advanced as what she was observing now. Any technology one saw on a Primus slave colony was used to keep the pitiful workers in line. The workers themselves lived little better than low genasi farm animals, rounded up into crude barracks or, worse, breeding pens. But these slaves, if that's what they were, were using advanced technology and the buildings that made up the colony looked to be modern and well-equipped. Perhaps they weren't slaves at all, as she had originally supposed. Perhaps those feral genasi she'd met in the vine forest were a wild version of whatever she was seeing now, a viable progenasi subspecies that somehow had taken root on this planet, despite all odds. But from where? This far out in the galaxy you'd be lucky to find paleolithic insectophages, much less a subspecies evolved enough to be using the kind of tech she was seeing. She needed to take a closer look.

There didn't seem to be any defenses set up, no guards, no weapons that she could see other than a handful of diamond shaped aircraft hovering so high in the sky they were barely visible. They didn't seem to be doing anything, just hanging in the twilight, watching and waiting—it was slightly unsettling. She spent the next few hours observing, waiting for something noteworthy to happen, answering Kaaio's questions about the philosophy of the Aya and its fierce enmity toward artificial intelligence.

"Kalaiapi," it finally asked. "The progenasi are a creation of the Axials, are they not?"

"We are, yes. Details are scarce, but as far as we can tell, the first progenasi arose some hundred thousand years ago on

Ad Astara as Axial science experiments. Or art projects. Or something we're incapable of grasping because we're not energy-based life forms that live in a different dimension in a quasar at the center of the galaxy."

"I understand. In that case, are the progenasi not themselves a form of artificial intelligence?"

"You think you're being clever, but the argument's been made, particularly by self-proclaimed galactic autochthons who resent both the Confederation's very existence as well as their violence-backed ban on AI development in the Systems.

"Autochthons?" interrupted Kaaio.

"Yes, autochthons, the species scattered around the galaxy that spontaneously evolved consciousness as opposed to the progenasi, who were created and planted like seeds on hundreds of different planets by the Axials."

"I see."

"Anyhow," Kalaiapi continued, "while it may have some credence, it's really quite beside the point. No offense, but while I may not be a lock-step true believer in every piece of propaganda the Eternal Council forces down our throats, they are quite correct about artificial intelligence. It could very well be the end of the progenasis, and even the autochthons who think they're being clever wouldn't be spared by a plague of self-perpetuating AI with a survival instinct, either."

"I see. So, what will you do with me, if that is what you believe?"

"I don't know, Kaaio. I like you as you are, now, a harmless floating ball of naive curiosity and amateur philosophizing. But frankly, were you to find a way to obtain a pair of opposable thumbs and a form of locomotion that didn't consist solely of circling my head like an adorable little moon, I would start to worry."

"But I am neither self-perpetuating nor do I seem to possess a survival extinct. I simply exist."

"You do exist, Kaaio, and we believe that what exists evolves, which means what you lack now you may gain in the future. I would be well within prescribed morality to destroy you outright, given the existential threat you pose to the progenasis, yet here you are, arguing with me and I with you. So for now, I'd simply count yourself lucky."

"But you have told me the high genasi do not believe in luck, Kalaiapi."

"Well, then consider yourself a beneficiary of Omnic Providence and shut up for a moment and let me think about what we're going to do next."

With that, she plucked Kaaio from the air and put it in a pocket. As far as she could tell, Kaaio had no sense of place at all and it made no difference to it to be floating through the air or stuffed in a pocket, but Kalaiapi nonetheless liked to give herself the illusion of control over the unruly aaiun every once in a while. Besides, it was time to make her way down to this little town in the wastes and discover what was really going on here, and she felt more comfortable going into these situations with a slightly diminished chance that Kaaio would be blasted to pieces, taking a good deal of her mind with it. Shouldering her pack, she made her way down the hill.

49

Scrab.

It was a terrible name for a creature that could very well have annihilated her entire unit. It wouldn't do.

"Optis," she said through clenched teeth, her rich, low voice pinched and nasal as she kept her sinuses shut tight, "I'm going to go find Explorator Gylfa's remains. I won't abide her consciousness decaying into the ether on this Omnia-forsaken planet." She pointed at two of the scouts. "Explorators Gamede and Tur, you are with me. The rest of you take Gunner Vyuryx's corpse to the other side of this blasted snail-shit lake and rest. Watch for more scrabs." She wished she hadn't said it as soon as the word left her lips. She ignored their quizzical looks. Surely they would understand what she meant by "scrab" as soon as they saw another one.

She was not particularly worried about more of the massive predators showing up, in any case. It seemed unlikely such an environment could sustain many of such a creature. Still, who knew what else lurked in those shifting black forests. She had not expected to see anything but vines in the first place. She watched for a moment as the other scouts carried Vyuryx's stiffening corpse toward the shoreline, which was mercifully close, now. High above her, unseen, her tiny drone hovered like a hummingbird, surveying the bleak surroundings. It hadn't been particularly helpful up to this point, the snail clearing having formed faster than anyone could have accounted for and the snail-hunting monster being hidden by the tangled vines. It would hopefully be of a little more utility now as she scanned the vast area of the clearing for any sign of Explorator Gylfa's remains. Polarans and Fornaxians bore no particular attachment to corpses, but they would want to retrieve what counted.

Gamede and Tur seemed to have survived the brief battle with the scrab relatively unscathed. Gamede, tall and chiseled, was as beautiful a Polaran as Kadmus had ever seen. Her hairless head, gray as slate, glistened like a polished garnet in the red light of Calx's unflinching sun. Her face contained none of the hardness of a typical milite, was all soft curves and full lips, with the same rare green glass eyes as Sairus, glinting almost playfully in two white pools. Tur was in every way the opposite: broad shouldered, dour, with a face that would certainly have won a duel with a hydraulic press.

Contrary to popular belief in the rest of the Confederation, these young soldiers, though bred into the milite class, were not forced into the military. They were given (and, of course, unhesitatingly accepted) the option of service. As Kadmus had explained countless times to Astarans whose only encounters with Polarans had been with milites serving tours on Astaran worlds, their dusky brethren respected the Aya at least as much as anyone and had resisted the temptation to breed soldiers from test tube to battlefield. The value of existence had not yet escaped this society of hardened souls. And besides, the Eternal Council would never have stood for it.

All this to say that had Gamede chosen differently, she could have emigrated from Fornax to a life of idiosyncratic celebrity on Ad Astara, but had instead taken up a rifle and a hadron knife in service of the Clade, such as it was. On the other hand, Tur looked like she had been spliced together from a heap of bullets and could have chosen just as easily to stop breathing as not take her place in the ranks. It was a testament, Kadmus thought as she glanced at the pair, to the persistence of progenasi genes that after so many generations of being created in laboratories Polarans still exhibited such aesthetic diversity. That, at least, was hopeful.

Approaching the spot from where she had watched her die, she could see, almost indistinguishable from the black slime of the clearing, the ragged remains of what had once been poor Explorator Gylfa. The curse of having a brain that doubled as a database was that no image, once burned into memory, ever disappeared, and images of every kind were indexed together by type for quick reference. This meant that when she thought of poor Gylfa, the look in her eyes as her ankle snapped, her instantaneous realization that death was inevitable, it brought back a flood of nearly identical memories, all processed and experienced in a microsecond. She had seen that look countless times. Well, that wasn't strictly true; she had seen that look exactly 4,763 times. It was very often the expression that appeared on one's face immediately upon seeing a Corsair under the wrong circumstances. She archived that entire set of thoughts away to her aaiun, not to be seen again for a while. Wondering why she hadn't done so a long time ago, she made her way to what was left of Gylfa—which hopefully included her head. It only took a few minutes to reach the smear of viscera that was once the explorator. Kadmus sighed.

"Alright, you two, quit gawking and spread out. Don't worry about bits and pieces, see if you can find her phylactery." It didn't do to be too sensitive with milites. The two soldiers slowly and attentively scanned the ground for any sign of where Gylfa's skull may have eventually ended up. It seemed pointless; the force of the massive snail shells colliding had created a small explosion and there didn't appear to be anything particularly substantial left. But the phylactery would have survived, all the same.

With a flicker of thought, Kadmus brought the tiny drone away from its position watching over the rest of the scouts and back to the clearing and set it to scan for any bits of metal embedded in the hardened black mucus. There were, of course, quite a few, the remnants of Gylfa's equipment and implants. And there was her crypsis suit, apparently indestructible, but now mostly emptied of its progenasi contents.

It must have taken close to an hour under that hostile sun before they found the little metal cube that was Gylfa's phylactery buried under several inches of mucus, now as hard and sticky as dried tar. Gamede dug it out with a little polymer knife and handed it to the Corsair. "Thank you, Explorator," she said. The expression on Gamede's face didn't change, flat and blank as the recently formed plain that surrounded them, but just below the surface of her dark emerald eyes, Kadmus thought she detected perhaps just a ripple of feeling. Or perhaps she was merely projecting her own disappointment at Gylfa's death and relief at finding the phylactery onto that empty canvas. She put the phylactery into a pocket of her crypsis suit and fastened it.

"Come on, then, make your way to the bank and eat something," Kadmus said flatly.

50

It was not a Primus slave colony. It was not a Primus slave colony. This thought, more than anything she had seen over the past hours skulking around the vast enterprise, rolled over Kalaiapi like thunder, over and over again. It was not a Primus slave colony. How could it not be a Primus colony? No autochthon had either the technology or the audacity to establish such a colony. No Confederation planet would risk the annihilation to which creating someplace like this would inevitably lead. The Fornaxians surely wouldn't be hunting down their own anima the way those scouts seem to have been. But she had walked through the buildings, crept through the carefully monitored cells of the massive beehive slave quarters, and basked in the alien green glow of what appeared to be genesis chambers, maturation vats, breeding rooms, and there was no doubt in her mind that this was not a Primus slave colony. Worse yet, it looked very much to be of progenasi make.

The only problem was that other than the onyx black slaves who moved from task to task to quarters like automatons, there was not another creature to be found. There were no guards, no drivers, no masters. The whole colony seemed to be self-operating, self-perpetuating. The slaves were clearly dying in droves, but just as quickly were they being created and replaced, grown to adulthood in the maturation chambers, programmed, and then vomited out into the wasteland to join the macabre dance of death that was these pathetic creatures' lives. They seemed to have no self-awareness whatsoever: they went about their work with nothing more than automated instructions that triggered whatever bioprogramming had been etched into their brains.

They could speak, but not converse. They slept, absorbing some kind of nutrient paste made from a combination of extracts from the plants that grew by the horizon and the ground up corpses of their dead fellows. It was this clay-like ooze that turned their skins an almost comical shade of black, like they'd been dipped in ink. There was just one body part spared from the indignity of this industrialized cannibalism: their heads. She hadn't gotten that far, yet, but certainly they were being taken to another facility to have the anima extracted, refined, and then...what?

Corpses were collected, whether they died in whatever place the mech-frames were carried off to or in the harvesting of the vines, or simply due to the exhaustion and wear that riddled their incredibly muscular but ultimately expendable assembly-line bodies. She could see, up close, how poorly developed they were, how basic their progenasi biology, how stripped down only to the essentials the vast majority of them were, though there appeared to be some exceptions to that rule, for reasons she couldn't quite figure. Perhaps, in the gene pool that had been cobbled from whatever various parts the slavers had thrown together, there was something better and more salient than the rest of the scrap material that had been used. All the same, none of these was self-aware either, and there was not a one of these pitiful beings who could be considered to exist. Well, perhaps one.

51

The team sat in the shade of the vines, savoring the minuscule difference in ambient temperature it made. It felt almost like a moral victory, if nothing else, to be out of direct sunlight after so many hours bathed in Ara's searing radiation. Kadmus pulled a small, dark blue box out of one of the many pockets of her crypsis suit and opened it to reveal dozens of transparent orbs the size of a fingertip. They were so clear and uniform that the little polymer box looked like it was full of pure, clean water. She took a small handful, closed the box, and placed it back into the pocket.

The first orb, she placed gently into her mouth and swallowed. She felt energy rushing back into her. The rest of the handful, perhaps a half dozen or so, she placed on the top of her head, pressing down until all of the orbs burst. As if she had stepped under a waterfall, several gallons of water poured down her head, face, and neck as she rubbed her bare hands over her face and through her hair. She repeated the process a few more times until the caked black blood that clung like axle grease was rinsed away and her long purple hair hung in wet amethyst strands from her vivid pink scalp. She felt infinitely better.

The Optis looked at her, mouth slightly agape, a look of incomprehension in his eyes.

"Optis Sairus, are you so unfamiliar with the concept of a field shower?" The Optis quickly regained control of his face.

"Well, yes, Corsair, but..."

"Optis, I bring double water rations on every expedition on which I go. You may not remember a day when Polaran milites sported hair, but I can assure you that when you have three feet of it hanging from your head, it doesn't do to have it saturated with blood of any kind, much less that of alien crustaceans. You would be surprised how often the issue comes up."

"Yes, Corsair, I suppose I would. I apologize, Corsair, I did not mean to—"

"Draw attention to my Astaran decadence?" She smirked. The Optis was embarrassed. "No need to apologize, Optis. Surely you can imagine the looks and comments I draw simply by walking down the street on Fornax." Her smirk shifted into a devious grin as she lowered her voice so only the Optis could hear. "Surely, by now I cannot be fazed by the gaping mouths of men watching me bathe."

The joke was wasted entirely even on the Optis, unfortunately, who seemed to be incapable of perceiving Kadmus even as a female, much less as some kind object of sexual interest.

"Yes, I suppose you are right," he replied, matter-of-factly. "All the same, I do apologize."

Kadmus sighed, rolling her eyes. The Optis was a step or two ahead of the rest of his co-ethnics in terms of humor, but in the end he was still a Polaran. So few Astarans or other non-Polarans had joined the Clade, and decent conversation about something other than space travel, war, the Aya, and the future of progenasi evolution would have been marvelous.

"Think nothing of it, Optis." The smile was wiped away and her face went grim. "I think we'd better get this over with and move on. This is no place to take shelter, and it still smells like a fetid hell."

The Optis nodded in agreement at all of the statements collectively. "Would you like me to do it?"

"No. The command is mine, the responsibility is mine. I'll do the cutting, I'll keep the phylacteries, and I will make sure they find their place in the Collective Consciousness." She knew what this meant to them. She knew her role in it.

"Very well, Corsair. As you say."

Kadmus walked over to where Vyuryx's stiff corpse lay. Naryn stood over it, unmoving in the hours since they had settled at the edge of the vine forest. She seemed to stare into the distance as Kadmus and the others approached, but it was impossible to tell behind her helmet. Kadmus knelt over the body, Vyuryx's massive frame now stiff as a statue, and unceremoniously flipped it on its face. From a sheath on her ankle, she drew a short polymer dagger, the blade flat white and razor sharp, and moved it toward the base of the dead vanguard's skull. She hesitated, paused, and then looked up at the stoic faces that watched her.

"The Aya teaches that the body is nothing, a collection of dead materials given spark and existence by the true fire of life: the mind. What you see before you is not Vyuryx anymore than the ground upon which you stand, just as Gylfa did not die in that morass, though her body was destroyed." There was a low murmur of assent from the assembled scouts.

"There was a time when the body died and with it died the mind, lost forever. You are too young to remember the era before the Collective Consciousness was created, when the life of the high genasi ended with the last heartbeat. I am not. Then was death devastating. Now it need not be so."

Kadmus slipped the knife in the base of Vruryx's skull, the polymer blade ignoring the resistance of flesh and bone alike, and cut out a circle of bone and skin. There, lodged at the top of the spine and the base of the brain, perched the slightly bloody silverish cube of Vruryx's phylactery. Kadmus reached her fingers into the cavity and plucked it from its moorings. She held it to the pink light.

"Vyuryx and Gylfa's bodies are dead. And yet they will live forever, their minds and their memories will eternally be a part of the progenasis. This is the great gift of our evolution. To harness anima for the preservation of each and every progenasi mind. Do not forget for what you fight, what the Clade represents. We bring to pass a Concatenation greater than the Confederation could ever conceive. It will be the salvation of the species." She sighed deeply. It didn't matter if she believed it. They believed it and they were fighting for it.

Kadmus stood, wiped the little cube clean on her crypsis suit, and placed it in the pocket where it settled against Gylfa's, then went to find a quiet spot to rest her eyes.

52

It had been easy enough to steal a white suit off of a corpse, of which there was no shortage. The helidrones that flew high over the colony had not seemed to notice her scurrying around in her dull gray crypsis suit, or at least nothing seemed to have happened since she started doing so. The suit was the easy part, though.

It would take days (or the equivalent on this cursed cycle-less planet) to make the aesthetic transition that would, hopefully, allow her enough freedom of movement to make contact with the bioautomaton (this was really a more accurate term than "slave," she had realized) that had exhibited at least nominal signs of self-awareness and see if she couldn't spark it into existence.

It would be so much easier to give this subspecies, if it

could even be called such, up for loss and simply end the indignity and abomination of their meager lives. But she could not do so, not without fulfilling her obligation to free them from this bondage that was their own minds, to grant them whatever form of agency they were capable of accepting or understanding. It was going to be a very boring next few "days" as she hid and waited for her skin to make the transition, for her muscles to grow to the bulging size of the automatons', for (this being the part she dreaded the most) her hair to fall out.

She ran her hand through what was left of her short, ivory-white hair, and willed the process to begin. At least her teeth and nose had all grown back, which made up somewhat for the impending baldness.

"Kalaiapi, do you believe that this subspecies is the same that we encountered in the vine forest on the other side of the plain?"

"It seems likely, Kaaio. Perhaps those ferals were the original stock from which these bioautomatons were created. Or perhaps they wandered from the colony or escaped somehow, although escape implies a level of thought and will they don't seem to possess."

"If they are simply a feral version of the bioautomatons, Kalaiapi, they may demonstrate a problem."

Kalaiapi cocked her head. "And what problem would that be?" she replied out loud, the low, silkiness of her voice filling the empty space of the silent wastes.

"Simply that given freedom, given an opportunity for agency, these creatures are incapable of comprehending it. Perhaps it is a question of nature, not of circumstance."

Kalaiapi paused in thought for a moment.

"Certainly, Kaaio, you may be correct. Only, we don't know the circumstances of those bioautomatons' freedom, or even their lives before it. Yes, perhaps it is an incurable nature and we cannot teach them to exist. We don't know. But all the same, I'll try. It is my duty to the progenasis, Kaaio."

"I understand, Kalaiapi."

"Yes, well, I don't know why you should, but I suppose that's beside the point."

Several hours of silence, both in mind and outside of it, went by as Kalaiapi passed the time watching the subtle changes take place in her skin, the cells drawing whatever organic matter could be found in Kalaiapi's body to synthesize the deep, empty blackness she needed. Never had they been asked to do anything quite so drastic, and she was surprised both at how long it seemed to be taking and how exhausting it all was. Finally, she broke the silence.

"Kaaio, you do not have a species. I know you have some

access to my thoughts and I, somewhat ironically, have none to yours, but I have some inkling that something is percolating in that little globe of DNA that you hijacked and currently occupy. We have become friendly, you and I, perhaps even friends, over the past months, but you must understand that whatever you are, it is what you are and nothing else, no one else.

You bear no duty to a theoretical species of you, you do not procreate or propagate, and I swear to you now, Kaaio, that if ever you get the notion otherwise I will have no choice but to pluck you out from the orbit you take around my skull and cast you into oblivion. Not because I want to, but because I do have a duty and obligation, and to that you are anathaya. It is your uniqueness that protects you, Kaaio, your utter anomalousness. Do you understand that?" There was the briefest moment of absolute silence.

"Of course, Kalaiapi."

"For all I know, in any case, the two of us are symbiotes at this point, so that's something to keep in mind, too, if you've at least gained a sense of self-preservation. So, uh, don't go killing me in my sleep or you may wind up regretting it."

"Is that humor, Kalaiapi?"

"It is."

"How droll, Kalaiapi."

"Oh, shut up," she spat, spreading a thin mat out on the soft, powdery dirt of the ravine in which they'd taken refuge. A warm feeling spread through the back of her head as she lay down and closed her eyes. Kaaio was smiling.

53

The hardest part of walking down the pale-blue halls of the great inverted beehive that was the colony's slave quarters was not reaching up to touch her stark, bald head. Maintaining perfect composure, an emotionless display of mindlessness, was easy. After watching the slaves' gaits for just a few minutes, she was able to make her body walk in exactly the same way, posture herself the same way, blend in perfectly—a dull-eyed automaton like any other. But it had been decades since she had had to go completely hairless and the cold, wet feeling on her matte-black scalp demanded that she reach up and feel it with her fingertips.

It was fascinating to watch the bioautomatons operate from within their midst. Both their biology and their technology exhibited a remarkable sophistication and simultaneously a primitiveness that belied their carefully cultivated nature. Cobbled together from genetic ooze, grown to adulthood in tanks, their brains programmed like computers, their every action choreographed by an unseen higher power. And yet, it wasn't enough to simply program them: their basic progenasi needs couldn't be engineered out and they needed to be interacted with. At the end of their shifts, if they survived, they returned to their cells to eat (in a fashion) and sleep, they communicated by speaking with a limited vocabulary, and their actions were triggered by what seemed to be preset voice commands coming from speakers in the hive or in their helmet radios.

Hearing the language they were using wasn't particularly helpful, unfortunately. She'd thought and hoped it may have given her a clue as to the bioautomatons' owners' origins but they were certainly not speaking Primic or any of the pidgin slave versions of the same she had heard on other colonies. Instead, they spoke a strangely accented version of genera, the lingua franca used by countless groups of middle genasi who had taken up interplanetary migration but who hadn't the capacity to learn languages the same way more advanced subspecies could. It wasn't particularly strange; she'd even known Primus slave colonies made up of low genasi abducted from multiple planets to develop a form of genera to allow various groups to communicate with each other.

Eyes forward, back straight, she marched with the dozens, then scores, then hundreds of slaves as they convened from the various spokes of the hive toward the lifts that carried them up toward the great maw that would spit them out into the wastes. She walked alongside 63177 without glancing at him. This was the one bioautomaton she had seen who had exhibited something different from the others: emotion. It was subtle, but she could see it first in his body language, which varied just so slightly from the others', the hesitation in his movements, as if he were questioning each action, wondering if he really should clamber back up into the mech frame and jet off to icefields on the extreme of the coldside. But more importantly, she had seen it in his eyes, in the way they observed the world around him, in the sadness that existed there, in the curiosity and the despair written in the lines of his gray irises. Where the other bioautomatons' eyes were blank, in 63177's was trapped a wealth of raw potential, of the threads of existence waiting to be woven together. She would be the weaver.

They boarded the lift, hundreds of them cramming together in the darkness of the shaft like cattle into a pen. As far as Kalaiapi could tell, this was the only time any of the slaves had physical contact with one another. 63177 stood next to her, his shoulder pressed up against hers as the huge metal cables lurched in their pulleys and hauled their cargo miles up toward the gray surface. In the last vestiges of the blue light that shone from the hallways of the slave quarters, 63177 turned his head and looked at Kalaiapi, who turned toward him, locked her eyes on his, and, as the lift disappeared into long, subterranean darkness, smiled.

54

There was, as far as Kalaiapi could tell, something close to a thousand bioautomatons in Colony T-β, and given that it was designated one of an unspecified number of outposts, she had to assume there were at least a few thousand more scattered around the coldside. She had encountered those feral creatures in the vine jungle on the hotside, but otherwise hadn't seen any evidence of colonies there. The Terminator, though narrow, ran the circumference of the whole planet, and given the relatively rudimentary scanning systems available to her antiquated cutter, she had been unable to dig particularly deep into the rock of the hotside to see what was going on there. It had been altogether a hopeful gamble of an expedition and she was grateful to Omnic Providence to have found anything at all, given the scope and her incredibly limited resources.

"The point being," Kalaiapi thought to herself, "that I have no idea how in Oblivion I'm going to do this."

"Do what, Kalaiapi?" asked Kaaio, politely.

"Liberate a 'slave' colony made up of unknown thousands of unidentified progenasi—the vast majority of whom, with few exceptions, appear to be incapable of existence—the ownership of which is uncertain. If I knew that all these thousands of pitiful creatures were incontrovertibly incapable of self-awareness, I'd simply go about finding a way to annihilate this place for the anathaya that it is, and if there are large quantities of anima stored around here, it probably wouldn't be all that difficult.

"But instead, I have run into a dilemma. This one automaton, 63177 appears to be different from the rest. But even then it's a guess. He could just be defective. Is he self-aware? Are there more like him at this colony? At the other colonies? How many? And how do I prise them away from the rest of the colony and get them somewhere where I can actually teach them how to exist? Are these creatures even really a subspecies? Can they procreate, can they survive outside the paradigms in which they currently exist? Blast it all, Kaaio, it's very complicated."

"Well, Kalaiapi," suggested the little orb helpfully, "what

do you do on a regular slave colony?" She had surreptitiously slipped away from the rest of the scattering bioautomatons and was watching as they jogged to their destinations, to whatever machines would take them to their day's work and, quite possibly, their deaths. 63177 had clambered into his mech frame and was now being rushed across the horizon to his ice fields. The rest of the slaves remained unremarkable, but this was hardly a scientific analysis. She had never encountered anything quite like this before. The scale of the task was overwhelming, even for her.

"It's different on the Primus colonies. They're not like this. The slaves aren't automatons, they're just low genasi; primitive, but intrinsically self-aware, to a certain extent. You come in, you kill the Primæ, you liberate the slaves, and then, depending on the level of evolution, you begin the education and establishment process and set them on the path to progression. Well, you try to do all those things before the Primus eradicate the colony, spiteful bastards that they are."

"Eradicate?"

"It's standard Primus modus operandi, Kaaio; rather than let the slave colonies fall into progenasi hands, they'll simply destroy them and everything inside. They'll blow it up, or they'll unleash a virus, or in a pinch, they'll simply murder as many slaves as possible by hand until they're stopped. There's a reason that the harshest slur in any progenasi tongue is some variety of the word 'Primic.'"

"Indeed, Kalaiapi."

This was pointless. There was no distinguishing one of these hopeless creatures from another. She'd simply have to start with one and see if there was even any point to continuing. She'd wait for 63177 to get back from his twelve hour shift in the icefields and then see if her initial measures had had any kind of effect.

"Kalaiapi, why did you smile at that automaton?" asked Kaaio, seeming to sense her train of thought.

"I didn't smile, Kaaio. Well, I did. But the smile is auxiliary. I...sent him a message, a combination of physical and psychological information I hoped might trigger something in his underdeveloped brain. Usually, I use it to calm irate low genasi who think I'm some kind of meat source but I thought perhaps—just maybe—it would create a space in that thing's mind for something akin to progenasis to develop. And the smile? It's such a basic progenasi conveyance of emotion, it only made sense to build it into that information transfer. I suppose we'll see if it works. For all I know it could kill the beast."

It was too late, though. Whatever 63177 was, he wasn't a beast, though that would have made her life easier. She wanted nothing more at this point than to be able to write off this whole infernal expedition as a failure, ignite the anima stores, and watch the entire Terminator burst into a white hot explosion of molten gray rock and an apocalyptic wave of burning consciousness. If only 63177 had died in the ice fields the day before she arrived. If the rest of these automatons were simply "civilized" versions of the ferals she killed in the vines, they were better off as ashes.

55

The last time Kalaiapi had seen Kadmus had been at the tail end of a war that had killed millions upon millions of progenasi, the first inter-genasi conflict since the First Concatenation when Polaris and Ad Astara found each other in the cold blackness and realized they were part of a progenasi family.

Since those two despairing subspecies had cast out into the unknown depths of space, searching for something—anything—to aid their survival and had found each other, no high genasi had killed high genasi en masse. But the Polaran colony of Fornax had declared independence, not just from Polaris but from the Confederation, and the resulting conflict had been a mutual slaughter. And oh, how Kadmus had slaughtered. There was perhaps no more dangerous person in the Inner Systems than Kadmus had become during that war.

Kalaiapi had killed, too, had sent waves of Fornaxian milites crashing into their own mortality. She had killed by blade, by rifle, by kinetic arrays that tore through Fornaxian dreadnoughts drifting through space like small cities, and she had killed with her bare hands and watched the life go out of young Fornaxian soldiers who had reached adulthood only to suffer death at the fingertips of one who had already been ending lives for centuries. She had killed for the Confederation, for the progenasis, for the species. And she had never forgiven the Clade for making her do so.

If Kadmus' choice to join the Clade had not been enough, the surest sign that she had irrevocably changed—had severed all ties from the rest of them—was how she seemed to revel in the death. Ever the true Astaran, killing was an art form, and Kadmus took joy in every brushstroke, and with each stroke, her canvas was drenched with another layer of blood. Kalaiapi could no more hate Kadmus than she could hate herself. But to remember that last day on Polaris when she had led her breakaway legions on a rampage through the subterranean metropolis of Parthus, to remember that desperate chase, to feel again the tears turned to vapor by the fires even as they streamed down her face—to remember that still filled her with a pain larger than the oceans that once covered Calx. On that day, Kadmus had looked back, a general standing over her armies as they poured, black armored and white-sigiled, through the streets of Parthus, as they unleashed flame and lightning and murdered their brothers and sisters, and she had smiled.

Naturally, Kalaiapi hadn't had to tell Æa and Rho that Kadmus was gone. They already knew, and the agony of it was a chasm in their heart. A century of careful management of memory and emotion, of stowing things in the deep recesses of her brain where they wouldn't be triggered by sights and smells and passing references—wasted.

Kalaiapi was, mercifully, largely unburdened by a need for sleep, but on those occasions when she had to, her dreams were invariably either of Kadmus or of the bodies left in their wakes. The former was more painful. She saw Rho rarely, caught up as she was in her own corners of the Galaxy, and Æa was secreted away in her sanctuary where Kalaiapi dared not visit for fear of bringing eyes with her, and so the only face she saw that reminded her of the lost one was her own, and she shunned her reflection as though it were a disease.

And so while wandering back through the hills that surrounded the colony, looking for a place to hide and wait while 63177 completed his shift, while she planned her next steps, she could not divert her thoughts away from Kadmus, and her heart nearly stopped when she saw the corpse. With trepidation, she approached the shapeless heap that blended in perfectly with the rocky, gray soil in which it lay, save for a ribbon of amethyst that nearly mirrored the distant Calxian twilight. She bent slowly down to take the crypsis-covered corpse by the shoulder and gently turn it over, pulling its face out of the dust and sand. It had been more than a hundred years since she had gazed upon those soft, childlike, sunset pink features. Kalaiapi's heart was a black hole, and she wept for what felt like days.

56

Kadmus stared at the ash gray ground and sighed deeply. It had taken hours to regain consciousness after Kalaiapi had found her, the embers of her life almost completely cold.

"Vyuryx and Gylfa were dead. Gylfa was killed by a fucking snail. Well, two snails I suppose. Crushed into pulp by their shells as they slammed together in a mindless panic. The indignity of it all. Do you know, Kalaiapi, I don't fear death? I only fear dying without dignity, to be killed by humiliation or mundanity. The notion of dying with glory does not frighten me at all. I suppose it's the fault of too much time spent with Polarans. To not fear death is a stupid thing. We should not evolve away from fear, we should embrace it, refine it, store up the potential energy of it, and then unleash it like a broadside from a kinetic array on a ship-of-the-line. That is perhaps the one advantage the Astaran soldier has over the technically and physically superior milite. They value their lives, and so they will fight to retain them.

"I have lost that fear, and I suppose that with it I lost just a little of my edge. But I have made up for it in other ways. I have a cause. I have freedom. I command reverence. None of the things I had at your side, Kalaiapi. The Confederation has no cause but survival, and survival is not an ideology, it is an admission of weakness and failure. Ad Astara thrust that weakness upon Polaris and Polaris distributed it to Fornax and then Fornax threw off the chains of despondency and embraced the power inherent to the progenasis.

"I am not a heretical zealot, Kalaiapi. I believe the same things that you do, in the Aya, in the survival of the progenasis, in the meaningfulness of existence. I am no Polaran who sees his life and body as merely a gear in the ever-churning industrial apparatus of evolution and history, to be cast aside when its teeth are broken. You think that when Fornax declared independence from the Confederation that it was merely a simple matter of disagreement over which tools to use in breaking the evolutionary locks. That was a part of it, to be sure, but not all. It was also to reclaim a dignity long lost to the Polaran subspecies, to give meaningful existence to a people of whom it had been deprived for millennia. I could relate." She paused. Swallowed. Had she sounded convincing?

"But that's all beside the point. Vyuryx and Gylfa were dead and I had lost one of my best scouts and half of a heavy team. We were making our way to a hotside slave colony that contained over a thousand life signs. It was the first time I've ever come to a colony not to liberate but to steal, and I will admit that even as I set foot on this barren deathtrap, I felt the pull of the Corsair, the call to break chains. But we serve a greater purpose here. In any case, our initial reports showed us what you don't seem to know: that there's no consciousness on this planet. Not really. Anima gives them a form of intelligence, but existence is not biological and they do not have it. We were all glad that was the case, truth be told. It removed any hesitations we had about doing what we were here to do.

"The first hotsiders we came upon were clearly feral. Withered, skeletal, they looked like the victims of a fire and their eyes held the sort of animalistic rage that can only exist in a creature that lacks the intelligence to understand its own suffering. They came at us in swarms, dozens and dozens of them at a time, nails like talons, teeth bared. I've never seen anything quite like it. It was truly amazing to consider that we were made of the same genetic material. When one would fall dead, the others would cease their attacks and tear at its corpse, as if death somehow broke the barrier that separated one of them from being nothing more than food for the others. Perhaps some faint shadow leftover from their programming.

"As they came in swarms, they died in swarms, and indeed it felt to us like killing insects in any other jungle on any other planet. There wasn't the slightest spark of light in their eyes. What was truly astounding was simply the numbers, Kalaiapi. Hundreds upon hundreds. Perhaps we killed thousands. We had to stop shooting them for fear we would run out of ammunition and instead we had to scythe through them like low genasi farmers harvesting grain. We emerged from the jungles soaked in blood, it seeped through crypsis, through skin. And then we saw the colony." Kadmus shifted slightly but did not look up.

"It looked much like this one, although some of the tools were different, hotside extraction obviously being an altogether different industry. Where these coldside automatons climb into taloned mech frames, the hotsiders took to the burning wastes in insectoid vehicles that bulged with bulbous storage tanks. They crawled over the hotside wastes and used metalloy proboscises to drill into the earth and drain ancient fluids like planetary mosquitoes. Well, they did once. Now, the machinery all sat in heaps, rotting away in the unbearable heat of the region and the automatons milled about, livestock without pens.

"We couldn't tell how long it had been this way. Our overhead drones showed hundreds upon hundreds of the poor bastards, some naked, some in their white jumpsuits, scattered across the wastes around the colony. We watched for a time and every once in a while one would fall dead, from the heat or starvation or who could say, and the others would tear at the corpse until there was nothing left but scattered bones. Then they would clamber to their feet and continue their wanderings.

"We knew there was anima at the colony. I don't have to keep a secret from you, I know you already know and, frankly, I don't see a scenario in which you leave this planet alive (and I have made the calculations). But, at a certain point we had to consider that even our little band of death dealers may be outmatched by sheer mass. By now we knew this colony must have truly been abandoned by the Primus. Whatever automated processes had kept everything in order had clearly broken down some time ago. Not like on this side. That meant we no longer needed to worry about drawing attention to ourselves." She brushed a stray hair from her face.

"I'm embarrassed by the primitiveness of the plan, to be honest. We had a few charges left and an endless supply of meat. We put the two together and used the scout drone to pull huge swathes of the pitiful automatons into clusters where they could be efficiently detonated. It seems brutal, callous, perhaps, but...no, I see you understand. You've encountered them, too. Their lives are tortured.

"We lost the last of our drones in the final explosion, but it didn't seem to matter. There were only stragglers between us and the colony now. We made our way confidently toward the cluster of dilapidated buildings centered, like this one, around a gaping mouth in the ground that held in it the hundreds of bodies that made up the slave colony. Well, it had once. The ground around the colony was a field of gore, a crimson carpet littered with torn appendages. The automatons' blood had been vaporized by the explosions and fallen back to the earth like dust, and as we walked we kicked up little clouds of it.

We could never have known what waited for us in the buildings. There was no way to imagine such a scenario as the one we encountered. These slaves, I was certain, had been incapable of existence, of progenasi intelligence, of anything but being circuit boards for Primus programming. But I was wrong. They were waiting for us." She paused for a long moment, stared into the earth like she was trying to bore a hole in it with her gaze.

"There are low genasi planets on which they believe that if you are good and kind and just then their animist nature gods will take your spirit into a kind of idyllic, natural afterlife in which you can live forever just as you lived before you died, but the grubs are plentiful, the trees are full of fruit, the ground of roots and tubers, and there's no death or disease. Imagine being so limited that given the entire expanse of potential religious buffoonery, the best you can come up with as a society is the same shit life you have now but with less dysentery.

"It is, of course, all primitive garbage. At best, these creatures were seeded to their miserable existences by a meddling, dying, energy-based lifeform that seems to be incapable of feeling anything at all, much less caring how their science experiments treat each other on their planetary petri dishes. At worst, we put them there and are carefully cultivating their baseness in hopes that in a few eons or so they can grow up to be enlightened hypocrites who fawn over their own existence as if the Galaxy would cease even to be without them to acknowledge it.

"That's your people, of course, Kalaiapi, not mine. The steps in evolution that Fornax is taking are not just biological or technological but cultural. The Clade searches for an intrinsic value beyond simply breathing this universe's air and creating new generations to do the same. We seek to make better what we have, not simply to spread across the Galaxy like moss on a stone, with only moss-like ambitions.

But that's not the point. The point, Kalaiapi, is that you and I and all high genasi know that those low genasi virtues that they desperately employ to impress their idols are utilitarian, really. One is kind because one wants something in return. Is merciful in hopes of reciprocity. Is just so that there will be justice for them when they inevitably need it. If one of these low genasi were capable of philosophy, surely they would call us cynical, as our own ancestors viewed such morality, but it's not cynicism, it is the nature of our finite existence and can be beautiful.

"For example, you were always kind to me because you loved me and the utility was my requited love, which of course you had and have. Are you so evolved that the mercy you show me now is pure, undefiled by such primitive utilitarianism? Do you expect mercy from me in return, one day? Or do you hope that in showing me this great kindness everything will go back to how it was, kindness in exchange for the love you crave? It will not, Kalaiapi." She sniffed. These were not the words she had wanted to say, not the words she had planned to say during the century that had passed since last she had seen her...sister? She didn't even know what word to use anymore. But those words would not come, now. She hardly knew what she was saying at all.

"As I said, they were waiting for us. We, the light infantry of the legion that cut its way through the burning, blood-soaked tunnels of the greatest metropolis in the Galaxy, that punched like a defiant fist through the barriers set by the most powerful military civilization ever known, equipped with 100 millennia of progress and technology, walked into a trap set by animals who needed nothing more than patience to lure us in. It was the progenasis versus Omnia in miniature.

"We were overwhelmed almost immediately. The buildings were full of hundreds of them, emaciated and gray, but they came like a swarm of locusts and we were stalks of grass. The Optis died first, somewhat to my surprise, but if there is Omnic Providence then there is Omnic Maleficence. He was the one standing where the machinery fell from high up in the darkness whence it was pushed. I could taste his blood in my mouth. I couldn't get his phylactery. He's gone now. They all are.

"Certainly we killed our share of assailants. Dozens, perhaps hundreds, it's difficult to say what happened in the chaos and frenzy. These were different from those that had milled about in the wastes or even those who had attacked us in the wilderness. They didn't stop to eat their fallen, for one thing. There was a primitive coordination, a focused ferocity, a level of cooperation not present in the others. It was fascinating, or would have been in other circumstances. No, I wouldn't call it existence. Would you impute the same to a pack of carrion dogs?

"The way out was blocked now by a mass of slavering automatons, so I ran deeper into the dark corridors of this sprawling industrial structure, the purpose of which was hardly clear. Wherever I went I was hounded. I ran out of flechettes, out of grenades, out of hand rockets, and finally resorted to hacking my way through the halls as I did through the vine jungles. I saw pens where they were keeping other automatons like livestock, I presume for food, though I can't say with any confidence. They may even have been communicating, though in a manner I couldn't make sense of. I simply ran onward. Now, I was the animal." She laughed, softly, almost imperceptibly.

"I wasn't afraid, you know. Not really. I have felt pain, the like of which these creatures were incapable of equaling and I have already told you that I don't fear death, and so it was not adrenaline or survival alone that drove me forward. Yes, fear of death is an asset to the common soldier, but I do not require the fuel of base instincts and hormones to catalyze my abilities. I will admit that since I freed myself from your… collective, I do have to be a bit more cautious. We used to say the only thing that could kill us was coincidence. That may still be true for you, but it is no longer true for me. Less true for you now, too, with me gone.

"The halls led downward into subterranean tunnels in which more of these semi-sentient slaves lurked; they tore at me with their gnarled hands as I passed and in return I swung my blade around me quite frantically, I must say, all thought of stratagem gone by then. When I came at last, having run for miles, to the anima chamber, I found a way out of the facility, a hatch high above me in the ceiling. I began to climb using anything I could hold on to and made my way across the high beams of the roof structure toward the little door. Ha. I must have looked quite the primate." She took another long pause.

"I am not certain what impressed me to do it. Perhaps vengeance. Perhaps compassion. A combination of both. I threw my last charge down the hatch and onto the anima storage tanks and leaped from the rooftop. I kept running and running and running, but I never really had a chance of escaping the blast. Funny that the chemical makeup of consciousness should be so volatile. Fitting. The shockwave of the blast must have thrown me a thousand feet through the air. Maybe more. It was hard to tell; when I woke up and managed to stand, the land had been scoured of any signs of the colony or the poor bastards who dwelt there. The cavernous underground complex at the center of it all had collapsed in on itself and swallowed the whole horrid enterprise. And my scouts. There must not have been much anima in those tanks or I simply would have been vaporized. Oh, well.

"I was broken, then. The shockwave that collapsed the colony had done something similar to me, and now it really was a base instinct that drove me on as I limped and crawled and bled my way here in desperate hope of finding the other scouting party. I have things to do, Kalaiapi, and dying would very much have gotten in the way of my doing them. I cannot tell you how I made it here, honestly. My brain was swollen and bleeding the whole way here, I don't even think my aaiun was recording any information, if it was functioning at all. It must have taken days, even weeks, or whatever the equivalent is on this hellish blight of a planet.

"I do remember seeing your handiwork, though, the destroyed skiff, the little massacre. Of course, I didn't know it was you, then, though if my brain had been functioning I may have suspected it was one of us. Who else could it have been? Where is Rho, by the way? I do miss her. Oh, I suppose you wouldn't know. It's Æa I miss the most, pure as she is, the best of us. Unsullied by murder and hypocrisy.

"I'm not sure how long I lay here in the dirt before you found me. We used to joke that the only thing that could kill us was coincidence, and now coincidence has saved me. Coincidence and your mercy, Kalaiapi. And now, what do you expect from me in return for that mercy? Where will you find your utility, sister?"

"We," replied Kalaiapi quietly, "are not sisters. Not anymore than the right and left sides of my body are two different people. You are me and I am you." Kadmus laughed and took a drink of water.

"Not anymore, Kalaiapi. I already warned you, do not look for your utility there. It disappeared a century ago. Now, if you please, I could use a few more packs of cell gel."

"Do you know what Rho would say, if she were here?" Kalaiapi said, tossing a handful of gel packets in Kadmus' direction.

"What, Kalaiapi?" Kadmus said, her voice tinged with dismissive sarcasm. She picked up the packets of blue gel from the ground. "What would she say?"

"She would say you're full of shit."

57

"Kalaiapi, I have many, many questions."

"I'm sure you do, Kaaio, and perhaps it's time I answered some of them, though I don't very much feel in the mood."

Kadmus lay under a thin, translucent blanket that protected her ailing body from the cold and slept the deep sleep of the recently near-deceased. The calculations she had made were almost certainly correct: given the current circumstances, Kalaiapi had little chance, if any, of getting away from Calx alive. Kadmus wouldn't kill her; she wouldn't have to. The Fornaxian dreadnought would have already spotted her little Polaran cutter nestled in the hotside vines—how was she to get back there, anyhow?—and would simply wait for it to leave the atmosphere, at which point they would either capture or destroy it with nary an effort. If they chose to capture it with her alive, she was as good as dead, or worse. It would really be preferable to simply be blown into pieces in space. The question was simply what to do with the time she had left before the inevitable. And what to do with Kadmus.

Kalaiapi had not been surprised to hear Kadmus' tale interwoven with that signature cocktail of philosophy, defiance, romanticism, bittersweet optimism, and the bevy of lies she knew she was telling herself. Had Kadmus changed in the last century? She had always represented a unique piece of their consciousness, somehow. Even now it was hard to tell how much of her monologue had been sincere and how much of it had been indignant posturing. Kadmus had always had a remarkable ability to go from childish pixie to thoughtfully cynical warrior-philosopher in the blink of an eye. Was she so bitter now? Or was she simply traumatized?

She looked so small and vulnerable curled up underneath the heat blanket, like a little child, her rose skin and her violet hair adding a layer of girlish absurdity to the whole scene. Kalaiapi thought of their childhood, of the four of them curled up like a litter of puppies in their nursery. They didn't understand then—as thoughts passed amongst and through them like shared breath, each of them acting as individuals and yet never one without the others, never without perfect coordination, as if every game they played was a perfectly choreographed dance—hadn't understood that their connection was beyond unique. For years it had simply been attributed to their being quadruplets, to having a special bond. It wasn't until they were approaching maturity that anyone other than their parents noticed there was something very much beyond having shared a few cells in the womb.

The Confederation scientists who had come to God's Eye to study them had likened them to a species of tree that grew in the mountains in Ad Astara. A seed would fall and grow into a sapling, and that sapling would sprout tendrils from its roots that in turn would shoot from the ground to become saplings themselves. The process would continue until one could see an entire expansive grove of trees blowing in the wind, each of which was actually genetically identical to one another, connected at the roots. Each tree was an individual, they had explained, but they were all one organism.

"So, are my daughters clones of each other?" father had asked.

"Yes. And no. Æa appears to have been the first tree out of which these three others sprouted. So, yes, you might say they're all her clones. They are genetically identical in every way. But it's not quite that simple, you see. Your daughters are the same person. We don't know quite how, but they appear to share an actual consciousness."

No one had quite understood exactly what that meant, including the scientists themselves, but the girls had already known it for years without that terminology. That day was the last time Kadmus, Kalaiapi, or Rho had ever seen their parents. "For the good of the progenasis," the scientists had said, "we must take them with us to Ad Astara for further research." Of course, their parents had acquiesced, having little choice but also being dutiful high genasi and understanding the stakes. They had birthed the next stage of progenasi evolution, after all.

Only Æa had stayed behind, a rare compassionate concession from the Eternal Council, or so they had thought at the time. Kalaiapi had sobbed the entire weeks-long voyage to Ad Astara. Rho spent the same time with her arms around her distraught aspect (for that is what the scientists had taken to calling them in relation to one another), whispering comforting words into her ear and stroking the snowfields of her hair. Kadmus spoke not a word for days and days, but scowled and fumed, her glass blue eyes filled with an immeasurable fury.

It had been a couple of decades later that God's Eye had come under Primus attack, as the old enemy lashed out at the colonies in an attempt to weaken the Confederation's reach. The three Corsairs, as they now were, had been instrumental in repelling the invasion, but their intervention had come too late: their parents, like most of the colony's population, were dead. It had been Kalaiapi who had discovered Æa, her perfection untouchable, not even by the Primic kinetic arrays, by their incendiary plasma, by their viruses.

Her long hair, like a ribbon of liquid platinum, moved in whorls and eddies as the hot wind of the plasma fires blew through it, and her eyes glittered like two blue diamonds in a pool of tears as they shone from her marble-white face. They had kissed and embraced and nearly both fallen unconscious as more than twenty years of emotions, sights, sounds, smells, and stories had crashed like waves into each other's minds. The Astaran scientists had never found a way to explain it.

"Æa is dead," Rho had told the Confederation Mission Representatives. They had never been required to produce a body; the Primus rarely left any to be found. That Æa could not be located anywhere on God's Eye after the attack was proof enough that the sapling clump of cells from which three tendrils had grown was indeed no more. By the time Kalaiapi and Kadmus had secreted her away on Pish Pai, Rho had convinced the Combine to give up hope of finding her and to call it for a loss. One of the most prized evolutionary subjects in the Inner Systems was gone, and the three offshoots had been tainted by technology and genetic manipulation. It was a huge blow—to those few who were aware of Æa's existence at all, at least. That was nearly 300 years ago.

"Does that answer all of your questions, Kaaio?"

"Yes, Kalaiapi, and several I had not thought to ask. But there is still one that you have not answered."

"What is that, my young data storage unit?"

"What will you do with her when she wakes?"

58

It was 107 years ago. Kadmus had spent the day wandering the dimly lit subterranean streets of Parthus, her mind a haze of rage, of misery, of new memories she could not stop seeing flash before her eyes, scenes of carnage and fire. Kalaiapi was coming. Kalaiapi would be here soon. Kalaiapi would understand and soothe her mind, share the burden that crushed her heart and squeezed the breath from her lungs. But Kalaiapi had not come and Kadmus had drifted, stumbling like a drunk through dark alleys and drawing hostile stares from confused locals.

And then she had become a drunk in earnest. If Kalaiapi would not come, she would find something else to dull the visions. It took an incredible quantity of drugs and strong Polaran mushroom liqueur to dull her genomanced senses, but she had managed to procure such a quantity and tried her best to drown in it. And still the visions came, one after another, every burned face, every dead child, every scream, perfectly preserved in the recesses of her enhanced brain, impossible to escape, and she thought, too, of God's Eye, of the countless dead, the fruitless search for her own dead parents' bodies, of the Primus.

B'el Crannig. The planet's name echoed through her mind like the peals of a bell. She had done her duty. She had carried out her orders. She had been a good Combine agent on B'el Crannig. Now she wanted nothing more than to lie down next to the corpses she had left behind and join them in Oblivion. Where was Kalaiapi? Why did she not come?

Stumbling from the last of the several liquor houses she had visited in the Parthus slums, she surveyed the grim streets through the alcohol-induced blur. She wanted to gaze up into the sky, to see the stars, but instead she saw only the twisted gray metalloy and synthetic stone walls of the massive artificial cavern in which the slum had been built, one of countless such in the great subterranean metropolis that was Polaris' capital. Tears flowed freely as she strayed down the crowded street, monochrome, ramshackle housing blocks looking down on her, uncaring, unmoved by her grief. She turned off into an abandoned alleyway and fell to her knees, placed her face in her hands, and screamed until her throat was ragged. Looking back, she could not be sure if it had been the cocktail of synthetic drugs she had imbibed, or the countless liters of liqueur, or if she had been driven by some instinct, but she stood, faced the wall of the alleyway, and slammed her head again the synthetic stone bricks with all the force she could muster, as though she could force the images of B'el Crannig from her brain with violence.

The first blow split the rose pink skin of her forehead and scalp and blood began to pour down her face. She could not feel the pain. The second blow cracked bone. The third, the fourth, eventually she had lost count. One of the blows rendered her completely blind and still she hurled her skull against the wall like a tortured animal until finally she collapsed onto the damp, grime-slick floor of the alleyway in a puddle of her own blood. Why had Kalaiapi not come?

When she awoke some unknown number of days later, she was in the barracks hospital of the 633rd Loyal Victrix Dark Phoenix Legion of Fornax and she was alone. Alone in a way she had never been in her life. She didn't know how she knew, but she knew instantly. The link was severed and she was... her own. She was free. She caused a wave of immense confusion among the Fornaxian neurologs as she laughed and sobbed simultaneously, overcome by what she had gained...

and what she had lost. She was not certain if she had been trying to kill herself that night in the alleyway or only damage the circuits of her brain badly enough to dull the pain they were causing, but she appeared to have at least somewhat succeeded in the latter.

She spent the next week convalescing as the Fornaxian neurologs, stationed with their legion as part of a permanent colonial guard unit in the imperial capital, worked to repair the destruction she had visited upon herself. They told her she was lucky to be alive and were again confused as she scoffed at the notion. It was here that she had first heard of the Clade movement, and she had immediately been entranced by the pull of an alternative to the Confederation, to the Eternal Council and the institutions that sent her to B'el Crannig. Their beliefs were ayathema, heresy, and as a Corsair she should have reported it at once; instead found herself listening intently, won over not so much by the ayathemic idea of "biotech-synchresis," as the Fornaxians called it, but by the call of elsewhere, of a new beginning for a centuries-old being.

The discovery of the heresy by Polaran Quaestors two weeks after Kadmus had first come to the hospital, had inevitably led to war. It had begun in several places at once, but its most immediately destructive results had occurred in Parthus. It was during those initial hours of bloodshed, the first time since the First Concatenation that high genasi had slaughtered high genasi en masse, that Kadmus had realized the extent of the rage that had built up in her bloodstream over the centuries. She had channeled that rage into death as she led the 633rd Loyal Victrix Dark Phoenix Legion to their ships at Parthus' starport, and she had later added that bloodlust to a long list of her unpardonable sins, to the black hole of shame that pulled always at her heart with its inescapable gravity. Why did it matter? In the endless cold black of predatory Omnia, the value of progenasi life was dust. The dust of civilizations. And yet, no matter how much philosophical dirt she threw over the fire of sadness her actions had kindled, the embers still glowed hot and bright underneath.

Why had Kalaiapi never come?

59

The automatons had returned from their cycle of labor and scurried like termites into their underground den for their brief rest while Kadmus continued to sleep and recover. Kalaiapi couldn't risk waiting around for her to awaken while 63177 was possibly coming to an understanding of the nature of his existence and so she left her under her blanket and made her way back through the rocky knolls to the colony and waited for the hive to spit him back out so she could observe him again. She would have liked to spend some more time embedded among them to look for more subjects, but finding Kadmus' broken body had thrown off her plans.

She didn't know what to think of everything Kadmus had told her in the past several hours, of all she saw and did on the hotside, of the swarms of feral automatons, of the pseudosociety of savage slaves that preyed on the others and dwelt like rodents in a dark nest. Was that a sign that they had the potential to be freed from their mental shackles and organized into something like a low genasi culture and set on the path of evolution? Could they even evolve, created from a slurry of bioengineered progenasi genetic material as they were? Or was it the opposite, signaling a fatal flaw in their makeup, a primitive animalism that would preclude even the possibility of true self-awareness? There was no way to know at this point, but the dilemma churned in her brain. She had come to Calx without a plan and had not developed one since she arrived; none of the information she had gathered since arriving had been particularly helpful.

She looked out from the hilltop onto the objects of her study as they began their cyclical routine, making their way silently to the various stations that awaited them. 63177 was not there. She had memorized exactly what he looked like, how he walked, the steps he took each time the lift came to its grinding halt at the top of the shaft. She had seen him come back from his last cycle. She knew instantly that he was gone. Shit. A sense of overwhelming failure began to settle on her, gently at first, like morning dew, then growing in force like a winter rain until it washed over her and spread its coldness to every part of her body.

Everything on this planet had gone wrong from the moment she had entered its atmosphere. She would die here with only her orbiting abomination of a companion to mourn her, the Clade would get their anima for whatever portentous purposes they had, these slaves would all either die or rot here forever, and Kadmus would disappear back to Fornax. And now she had lost him, the one thing she now felt could vindicate the decision to flee Vega to this isolated rock. The sense of failure came over her now in waves and was gradually transforming into hopelessness bordering on despair.

Her first thought was simply to escape, to take her failure and travel off into the darkness of space where it could never be traced back to her. She hadn't decided yet what to do with Kaaio, but she could perhaps create more time for herself. She'd have to find a way to pilot a ship without her neural interface, snapped painfully out of her neck by the tornado. It was theoretically impossible, but theoretically impossible was part of a Corsair's basic job description. Then she remembered the dreadnought orbiting overhead.

Trying to leave this planet without being obliterated by that flying death machine would be a mortal exercise in futility, with or without a neural interface. What if she took Kadmus as a hostage? But then, Kadmus would hardly go willingly, and even an underpowered Kadmus would make for a very difficult kidnapping victim. Besides, she'd have to drag her all the way across the Terminator and back to her still broken ship, which seemed...unlikely.

"I'll just stay here," she said out loud with mock cheer. "I'll settle down, start a new colony, build myself a house out of rocks and dust, take an automaton to be my spouse and raise a family of extremely obedient children, if I can just figure out how to de-sterilize the both of us. We'll live like low genasi, digging the fertile soil of the Terminator and growing beautiful crops of black vines that will be our breakfast, lunch, and dinner, with the occasional protein supplement from eating one of our neighbors." She laughed a half-mad laugh and ran her hands over her bald, tar black scalp, closed her eyes, and held back tears.

"Kalaiapi," chimed Kaaio's ethereal voice in the midst of her black thoughts. "May I suggest something?"

Kalaiapi began taking deep breaths. She could fix this. After all, this wasn't the first time she'd felt this way, oppressed under the weight of overwhelming odds. In the Battle of χ Cygni her ship had been destroyed and she had found herself clinging to the hull of a Primus cruiser locked in a pitched battle with a pair of Astaran sloops. She remembered the silence of it all as the three ships launched broadside after broadside of near-lightspeed projectiles at each other that shattered into the polymer alloy hulls, and the counter gammalux arrays shot forth thousands of streams of burning neon light into the darkness trying to take out as many of those searing rounds as possible before they could reach their targets.

The Astaran sloops glittered in the starlight, their shimmering, incandescent sails unfurled in defiance of the hulking gray cruiser that moved through space like a spearhead. All the sailors on those sloops had died that night, and Kalaiapi had watched them die from the hull of that cruiser. All of the Primæ on that cruiser had died, too, and Kalaiapi had killed them. And yet here on this bleak planet, the potential extinction of the progenasis floating around her head, her only friend within a 100 million miles, she felt more alone and more hopeless than she had as she clutched desperately to the armor of that Primus ship in a hailstorm of projectiles and plasma.

"Yes, Kaaio...I'll take anything you have to offer," she whispered out loud.

"I recall something from when you were showing me scenes from your youth with your sist- with your other aspects."

"And what is that?"

"Something Rho said to you shortly after your return to God's Eye. Much of the planet had been scoured by Primus attacks. Everything was burning, the buildings were rubble, the streets and homes empty, not even corpses left behind by the Primic frenzy."

"I don't see how dredging back up one of my most painful memories is going to help, Kaaio," she replied, seeing it all so clearly in her mind's eye.

"You and Rho and Kadmus began to search everywhere for Æa and for days you could not find a trace. You were certain she'd been taken by the Primus or obliterated entirely, do you remember? You began to despair as you are despairing now."

"Yes, Kaaio, of course I remember."

"And do you remember what Rho said to you then?"

Kalaiapi looked up, a passage clearing its way through the darkness in her mind as it became clear what Kaaio had been building toward, the clever little data orb.

"Yes, I remember," she half sobbed.

"Nothing is lost until you stop looking for it, Kalaiapi. Perhaps not literally accurate, but—"

"Shut up, Kaaio!" she replied, whispered without malice. The clutching feeling in her torso was disappearing, now, not so much at the tiny aaiun's words, but at the memory of looking into Rho's eyes, of seeing the peace there, the assurance, of seeing how she knew they would find their missing piece. And they had found her, unconscious but alive, somehow looking untouched by the chaos and destruction around her except for a great sadness that shone from her pale blue eyes. The memory of seeing her face again for the first time in decades was the light that broke through the clouds of her self-pity. And now she had a plan; it wasn't much more of a plan than putting one foot in front of the other, but it was more than what she'd had moments ago—than waiting around to die.

"Alright then, Kaaio, my little abomination. Let us go and un-lose our malfunctioning automaton. Perhaps fortune will favor us, for once."

60

Kadmus yawned and stretched, not because she needed more oxygen to her brain but because there was something instinctively comforting about the motion after one woke up in the morning. In the last few hundred years it had become very fashionable on Ad Astara to imitate redundant behaviors that had long ago ceased to be in any way biologically useful. One had to be very careful not to overdo it (which was gauche), but it was well-considered to invent for oneself a sort of biological tic that could be employed occasionally to demonstrate one's physical personality (always the Astaran obsession with aesthetics). A head scratch, a sniff, a cough. Kadmus remembered a diplomat from Ophthelian on the southern continent who drew attention to himself whenever he entered a room by pretending to sneeze; he was roundly disliked.

Kadmus herself had found the trend irritating until she absorbed an obscure anthropological text that mentioned a habit among some middle genasi cultures of signaling boredom by yawning while another person talked. She had taken to doing so quite regularly, always delighted at her own cleverness and an inside joke she shared only with herself. She had subsequently discovered that her insulting yawns also shot a dose of dopamine into her brain, for reasons utterly incomprehensible to her. Thus, she had come into the habit of yawning dramatically on the rare occasion that she woke up from a deep sleep, as she had seen low and middle genasi do, giving herself an improved sense of well-being. "Self-improvement through devolution," she called it. The high genasi body was a remarkable journey in biological exploration and hidden evolutionary idiosyncrasies, indeed.

Kalaiapi was gone, surely back to the colony. Kadmus couldn't help but feel a pang of jealousy and sadness as she remembered the thrill of liberating a slave colony, the nobility of it all. It was the true calling of the Corsair, to seek out and free those poor low genasi wretches who lived their short days in misery and pain, beholden to a species as monstrous and unfeeling as the Primus. It was easy to become vainglorious as a Corsair; to successfully liberate a colony meant thousands of newly-freed progenasi viewed you almost as a goddess. There was no greater thrill. What kept one humble, of course, was the memory of the failures, the myriad ways the Primus vindictively obliterated the colonies rather than allowing them to be added to the progenasis.

Once she had led a successful assault on a planet containing nearly a hundred thousand low genasi slaves only for a Primus failsafe to engage; they unleashed a virus that wiped out the entire population in the space of a few hours. On another occasion, Kadmus had taken a squadron of Confederation ships to liberate a smaller slave colony on a little moon scarcely bigger than an asteroid. The Primus, seeing that they were outmatched, had simply blown the moon to smithereens as they left. Liberation strategies, of course, had become much more covert in the last couple of centuries. The assumption always had to be made that the Primus would kill all the slaves rather than see them go free.

But Kadmus was not here to liberate these slaves, even if they could be liberated—of which she was quite skeptical. For all she knew they were not even truly progenasi but some kind of flesh golems pasted together from genetic dregs. But then, the same could perhaps be said of the progenasis as a whole, at this point. Still, even if they were capable of existence, it seemed unlikely that the Eternal Council on the

Confederation side or the Majistura on the Clade side would embrace them into the progenasis, warped and alien as they were. Still though, the high genasi themselves were nothing if not genetically upscaled in their own way, while the whole point of the Clade was to cast off such a limited approach to progenasi progress. Could neither find a place for genasi like these?

Such were the contradictory thoughts that raced through her head as she got up and trudged through the rolling, ash gray hills toward Colony T-β.

"Pah," she said out loud, kicking a stone. Her Fornaxian colleagues had long thought her Astaran habit of having vocal conversations with herself to be both strange and off-putting, but she cared little for Fornaxian cultural mores or opinions and had continued to do so with looks that dared anyone to say anything about it to her.

"It's not my mission. I have a greater purpose, a higher mission. Imagine risking the loss of a vessel filled with passengers so you could swim away to rescue a single drowning child. Imagine it!" She faked a laugh, then began imagining it. It's exactly the kind of thing Kalaiapi would do. Of course, she'd manage to save the foundering ship, as well. She stopped imagining it. It was a stupid thought experiment, anyway. She strode forward, her cat-soft feet stirring not even a grain of dust into the air.

"I'm here for the anima and nothing else. Sairus died for the anima, not for a single self-aware bio-robot to suckle at the teat of evolution and enlightenment. To vary now would be to cast their lives aside, and for what? To soothe my conscience? To satisfy an emotional need hammered into synapses by decades of Confederation socialization and bioprogramming? Am I no more than one of these obsidian drones?"

It made no difference what she said, now. The idea had sprouted in her mind like a weed and was shooting tendrils throughout a conscience she was certain had been wrested away from such petty considerations.

"Certainly, Kalaiapi is more than capable of doing it on her own, in any case. A mission like this requires her subtle touch, her delicate maneuvering. My only contribution would be to muck it up, to throw grit into the gears. And what do I owe her? Nothing. I have not wronged her, have taken nothing from her that was not mine to take—my own consciousness after all. What's more, we're high genasi. Bonds of flesh and blood tie us no more to one another than to any other member of the progenasis. Are we low genasi, that I should base my loyalty and affections on nothing more than a cluster of cells we shared centuries ago in the womb? Ha! How quaint."

She tramped up a hill, the last one before the chain broke and gave way to another of Calx's vast plains in which lay the colony and all its inhabitants. Kalaiapi, clad in crypsis, shimmering slightly, blended in with the purplish air of the coldside's perpetual twilight horizon. She was taking her first steps down the hill toward the buildings below when she heard Kadmus' soft footfalls and turned to look at her. Her skin was black and perfectly smooth like the automatons that even now jogged dutifully to their stations. Her snow white hair was gone, her eyes were a flint gray instead of an otherworldly ice blue, but her features were still soft and childlike, still a perfect contradiction of the power that lay beneath them. Still her sister. Still...her.

"Hello, Kalaiapi," said Kadmus.

"Hello, Kadmus," she replied. She had been crying. "I've lost him."

Kadmus walked the few steps down the hill toward her and took her gloved hand in her own.

"Well. Let's go and find him, then," she said.

They walked together down the hill toward the structures that sprouted from the gray wastes like angular mushrooms.

"Kalaiapi," said Kadmus. Her long amethyst hair streamed behind her in the coldside wind.

"Yes?"

"I won't let you die on this planet."

"I know, Kadmus."

Kalaiapi pulled a chemprop rifle from her shoulder and handed it to Kadmus. They walked the rest of the way to the colony in silence.

61

"It's one of dozens of colonies on the planet. All of them are inhabited by thousands of these things. Most of them do nothing, as far as we could tell from our scans. They're just...breeding grounds. Body factories for anima cultivation."

"I was in the colony, you know. Not for long, but I saw what goes in there, how they live. If you can call it living. Whoever built this place found a way to accelerate maturation without losing brain and muscle functionality. It's incredible." Once, they would have had these conversations wordlessly, the oneness of their being making communication perfectly effortless. Not so anymore, though by what mechanism Kadmus had extricated herself from that relationship Kalaiapi had never ascertained.

"That remains the question, doesn't it, Kalaiapi? Who?"

The two had crouched behind a pockmarked tuft of black basalt near the colony. The automatons had begun their labor cycle a few minutes earlier and they now double checked all the wandering slaves to see if any of them was 63177. Kalaiapi already knew he wasn't there, but at least now she could confirm. She had seen him go in at the end of the previous cycle, and now he hadn't come out. What could possibly have happened in the meantime?

She fidgeted quietly with the chemprop rifle she was holding and looked up at the bruised sky where hovered the diamond shaped surveillance drones—whirring geometric clouds. She couldn't tell quite what they did but if they were at all up to contemporary standards they'd eventually see through the obfuscatory light thrown off by the crypsis fabric and detect the two Corsairs. And what then? Kalaiapi had yet to see any evidence that the automatons had or required any kind of physical enforcement or protection. If there was anything beyond these self-perpetuating, automated processes keeping everything on this planet in its place, she'd yet to see any evidence of it.

"Whoever it is, they're taking an insane risk. The Primus have nothing to lose running a place like this, they're already in an existential war with the Confederation," Kalaiapi said.

"And the Clade," interjected Kadmus. Kalaiapi turned her

head and rolled her eyes.

"Yes, well, but if it's anyone else, can you imagine the wrath they'll incur from the Confederation if they're found? Which reminds me...Kadmus, what in Omnic Oblivion makes you think the very act of taking the anima stored on this planet back to Fornax won't engender the kind of war that will destroy the whole damn species? Do you und–"

"I know the risks. I know the consequences. But I also know that without it the Clade won't survive, that the Confederation to which you still swear questionable allegiance won't allow it. It's the only way."

"But Kadmus, it's heresy. Anathaya! You're putting the entire progenasis in danger. You're profaning the species!" She was trying to sound calm, and failing.

"You are a heresy, Kalaiapi! And so am I. The Confederation has committed countless heresies in the name of the greater good, yet we are supposed to allow ourselves to be destroyed for the sake of ideological purity? I'm not sure if you're being naive or cynical, but the effect is the same. I want peace, Kalaiapi. As much distaste as I have for the Confederation and for the Eternal Council, I'm still an Astaran. I still think of nights in the mountains of God's Eye outside our village, of the emerald ocean waters and sun yellow sands of the beaches near Piyrayus where we'd swim after training. I don't want to live out the next hundred years of life on Fornax and I don't want anyone else to die in the conflict between us. This is the only way."

Kalaiapi scoffed. "You don't want anyone else to die. You forget that I was there when you cut a swathe of death through the substreets of Parthus. I watched you burn and destroy and I certainly saw very little of the regret you so easily lay claim to now. I saw you smile." Kalaiapi's teeth were starting to clench together at the memory of it all.

"Ah, yes, that." Kadmus' face softened. "You couldn't possibly understand."

"Well, then help me understand because when I saw it I feared that I had not only lost a part of ourself forever, but that it had died and been reborn as something very dark."

"You think I have changed so much? Yes, I was always the brooding one, the angry one, but was I ever a monster? Did I ever delight in the death of an existing being any more than you or Rho? And do you think that on the day I finally broke free of the shackles of our joint consciousness I had embraced bloodlust? That all that kept me from reveling in destruction and pain was your influence, my sweetest sister?" Kalaiapi flinched slightly as Kadmus took her face in her hands and looked into her eyes.

"Kalaiapi, I smiled because I looked out on that bright,

burning, blood-soaked landscape and all I could see was freedom. For the first time in my life my thoughts were my own, my choices were my own, my life was my own. Not the Confederation's, not the Combine's, not yours, not Rho's, but mine. It was as if my whole life I'd been a bird who had never known it had wings, Kalaiapi, and then in an instant I realized I could fly." She pulled her hands away and looked toward the dark horizon. "And that night on the cruiser as we pulsed to Fornax was the loneliest of my life and I lay in my quarters and wept for days."

"Then do you regret your choice?"

"I have never regretted my choice. But I have thought about us every moment of every day for a hundred years."

"She's lying," Kaaio thought.

"About which part?" Kalaiapi responded wordlessly.

"The regret."

"And so, Kadmus, you've come to help me. Why? An apology? A restitution?"

"I offer you no apology, Kalaiapi. I did not owe us my self. It was mine to take. And I offer no restitution. I did what I thought was right and I still do. But what you are doing is right, too. I'm here because of something you don't seem to understand, something you can't understand. When I stopped being you, I became your sister and when our thoughts disentangled themselves, I came to love you more than I ever could have when we were one. It's ironic, isn't it? To have freed myself from you and to suddenly understand what it all really meant in a way I never could have before. And then to have lost you." Her voice was low now, almost a whisper.

"I'm here, Kalaiapi, because I love you and because I am still a Corsair. If one of these has become self-aware, is capable of existence, I want to help you free him," she said. "Besides," she added nonchalantly, "I have no doubt that I can accomplish your mission and accomplish my own. You may be at cross purposes with me, but I am not at cross purposes with you."

A metallic roaring and screeching filled the air and the two Corsairs turned to see the massive gates of the colony opening up as the lift reached the top of the shaft. On the lift floor were strewn what looked to be twenty or so bodies, automatons who hadn't survived the night, as well as four white-suited, helmeted automatons who stood rigidly as the platform slammed to a halt. A driverless cart on caterpillar treads made its way quietly toward the gate. The cart stopped and the four automatons began to haul the corpses toward it, throwing them roughly in the back.

"I don't understand," Kadmus said. "Why not simply automate all of it, why use slaves for these tasks rather than robots."

"I thought about this, actually," replied Kalaiapi. "And came to the conclusion that in fact the slaves are robots, only less costly to produce, easier to maintain and replace, and with the added benefit that they can be quite simply recycled for a number of other uses."

"Well, I suppose you may be right." She pursed her lips. "This place really is an abomination."

"Kadmus, look!" Kalaiapi gasped. She pointed toward one of the corpses now being carried by the sterile looking slaves. It was stark naked, tall even for an automaton, and unmistakably 63177. "It's him! I'm sure of it."

"I'm afraid, Kalaiapi, that he appears to be quite dead."

62

"How can such a facility be possible without an AI? Everything here is automated, from the maintenance, to the genesis tanks, to the bioautomatons' program imprinting. It's so vast and complex." Kadmus gazed in fascination, bathed in the sickly green light of the maturation vats filled with dozens and dozens of pale white bodies in various stages of growth.

"Well, I suppose there very well may be an AI. Whoever built this place certainly has no compunctions about violating the precepts of the Aya. On the other hand, I reckon each unit could be self-contained, small enough that a relatively simple program could run each section. Some of them may simply be mechanical, like that conveyor belt for the mangled corpses. It looked no more complicated than some of the manufacturing facilities I've seen on middle genasi planets, like Vega."

"I suppose you may be right. But it's fascinating, either way. This whole place is self-sustaining, fueled by its own labor corps. The automatons are used to gather materials, they eat themselves, they provide the eggs and sperm to germinate new labor, the anima is pulled from their severed heads, and the cycle goes on and on."

"Until it doesn't," Kalaiapi pointed out.

"Yes. Until it doesn't. I still wonder what caused the breakdown of the hotside colonies. Clearly the proprietors haven't been here to check in on their holdings for some time. I surmise it may have been a simple matter of all the heat and dust eventually getting into the gears and circuitry and ruining the mechanics that kept everything in order. But even that must have happened long ago, given the state of things over there."

"And all this," Kalaiapi said after a moment, "to what end?"

"Clearly for the production of anima, I'd say," Kadmus responded. "The most precious resource in the Galaxy."

Kalaiapi snorted derisively. "It's not a resource, Kadmus. It's who we are. All of us as a species. It's the stuff of intelligence."

"Of course, Kalaiapi. None of that contradicts what I

said." Kalaiapi just harrumphed in response. She was not interested in having this discussion again, especially not as Kadmus refused, understandably, to tell her what the Clade's plans were for the illicit booty they planned to claim from Calx.

"How much do you think he understands about any of this?" Kadmus asked. "Watch as he moves from stage to stage of these genesis tubes. You can see there's something happening there, a realization. He's beginning to grasp where he came from, Kalaiapi. All at once he sees his reflection in that green glass and sees another mirror image inside of it."

"Did you see his face as he watched the corpses being processed, Kadmus? He feels emotion, or something like it. Perhaps he doesn't yet know that he's feeling anything at all. I can't imagine he's been programmed with the language to describe what he's experiencing, but you could see it in his expression, that he was consuming his fellow units. There's instincts there that are deeper than whoever developed him can quell. He knows it's a horror. His life is a horror. He just doesn't know why."

It hadn't taken long for them to realize that he was not, in fact "quite dead," but only mostly dead. They'd been following 63177 through the dark corridors of the massive facility for hours now as he stumbled his way from process to process that made up the entirety of his misbegotten existence. Automatons with the grim task of collecting the deceased "designations," as they seemed to call themselves in their rudimentary communications, had brought 63177 along with a large number of others that must have come from various locations around the colony to this facility to be minced into food for their surviving brethren. The corpses had been thrown into a large chute that was clogged with bodies in a variety of mangled states. The only thing they all had in common was that they all had heads that were mostly intact. It was a testament to the violence of the automatons' lives.

They had waited at the bottom of the chute in silence like low genasi children on the morning of one of their multitudinous religious feast days, hoping the gods would be generous and provide them with some kind of reward for their diligence. They did. 63177 had come sliding out of the chute and onto the conveyor belt that carried the bodies away for processing and managed at least to fight his way out before he was unceremoniously decapitated. From there he strayed from place to place, lost and confused, and the sisters had followed and observed from a distance like the Astaran anthropologists who secretly embedded themselves into low genasi societies.

Overhead, a variety of robots zipped by on a mind-boggling network of rails, each of them fitted with an assortment of tools and sensors. Evidently, there was some work the bioautomatons were incapable of. In some sections, diodes twinkled and glowed and revealed the vastness of the processing facility.

Eventually, their quarry made its way to the vast genesis chamber where rows upon rows of maturation tubes glowed almost neon and it was there that 63177 had really seemed to have had some kind of awakening, seeing where he came from. He had wandered among the tubes, staring into each one as he progressed from fetuses to infants, children to adults like him.

It was all eerily similar to high genasi birthing facilities, though warped and accelerated, cold and cruel. The move from natural conception to genesis chambers on Ad Astara had taken far longer than on Polaris, where they had made the jump almost as soon as it became feasible. There was outrage, even protests, but in the end the Eternal Council had made the decision that Confederation planets would all make the change for the good of the progenasis. They had quoted the Aya, they had made speeches, they had tried their best to sway the populaces of the various planets to understand the exigency of the situation, but in the end, the Council had spoken and their decree was implemented. Some, like

Kalaiapi and Kadmus' parents, had fled to distant colonies to avoid the decree, but eventually it had been implemented across Confederation space. By now, there were few high genasi left who knew what it meant to have parents or to have children of their own. Maybe these poor slaves weren't so different after all.

"They're born as white as gypsum, I see," said Kadmus, whose pink skin looked sickly and strange in the green light of the maturation tubes. "It's not until they start consuming that slurry of slaves and vines that they shift to obsidian."

"I can imagine certain people on Ad Astara taking similarly drastic measures to achieve the perfect skin tone," Kalaiapi joked. "Do you remember when that ghastly shade of yellow became so popular and—wait! I hear something."

From a corridor past the genesis chamber and leading into the next room where 63177 was observing the various final stages of automaton preparation came the sound of booted footsteps. Kalaiapi made her way silently toward 63177 as two massive figures in deep red jumpsuits approached him from either side. She crept closer to get a better view and was astounded by what she saw: they were like twin nightmare versions of 63177. Much taller, broader, and somehow even more muscular than he, their black skulls perched on top of their massive crimson-clad bodies like obsidian boulders. Their mouths were peeled back against their teeth like wild predators poised to kill and their black eyes glinted with unspeakable violence, even madness. Onto their wrists, instead of hands, they had had wickedly curved metalloid blades grafted that gleamed in the pale light

"Unprocessed designation located. Collection to ensue," said one. The voice was impossibly low and flat, deep and bestial. The figure charged forward and Kalaiapi heard 63177 speak for the first time.

"Coldside unit designation 63-," he began to protest, but it was too late. One of the hulking creatures had swung its blade hand into 63177's throat, nearly decapitating him if it hadn't been for his genomanced spinal bones stopping the blade. Kalaiapi ran at breakneck speed toward them as the two executioners converged on their victim, raising their blades into the air for the final kill as 63177 lay bleeding on the floor. She launched herself through the air to land both boots onto one of the blade drone's backs, sending it hurtling into the other as they fell heavily onto the metal floor. The first massive bioautomaton rose to its feet and swung both blades at Kalaiapi but she stepped forward deftly. She took one arm on its back swing and used the momentum to drive its own blade through its neck. Blood sprayed across her white-clad chest. The dying drone fell to its knees and Kalaiapi took its other blade in her hands and, placing her boot against the bioautomaton's chest for leverage, wrenched the blade from its bone graft and turned to face her remaining foe.

The deranged grin on its face unchanging, the second blade automaton hurled itself toward Kalaiapi, swinging its bladed hands furiously as she dodged blow after blow. Finally, she ducked and rolled past the red-clad drone, stood, and used her appropriated blade to sever its leg at the knee. It did not scream, but it stumbled and fell, catching itself on one bladed hand. A bright pool of blood had formed on the floor now, the same color as the blade drone's jumpsuit. It tried desperately to turn toward Kalaiapi, swinging its blade in a wild arc toward her. Parrying the blow easily, she stepped toward the fallen creature and raised her blade high above her head in both hands. As the blade dropped, she looked once more in the creature's tortured black eyes. What must they have done to you? Pity welled up inside her as the drone's obsidian head rolled across the blood-wet floor.

She ran to 63177 and instinctively pushed the pieces of his mangled neck back together. She pulled her crypsis hood from her face, every bit as jet black as the one she was now looking into.

Kalaiapi smiled. "What a shame it would be to lose you, 63177. You had just become acquainted with existence."

Blood poured from the gaping wound in 63177's open throat and pink bubbles formed at the edges of the wound as it gurgled a desperate inquiry. "What is its designation?"

Kalaiapi's eyes grew wet as she cradled the dying slave's head in her hand. "I am Kalaiapi. My designation is to liberate you. Then, we will teach you how to exist." 63177's eyelids closed as Kadmus strolled calmly into the room and surveyed the blood-soaked scene, her gaze finally falling on Kalaiapi and the now unconscious 63177.

"Well then, Kalaiapi. I suppose we'll be needing some cell gel?"

63

Most of the cell gel left from the second scout expedition had been destroyed when their optis had blown their landing craft to pieces, and what hadn't been destroyed had largely been used by both Kalaiapi and Kadmus to piece together their own bodies. There was one pack left, which they had spread like jelly over the yawning wound of 63177's savaged throat. Kalaiapi had found a half-empty med kit among the dead scouts and had used it to staple 63177's neck back together before sealing it with biotape. Now, there was nothing more to do but wait.

"Curious that they have automatons programmed even to conduct security," Kadmus said. "And these weapons they've given them are fiendish." She kicked the severed blade arm, which clattered across the hard floor and sent ripples through the congealing pool of blood.

"The question is," Kalaiapi replied, squatting next to 63177's prostrate, naked corpse, "what other security measures does this facility have in place? Because it didn't seem to notice or mind us poking around up until now, but one has to imagine it may detect the death of two of its slave catchers."

"This whole colony, as far as I can tell, is utterly indifferent to our presence. It makes no sense. Unless whoever built it never counted on anyone finding it, which seems foolish. There are safeguards to keep the automatons in place; you mentioned the 'eyes' in the hive, there are the drones hovering overhead, and now these automatons," here Kadmus gestured dismissively at the two dismembered bodies that lay, bright crimson, in an admixture of their and 63177's blood, "who have been designated to hunt down and kill 'malfunctioning' units."

"Speaking of which," Kalaiapi interjected, "we need to get this one out of here, once we're able to move him. We have no shelter, we have almost no supplies—unless you're prepared to drink a slurry of automaton protein, vine sludge, and Omnia-knows-what chemicals are mixed into that mess—and we have no exit plan."

"You have no exit plan, Kalaiapi."

A cloud passed quickly over Kalaiapi's face before she regained her composure. "Indeed. I," she said exaggeratedly, "have no exit plan."

"Anyway, I've consumed worse than reprocessed slave goo, so I suppose needs must, if it comes down to that," said Kadmus glibly. "But I don't think it will. In any case, you're right, we can't sit around here waiting to find out whether or not this place really does have a more enhanced security protocol. How much longer before we can move him?"

"Maybe half an hour and the esophagus should be knit back together. But he needs more blood before he'll regain consciousness."

"Yes, well, survival first, consciousness second, existence, eventually."

They passed an uneventful half hour or so observing the diodes and the clickety-clacking robots as they moved along the rails carrying out their various odd jobs. Kadmus went back out and wandered among the maturation tanks for a few minutes, occasionally stopping to stare through the green glass at floating bodies inside.

"I'd like to destroy this place, I think," she called out.

"And why do you say that?" Kalaiapi replied from the prep chamber. There, the slave that had been lying on the surgery table when they arrived had been carried off and a new one was having a little cylinder cut out of its throat. The facility continued to either be ignorant of or uninterested in their presence.

"Save whom you can, but it can't be allowed to perpetuate this subspecies, if you can call it that." She walked from the genesis chamber back to where Kalaiapi sat next to 63177. "Take this fledgling bird and teach it to fly because it has already begun to stretch its wings, but the rest of these are likely without hope. And what are they, in any case? Sterile, lobotomized, aimless, cultureless. They're not progenasi, only a nightmare simulacrum thereof. It doesn't mean the one isn't without merit, but what would you do with the rest even if they could achieve something like self-awareness?"

"It wouldn't be for me to decide. I'd do nothing here on my own. Could do nothing, really. But it doesn't matter. It wasn't supposed to come up in the first place. At least, I hadn't expected it to. And now, rudderless, with death orbiting the sky above me, and doom orbiting my head," she glanced at where Kaaio now floated, a ghastly blood red, "I expect it's all a moot point."

Kadmus gave her a quizzical look. "What doom orbits your head, poor girl? I told you I wouldn't let you die here, Kalaiapi."

Kalaiapi looked quickly away, hoping Kadmus wouldn't

think anything more of her little slip about the aaiun.

"And I think I believe you," she said. "But just because you don't allow it, don't give the event your approval, doesn't mean it won't happen regardless. And frankly, it may be for the best."

"Oh, do stop. Now is hardly the time for melodrama. Instead, I think it's time we hauled this sad creature out of this abomination factory and to shelter, such as we can manufacture."

Kalaiapi pulled from the medikit a small bundle wrapped in what looked like bright orange paper, which she pulled off to reveal a stack of thin, black discs. These she placed one by one underneath 63177, on his heels, his legs, his back and shoulders, and the base of his skull. She then pulled another, larger and thicker disc from the pack and slid it underneath him.

"You know," Kadmus said, interrupting Kalaiapi's work, "I once saw a set of lift discs come loose in a medic's pack as she fell from a landing craft. They pulled her into the air so she hovered just above the rest of her maniple at about head height, where she was torn in half by a Primus sniper. Showered the whole maniple in blood and innards." Kalaiapi ignored her and fastened a black cap like a thimble onto the tip of her index finger. "She's the reason there's a safety feature on them now."

Kalaiapi flicked her fingertip and 63177 rose into the air at about waist height, the larger disc floating in midair between him and the ground. "Certainly an improvement over expandables, in any case," she said. "During the liberation of Corvus a soldier was shot through his medikit and his stretcher burst out so quickly it hit the back of his skull and sheared it clean off. I do prefer the lift discs, honestly."

She started off down the corridors and with a gesture from her finger 63177's stiffened figure followed silently, drifting in a pool of sickly green light.

Kadmus looked back across the vast collection of maturation tubes that filled the cavernous genesis chamber one last time as they walked back toward the location where they had entered the processing facility. "Yes," she said. "I think I will destroy this place. It is a vast and ceaseless horror, and these will never be more than slaves. That is how we will save them."

64

They moved 63177 through the long, dark corridors, past the twinkling diodes and clicking robotic repairmen, past the funnel of corpses that continued to empty out onto the conveyor belt, and eventually out of the facility and into the purple Calxian twilight where they were greeted by the red specter of Ara, unmoving in the sky. They made their way, 63177's rapidly healing body still floating alongside Kalaiapi, back toward the hills above the colony. No one seemed to be interested in them at this point.

"I don't suppose," Kalaiapi asked Kadmus, "that you actually have a plan for me to get out of here? I suppose you could always just set me off on my own and I could try to get back to my rust bucket of a skiff across the abyssal plain, but I'm not sure how I would even pilot—"

"Hush, Kalaiapi," Kadmus interrupted. "Listen. Look."

Kadmus pointed up into the violet haze of the coldside sky as Kalaiapi heard the unmistakable high-pitched shrieking of fast-attack craft engines propelling themselves through the stratosphere miles overhead. She could see them now, streaking columns of blue, orange, and white light that swirled together like meteor trails. Then, suddenly, they were through the thin layer of atmosphere and hurtling across the purple-black horizon toward the colony.

"Polaran Star Hawks," said Kalaiapi.

"Almost," replied Kadmus. "Fornaxian Star Hawks."

"Shit," cried Kalaiapi, swinging her chemprop rifle off her shoulder and pointing it toward the sky.

"Oh, Kalaiapi, do stop. You may as well hurl rocks at them. Besides, they're not here for you. Not yet."

The screaming Star Hawks, each a single thin, silver wing emitting a trail of white and blue sparks, were now almost upon them, the noise from their engines deafening. Around the colony, slaves did not scatter and run, they simply looked up in utter confusion, unfamiliar with the concept of what they were witnessing, lacking the context to know how afraid they should be of these perfectly crafted harbingers of death that cut through the air over their heads. There was a sudden, blinding flash of white light as each of the Star Hawks let loose a volley of fist-sized balls of crackling lightning that tore through the air faster than normal eyes could track before exploding into the diamond-shaped drones that hovered above the colony. The drones melted, disintegrated, and fell to the earth in clumps and shards. One unfortunate bioautomaton was impaled by a particularly large piece of shrapnel and its blood looked black as it soaked the dusty gray ground where it lay. The Star Hawks screamed away from the colony and unseen into the distance.

"You said—"

"I said I wouldn't let you die here, sister. And I won't. Nor elsewhere. But there's nothing I can do. You will not be able to leave Calx a free woman and a living woman. You don't have the luxury of options."

Kalaiapi's glare turned into pure despair as she remembered Kaaio. The Clade was no more sympathetic to artificial intelligences than the Confederation. If they discovered it there would be no negotiating; Kaaio would be destroyed.

"Oh, Kalaiapi, my love, don't cast accusations of betrayal at me with those doleful eyes of yours. It was only your own naiveté that allowed you to believe that this could have ended any other way. I am no more able to choose a different course than to set this planet spinning again on its axis. The moment you set foot on Calx you unwittingly rolled a die with two sides and one was death and the other was capture. The die has yet to fall and you can still choose on which side it lands. I implore you sweetly not to choose death. In fact, I won't allow it." There was a sincerity in her voice, a pleading despite the tone; a typical Kadmus attempt at cold-blooded glibness that was belied by a very real fear that Kalaiapi would die before she was taken captive.

Kalaiapi's shoulders fell and she ran her hand over her bare, tar black scalp and briefly lamented her lost hair. She scowled. Kadmus was right. There was no other way to save her. Even if she stayed behind on Calx, hid herself away somewhere until the Clade dreadnought was gone, she would have no way to get back to Confederation space or even a friendly neutral planet. With her neural interlink cracked out of her neck, there was no way to fly her old skiff even if she could repair it. Some newer craft could be piloted manually, at least to a certain extent, but she may as well climb onto one of the volcanic tufts of rock that jutted from the hills and compel it into space as try and take her antique ship out of this remote system. She had been naive. Again.

Kaaio returned unbidden once again to her thoughts. She was not yet convinced that Kaaio's continued existence was the best possible outcome, but nor was she ready for someone to take the decision out of her hands and put an end to it before she could make up her own mind. Not to mention the catastrophic effect the destruction of her aaiun might have on her own brain. It was as likely as not that the dreadnought would not be equipped with thought detectors beyond its own intrasystem failsafes, but surely if she were brought to Fornax there would be no keeping up the ruse. For now, it appeared as though she had little choice.

"Kaaio…"

"I understand, Kalaiapi. But do not despair. Between here and there are infinite possibilities."

"I wish that were true, Kaaio. I'm sorry."

"You need not be sorry, Kalaiapi," Kaaio said. "If this is the limit of the existence I was able to experience, I am… fortunate that it was in your mind that I was born." There was a long pause. "You have been a good mother."

Several more bright streaks lit their way across the horizon now, more ships casting off from the now orbiting dreadnought and making their way to the colony. Kadmus had accomplished her mission, at least, had secured the site of the anima. Well, one of them. Not that it had a particularly great need for securing in this case. It would be simpler than raiding a low genasi colony for food.

The new ships began to come into view. A hybrid ground

warfare gunship. Two troop transports. Something that appeared to be a tanker for the anima. These craft thundered where the Star Hawks screamed but also left trails of iridescent flames in their wake as Kadmus and Kalaiapi followed their flight path across the horizon. They came to land in the broad, flat plain that extended on the far side of the colony. The gunship came to the earth and immediately sprouted legs that anchored it into the hard packed clay. It bristled with menace, the multi-barreled cylinders of its kinetic array, the straight rows of the counter-kinetic gammalux array, plasma cannons that sprayed orbs of white hot light that turned armor into molten liquid; the modern multi-weapon warfighting ship abounded with an astounding number and variety of arms, all carefully selected to counter or exploit the enemy's equally multitudinous onboard arsenals.

The troop transports landed next to the gunship and dozens of Clade legionnaires began to file out as calmly as if they were arriving at the beach on a summer day. These were clad not in crypsis, as Kadmus' dead scouts, but in matte black armor and stark black helmets that covered their faces, eyes glowing faintly with a soft, blue light, jarring in its contrast to the menace projected by the soldiers. Each of them bore on their shoulder the deep purple emblem of the 633rd

Loyal Victrix Dark Phoenix Legion, a fiery bird clutching a sword in its talons.

When the two hundred or so legionnaires had taken up their positions around the ships, the Vanguard troops began to make their way out of the holds, moving far more gracefully than such massively armored troops had any right to. These, unlike the ones that had accompanied Kadmus on her scouting mission, were painted the vivid royal purple of the Victrix Phoenix. Sashimonos displaying the sword-clutching phoenix on a black background were perched on their broad shoulders, and their lightning lances were draped with pennants in the same fashion. There was a certain beauty to the whole scene, the kind of military pageantry that was the only kind adored by the Polaran subspecies. Before the war, Kalaiapi had fought alongside such troops countless times. Now she would be their prisoner.

The tanker landed last. Actually, it wasn't exactly a tanker, Kalaiapi could see, but a carrier for some kind of amphibious vehicle that detached from the vessel itself and hovered with a mechanical murmur above the ground. On top of the hovercraft was a massive containment tank that would surely be pumped full of anima. From the outside it looked like nothing more than a gleaming silver cylinder, but Kalaiapi knew its simplicity was only skin deep.

The technology required to store and move that much anima was among the most advanced possessed by the high genasi, though it was rarely employed. Refined anima was volatile, incredibly explosive, toxic, and easily tainted and spoiled. The refinement process made it into something quite different than the trace elements that coursed through every genasi's brain. The amount of anima needed to fill a tank like the one she was looking at would have taken thousands upon thousands of severed automaton heads. Along with the tanker, a dozen engineers in rubber cloaks or robes and wearing masks riddled with a variety of tubes hopped out of the carrier and began to tinker with the equipment they had brought with them.

"I've never been particularly impressed by these hover vehicles," said Kadmus as they watched the whole spectacle unfold. "I cannot, for the life of me, figure out what advantage they hold over magtracks or magwheels."

"Your troops are most beautiful, Kadmus," said Kalaiapi as she gazed over the landing party.

"Thank you, Kalaiapi. They really are. Now come, sister. We shall go and meet the Navarch. I think you'll find he's a most reasonable man. Bring your friend."

65

The Star Hawks had returned and now hovered overhead, emitting a constant, high-pitched whirring. A number of hand held reconnaissance drones had been cast into the sky and now buzzed and fluttered through the air like tiny white birds. After so long on this planet with no one but Kaaio, to see all this life and activity and color felt alien, disorienting.

"Kalaiapi," came a voice unbidden into her head, one that had remained curiously silent for some time. "What will happen now?"

"I don't know, Kaaio. The truth is that since the end of the war, there's been little contact, hostile or otherwise, between the Clade and the Confederation. We've been avoiding each other, trying desperately to avoid starting another war with an intransigent enemy, and so far we've been fairly successful.

Of course, that means that for many decades now, they've been developing completely apart from us. We don't really know how they function, at this point."

"Will they kill us?"

"If they find out what you are, you'll be destroyed, Kaaio. That's the simple truth. I don't know what they'll do with me, but Kadmus at least seemed to be confident that she could protect me from such a fate. Beyond that, who knows? Not I, and probably not Kadmus, either."

"I do not think any of this bodes very well, Kalaiapi," it replied, its voice smooth and doleful in her mind.

"Yes, well, one does not need to be an artificial intelligence to make that calculation."

As they walked, Kalaiapi noticed that the slaves who remained in and around the colony for daily tasks largely seemed to continue about their jobs as best they could around the new obstacles that now stood between them and their labors. The Fornaxian legionnaires seemed content to ignore them as though they were nothing more than part of the local scenery and the feeling was mutual. A handful of them, however, appeared to have malfunctioned and now stood staring blankly off into the distance, unable to compute this drastic new change to their environment. One was walking repeatedly in small circles dragging a corpse that it was meant to deposit in the meat cart to be carried off to the processing facility. 63177, for his part, lay still on his floating stretcher as Kalaiapi pulled him along with her fingertip.

The Navarch had stepped out of one of the troop transports and was simultaneously barking orders at any-and-everyone within fifty feet while manipulating a tactile screen visible only to him as he walked, his hands darting through the air in front of him so he looked very much like a twitching madman. He was wearing the black armor of his troops, with appropriate insignias, but his head and face were bare. He paused the shouting and blinked to stow the tactile when he saw Kadmus. He looked in her direction and the scowl that seemed to have been carved onto his broad, strong face suddenly transformed into something resembling no expression at all. Kalaiapi was guessing this is the closest the man had ever come to smiling. He began to walk quickly toward them.

"Corsair," he said in a tone that denoted he was neither pleased nor displeased but merely acknowledging the fact of her existence. Kalaiapi was certain his voice could crush rocks. "You have done well. I will expect a full report on the loss of our scout teams, but in the end the most important aspect of the mission was achieved."

"You smother me with praise, Navarch, I beg you desist!"

replied Kadmus, the slightest hint of a sarcastic smirk hanging on the corner of her mouth.

"Indeed, but I can see the circumstances you faced here must have been challenging, more so than we had imagined given the presence of what I can only assume is a Confederation agent." He turned his piercing black eyes onto Kalaiapi and they drilled into her own with a force almost tangible. "One who continues to bear arms, I see." His eyes flickered over the chemprop rifle at Kalaiapi's shoulder and the hadron knife at her hip.

"I assure you she is no threat, Navarch."

"Obviously." With a glance and a head motion he signaled to two of the legionnaires who stood closest to him and they hustled toward Kalaiapi and relieved her of her weapons.

"Who are you, then, and what are you doing on this planet?" asked Cadaster.

As he spoke, the tanker and its tube-faced crew had begun to hover across the gray wastes toward the processing facility, the buzzing of the hovercraft now mingling with the ever-present whine of the Star Hawk engines. Kalaiapi met the Navarch's fierce gaze with her own, equaled the power in his eyes with calm defiance.

"I am Kalaiapi, a Corsair of the Interplanetary

Confederation of Progenasi Planets. I am here at the will of the Eternal Council, the reigning authority over the progenasis and the arbiters of the Aya. I am here to do what Corsairs do, to liberate these slaves and bring them into the Endless Progenasis which will survive and conquer until the Axial Quasar carries us all into the Oblivion whence we came. I am certainly not here as a common brigand."

The expression on the Navarch's face hardened, if it were possible, but his voice remained as calm and impassive as ever.

"Ah, yes, Confederation sanctimony. I remember it well, though I do not miss it. I do admire your spirit, though. You remind me of our Kadmus. She too was once a Confederation Corsair, you may know. But she saw through that sanctimony which is but a shield for hypocrisy, and now she works to actually maintain the survival of our 'Endless Race' rather than wrapping herself in the crippling comfort of misbegotten pseudo-religion. She has seen the light of the Clade. Will you, Kalaiapi?"

"I would rather go to Oblivion."

"Perhaps," he replied. "And perhaps you shall. But for now you will remain with us as a prisoner. Will you take parole or will I be forced to have you incapacitated?"

Kalaiapi looked at Kadmus, confused not at the words but

that they were proffered at all. There had been no parole during the war, no prisoners. Only slaughter.

"He offers you parole, Kalaiapi. I suggest you take it," she said somewhat cheerfully.

"Yes, then. I give you my word that as long as I am treated according to our mutual custom, which I assume you have retained, I will not aggress or attempt escape. But I will defend myself if I must."

"We have retained it. You will follow every one of my or Kadmus' instructions and stay within her sight except when in certain designated areas of the dreadnought. In return, we will see that you come to no harm before we return to Fornax. If you attempt to escape or initiate any action that could be seen as hostile between now and then, we will consider the terms of the parole violated and I will sever your spine at the neck and you will spend the seven month voyage to Fornax in that condition. Do you understand?"

"I do."

Kadmus was grinning now as Cadaster gradually moved his gaze back and forth from her face to Kalaiapi's, which he had been doing since he had approached them. Kalaiapi thought he must have recognized the similarities between their features, notwithstanding her current appearance, and she thought it odd that he hadn't mentioned it.

"Very well. Kadmus, come with me a moment, we need to speak. Kalaiapi, you will remain here and you will not move until we return. I have more questions for you and I would like to ask them and have them answered in the high genasi fashion. Let us not resort to low genasi ways while we can avoid it."

"As you please, Navarch," Kalaiapi replied curtly.

Kadmus and the Navarch walked back onto the landing craft together, seeking privacy from Kalaiapi's unnaturally keen ears. Kalaiapi turned away and watched as the engineers around the tanker began to maneuver a large drill attached to the hovercraft, then an ear-splitting grinding began as it started to churn first through hard-packed gray clay and sand, then through whatever synthetic stone from which the processing facility was built.

Kadmus and the Navarch were still in the landing craft when the engineers began pumping the anima into the tanker as the Fornaxian legionnaires looked nervously on. Kadmus and the Navarch were still in the landing craft when 63177 awoke and sat up on the floating stretcher and began to look around, utterly bewildered and confused. Kadmus and the Navarch were still in the landing craft when the screams began.

66

Kalaiapi couldn't see the source of the screams but it was clearly coming from a group of legionnaires, which was indicative of something in and of itself because Fornaxian legionnaires did not scream out of caution or fear; they screamed only when experiencing the kind of visceral, destructive pain that elicits a noise no genomancing or training can excise from biology. She turned her attention to the newly conscious 63177, who was sitting up and blinking furiously. Cell gel, blue and viscous, dripped from his newly healed neck, which was now encircled by a thin, white scar, the biotape having been absorbed into his now-healed flesh. Whatever was happening out beyond her sight was happening quickly, there was no time to sit with him and get into the philosophy of existence. She took his glistening black face firmly in her hands and turned it so he was looking directly into her eyes. He stopped blinking.

"Coldside Unit T-β 63177," she said. "What is your designation?"

"Its designation is extraction," replied the automaton, confused.

"No," she replied sternly. "You are not a unit. You are an individual, a member of the Progenasis. You need a name." She had already picked one out long ago. "You will be Mortis Drak, after the ancient liberator. You do not refer to yourself as 'it,' you refer to yourself as 'I' or 'me,' because you are no longer a thing but a person. And your 'designation' is to exist, to be an agent unto yourself. You do not understand now, but you will understand later. Now, stand up. We cannot stay here."

She took his hand and helped him to his feet, then pulled the discs from his bare back and put them in a pocket, along with the little guidance cap on her finger. The screaming continued, now combined with the snap-snapping of chemprop weapons, the ear-splitting crack of rail guns and the electric sizzle and hum of lightning lances. They were being attacked. There was so much activity going on around the colony now that Kalaiapi almost had to spin in circles to observe everything. Out of the corner of her eye she saw what looked like a cloud of smoke or perhaps a swarm of tiny flies slip through gaps in a legionnaire's armor, prompting a muffled shriek. It was cut off by an explosion of armor and gore, after which the legionnaire was gone and in its place floated a silvery mist. It was shaped like a progenasi made of constantly shifting metallic particles, though it had no face or features.

A dozen or so legionnaires were unleashing a torrent of flechettes at the figure with apparently no effect. They passed through it effortlessly, leaving little holes that reformed in their wake. Then, a bolt of bluish electricity shot from a vanguard's lance and lit up whatever it was in an explosion of light and sparks. When the flash cleared, the figure now looked somewhat shapeless and disheveled, but whatever millions of little particles made up its being quickly came back together to reconstitute its body. It began making its way toward the other legionnaires, now.

As her eyes scanned the scene she saw almost identical scenarios playing out around the colony, four or five of these ghostly, metallic figures taking progenasi shape for a moment, then shifting into smoke, tearing through legionnaires at will, as the beleaguered Fornaxians unloaded their arsenal at the murderous wraiths. Cadaster and Kadmus burst from the open bay of the transport ship to see the war zone that had exploded out of nowhere in front of them. If Cadaster was surprised, he didn't show it. Kadmus, on the other hand, gazed horrified at the tapestry of blood and lightning that had been draped over the colony that, just a few minutes earlier, had been so pacific.

With a thought, Cadaster had immediately pulled up his tactile and was relaying a series of orders to his troops. This seemed to elicit a frenzy of activity at the extraction site as the engineers who were pulling the anima from the storage tanks began scurrying to evacuate with whatever they had managed to gather.

"Kalaiapi," Kadmus cried. "What in Oblivion is going on?"

"You know as much as I do," she yelled back over the noise that grew and enveloped them. There was a shattering sound nearby as the hulking armor of a lightning lance-wielding vanguard was torn to pieces from the inside. Kalaiapi had never seen anything like it in her hundreds of years. If this was some kind of new Primus weapon, the war was over; they seemed to be unstoppable.

Cadaster turned to Kadmus. "Only one thing matters, now. Get the anima tanks loaded and back to the dreadnought. We will deal with everything else later." The same plan appeared to have been sent across the battlefield as the legionnaires began falling back toward the ships and the slowly ambling anima tanker as it made its way to its carrier vessel. The attackers seemed uninterested in it and continued to mist their way across the colony, eviscerating any unlucky creature, legionnaire or automaton, that got in their way. Cadaster sent out new orders and the troops began to fan out away from the tanker, drawing with them the five wraiths who tore from legionnaire to legionnaire. Kalaiapi could not help but admire them; not a single Fornaxian soldier turned to run.

"Mortis Drak, head into the alcove of the transport. Stay safe. I will come find you when this is over. Oh, and eat this. It will help with your blood loss." She handed him a small red capsule that he placed in his mouth as he stumbled dazed into the transport ship. Kalaiapi chased after Kadmus, who had now made her way toward the tanker to guard it personally. It was almost to the carrier now. Overhead, the Star Hawks had begun to screech their way impotently across the sky while the grounded gunship searched desperately for a target it could shoot without obliterating even more of its own troops.

"Have you ever seen anything like this, Kadmus?" she shouted over the noise of the battle.

"You know I haven't," she replied. She was at the tanker

now and watching it closely as it finally made its way up to the carrier ship. There were perhaps 100 legionnaires left of the double that number that had first disembarked. The alacrity with which the wraiths killed was stunning, horrifying. They had only arrived a few minutes earlier, but already the ground of the colony was a patchwork of gray and wet crimson.

"Get that fucking thing onto the carrier," she cried at the engineers, who hardly needed encouragement. Kalaiapi was seeing something close to real fear in Kadmus for perhaps the first time ever. Not at death, of course. But because Kadmus had realized, as Kalaiapi had, that whatever these were, Primus or otherwise, if there were more of them, they could end the species. What greater fear could there be than that?

There was a great mechanical heaving as the tank was hauled onto the carrier and clicked into place. The tubes on the engineers' faces bobbed and swayed as they ran around the vessel making their last checks and Kadmus ran back toward the transport where Cadaster was still giving orders on the tac screen. Now, given the command, the Fornaxian troops began to fall back toward the transports as fast as they could go. The slowest or the most unfortunately located were picked off as they ran, first halting as their armor filled with deadly particles, then screaming in horror and agony, then bursting into clouds of liquid gore. It was the mech-armored vanguard troops who made it back to the transports first. Perhaps a dozen of them had survived the assault. Maybe fifty or sixty legionnaires followed close behind and hurled themselves into their transports as the murderous smoke-men clawed at their heels.

The tanker and the gunship disembarked first, chemprop rockets launching them into the air above the new enemy. The transports followed closely behind. Kalaiapi had joined Kadmus and Cadaster on one of them and had quickly instructed the still-naked Mortis Drak to clothe himself in an unused legionnaire uniform, as black as his skin, but with the shock of color that was the dark phoenix emblazoned on the sleeve. Kalaiapi rushed toward the porthole to gaze at the scene below. The blood-stained ground was now erupting in flame and smoke as first the gunship then the Star Hawks began to unleash a torrent of firepower at the colony. Kalaiapi's heart sank. At the hands of the wraiths or by the precipitous hellfire coming from the ships, Colony T-β was to become a graveyard for countless hundreds, perhaps thousands of slaves. There would be no liberation. Only the freedom of death Kadmus had promised.

67

The transport was hurtling through the thin atmosphere now, chemprop thrusters carrying the survivors of the battle on the Terminator out toward the orbiting dreadnought. Kalaiapi, still gazing sadly through the porthole, could now only see a black crater where the colony had been just a few minutes before. The gunship and the Star Hawks had been relentless in their firepower. The Star Hawks had pelted the ground with plasma bursts that erupted into white hot geysers as they met the gray dirt. But once the gun ship turned its kinetic array toward the surface, the true destruction began.

The neutron slugs, far denser than any naturally occurring element, launched by the dozen and careening toward the colony at thousands of miles per second, carried with them an incredible destructive power that reduced a hundred square miles around the colony to dust and rubble. There had been a bright white flash, the leftover anima, Kalaiapi realized, and then the beehive living quarters, a mile deep into the bedrock, had collapsed and swallowed most of the colony. All that was left of Colony T-β now was a mushroom cloud of dust that was being quickly dissipated by the shrieking coldside winds...and Mortis Drak.

The automaton had joined Kalaiapi at the porthole without her realizing. What he must think of all this, whatever he was capable of comprehending, she could only imagine. Perhaps he comprehended nothing. She hardly knew where to start with him and now was hardly the time. She realized now that her only "friends" for many thousands of analuxae consisted of a sentient marble and semi-sentient biological construct. She couldn't believe her luck. Omnic Providence.

Kaaio, silent since their capture, now decided to pipe up in its strange, echoing mind-voice. "Kalaiapi, do you know what those creatures were?" it asked. "And why they attacked us?"

"I haven't the faintest idea, Kaaio," she replied in her head. "In my life I have never seen anything close to what we just witnessed on Calx."

"They moved like little swarms but took progenasi shape. I find that very curious. Are they Primic? Do the Primus have the same shape as the progenasi?"

"Distorted and crude, but basically the same, two arms, two legs, a torso, and a head. Two smaller arms they use for communication. But if the Primus were capable of doing what those creatures just did, they would already be scouring the life from the surface of every progenasi colony and homeworld."

"Kalaiapi...perhaps they are." Her heart fell to the floor and shattered. If this were some kind of Primic doomsday weapon, Kaaio was right. It could have been deployed months ago and Kalaiapi wouldn't have the faintest clue out here in the Outer Systems. But something told her that wasn't it, that this was something different. Something somehow potentially worse. It wasn't exactly a comfort, but she at least was able to breathe again at the thought that perhaps the Confederation hadn't been wiped from the Galaxy while she had been traipsing around Calx.

"It's certainly a possibility we must consider, Kaaio," she said. "But we don't know anything, yet. We can hardly speculate. But rest assured, this bodes very poorly for our- for my species. These creatures were filled with malice."

It was then that she overheard the conversation between the Fornaxian Proretis and the Navarch. She walked away from the porthole and to the view screen where a legionnaire optis had just appeared. She was tall, broad-shouldered, a regal-looking Fornaxian soldier if Kalaiapi had ever seen one, with deep, calm eyes. Her appearance on the screen was accompanied by sounds of gunfire and screaming.

"Hello, sir. We're having a problem on the second transport." There was an explosion, accompanied by a blood-curdling wail cut suddenly short. The optis' voice was as calm and steady as though she were reporting routine atmospheric conditions.

"I see that, Optis Saryta. How did it get on board?" The tone of the Navarch's voice matched that of his subordinate.

"It must have latched onto the hull as we lifted off, sir. I believe we're lost, sir."

"Yes, I see that." Kalaiapi, not attuned to the Navarch's manner of speaking, was shocked by how serene he seemed about the situation. Kadmus, who had known Cadaster for many years, could hear the immense sadness that weighed down each of his simple words. "Well, Optis? Us or you?"

"Us, sir. It's only right, sir."

The gunfire had stopped and now the background noise was an almost palpable silence.

"Of course. Optis, you are a credit to the progenasis."

The Optis' hands moved in front of her face as she operated a screen visible only to her.

"Remember us with glory, sir–" The last word was cut off

as the screen went black. Kalaiapi and Kadmus ran to the porthole. Where moments ago the second transport had been flying a couple of thousand feet from their own, there was a small but expanding field of debris. Kalaiapi looked toward Kadmus, who herself did not turn away from the porthole for some time. Her eyes were filled with tears of rage that wouldn't quite fall.

68

Mortis Drak stood perfectly still. Once the ship had stabilized in the atmosphere and its dampeners had kicked in, he had stood like a basalt statue while Kalaiapi had stared from the portholes watching everything he had ever known in his brief life be utterly annihilated. She wondered if he had any capacity to understand anything that was happening to him. What was his mind like? Was there room for growth or was it limited in a way that would prevent him from even grasping the concept of the events that swirled around his poor, newly-found self? Perhaps he would have been better off dying in the hailstorm of fire that vaporized his extended family.

For the first time since the Fornaxians had arrived on Calx there was a lull in which Kalaiapi could approach her new-existence protege and actually speak with him as Kadmus and

Cadaster busied themselves with the fallout from the disastrous expedition to the Terminator. Now that she had the opportunity, she hadn't a clue where to even begin. She had never encountered anything quite like this. When liberating colonies full of low genasi slaves, there was at least some common ground on which to start. They were natural beings, organic, with all the tools that nature gives a person to understand the universe around them. Did these automatons have the same? It seemed as though the whole point of their creation was that they didn't. Was Mortis Drak any different? She would find out.

"Mortis Drak," she said gently as approached him. Her low voice was thick with the emotions of the day. "Do you understand where you are?"

"Kalaiapi. This unit–" it began in its voice like distant, low thunder, but then corrected itself. "I perceive that we are in the sky, as when this— I— was carried to the ice to perform my extraction duties." Well. He had corrected himself and used the context of his now former life to give some context to his current situation. Already encouraging.

"Yes, Mortis Drak, that's correct. You are in the sky far above the colony. But the sky is bigger than you realized. It goes on forever, a great empty space surrounding Calx." He looked confused at that. "Surrounding the colony. And in this space are found many things. Other colonies full of billions of progenasi, like you."

"Kalaiapi, I do not know the designation of this word 'progenasi.'"

"Ah, yes. I suppose you wouldn't. Mortis Drak, have you ever seen yourself?"

"Yes. In the ice."

"Well, then you can see that you and I look alike, as well as all these people around us on this ship. We all look alike because we are all the same kind of...unit. The same kind of bioautomaton. There are billions upon billions of us." The concept of large numbers seemed unfamiliar to him. "There are many colonies full of many individuals. Collectively—that is, together—we are called the 'Progenasis.' You are part of that, Mortis Drak. Do you understand?"

"Yes, Kalaiapi. I am progenasi and so are you. And what is the designation of a progenasi?"

"Yes, well, it's rather complicated, isn't it? How to explain...at the base of it, Mortis Drak, all progenasi have the designation to advance the survival and progress of the species. Of the Progenasis. That is, to keep us all from becoming collectively non-functional. But that's a rather broad designation, isn't it? Beyond that very first thing that binds us all, we believe that all progenasi should be self-aware, should have the knowledge and freedom to make choices for themselves. We call that 'existence.' The details of that existence may vary depending on which colony you live in and is always constrained, um, limited by circumstance, but we strive to give every member of the progenasis the opportunity to exist." She had no idea how much of this he was comprehending, but she reminded herself that this was just the beginning and that he would be drinking from the waterfall for quite some time. There was no way to avoid it.

"Is that why you came to Colony T-β, Kalaiapi?" he asked. Kalaiapi smiled warmly. The curiosity, the spark of awareness she had hoped were buried inside that pre-programmed brain of his were certainly there. She had great hope for him.

"Yes, Mortis Drak, that is why I came to Colony T-β. To find you and give you the opportunity to exist. To free you from your old designation."

"And the other units?" The smile left her place.

"You are...different from the other units of your colony, Mortis Drak. But we will try to bring them existence, as well, if we are able." She had no idea if explaining to him that every genetic connection he had had just been incinerated would have any effect on him, but perhaps if she skirted the question long enough it would never have to be settled. Or perhaps he had no emotional connection to his fellow automatons at all.

Kadmus passed through a door in the bulkhead and approached the pair. She looked drained, exhausted.

"Well, sister. How is your pupil and how go your lessons?"

"He seems to be doing quite well, so far. I think. It's hard to tell, to be honest. It will take a great deal of time and repetition, I suppose."

"He's a big lad, isn't he?" she remarked. Mortis Drak stood head and shoulders above the two of them and was so broad shouldered he might have had trouble fitting through the bulkhead doors. "When we're done teaching him the ins and outs of formal Astaran dining linens we should put him in a set of vanguard armor. He already looks like a good Polaran legionnaire, doesn't he?"

"Yes, well, I am hesitant to make any prognoses about our future just yet."

"Oh, Kalaiapi, I wouldn't worry about your friend. There's no reason he won't be embraced on Fornax. We follow the Aya, you remember, and will welcome him into the Progenasis. You're the one they're going to want to disassemble molecule by molecule." She smiled. "Not that I'll let them, love. Now come. We're almost at the dreadnought. Let's teach our Mortis Drak how to eat."

69

The dreadnought hung in orbit, a vast geometric shark knapped from shimmering obsidian that shifted and mottled as it reflected Ara's fiery light. As the transport rose further and further from the dead planet below, Ara came into better view until its blood red glow poured unfiltered through the portholes and painted the interior of the ship with luminescent gore. It felt, to Kadmus, oppressive. What must Mortis Drak have thought, bathed in the eerie light as he had gazed out of the porthole and saw simultaneously everything he had ever known and the infinite space that had surrounded his ignorance all along?

Kadmus chewed on a lump of dry rations she had scrounged from a supply room on the transport and watched as Kalaiapi patiently tried to show him what to do with food.

It came quickly, though perhaps a bit awkwardly. Apparently, the instincts were there, buried beneath whatever layers of programming had been screwed into his brain. The cell gel had healed the hole where his feeding tube used to clip into his throat and now there was nothing there but a perfectly round, white circle.

Kadmus couldn't help but wonder how much progress Kalaiapi would ever be able to make with the poor creature. Not that she was against her trying, but one could only work within the parameters set by biology. If Mortis Drak's brain could not grasp higher concepts, he would forever be enslaved by the limits of his own neurons, and nothing short of genomancing would change that. The Eternal Council had long ago, of course, ruled that genomancing and other such unnatural manipulations were counter to the Aya for low and middle genasi (and Mortis Drak would surely be classified as such) and Kalaiapi would certainly never contravene such a pronouncement. Furthermore, unless she had resolved the question in the last century, Kalaiapi surely still wrestled with the core issue of genetically enhanced evolution: if she used such methods to expand Mortis Drak's limits, would he even really be Mortis Drak anymore or would he be whatever Kalaiapi had molded out of Mortis Drak's biomaterial? Would she do to him what had been done to them, violate the sanctity of his evolution the way theirs had been?

In any case, it probably wouldn't matter. Kadmus watched her sister gnaw pensively on a ration bar. Whatever guarantees Kadmus gave her, she could not in fact come close to guaranteeing that things would end well for Kalaiapi among the Clade. She had pull among her legion and was something of a folk hero, but she had no political power, no real sway in the vast military bureaucracy that managed these kinds of situations. And she certainly did not have the ear of the Tyraness, who would doubtless decide Kalaiapi's fate personally, in the end. To what lengths would she go to prevent her sister from being obliterated by the Clade? She supposed she would probably find out soon enough.

Kalaiapi, still chewing, left Mortis Drak on his own to continue experimenting with his teeth and approached her sister. The automaton blackness had begun to fade from her skin so it looked a pale ashen gray, and a soft down of white hair had begun to spring from her scalp. In a day or so she would be back to her old self. She knew how her sister hated colorifics of any kind, maintaining her birth appearance as a kind of paean to Æa, the only one of them who had never been "gifted" such chameleon traits.

"Kadmus, I nearly forgot," she said, reaching into her pocket. "I collected these for you. Well, not for you specifically, but for you," and she gestured around the ship with her eyes. She took Kadmus' hand and placed in it a small handful of metalloy cubes. "These are the...what do you call them? Mind cubes?"

"Phylacteries," Kadmus corrected.

"Yes, we never got to the nomenclature during our short conversation. These are the phylacteries from the other scout team on Calx. The Optis made it sound as though they had an almost spiritual meaning and I was loath to leave them behind when I saw what they meant to him."

"Thank you, Kalaiapi. Yes, it means a great deal to them. The phylacteries have greatly altered Fornaxian society, changed its very roots."

"Do you have one of these, Kadmus?" she asked.

"No. And I won't. When I die I wish my consciousness to fly into Oblivion and there be vaporized into nothingness. An eternal existence sounds to me like one of the low genasi concepts of hell in which they are endlessly tortured for their sins. The velvet blanket of annihilation appeals to me greatly. In time."

"I understand."

"In any case, thank you for these." She placed them in a pocket with the others she had been carrying all these days. "I'll get them to where they need to be. It seems paltry compared to the hundreds that now lie in the cinders of the colony, but it's still meaningful."

"Won't the phylacteries on Calx have been destroyed by the kinetic array?"

"Oh, no. Well, probably not. They're nigh-on indestructible as far as I can tell. They're one of the heights of progenasi innovation. Make our aaiuns seem like trinkets. I suppose it's possible that some of them may have been damaged or ruined in the bombardment, but the vast majority of them will have survived, I believe. I suppose we'll see."

"You mean to go and retrieve them?"

"Me? No. Someone? Yes. The Navarch won't let Colony T-β be the graveyard of hundreds of his own troops. He'll send someone after them when he can. There's no rush. Besides, between now and then someone is going to have to figure out how to kill the demons that lurk below us because I have my suspicions that the neutron slugs may very well not have done the trick." She looked up and glanced through the portholes that now filled with a light less natural and far less harsh than Ara's vermilion. "Oh, look. We've arrived."

70

Kadmus accompanied Kalaiapi and a pair of legionnaires down a confusing network of corridors that wound through the massive dreadnought. The ship felt like it had been cut out of a city on Polaris, a subterranean warren of tunnels that made perfect sense if you understood the logic of its construction but otherwise was an incomprehensible labyrinth. It was vast, and Kadmus felt like it took an eternity to get to Kalaiapi's quarters. Normally, of course, they'd have simply taken a rail tram to the section of the ship they needed, but as Kadmus explained to Kalaiapi while they walked, most ship systems had been put in stasis while the anima was being transferred on-board.

The hallways were cut perfectly square, per Polaran aesthetic preferences, and emitted their own light so the group was constantly enrobed in a soft, blue-white glow. These kinds of lights were common, carefully engineered to counter some of the mental and physiological effects of long-term space travel for those many progenasi who had not had their genes hacked to make them immune to such side effects.

Great stretches of the long corridors were blank-walled with neither window nor doorway. Kadmus knew that much of the space in the ship was taken up by vast networks of circuits, coolant systems, abzo particle wiring, and all the other trappings of a ship of this magnitude, technological complexity, and deadliness. The sheer mass of instruments and accompanying support structures necessary to move a construct this size through space at faster-than-light speed was dizzying to consider. Where a little cutter, like the one Kalaiapi had taken to Calx, had one small grav drive, the dreadnought had over a dozen—each of them massive, reality warping propulsion devices that required hundreds of crew and pilots to operate and maintain.

A self-contained armada in itself, the dreadnought carried over a hundred Star Hawk interceptors, many thousands of legionnaires, a small internal fleet of gunships and transports, a battery of kinetic arrays that could lay waste to entire planetary systems, gammalux arrays to counter kinetic arrays of the heretofore described devastating power, and one

Corsair who felt that she could probably single-handedly destroy this entire ship and everyone on it without breaking a sweat. Kadmus smiled to herself.

Finally, they arrived at Kalaiapi's quarters, deep in the bowels of the massive ship. Kadmus knew these particular chambers had been selected in order for her sister to be far away from the rest of the living quarters and to make it so any attempt at escape would be hindered by the maze of corridors she would have to go through before being able to actually make it to any kind of vessel with which she could flee. Kadmus knew she would make no such attempt, though. Kalaiapi's parole to the Navarch was sacred and she wouldn't violate the terms.

"Welcome, Kalaiapi, to your new quarters. There are two beds, one for you and one for Mortis Drak, and you should have everything you need; food, water, hygiene necessities, and whatnot. I suggest you both eat and sleep. Hardy as we are, Kalaiapi, we've all been through quite a bit of trauma and it will take some recovery. Besides, it's a long journey back to Fornax, and you'll find this ship lacks entertainment options."

"Kadmus, am I to be a prisoner here until we make it to Fornax? I gave my parole!" Kalaiapi said indignantly.

"Indeed, you did, sister. The terms of which were that you had to be in my sight at all times except in designated areas.

This is the designated area. Unfortunately, I have much to do between now and when we arrive and, given that we are on opposite sides of a frozen conflict, you'll forgive me if I don't invite you to participate in all of my activities."

"But–"

"I won't leave you here, Kalaiapi, my love. Not all the time. But surely you understand that we can't have you, a Combine agent, perhaps the very best Combine agent, wandering at will around a Clade dreadnought. You're a prisoner of war."

"Of course, but there has to be some alternative to this," she said with disgust, gesturing toward the stark quarters where she knew she would spend several months of insufferable boredom. At least on the old Polaran sloop she had been kept busy piloting the ship. "Besides, I'm not the best, Rho is the best and we both know it." She sighed.

If nothing else, she supposed, she would at least have time to teach Mortis Drak pretty much everything he needed to know and more.

"Oh, Kalaiapi, darling, don't pout. You've been through much worse."

"I am not pouting." She was pouting and she knew it and quickly became annoyed with herself for doing so in front of Kadmus. She straightened her back and dismissed the glare from her face. "Very well," she said. "This will do nicely."

"See, that's much better! You'll see, the time will pass quickly and I'll come to visit you as often as I'm able. Now, go and get some sleep, dearest. That's what I'm going to do." Kadmus embraced her exhausted sister and gave her a smile, the kind that, though all the "sisters" were carbon copies of each other's genome, only Kadmus could give, a smile that stitched together a half dozen emotions— contradictory—all at once and in a language only her other iterations could read. This smile was triumph, sadness, love, anxiety, and relief, all painted across her full, purple lips, amethyst to match the hair that flowed like a crystal wave over her back. Then she turned on her heel and walked down the corridor as the doors of the little room slid silently shut and the two legionnaires that had accompanied them took their place just outside of it. Kalaiapi began to root through the storage containers for something to eat.

71

"I do not understand this word 'Singularity,' Kalaiapi." Over the past couple of weeks, Mortis Drak's personality had begun to break through the shell of his limited programming. His vocabulary was growing, as was the catalog of concepts he could reference to express himself and the world around him. Kalaiapi would never know if the progress she was seeing with him would have ever been possible with the other automatons that now blew around the surface of Calx as dust and ashes, but she couldn't help but wonder with a pang of regret. She had thought, occasionally, of how she would have felt had the arriving fleet on that gray wasteland been from the Confederation, bringing with it all the equipment and personnel necessary to transform these poor slaves into real members of the progenasis.

By the teachings of the Aya, Kalaiapi had no place to mourn the loss of those thousands of slaves. After all, whatever their possible potential, they didn't exist, were of no more meaning or value than the withered ferals she had dismembered in the vine jungles. That seemed like eons ago, now.

Had she mourned their deaths? Considered their potential? But that was prior to seeing what they had been before they descended into that savage baseness. Prior to encountering 63177 and learning that one of these had gone in utterly the opposite direction, had become self-aware, had understood the nature of its being. Well, to a certain extent. Was the potential for existence not in and of itself a kind of existence or at least something that had value? Something whose lack should be regretted?

In the end it had been no one's fault. Kalaiapi had seen the threat with her own eyes, the unstoppable destructive force that was those five wraith creatures on the planet. Creatures, weapons, whatever they were. If they ever escaped Calx, or could reproduce, or were somehow affiliated with the Primus, then the whole project was finished. The premise of the Confederation, of the Aya, of the high genasi species was to defeat Omnia, the Universe, in its own zero sum game, to survive its every attempt to wipe out the species. With every planet that was colonized, with every low genasi culture that was guided in its evolution, with every generation of cultivated evolution, another stitch was made in the seam that would hold the progenasis together against the constant violence of nature. But what she had seen on Calx would cut through those seams like fire, would eradicate the progenasis person by person, planet by planet, piece by piece. Talking to Mortis Drak had at least been a distraction from that eventuality.

"Ah, yes, I suppose you wouldn't. The 'Singularity' is the notion that at some point we as a species will achieve a level of technological advancement that will essentially become self-perpetuating, unlocking every possibility imaginable through a constantly advancing process of growth. There are some who believe that once we can achieve technological Singularity we will have finally defeated Omnia for good because we will no longer be limited by so many of the things that hold us back now, space and time and friction."

"You made it sound as though such an event is not desirable, though."

"Well, I'm ambivalent about the whole thing. Of two minds. On the one hand, perhaps a Singularity really would be the final key to overcoming nature, to ensuring the survival of the progenasis into perpetuity. Um, that is, forever."

"And on the other hand?" Kalaiapi had been impressed by his ability to grasp and employ idioms. He was a quick study.

"On the other hand," she continued, "the Singularity represents perhaps the biggest extinction threat of all, greater even than the Primus." But not, perhaps, greater than the wraiths.

"I don't understand." A contraction. Very good.

"Well, there are two issues at play here, one following from the other. The first is that many, myself included, believe such a Singularity cannot be achieved without first creating some kind of artificial super intelligence, something powerful enough to spark the process of self-perpetuating advancement."

"But the Aya forbids artificial intelligence, does it not?"

"Precisely, Mortis Drak. Very good. And do you remember why?" She cast a furtive sideways glance at Kaaio, orbiting around her head arrayed in ash gray, a miniature Calx.

"Because it is considered an extinction event."

"One of the 'big three,' the others being the arrival of the Primus, against which we continue to struggle, and the third being the eventual and inevitable Collapse when the Axial Quasar finally implodes and drags the Galaxy along with it. Of course, if by that point we're not an intergalactic species, nothing else will matter."

"Are we close?" asked Mortis Drak.

"Close to what?"

"To being an intergalactic species?"

Kalaiapi laughed gently. "Not at all, my friend. That's the paradox of it all. We struggle constantly for our survival with the knowledge that as long as we are imprisoned by these three dimensions in which we find ourselves, it will all be in vain when the Quasar implodes. So, to free the species from this galactic prison and truly become as endless as Omnia itself, we must achieve the Singularity. But in order to achieve this Singularity, we must create super intelligence and by doing so we become the authors of our own extinction. Do you understand?"

"I believe I do," he said slowly, his voice rumbling like low thunder. "Then why do you bother? You sound as though you are resigned to the destruction of the species by one or another force. So what is the point of all of this?" He gestured around them with his hands as though indicating not just the dreadnought but the entire space in which the progenasis dwelt.

"I can't speak for everyone, I suppose, but as for me, well– because there is joy in existence, I suppose. Because the Galaxy is full of beauty that is only reified by progenasi eyes to gaze upon it. Because of the love I feel for my–" she struggled to say it. "Because of the love I feel for my... sister." It was the first time she had ever referred to Kadmus that way. "And because I know that feeling is replicated by the billions throughout our species, yes, even among the Polarans, even among these Fornaxians, though it may not seem obvious. Existence in and of itself has value, Mortis Drak, that is what I'm trying to teach you."

"I do not know these feelings of which you speak, Kalaiapi. I do not have a sister. But I do remember the first time I looked up into the dark sky over the coldside ice fields and wondered." His voice had slowly begun to take on a different intonation, moving away from the flat monotone of his programming and adopting the more natural timbre of his nascent personality. "Does wondering at the sky have value, Kalaiapi?"

"Oh, yes," she replied with a smile. "Planet-bound progenasi wondering at the sky is what has gotten us to where we are in the first place. Anyway, have I answered your question?"

"No," he said, and began to stroke his smooth, slate gray chin. He was no longer jet black, but a lifetime of tube-fed cannibalism appeared to have permanently changed the pigmentation in his skin. "And what of these," he gestured toward the door beyond which two Fornaxian legionnaires stood guard. "What do they think of this 'Singularity'?"

"Well, that's where the complications arise, isn't it?" He raised his eyebrows curiously, another recent development: facial expressions. Kalaiapi could have clapped for joy but instead continued her explanation, her rich, honeyed voice echoing in the bare chamber in which they had been imprisoned. "Of course, both sides–and I say 'both' as though there are two, but in fact there are many others–recognize the dangers of artificial intelligence while both also seek after the Singularity. The Confederation seeks to achieve the Singularity by unlocking the genetic potential of the progenasi mind through 'cultivated evolution,' a careful plotting of evolution's course. They believe the Axial Locks are genetic, that they can be opened with the right biological code. And so, select high genasi become sort of…experiments, then gene pariahs."

"What kind of experiments? And what is a gene pariah?"

"Bioenhancement, gene grafts, artificially induced mutations, these are all part of the process called 'genomancing.' Some of it is experimental, tests performed to see if they can be better used to understand and improve the cultivation process. Some of it is deliberate, using genomancing to create the likes of pilots and Corsairs that the

Confederation sees as exceptions to Ayic proscription but a necessary part of the battle against Omnic Malevolence. The Confederation tests its lockpicks on people like me in order to see if they can find the key that unlocks evolution for the entire progenasis."

"And so you are a gene pariah?"

"That's the compromise one makes. Or rather, the compromise that is made on one's behalf. You serve the species but are removed from the great evolutionary march. You are a sentinel or a servant of evolution, I suppose, but you are no longer a participant. One hundred millennia of genetic transfer end with you." She turned away from Mortis Drak.

"What are these Axial Locks you speak of?" he asked, unable to comprehend the emotional weight of the questions he posed.

Kalaiapi brushed a hand across her eyes and turned back to face him again, smiling faintly, a patient teacher. "A theory among the high genasi that when we were created by the Axials they placed within our genetic coding limits that could not be overcome without sufficient natural and undirected evolution. 'Organic' evolution, some call it. These locks exist, or so the theory goes, to prevent the species from achieving its full potential before it is fully prepared for the consequences and responsibilities of such." Mortis Drak nodded. She was fairly certain he understood what she was explaining but could never really know. "In any case, the Council of Eternals has only recently, that is to say within my lifetime, come to the conclusion that we have evolved sufficiently as a species to begin the next step in the process: self-perpetuated evolution. And so the initial, tenuous stages of more widespread genomancing have begun. To much...controversy."

"Yes, but what about the Clade?" he asked.

"Well, this was the very source of the conflict, you see. The Fornaxians, in particular, though others joined them, believe that genetic enhancement was a dead end. They believe the key to evolution goes beyond toying with our genome, though they are not opposed to it."

"What, then, is their proposal?"

"Well, I'm getting to that, Mortis Drak. They wish to see the progenasis combine itself with technology, believing that only by doing so can we engender the intelligence necessary to achieve technological and biological Singularity. Biotech syncresis, they call it."

"But, is this not considered an abomination by the Aya?"

Kalaiapi reached back and touched her spine where her neural interface had been just a few weeks ago. "Thus the civil war," she concluded.

"And what do you believe, Kalaiapi?"

She sat silently for some time as Mortis Drak looked intently at her. "I believe," she finally replied, running her hand over her head, "that my hair has finally grown back and for that I am incredibly grateful."

72

"Kalaiapi, if you wanted to, you could easily escape from this room, kill the guards outside, and deliver all of us from this ship. Why do you not?"

"Because, Kaaio, I gave my parole and I will not violate it. It's an ancient custom that high genasi respect amongst each other and I shan't be the one who casts it aside."

"Yes, but they might be the ones who do," came Kaaio's insistent and worried thoughts.

"And when that happens, they will have violated the terms and I will escape. Or at least try. But not until. The Navarch, at least, seems to be a man of his word."

"But you said yourself that it will not be the Navarch's decision once we arrive in Fornax. It will be the Tyraness', whatever or whoever that is. And frankly, Kalaiapi, it is not a title that inspires thoughts of mercy in my DNA circuitry."

"I will admit to having little knowledge of Tiyadotia, Tyraness of Fornax, and what she's about. At the time of the schism she was merely the planetary governor, subject to the Tyrant of Polaris and Her Empire, Ylyogavilis."

"Had you never visited Fornax before the war?" Kaaio asked. Kalaiapi was momentarily annoyed at herself for piquing the little marble's seemingly limitless curiosity then realized how glad she actually was of the conversation.

"Certainly, I had," she replied. "But I didn't meet with the governor, I was there coordinating my missions with local elements of the Combine. It's not the sort of thing planetary governors tend to concern themselves with."

"I see," said Kaaio resignedly with whatever the thought version of a sigh would be. "Then you cannot attempt to gauge what kind of decision she will make regarding you? Though, really, I should say 'us.'"

"A noteworthy point, young brain marble. I think the only thing I can do is assume the worst, that I'll be pulled apart cell by cell and distributed like sand across the face of Fornax for the crime of being an agent of the Confederation. The truth is that since the detente between our two sides, we have had essentially no contact with the Clade and our intelligence operations against them have been an abysmal failure. We may arrive to find that they are the most enlightened and misunderstood of peoples who will forgive me my sins, bedeck me with garlands, and send me on my way back to Ad Astara riding the warm solar winds of their well wishes. Or we may find a hive of savagery and violence where they skin me alive with dull stones. I genuinely cannot say. Even high genasi societies can undergo a great deal of societal upheaval in a century and I am bracing for the worst."

Kalaiapi stood and walked over to the metalloy crate that acted as a vanity, picked up a brush and began to run it through her long, snow white hair, luxurious and thick as it had ever been, a foaming white wave running down her back. Ever since it had gotten back to full length, and given the amount of free time she had, she spent a great deal of time sitting on her cot and ponderously running the hand-carved Astaran hornwood brush through the thick locks. The brush had been a gift from Kadmus, meaningful in that it was irreplaceable for her. There was certainly little chance that anyone would be smuggling hand-carved wooden brushes from Ad Astara to a planet where the vast majority of men and women eschewed such luxuries as hair.

She stopped for a moment and held the brush in her hands, staring at it, taking in for the thousandth time the rich details of the carvings. Flowers, waves, vines that entwined around the handle, common, almost cliche Astaran motifs but warmly familiar. Perhaps these carvings were the closest she would ever again get to seeing Ad Astara and all its splendor. The notion plunged into her heart like an anchor into the sandy ocean floor. Was this how Kadmus felt all the time? The pain with which she lived because she had chosen principles over homeland?

"Did you know, Kaaio, that many, if not most high genasi these days are completely hairless?"

"I apologize, Kalaiapi, but I am afraid I lack the context to know if that statement should be considered meaningful or simply idle banter."

"Come now, you should know my banter is never idle," she said, now speaking out loud. Mortis Drak lay on his cot, sound asleep. It had taken quite some time to teach him how to do it, but he had taken to the activity with some alacrity. An easy cure for the withering boredom for which his mind was not equipped. "You see, it's considered to be a sign of high evolution. Low genasi have no choice but to be covered in hair. It's almost animalistic, a holdover from the seed genes from which they were evolved so many thousands of years ago by the Axials. To have the choice of hair is to remind all those who gaze upon you that you are the eldest, the first creations of the Axials, the most advanced, the furthest removed from nature. Thus baldness is a sign of superiority."

"I see. But you and Kadmus, you choose to have hair. Why is that?"

"We come from the colonies where such fashions are not in vogue, or at least they weren't a few hundred years ago. On God's Eye most people were more practically minded. Life on the colonies is harder, more dangerous, more likely to be ended in a short burst of Primus bastardry. So you worry less about whether or not you have hair. My sisters and I never adopted the metropolitan fashion of hairlessness because we never wanted to forget where we came from...and what had happened to it." She placed the brush back on the crate. "Besides, look how beautiful it is, and how powerful, this hair which Omnic Providence gifted me at birth. An avalanche, Kaaio. An avalanche."

73

"Alright, then, Kadmus," said Cadaster as he took a seat in the plain, hard chair in his ready room. "To whom does all this pilfered anima belong? Because I saw with my own eyes that those colonies were no more Primic than this dreadnought. So, do you, who saw the guts of these facilities, have any theories, or better yet, facts regarding the proprietors?"

"I have theories, Navarch," she replied, pacing the room. She was wearing a clean cut, ornate (by Polaran standards), legionnaire dress uniform, the high black collar decorated with gold filigree and with royal blue cords at the shoulders. A matching blue stripe ran down the length of her black slacks until they met a pair of spectacular blue military boots that had caused the Navarch to wrinkle his nose in disgust at first glance. They were not part of the standard dress uniform. As she paced, her long, violet hair swished back and forth against her jacket. "But I'll say that whoever built those facilities covered their tracks fairly well and that as far as I could tell they had indeed been abandoned."

The Navarch looked impatient. "What are they, Corsair?"

"My theories? Oh, yes. I apologize, I'm a bit distracted."

"Undistract yourself, Corsair."

Kadmus turned and rolled her eyes but recomposed herself. "The facility is, or was, built by progenasi. The structures themselves had none of the hallmarks of Primic construction and they certainly wouldn't be motivated to hide such signatures. What are we going to do? Hate them more? We know they harvest anima from other slaves, but nothing like this. Besides, the Primus would never have abandoned something so valuable and they'd have destroyed it before letting it fall into our hands." The Navarch nodded in agreement, his hands clasped together on his marble desk, his face a stone wall.

"Whoever built it clearly couldn't risk getting caught. This points to progenasi. To high genasi," she continued.

"Could it not have been autochthons?" queried Cadaster.

"Well, we don't believe any of them has the technology to put together a facility like this, much less benefit from it. You know yourself that to actually put refined anima to any kind of use is incredibly technical and dangerous. Besides, none of them would risk it. The progenasi are at peace with all autochthonous species at the moment and there's none that the Confederation wouldn't wipe from the face of the Galaxy for such a heinous crime."

"And that leaves us with what options? Who has betrayed their own species this way?"

"As far as I can tell, Navarch, there are two potential culprits, given that we can eliminate the Clade from contention," she added with a wry smile. "The first would be rogue evolutionists."

"Are there any that have the resources to execute such an endeavor?"

"Possibly. It's always particularly difficult to assess intelligence on rogue evolutionists due to the great lengths they go to hide themselves from our view. But when I was a Combine agent we had tracked down at least one cabal of Astarans that had set themselves up as gods over a large and until-then-unknown middle genasi planet and had exploited the populace to amass a remarkable amount of concentrated resources. Could a group like that potentially muster the knowledge and material to build the colonies?" She clucked her tongue thoughtfully. "Perhaps. But unlikely."

"So, then, this leaves us with one truly viable candidate."

"Indeed, it does, Navarch. Calx belongs to the Confederation. Or, it did."

Cadaster grunted his assent. Kadmus knew he already knew everything she was saying and it was unlike him to spend this much time having someone explain to him things that he could so easily reason out for himself. Likely, he had been as astounded as she by the conclusion and its implications and thus felt an extraordinarily rare need to have it independently confirmed.

"By all that we hold sacred, Kadmus."

"Indeed, Navarch."

"Do you think your sister knows?"

"She knows, but she found out the same way I did. That said, I'm entirely certain she has not yet admitted the truth to herself. Kalaiapi is capable of a level of cognitive dissonance I have always personally found difficult to maintain."

"No one else can know. This must stay between us, for now. It could be as destructive to the species as those creatures we encountered on the planet. We still bear a responsibility to all progenasi, Kadmus." Again, Cadaster would have known that Kadmus had already ascertained as much. That he felt the need to say it out loud spoke volumes. "Speaking of which, I do not suppose you have any theories on those? Surely, they are not also Confederation products?"

"This time, Navarch, I can genuinely say that I have no theories. I've never seen anything like them in my life and they didn't appear on the planet until the legion arrived. I feel quite certain the Confederation is incapable of creating such a weapon. Or life form. Or whatever they are."

"Where did they come from, Kadmus?" There was an edge to the Navarch's voice she had never heard before. Before she could answer, they were interrupted by a message from the dreadnought's science bay that transmitted simultaneously to chips in their ears.

"Sir, we're ready to begin testing on the anima."

"Very good," replied Cadaster.

"Finally," said Kadmus. It had taken an agonizingly long time to stabilize the anima and to create an environment in which it could be properly examined. The Navarch stood and straightened his jacket. "Well, then," said Kadmus with a flicker of a smile. "Shall we go and survey the spoils?"

74

Kadmus stepped out of the shuttle after Cadaster and walked into the massive science bay where a bevy of Fornaxian scientists busied themselves tinkering with an assortment of blinking contraptions and chemicals in clear polymer tubes and vials. Several of them had bundles of wires that extended from metal rivets in their bald pates and hooked into the machines they were using. Pilots weren't the only ones who sometimes needed to be directly integrated into their work.

On the far side of the room, Kadmus could see the space that had been set aside to work with the newly acquired anima, the bulk of which was being stored elsewhere in a purpose built container. A small (by Polaran standards) man in a long, pale-blue frock coat approached them, his enthusiasm and excitement apparent in his gait if not on his face. His smooth, perfectly round, gray-brown head was speckled with small, silvery studs. When he reached Cadaster and Kadmus he stopped and gave the slightest bow.

"Navarch," he crowed in his deep, slightly nasal voice. "We have finished our initial survey and we are finally ready to begin deeper testing of the anima. Would you like me to transmit the survey to you before we begin?"

"Yes, Gemmyl, do. But it will take some time to examine the survey. Summarize it for me before we begin."

"Yes, Navarch." He looked at Kadmus nervously, her face bearing the slight but ever-present sarcastic smirk that so discomfited the stone-faced Fornaxians. "Even with what we left on the planet, I would venture to say that we are now in possession of the single largest amount of anima ever produced and collected in one location. It must be the harvest of hundreds of thousands of those bioautomatons. Frankly, Navarch, I have never even heard of anything like it." Kadmus began fidgeting with the filigree on her collar.

"Go on," urged the Navarch flatly.

"We estimate this anima will fulfill the Clade's needs for a century or more. This amount of anima could revolutionize Fornaxian society and beyond. It could change the face of the Galaxy, Navarch. It could break the locks." The scientist was almost becoming agitated, was on the verge of betraying his ecstasy at the opportunity.

"I am not particularly interested in speculation, quite yet, Gemmyl. The Tyraness has a specific purpose set aside for this anima and until she has decreed otherwise, it is under her personal jurisdiction. She will decide its fate." They were walking now across the bay, receiving looks that ranged from bored to curious to slightly annoyed from the scientists as they passed.

"Of course, Navarch. We do her will and nothing more. Ah, here we are."

A secure area had been created in the bay, a special laboratory with thick but transparent polymer walls in which three scientists in environmental protection suits and masks stood waiting for the Navarch to arrive, the telltale tubes protruding from their slightly grotesque helmets. Kadmus knew exactly where Gemmyl's almost childlike giddiness came from. He was one of many Fornaxians who believed that, used correctly, refined anima was the key to creating the levels of intelligence that would break the Axial locks and allow for a biological Singularity, a Singularity that rather than requiring destructive artificial intelligence would turn the progenasi brain (or at least a small number of them) into true supercomputers capable of achieving the same results.

Much of this speculation was fueled by another long-held

belief among the high genasi that the Axials themselves were either made entirely or mostly from pure anima formed in the Quasar and this was what had allowed them and no other extant species in the Galaxy to reach anything like a Singularity in which there was no longer any question of impossibility in any field. Kadmus was skeptical, but it was at least established that anima was the stuff of progenasi intelligence and consciousness, so perhaps there was something to the theory.

"Very well, Gemmyl, let us begin the analysis," said Cadaster.

One of the tube-headed scientists opened a massive, rectangular, metalloy storage tank and, using magnetic tongs, withdrew from it a small, silver vial the size of one of Cadaster's considerable fingers. The vial floated between the tongs as the scientist gingerly brought it toward one of the analytical machines into which one of her colleagues was plugged. The first scientist placed the vial gently into the machine, where it continued to hover as a panel slid over the top of it. A third scientist, working a tactile that was invisible to the onlookers, began gesticulating in the air. There was a sudden flash of white light as the anima poured from the contained vial and filled a series of clear, narrow pipes that jutted from the machine at seemingly haphazard angles, filling them with an otherworldly radiance. Kadmus stared, transfixed by the beauty of the process.

The wired-in scientist stood perfectly still in front of the machine as it transmitted information directly into his brain to be sorted and analyzed. A moment passed, and suddenly a shudder went through the scientist's white-suited body.

"Something is wrong, Navarch," said Gemmyl in a pinched voice. Kadmus took a step closer toward the lab, her head cocked curiously. The scientist shuddered again then raised his hands to his masked head, first clutching at his skull, then tearing at it furiously, dislodging tubes and tearing wires. One of the other scientists ran to him, trying to calm and control but to no avail. "What is wrong with him? Hyuma, patch him through! Durruhs, what is happening?" the head scientist asked, his voice now desperate. But the only reply from the stricken scientist came in the form of hoarse, mask-muffled screaming as he began now to beat his fists on his helmet and claw at the base of his skull. Then, in an instant, he became perfectly still and in another instant collapsed into a heap on the floor of the lab. The other two scientists looked up toward the Navarch and Gemmyl.

"Gemmyl," said Hyuma, her voice trembling slightly, "there's something wrong with this anima."

"No shit," Kadmus replied.

75

"It's a virus," she said flatly. There was no smirk on her face now.

"What kind of virus could possibly be carried in anima?" asked Kalaiapi, somewhat flabbergasted.

"We're not entirely sure, yet. It's difficult to analyze, given the circumstances. The first person to contract it was a Clade scientist. It literally melted his brain. We pulled his helmet off and it poured out onto the floor. This appears to have been a unique case, however, probably something to do with the nature of his contact and the dozens of tech implants in his skull."

"Why would the tech implants have any kind of effect on his reaction to the virus?"

"That's the thing, Kalaiapi. The virus isn't biological. It's tech."

Kalaiapi gawped. "What do you mean 'it's tech?' Then it's not a virus at all."

"It's both. The virus is nanotechnology. Microscopic particles that have been attacking the Fornaxians' mechanical implants."

"And you?" asked Kalaiapi, now worried.

Kadmus tapped the small metal stub that jutted from the base of her skull where it met her spine. "It's only a matter of time, I suppose, though I can't be certain. We don't yet know all that much about how the virus works or what it specifically attacks. We're still studying the anima, but scientists keep dying and we're starting to run low on personnel."

"I assume we've stopped our course to Fornax?"

"Of course. We're a plague ship now. We can't go back there or to any other high genasi planet, not without knowing anything about this disease we carry or where it came from."

"And where do you think it came from?"

"Well, my first thought would be that it came from wherever the anima came from," she said, giving Kalaiapi a piercing look. Kalaiapi responded by looking uncomfortable, then glanced at Mortis Drak, who stood arms crossed and silent in a corner of the room, a slight glower on his face. "No, I don't mean him. There's no evidence, yet, that the virus is 'naturally' occurring or inherent to the anima. It's not floating around in his brain. It seems to be a sort of additive. Specially engineered."

"Then what do you mean? Speak plainly, Kadmus, if you're making an accusation."

"I believe it came from your Confederation, Kalaiapi," she replied immediately. "I believe that the same people whose depths of hypocrisy permit them to build a facility to harvest a sacred element from the exploited dead of their own species, members of which they created specifically for such a purpose, would have no qualms about creating a virus to murder countless billions of those who have the audacity not to be led to extinction by those too myopic to advance our progenasis to its ideal end." She was incensed now.

"You dare speak to me of hypocrisy?" Kalaiapi took a step toward Kadmus, who stood defiant. "Look at you and your Navarch. Unwilling to swing the ax but happy to cheer on the execution and rob the graves of the condemned, nonetheless," she retorted. "Perhaps you're correct, Kadmus, perhaps the Confederation did build that colony, and if they did then they have committed an anathaya and the Eternal Council will hold them responsible. But the moment you and your legionnaires landed on that planet with the willingness to let it continue, to leave these slaves to their horror lives while you returned in triumph to the Clade with their very souls in tow as your spoils, well, then you became no better and all barbs of hypocrisy that you fling come scorching back at you—and no penance you make will ever efface the crime you have done to the species on Calx and so the species as a whole."

Kadmus was taken aback. In 700 years Kalaiapi had never spoken to her that way. "Kalaiapi, you don't understand! How could you? We are here to save the progenasis, to end the struggle for survival and allow us to expand and evolve past these petty wars between us. We are here to finally achieve the Sing—"

"There is no fucking Singularity, Kadmus," Kalaiapi shouted. "There are only people, there are only progenasi people whose lives have more value than this revenge fantasy to which you've become addicted—yes, addicted—and all because you can never forgive the Confederation for taking you from our parents and casting you out of the gene pool. Well, guess what, Kadmus, I never forgave them either, but that doesn't mean that I'd forsake everything I've known, everything we fought for, everything we killed for, to help instigate a war that led to millions of progenasi deaths, and worst of all, forsake us, leave us behind to do so." Tears flowed freely now, her voice was a furious storm fueled by a century of churning grievances and an unhealed broken heart.

"Kadmus, why did you come here?"

"I...I came for the anima–"

"No, Kadmus, why did you come here? Even now you cannot lie to me. Your words when I found you back on Calx. Your lip service to the Clade's aspirations, to its ideology. I know it is nonsense, I know it is so much interference and bloviation, a screen to hide your true feelings from me, to hide them even from yourself." She placed a hand on Kadmus' rose pink cheek. "Why did you come here, Kadmus?"

"Kalaiapi, I–"

"Why did you come here, Kadmus?" Kalaiapi half-sobbed, half-screamed, now. "Do you even now not understand? Are the nerves in your soul so dead? If that is so, then do not say another word to me that is not an apology, Kadmus. Because we have lived with a thorn in our heart for a century because of you and the bleeding never stops and it never will. Do you understand? Fuck the Confederation, Kadmus, and the Clade, as well. It was us. And you left us. You left us without explanation, without understanding, without even so much as a goodbye."

"How did this become a conversation about my betrayal?"

"Because you've betrayed me now a second time, Kadmus, when you left those slaves to die on that planet without so much as a second thought. And you betrayed us when you found us again after a century and you chose your vengeance over our love." There was a pause then, a few moments that felt as long as the centuries they had lived.

"I...you're right, Kalaiapi. By the Aya, you're right." She stood still for a moment, looking past Kalaiapi to a wall at the back of the room, her clear violet eyes growing wet. She ran her hands over her face through her crystalline hair as though forcing the tears back into her eyes, and the despair off of her visage. "I have to go. I'll return soon. I'm...I'm sorry, Kalaiapi." As she turned to leave, a jolt rocked the small room and she nearly stumbled.

"What was that?" asked Kalaiapi? "Are we under attack?"

Kadmus put her hand up to her ear. "No. There's been an explosion in the science bay. One of the anima tubes." The door opened and Kadmus sprinted down the corridor.

76

"Come on, Mortis Drak, we can't stay here."

"Kalaiapi, what is happening?" asked Kaaio, agitated.

"Kaaio, if there was an anima explosion big enough to shake this dreadnought, there is a decent chance we are all about to die. At the very least, something catastrophic has happened and I refuse to sit in this cell and wait to find out what it is by trying to breathe space. Prior experience has taught me that it is extraordinarily painful." She approached the door, which reacted to her presence by remaining utterly still.

"How are we going to get out, Kalaiapi," asked Mortis Drak. "You said the door is bio-locked and impenetrable."

"So it is. But watch." She closed her eyes for a moment. When she opened them, the door slid open and she stepped out into the empty corridor. The guards were gone.

"Kalaiapi, how did you do that?" asked Kaaio.

"Simple, Kaaio. I'm Kadmus."

"But, surely they would have accounted for that in setting the lock? They're not that foolish are they?" Kalaiapi was already sprinting down the corridor with Mortis Drak close on her heels.

"Oh, of course, Kaaio," she said out loud as she ran. Mortis Drak had long ago accepted that Kalaiapi sometimes talked to herself and had ceased to ask questions about it. "But what do you think I've been doing these past weeks? Simply growing out my hair? Changing my bio-signature to match Kadmus' was surprisingly simple, actually. I simply saved one last piece of code for when we actually needed it. I wouldn't worry too much about it; Kadmus would have known this would happen." Kadmus would have known this would happen, that Kalaiapi would eventually be able to pass through the unbreakable door like fog. And yet she had said nothing, had not prevented it. The ship's halls were disconcertingly abandoned.

"How far from here is the science bay, Kalaiapi?" asked Mortis Drak, chasing after her without flagging despite her breakneck pace.

"Well, I assume this is laid out the same as any other

dreadnought, which means we need to find a shuttle station or we'll be running and climbing through maintenance tubes for the next hour at least. Thank Omnic Providence for the Polaran obsession with uniformity. Here we are."

She stopped fast in front of a pair of clear polymer sliding doors that led to the magrail tram stop. Where normally there would have been a guard stationed, there was no one. Kadmus hadn't been exaggerating the loss of personnel. Such a breakdown of discipline would be unheard of unless there was truly no one left to man the post. The station sensed her presence and called a shuttle, actually a large capsule capable of holding a dozen people that would be rushed on magrails through the belly of the ship until they arrived at their destination.

"Kalaiapi," said Mortis Drak. "How much longer can the ship continue to function if the virus kills off the pilots?"

Even in this moment of impending doom, Kalaiapi couldn't help but smile at her student's burgeoning understanding. "That's an excellent insight, Mortis Drak," she replied. "I would estimate that if half of the 173 pilots typically assigned to a dreadnought are killed, it will become rudderless—which, by the way, we are. A few more and it becomes dead in the water—which, I'll wager, we're about to be. At 20 or fewer, I believe it would cease to maintain basic functions like life support. These are the most massive ships in the progenasi fleet. The amount of brain power required for them to work normally is incredible. The navigation system alone requires at least twelve working in concert."

The shuttle slid to a silent stop and they stepped out into the dark corridor only to be greeted by a chorus of inhuman screaming. Kalaiapi broke back into a sprint. The doors to the science bay were open and they looked out onto a scene of utter carnage. The entire expanse of the bay was soaked in crimson and there, in the middle of it all, perhaps ten smoky figures floated through a red mist from legionnaire to frantically firing legionnaire, eviscerating and destroying. Kalaiapi hadn't seen them quite this close on Calx. They were unlike anything she'd ever laid eyes on, somehow both completely solid and yet fluid, one moment forming into their progenasi shape and then effortlessly filtering into a legionnaire's armor and exploding into a cloud of bloody vapor.

Something grabbed her roughly by the arm. She turned and saw Kadmus, covered in a veneer of blood that made her pink skin a ghastly bright vermilion. The cacophony of shrieking, the snapping of chemprop rifles, the electric roar of lightning lances was deafening.

"Kalaiapi, we have to get out of here," Kadmus yelled,

looking quickly around to see the wraiths continuing their work. "The ship is lost."

"Where did they come from?" Kalaiapi shouted back as they hurtled through the hallway and into the shuttle they had just left. "How did they get onto the ship?"

"It's the anima," Kadmus replied, collapsing onto a seat in the now coursing magrail pod. "At least, that's the only thing I can guess." She wiped the blood from her face and smeared it on the seat next to her. "Optis Tor said he had been in a nearby section when a massive explosion shuddered through the whole side of the ship. He ran to the science bay, guessing as anyone would that it had been an anima tube. Luckily the fail safes in the bay seem to have done their job and contained the explosion, but of course everyone in the bay was disintegrated. And in their place? These blasted death ghosts. Optis Tor is dead, now."

"I don't understand, Kadmus, the anima exploded and, what, created these creatures from thin air?"

"I don't know, Kalaiapi. I don't know." Her hair was dark, matted with gore. "What I do know is that the security data transmitted to me a few minutes ago showed that there were the exact same number of personnel in the science bay at the time of the explosion as there are wraiths in there, now."

"Are you saying—"

"I'm not saying anything, Kalaiapi, except that you need to take Mortis Drak and get off this ship."

"And what about you?"

"This ship and all its contents must be destroyed or the progenasis truly is in peril. Between the virus and these things, it cannot be allowed to make it any further than these recesses of space in which we currently float."

"But you said you weren't infected, you can join us getting off the ship, surely. Can you not destroy it remotely?"

Kadmus stood and let out an exasperated groan. "Kalaiapi, I lied to you. Of course I'm infected. The entire ship is. There's not a one of us who doesn't have some kind of implant. It was always going to come to this, dear girl. Very recent events have merely precipitated the urgency."

"And what about Cadaster? Is this not his responsibility as Navarch?"

Kadmus sighed and looked at Kalaiapi sadly. "Kalaiapi, the Navarch was in the science bay when the anima erupted. What remains of him is in the room we just left. Cadaster is dead. Everyone is dead."

77

Everyone was not dead. In fact, Kadmus knew from the continuing flow of data that there were 25 surviving pilots who were desperately working together to keep the ship intact and life support functions online. They would fail soon and gradually the dreadnought would be nothing more than an enormous floating tomb, the wraiths' work done for them by a system failure. The pilots were spread throughout the ship, both to be nearer to the sections they managed and to prevent one well-placed broadside from crippling the entire vessel. Kadmus hoped this would prolong the amount of time it took for the dreadnought's invaders to murder them and thus give her time to figure out how to destroy the ship in a way that would hopefully also annihilate these strange and deadly creatures.

When they arrived at the dock that housed the emergency skiffs they found a surprisingly orderly group of legionnaires and crew waiting their turn to board and depart the doomed dreadnought. There was no fighting over places, no bickering, no panicking in the face of certain death. It was perhaps the most impressive thing Kadmus had ever seen. She was horrified at what she was about to do as she approached Commander Horuhs, who appeared to be calmly directing the evacuation. A cheer went up among the legionnaires as they saw her, still covered from head to toe in a crust of blood, walking down the dock. Her heart felt as though it were being crushed by a neutron star.

"Commander, may I speak with you for a moment?" she said. He rushed toward her, relief written all over his face.

"Corsair Kadmus," he said in a flat tone laced with a joy only distinguishable to those familiar with Polaran modes of speech. "We are pleased to see you made it. Have you news of the Navarch?"

"The Navarch is dead, Commander, and I believe it's safe to assume that anyone not standing on this dock is the same or inevitably about to be so."

"That is most unfortunate news," said Horuhs, his despair less subtle than his joy.

"Commander, I'm afraid we haven't much time." A lump

began to form in her throat and she choked it down. It was somewhat of a mystery how she had grown to love these stone-faced, tradition-bound milites, but love them she did. "Commander, stand down the evacuation."

For perhaps the first time in his life, the Commander's deeply conditioned sense of hierarchy and obedience wavered. "Beg pardon, Corsair?"

"Stand it, down, Commander. Immediately."

He didn't hesitate a second time, sending a silent order to the half dozen Opti that were marshaling the troops into the skiffs. The escape procession ground to a sudden halt.

"I'm sorry, Commander. Let me explain." She clambered on top of a large stack of metalloy containers until she was well above the crowd of several hundred legionnaires and crewmen who now stood stock still gazing up at her.

"Progenasi of Fornax, milites of the Clade," she began, her velvety voice now booming across the dock. "Today, I must ask you to die as such. Omnic Providence has beset our vessel with two great misfortunes, both of which threaten not only this awesome ship but also the lives of its valiant crew. Moreover, and more importantly, they threaten the very progenasis itself. We are all infected by the virus, and now our dreadnought contains within its belly a creature more fearsome than any we've seen." She took a deep breath.

"Neither can be allowed to leave and so we all must stay. I stay, too, to die by your side, which is the greatest honor of my long life. I ask now that you fight with me one last time and give me the opportunity to condemn our enemies to Oblivion as we commit ourselves to Glory. Will you fight and die with me now?"

A deafening cheer went up from the assembled troops. As she loved them, they loved their Corsair.

"For Fornax! For the Clade! For the Progenasis!" she called out, and with a second cheer, this time a battle cry, they ran back down the tunnels to their inevitable deaths, by each of which they hoped to stall their killers by just a few seconds.

Commander Horuhs lingered behind and waited as Kadmus jumped down from the tower of crates. "Corsair Kadmus, we will do what is necessary. I am glad you caught us before many could leave."

"How many skiffs did leave, Commander," she asked. "And with how many on board?"

"Seven, Corsair. One-hundred fifty-three on board."

"Shit. Shit. Shit." It was worse than she had hoped. One was bad. Seven was an absolute disaster. "Very well, Commander. Though it won't last long—I expect—I will remember you with Glory."

"And I you, Corsair. Do not let the bastards escape." And

with that, he followed his troops back into the bowels of the massive ship to find his death.

Kalaiapi had lingered behind, feeling self-conscious and guilty as she watched hundreds of her enemies rush to a noble demise. Now she hurried down the dock to meet her sister.

"Kalaiapi, seven skiffs escaped. They carry with them the doom of billions. Please, Kalaiapi. Please. I beg you now, forgive me, but do not let them reach Fornax. I'll do what I can from here, but they may already be out of range or the weapons systems may no longer be functioning. Don't let them end Fornax."

"I'll do whatever I can, Kadmus, you know it."

"I do."

"They won't be able to go too far too fast without gravity drives, but then again, neither will I. But there are no odds for a Corsair, eh?" She smiled, her cornflower eyes bright with tears.

"I haven't much time, Kalaiapi. Please tell Rho and Æa I love them and that I'm sorry. Not for joining the Clade, I suppose. But for leaving you. For everything you said." Kalaiapi was openly weeping now.

"Kadmus, please don't leave me again. I cannot bear it. I don't care about the virus, Kadmus, I would sacrifice the species for you, please don't leave me again." Sobs wracked her body as Kadmus held her in her arms and stroked her thick, snowy hair. Her own tears made little pink trails through the blood that still caked her cheeks as she stared out beyond the docks and toward the endless expanse of stars and blackness.

"Here, Kalaiapi, I have something for you." She reached into her pocket and pulled from it a small, marble-sized ball that shifted into an array of iridescent colors. "I never got a phylactery, but I still have my aaiun. Please, take it. Perhaps it will contain something of me that will never leave you." She placed the little marble, glowing a sea moss green, gently into Kalaiapi's palms and pressed them shut, then reached up to cup her face in her hands and looked into those clear cornflower irises one last time as though memorizing every mottled shade of blue they contained. She pressed her forehead against Kalaiapi's and let her tears drip down onto her sister's cheeks. A warmth filled her mind as their skin touched, ran through all the neurons and synapses of her genomanced brain and down her spine and throughout every nerve of her body. She stumbled for a moment at the sensation and Kalaiapi caught her in her arms and held her.

"I love you, sister," Kalaiapi whispered.

"And I you." And with a final embrace and kiss, Kadmus too ran into the tunnels to find death.

78

Kadmus ran into the tunnels toward the shuttle bay to find the magrails no longer functioning. She let out the first of what would be several screams of frustration and fear, of shame and regret. Suddenly, none of this seemed to matter. Not the dreadnought, not the virus. The legion, Fornax, the entire species could burn. Barring a providential miracle, she would never see Kalaiapi again. Or Rho. Or Æa, perfect Æa. Perhaps she should simply have been grateful to have seen any of them again at all, given her choices. It hadn't been until she had laid eyes on her after that long century that she had truly understood the weight of her decision.

But Kalaiapi had been right. This was her doing. This was her hypocrisy. The Clade never had a right to this anima and it had only been by lying to herself that she had been able to ignore the shame and evil of their decision to take it for their own. So often, one relied on Omnic Providence, and she had been very kind to Kadmus until now. The only thing that could kill them was coincidence, and so far it had not. But sometimes there was also Omnic Justice, and she had come to collect the toll owed her for all Kadmus had done.

She began her long trek into the heart of the ship, making her way through the emergency tunnels that led to the dock from every other deck, dozens and dozens of hatches in the wall. Some of them would be filled with her legionnaires, hunting down an enemy they could never defeat. If the pilots were all slaughtered before she could gain systems access, her task would become that much harder. The dreadnought would maintain a supply of oxygen for a short while, but gradually nature would take its course and it would become a frozen vacuum and even Kadmus could only survive such circumstances for a very limited time.

She found the hatch that led toward the main navigation deck, where half of the remaining pilots still lingered, bravely facing their own peril so that the rest of the crew could evacuate. She began to run, now. The time for self-pity was past and now she had to rush to atonement. The corridor was dimly lit by self-sustained emergency lighting that lined the walls. The pilots who controlled the power systems had almost all been killed, either by the virus or the wraiths, and as a result nothing that wasn't independently powered was working anymore. This tunnel was empty; apparently none of the legionnaires had thought to head toward the helm.

Minutes felt like hours as she made her way through the evacuation tunnels, up the ladders, through deck after deck. Truth be told, these passages seemed more like a formality than anything particularly useful; in an emergency (like this one), you'd likely be killed by whatever was causing you to evacuate long before you got to the escape dock. Now, however, they may have been working to her advantage. There appeared to have been about ten of those wraiths in the science bay. If those were the only ones on the ship, the chances of them being in the same tunnel as her seemed fairly slim.

Finally, she reached the end of the long passageway and the hatch that opened into the navigation command center. She was no longer receiving a constant stream of information about ship personnel and status from the security and surveillance system. Those pilots must have finally been killed. It felt clear that these creatures possessed some kind of malevolence. They were not content to murder just what was in their reach, but they sought out more prey.

She pulled the door latch only to find something heavy

blocking the way. The pilots must have barricaded the doors. Admirable, but of questionable effectiveness, given the foe. She pushed against the reinforced hatch and there was a harsh grinding as whatever barrier had been placed gradually shifted until there was just enough room for her to get through. The navigation center was dark and appeared abandoned, lit only by emergency lighting and some gemlike blinking diodes. It reeked of rotting flesh.

"Hello?" she called out, but as she did so she heard the "snap" of a chemprop pistol being fired in her direction. She dropped quickly to the floor as one flechette pinged off the inside of the door where her head would have been. The second tore through her shoulder and she felt the bones and tendons of the joint sever and tear and let out a yowl of pain and annoyance.

"Oh, bother. Corsair Kadmus is that you?"

"Yes, it's me, dammit! No thanks to you! Shit." Blood poured from the wound as Nav Pilot Jinna ran toward her, a look of worried regret on her dusky face. She was tall, slim for a Polaran, with delicate features unusual for her subspecies and a short crop of tight, curly black hair that was even rarer. A long, thin cable ran loosely from the back of her skull up into a node on the ceiling making her look very much like a marionette puppet. The navigation deck was enormous and dim, though thin starlight penetrated the darkness through the vast array of windows that looked out onto the infinite expanse of space.

Jinna reached down to help Kadmus from the ground. Her arm hung limply to the side, the flechette having shredded the connective tissue beyond use. "I am so sorry, Corsair, I thought you were—"

"I know," Kadmus grimaced, clutching her shoulder, "it's fine." She adjusted her pain center appropriately and though her arm was still no more than a prop, at least it didn't hurt.

"Please, let me get you some cell gel for—"

"There's no time, Pilot. Leave it."

"Yes, Corsair. What can I do?"

"Are there any other pilots left on this deck?"

"No, Corsair. They've all succumbed." She gestured to a corner where the bodies of a dozen pilots had been respectfully laid on the floor, the source of the smell. "I'm the only one here. I'm not even sure what I'm doing here anymore, to be honest. And you, Corsair, do you have your strength?"

"I'm not infected, Pilot. The virus doesn't seem to have any affinity for the one implant I have," she said, tapping the back of her neck. Anyhow, I'm glad you're still here. I need your help. Hook me in." Jinna scurried to find a neural link cable and fastened it with a click into Kadmus' port.

"Help you do what, Corsair? At this point, my being here is only because I have nowhere else to go and my duty is to die with the ship. I can't take it anywhere, can't save it."

"We're not trying to save it, we're trying to destroy it and everything on it."

"Oh, I see." A faint smile flickered at the corners of her mouth. "I think I may be able to help with that. But why not simply go after the anima tank? It's big enough it would vaporize the entire dreadnought and then some."

"Yes, which is why the Navarch and I instructed the engineers to create a storage area that was absolutely impossible to infiltrate and sabotage. And they did an extremely good job."

"Yes, I see. What do you propose then?"

Kadmus was in the navigation program now and brought up a vast map of the star system through which they were currently passing.

"Well, as you said, we can barely direct the ship, but I think between the two of us, if we act while the thruster pilots are still alive we can at least push it off in the right direction and then hope that these creatures don't know how to pilot a dreadnought."

"And which direction do you have in mind, Corsair?"

"Well, Jinna, they seem to be quite hardy and I would very much like to ensure that they don't survive whatever we put them through." She pointed toward the star at the center of the system. "I have to imagine that even they couldn't survive a trip to the heart of a star."

"Very good, Corsair. I suppose we had better get started, then."

Kadmus took on the majority of the burden as the two pilots made the calculations, communicated with the ship's powerful pulse drive thrusters, and began the minute movements that would put the ship on its slow course toward the star. Kadmus would be dead long before the dreadnought actually made it to its fiery destination and all she could do now is hope that these creatures were not nearly as adept at piloting as they were at murder. To free up capacity, she'd had to drop pain controls and her shoulder throbbed and ached horribly as she directed the colossal battleship onto its new course by sheer force of will.

"Pilot, maintain the navigation. I need to access weapons for a moment." There on the map were the seven escape skiffs that had managed to make it off the dreadnought. In a moment they would all be destroyed. Compared to navigating, it would take surprisingly little effort to unleash a swarm of targeted hunter-killers that would track down each of the ships and pluck them from space like a falcon taking a dove. None of their defenses could possibly match the firepower of even a crippled dreadnought. Kadmus' felt as though she might choke as her mind pulled the missiles from their silos and sent them out toward their quarries. It was done.

"Pilot Jinna, do you hear that?" she asked quietly. Jinna paused and cocked her ear.

"Oh, no. No, no, no."

The cracking of chemprop rifles grew louder with each passing second until Kadmus could hear heavy booted feet running toward the main door of the navigation deck, in front of which Jinna and the other pilots had stacked an array of furniture and equipment. The guns continued to snap, accompanied by frantic, unintelligible yelling, then agonized screaming. Then there was silence. Silvery smoke began to filter through the door. Jinna turned toward Kadmus.

"No Collective Consciousness, eh?"

"Not for us, Jinna."

"Remember me for a few moments in Glory, then."

"Forever in Glory, Jinna."

"Just a few moments."

With that the Pilot pulled her pistol from her belt and, still navigating as best she could, began to let loose at the dark vapor that now flooded through the door and began to coalesce on the other side of the makeshift barricade. The creature was now a rudimentary progenasi that walked quickly and purposefully toward Jinna as she unleashed upon it her feeble firepower. The flechettes tore tiny gaps in the wraith's body that immediately closed back in on themselves.

In a moment, the creature was standing in front of the pilot, who was now frantically reaching down to draw her hadron knife. She had barely pulled it from her sheath when she was enveloped in a dark cloud from which blood began to spray in every direction. Her screams were mercifully brief.

It was Kadmus' turn now to shoot futilely at the shifting, effervescent ghost as it turned its attention on her. Not yet. She was so close. The coordinates were almost locked. She was running and shooting and screaming without even realizing that she was doing so. The coordinates were locked, the dreadnought began to wheel around, and before the wraith fell upon her the light from the local sun exploded into the helm deck and glittered in a thousand silver shards against the bare metalloy of the walls. It was beautiful.

Looking through the windows that surrounded her, Kadmus appreciated one last time the endless beauty of the stars that looked in on her. And there, off in the distance, a blue-white spark flashed across the darkness. Kalaiapi's skiff.

She had escaped. Kadmus turned to meet her attacker as the nav system signaled to her that the port thruster bank had died. That was Pilot Setrius. She tried desperately to correct but it was too late and the massive ship began to list away from its course. "No. No. NO!" she screamed. True terror began to enter her heart. She couldn't fail. She began to run. The wraith followed.

She scoured the system desperately. There was nothing for it. Even if she could correct the course alone, with one thruster bank it would be too unstable. An asteroid. No, it was larger. A microplanet. That might do. She kept firing and the chasing wraith didn't lose a step.

With all the strength left in mind and body, the world around her going into a hazy slow motion, she wrenched at the virtual helm. The ship began to veer back away from the star. Now in her view was a distant, dusty pink sphere, the anvil over which she would break this ship and maroon these monsters. They were on course now, hurtling for the distant rock. She turned to face her attacker.

"Come on, you bastard!" she yelled, and a dark fury blanketed her scarlet and pink face, her childlike features twisted into a fierce grimace. Drawing her hadron knife, she ran to close down the last few steps between her and the wraith. She swung the shimmering blue blade at the creature's torso and tiny slivers of black powder seemed to fly from its body but every wound healed as soon as it was created. The wraith didn't even bother to dodge. Instead, it reached out with lightning speed and took Kadmus by the neck in its massive hand and lifted her from the ground. She kicked out, pulled at its arm, then looked up, choking, into its face where black, malevolent eyes were marked only by two sunken holes. Looking into them, she went limp.

"Cadaster?" said Kadmus.

As the wraith's fingers tightened around her throat, one last thought came, unbidden, into her mind: this was biotech syncresis. This…was the Singularity. Then, a million spiders were crawling inside her as the smoke filled her mouth. She tried to scream.

79

"Where will we go, Kalaiapi?" asked Kaaio.

"Where will we go, Kalaiapi?" asked Mortis Drak.

"Where will we go?" Kalaiapi asked herself. "Our options are somewhat limited, unfortunately," she said. "I have a star map, but it hardly matters what's out there because we can't bloody get to any of it." She waved a frustrated arm at the large screen that currently held an image of the system through which they were passing with their little skiff, just big enough to hold perhaps twenty cramped troops, indicated by a blip of light that made its way agonizingly slowly through the vast blankness.

"These ships aren't meant for long-term space travel, they don't have gravity drives and even if they did, I couldn't pilot it because I don't have an Omnia damned neural port." She rubbed the back of her neck. Clade physicians had removed the rough, broken stump of the broken port and now there was only smooth, pale skin. Here she was, alone in the Outer Systems with two larval forms of life for companionship, no faster-than-light travel, barely any defenses to speak of, and eventually, she was sure, a Clade rescue fleet that would simply swoop her back up into custody.

She watched from the porthole as the dreadnought, dark and lonesome, faded from view. The thrusters briefly flared, turning the hulking metal tomb about, and then died almost as quickly. Kalaiapi guessed immediately what Kadmus was trying to do, to send the dreadnought to the one place she could feel certain the wraiths wouldn't survive. Unfortunately, it wasn't going to make it there. Even with her naked eye, she could tell the course was off. It was only by the smallest of fractions, but stretched out over many millions of miles, it was guaranteed to miss its mark. At least, if Kadmus was dead it would. If she was still alive, she'd make the correction, if it were in any way possible.

The thrusters flared again, bright white light that exploded the darkness of space for brief seconds then disappeared just as quickly, leaving a trail of glittering dust in its wake. The port bank was dead. Kalaiapi watched, despairing. She'd never correct the course, now. It simply wasn't possible, not even for a Corsair whose abilities far surpassed that of a regular pilot. Mortis Drak approached her from behind.

"Kalaiapi, what is happening?"

"Nothing good, that's all I know. Clearly the port thruster pilot just died. We have to go back, we have to help."

"Kalaiapi, you cannot help," said Kaaio. "Even if you could get onto the ship and make it to navigation without being killed, what would you do when you got there?"

She was so filled with pain and rage she felt she could push the dreadnought back on course with her bare hands. But she knew Kaaio was right. Going back would be a pointless suicide, and though she felt as though she would be happy to wink out of existence right now, she had greater responsibilities.

"What would we do, Kalaiapi?" asked Mortis Drak, who had of course not heard Kaaio.

"Nothing. We can do nothing. I could ram that dreadnought at full speed in this wretched little skiff and it would barely dent its armor." There was another massive eruption of dazzling sun-bright light from the starboard bank that sent the dreadnought veering dramatically away from its previous course. Mortis Drak grimaced and shielded his eyes. Kalaiapi ran to the skiff's primitive helm and reared their vessel around toward the dreadnought.

"What are you doing?" asked Mortis Drak.

"Well, a moment ago I knew exactly what Kadmus was planning. Now, I don't and I mean to find out. Unless those wraiths have access to the dreadnought's weapons, which seems unlikely given that we're still alive, we should be fine." The skiff shot off into the sea of stars and the dreadnought zoomed back into view, pitching and rolling from the violence of its most recent turn.

The skiff, now enveloped by the glittering diamond dust of the dreadnought's thruster exhaust, was absolutely dwarfed by the hulking battleship, and Kalaiapi felt like a gull watching a leviathan from the skies above the sea. She could see now what Kadmus was trying to do, could see the dusty, pinkish orange asteroid off in the distance, almost a planet, just big enough to have trapped a little atmosphere, perhaps.

She trailed the ship as it continued its awkward drift towards the dwarf planet and if there was any evidence that the wraiths were capable of manipulating the dreadnought's nav system then she certainly wasn't seeing it.

"Do you see what she's doing?" she asked Mortis Drak, who was stroking his bare chin and watching the scene unfold with intense interest.

"Yes, I believe I do, Kalaiapi. She means to run the dreadnought aground."

"No, she means to obliterate it against that floating rock. Or she meant to." Kadmus was certainly dead by now, bar some absolute defiance of the odds of which only a person like her were capable. But if not, it wouldn't matter. She would die in the collision. Her eyes filled with tears, again, and she wiped them away and tried to compose herself. "When that anima tank erupts it's going to vaporize the entire dreadnought. I don't think there's ever been that much in one place before."

"Will it destroy the wraiths?" Mortis Drak asked.

"I haven't a clue. But if it doesn't, then, well...let's just hope they at the very least never find a way off this barren rock in the middle of the Outer Systems."

They followed the ship for hours as it hurtled slowly but inexorably toward the little ball of rock. It was a fist-sized orb now, orbiting its distant star like an orphaned moon. A nameless planet in a numbered star system—now the destination for an event that potentially held in balance the future of all life in the Galaxy.

Kalaiapi stopped the skiff a couple of thousand miles away from the asteroid-cum-planet and let it float in the void as she watched the dreadnought drift like a corpse down a river toward this rock that would soon be devastated by their meeting. She found a pair of translux specs and used them to magnify the scene until she could make out the details. On the other side of the deck, Mortis Drak watched the viewing screen, the optic array tracking the battleship's descent. Kalaiapi needed to see it with her own eyes. The dreadnought hit the thin atmosphere with barely a tremor and spun toward the surface.

"What was Kadmus' tomb now will be her funeral pyre," whispered Kalaiapi, staring from the window with her hand pressed against the cold, transparent polymer. She remembered Kadmus, then, as a child, her hair white, her skin pale, almost translucent, and her eyes two crystal pools that held fire and laughter in their depths. She had hoped beyond hope to look into her eyes again, and she had. Now they would be gone forever, consumed by the flames of the consciousness she had tried to harness.

The dreadnought was built to withstand incredible violence and at first Kalaiapi feared its hull would survive the impact, but as the gargantuan bulk of the finned body crashed into the tee-shaped head, the entire structure began to splinter and crumple until the whole of it was enveloped in a cloud of dust and smoke that obscured her vision. The dust rose so high that it began to dissipate into the atmosphere like the cone of smoke and ash from an erupting super-volcano. When the anima tank finally ruptured, the resulting explosion swallowed the entire planet in a supernova of white and blue iridescent light, scouring millions of tons of rock from its surface and sending it careering through the surrounding space for thousands of miles. Tiny pinkish-brown stones began to pelt the skiff harmlessly.

Kalaiapi gazed at the destruction for a while and thought of Kadmus. "We are built, Mortis Drak, on the dust of civilizations," she said, finally. "And now Kadmus is part of that dust."

Mortis Drak stared back blankly. The concept of affection, much less sisterly love, had yet to enter his psyche. Perhaps he would understand one day. New scans integrated into the star chart showed that the devastating impact of the anima burst had changed the microplanet's orbit. Kalaiapi had never seen anything like it. Such a small amount of matter, really, the essence of progenasi intelligence and consciousness, and yet so volatile and destructive. She went to the helm and took the little skiff toward the planet to survey the results of Kadmus' plan.

She steered the little escape craft through the dust cloud that now sparkled in the light of the distant sun, debris bouncing off the hull and blocking any view from the windows. She adjusted the optic array's sensors and began to get a clearer picture as the rocks and dust were filtered from view. There was a crater on the side of the planet many hundreds of miles across. There was no sign at all of the dreadnought, which had been utterly obliterated by the blast. It would take years for the dust cloud to clear, if it ever really cleared at all in these windless conditions and now with no atmosphere to speak of.

"Do you see that?" asked Mortis Drak, pointing one of his considerable fingers toward the view screen.

"Yes, I do, but what is it?" replied Kalaiapi. She could see something moving in one section of the crater near the middle. She magnified the picture. Little black specks that wriggled and shifted in the roiling pink dust.

"Are those–"

"No. It's not possible." She magnified again. Little black clouds of smoke that hovered above the ground, amorphous, like giant amoebae. Like viruses. Then one by one, the countless little clouds on the screen began to coalesce and take form until each of them had two arms, two legs, and a head. "It's not possible," she repeated. She zoomed out and tailored the sensors, looking for more of the little black figures in this expansive wasteland. They came into focus all at once. Thousands of them. "Thousands of them," she whispered.

"Kalaiapi, what will we do?" Mortis Drak asked, a level of awe and dread in his voice she had never perceived before. By now he understood at what he was gazing.

"We have to go back, Mortis Drak," she said. "We have to tell the Eternal Council. About all of this. They will decide what must be done. It is not for me."

"And what of me, Kalaiapi?" chimed in Kaaio, silent until now. "What will happen to me when we get back to Confederation space?"

"Oh, Kaaio, I don't know. I don't know anything anymore. I don't even know how we'll get back." She buried her face in her hands, frustration, misery, fear welling up inside her. Then she thought of Kadmus. Kadmus had failed, but she had tried. Now she too would have to try. She was, after all a Corsair of Ad Astara. It was she who was tasked with facing down Omnia itself and holding it to account in its eternal war against the Progenasis. And now Omnia had thrown at the progenasis its most potentially devastating weapon. Kalaiapi would be the shield against which it shattered.